P9-CFT-250

Place your initials here to remind you that you have read this book!

η·L· OR			8cm
BS			

DISCARD

A
MATTER OF
TRUST

Center Point
Large Print

Also by Susan May Warren and available from Center Point Large Print:

When I Fall in Love
Always on My Mind
The Wonder of You
You're the One That I Want
Wild Montana Skies
Rescue Me

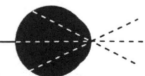

A MATTER OF TRUST

Montana Rescue

Susan May WARREN

CENTER POINT LARGE PRINT
THORNDIKE, MAINE

This Center Point Large Print edition
is published in the year 2017 by arrangement with
Bethany House Publishers,
a division of Baker Publishing Group.

This book is a work of fiction. Names,
characters, places, and incidents are the product of
the author's imagination or are used fictitiously.

The text of this Large Print edition is unabridged.
In other aspects, this book may vary
from the original edition.
Printed in the United States of America
on permanent paper.
Set in 16-point Times New Roman type.

ISBN: 978-1-68324-477-6

Library of Congress Cataloging-in-Publication Data

Names: Warren, Susan May, 1966– author.
Title: A matter of trust / Susan May Warren.
Description: Center Point Large Print edition. | Thorndike, Maine :
    Center Point Large Print, 2017. | Series: Montana rescue ; 3
Identifiers: LCCN 2017018791 | ISBN 9781683244776
    (hardcover : alk. paper)
Subjects: LCSH: Man-woman relationships—Fiction. |
    Large type books. | GSAFD: Love stories.
Classification: LCC PS3623.A865 M38 2017b | DDC 813/.6—dc23
LC record available at https://lccn.loc.gov/2017018791

SOLI DEO GLORIA

I

Gage Watson blamed the trouble on the bright, sunny day. A day when the sun arched high against a cloudless blue sky, and light gilded the snow-frosted, razorback mountain peaks with showers of gold.

Days like this lied to people, told them they could fly.

The air wasn't so cold as to frighten the hordes of skiers into their condominiums or the après-ski bars, nor so warm as to turn the mountain into a river of slow-moving slush. Instead, a perfect day, rich with the fragrance of white pine and cedar, the powder dusting up behind him as he shredded the fields of untarnished snow, as his board carved through the white, soundless and free.

Dangerous. Because this kind of weather seeped into the bones of the extreme skiers who dared the back bowls and mogulled faces of Blackbear Mountain and turned them . . . well, as his father would describe it, reckless.

Or, more precisely, into idiots out to get themselves and others killed.

Like the kid dressed in an inflatable T. rex costume that Gage had chased down the mountain this morning.

Once upon a time, Gage had been that reckless T. rex. Maybe not wearing that ridiculous outfit—not when he had sponsor gear to display—but chin-deep in the lifestyle of the epic snowboarder, grinning for the cameras, basking in the limelight and cheers that came with the sport of backcountry skiing called freeriding.

Now he'd turned traitor, donning the red coat of a ski patrol and chasing down the renegades who sneaked past the roped-off areas for the run of their lives.

He stood at the edge of the perimeter of Timber Bowl, binoculars pointed to the tree-rutted, cliff-cut powder, scanning the undesignated area, just to make sure that hotshots like T. rex and his buddy hadn't returned for a late-afternoon run.

The sun glistened off snowfall so deep it could bury a man, a condition unbearably tempting for a true powder hound. Gage could hear it calling to him, the vast, crystalline fields of white, feel his board cutting through the snowpack like it might be frosting.

Never mind the deadly, concealed ledges, drop-offs, and steel-edged boulders.

Or the threat of avalanche. No one thought about death chasing them down a hill as they attacked the powder, but with the five inches of fresh, heavy snow layering the snow pack, the cornice ached to break free and rush down the hill in a lethal wave.

And if tonight's forecast was correct, he and the avalanche control team would be blasting another layer of powder off this slope come morning.

Gage had risen early with the rest of the Blackbear ski patrol, ridden the gondola up, and bombed the crust, the snow falling behind him, scarring the bowl. Then he'd skied through the layers, cutting into the pack to loosen it.

Still, it posed enough of a danger that they'd closed the slope and put up an orange safety line cordoning off the area from the early morning skiers sliding off the Timber Bowl express lift.

And that's when T. rex showed up. Gage pegged the snowboarder at about nineteen or twenty. His buddy was attired with the appropriate GoPro, which made their intentions clear.

Gage had caught them just as they edged near the tape.

"Dude—the bowl is closed," Gage said, keeping it easy.

T. rex gave him a face, like, *C'mon, really,* and Gage saw himself, not so long ago. So he put a growl into his reply and threatened to confiscate their tickets.

Which apparently meant nothing, because not fifteen minutes later, as he'd scanned the mountain, he'd spied the duo some two hundred feet downslope, cutting through the pristine powder, catching air off a cliff, then disappearing into the treed perimeter below.

The dinosaur had slipped out of his radar, but Gage promised himself that he'd hunt the two hotshots down and kick them off his mountain if it was the last thing he did today.

"Ski patrol, we have a downed snowboarder just below the Timber lift, tower 37."

Gage lifted the radio attached to his jacket. "Ski patrol, Watson. I'm just below the lift, on Timber Bowl."

"Roger, Watson. The lift stopped, and apparently he jumped for the pole and missed. Possible fracture. We have another hanging from the chair."

Oh, for crying out loud. "I'm en route. Watson out."

Gage clipped on his radio, then unsnapped his splitboard and pulled out his skins.

Faster to climb his way to the top and ride his board down through the trees.

He put oomph into his climb and in a few moments spied the tower through a scrim of pine trees.

"Ski patrol, Watson. I'm on slope and heading down to the victim." Gage snapped his splitboard together and shoved the skins into his backpack.

Sheesh, he could have found the boys with his eyes closed, the way they were shouting. Keep it up and the Blackbear patrols wouldn't have to set off charges to bring down the mountain.

Gage snapped into his bindings, then pushed

off, cutting through the soft, albeit dangerous, treed terrain. He ducked under a branch and emerged into the free, catching air. No fancy stuff, just necessity, and he landed easily.

Two more turns and he'd reached the first victim.

The kid had fallen nearly forty feet. His screams echoed through the valley of the Timber Bowl, bouncing off the edges and back to the terrified passengers of the stalled lift who were witnesses to the carnage as he lay broken below his chair.

His buddy, clearly possessed with the same tankful of smarts, had probably tried to stop him, lunging forward and slipping off the chair. The hero now dangled half on, half off the chair, his arms wrapped around the bar, his leg hooked on the seat, his boot wedged in to the side rail to secure him. Still, the kid was perilously close to joining his buddy below in a pile of broken bones.

Gage snapped out of his gear in seconds, lifted off his goggles, and dropped beside the kid who writhed in pain in the snow, his leg brutally twisted under him.

"Ski patrol. I'm here to help," Gage said. He didn't want to move the kid or splint his leg until he could get a neck collar on him. However, blood already saturated his gray ski pants, and the protruding bulk of bone from above his knee suggested a compound fracture.

"What's your name?" Gage pulled off the kid's mitten and reached for a pulse.

"Hunter Corbin." He wore a ski helmet, and blond hair trickled out the sides and back.

"How old are you?" Gage timed the beats. A little high and thready.

"Fifteen. It's my first time out West."

"Your parents around?" Gage kept his voice even, calm.

In the meantime, Hunter's friend dangled, screaming, forty feet overhead.

Gage wanted to feel sorry for Hunter, but whatever had possessed the kid to—

"They're at the bottom." He groaned, tears filling his eyes. "My cell phone. It fell—I wanted to get it before it got lost. It's a brand-new iPhone."

Gage took out his radio. "Ski patrol, this is Watson. I have a fifteen-year-old male with what looks like a compound femur fracture. Possible neck injury. I need a dual sled, a neck collar, leg splint, and a lift rescue team." He looked up. "And fast."

"Copy, Watson. We have a team on the express lift en route."

The express lift, on the other side of the mountain. Ten minutes, at least.

Gage glanced up at the dangling victim, assessing. "What's your friend's name, Hunter?"

"Adam. He was just trying to help me."

12

"Right." He got up, cupping his hands over his eyes. Overhead, spectators watched in silence, two or three to a chair, probably traumatized by the tragedy that had occurred on their vacation. A few held up their phones, and he wouldn't be surprised if the event made YouTube.

Hopefully no one would recognize him, or worse, tag him.

Just when he'd put the past to rest. Or tried to. "Adam, how you doing up there?"

A stupid question, but he hoped to keep the kid calm.

"I'm gonna fall!"

"Keep holding on, we're going to get you out of this."

Gage could see the lure of the stunt—the chair had stopped parallel to the tower, a mere three feet from the lift. And, with the rungs affixed to the side, Hunter might have landed that leap if he hadn't been wearing snowboarder boots and bulky mittens.

Or, if he were a trained mountain climber.

Gage had a lift letdown system in his pack, a weighted ball attached on one end, a sling on the other, but he strongly doubted that Adam could either catch and throw the rope over the lift cable or get the sling around his body.

"Don't let go!" Gage yelled again and grabbed his pack, retrieving the assembly. Then he headed over to the tower. "I'm coming to you, Adam."

He jumped and grabbed on to the lower rung, pulled himself up to the next rung, and got his feet on the lowest bar. He began to climb.

The kid was swinging his body in an attempt to slide back onto the chair seat. The chair began to sway, moving the other chairs around it. Screams lifted from the riders.

"Stop swinging, dude!" Gage yelled, seeing in his mind the entire rig detaching and crashing to the ground, crushing Adam's already injured friend.

In fact, they might have an entire mountain full of injuries.

Gage pulled himself up parallel to the kid. He could just barely reach out and touch him when he extended himself. His grasp wasn't enough to pull the kid in, but he could help secure him.

He threw the weighted ball over the ski lift cable. It fell to the ground.

"Listen up, Adam. I'm going to put this sling over your head, and very carefully you're going to work it down under your armpits, one arm at a time. Then I'm going to climb down and secure the line to the tower. The sling will keep you from falling."

"Aren't you going to lower me down?"

He had hooked the sling over the boy's head, a little nervous at the way the kid turned to him with big, terrified eyes. Adam was a stocky kid in gray snow pants and a yellow jacket, and Gage

14

had to give him kudos for hanging on as long as he had. He drew back fast, however. He couldn't get any closer or Adam might grab him, pull them both down.

"Wiggle it over yourself," Gage said.

The kid put one elbow up, through the opening in the sling.

"Good job, kid," Gage said as he scrambled back down the ladder and hiked over to the weighted line.

No sign of his patrol buddies on the ridge above.

Dragging the line back over to the tower, he glanced up and saw that Adam had worked the sling under both arms.

Gage threw the line over the bottom rung and slowly began to pull it taut. It tightened around Adam's chest.

"Don't let go! This is just to catch you if you fall." He secured the line to the tower.

"Let me down!"

"Help will be here soon. I can't lower you on my own."

Well, maybe he could, if he used the tower as both leverage and an anchor. But for now, Adam wouldn't fall, and Hunter was running out of time.

Gage knelt next to Hunter and checked his pulse. Gray, clammy skin, dull eyes. A pool of blood formed under his leg, saturating the snow.

The kid could lose his life to shock long before he bled out.

He lifted the radio. "Ski patrol, Watson. Where's my sled?"

"Just getting off the lift," came the answer.

Perfect. Gage pulled his pack over to himself and pulled out scissors and a tourniquet.

He took the scissors to the boy's pants, cutting away the bloody fabric to get to the source.

The jagged edge of his femur jutted out of his skin just above the knee.

Gage searched for a radial pulse from the posterior tibial artery and found none. The broken bone had cut off blood supply to his foot.

First, he had to stop the bleeding and then get the kid down the mountain before Hunter lost his leg.

Gage threaded the tourniquet under his leg and worried when Hunter didn't move. In fact, the kid had stopped writhing altogether.

"Hey, Hunter, stay with me here. Tell me, is that your Lib Tech board? A Snow Ape C2 BTX? One of the best power freestyle sticks on the planet. It's a dream on the snow, right?"

Hunter opened his eyes, tried to find the voice.

Gage finished the tourniquet and leaned up, meeting Hunter's eyes. So young and rife with fear. "Don't worry, I'm going to get you down the mountain. And I know this awesome doctor that will fix you right up. You'll be doing a half-cab quadruple backflip by this time next year."

16

"A what?" Hunter whispered.

"Google it and then come back here and I'll teach you myself."

"Really?"

"Yep."

"Ski patrol, Remington at the ridge." Ty's voice came through the walkie. "I see you, Gage. Coming down."

Gage looked up and spotted the two ski patrollers, red jackets against the glare of light and brilliant white, carving a trail through the powder. One of them guided a two-person sled.

They slowed before they reached the accident site, leaving the powder drifting safely away, and snapped off their skis. Ty reached him first. "Hey there, kid," he said to Hunter, pulling off his gloves and kneeling next to Gage. He carried the splint as the other patroller brought over the sled.

One of their rookies, Skye Doyle—Gage recognized her as she brought the sled closer. Blonde, in her early twenties, she'd joined the patrol as a volunteer. Gage didn't ask why Ty had let her lead the sled—probably practice. But she didn't have nearly enough experience to steady it going downhill. And she'd never be able to lower Adam on her own—she'd need Ty's strength.

"Let's load him up. Then we need to get Adam off that lift." Gage reached for the splint, a high-tech, emergency fracture response system. It moved to the shape of Hunter's fractured leg, and

Gage strapped it into place to keep it immobilized as Ty affixed a neck collar on him. Skye brought over the backboard, and they eased it under Hunter, sliding him onto it and strapping him in.

Ty and Gage moved Hunter to the sled and zipped him inside the emergency blanket. Skye secured the boy onto the sled as Gage and Ty returned to the problem of Adam.

"How are we going to get him down?" Ty said.

"We could use the pole as leverage, with you wearing the descender. I could lower him down while you let out the slack."

"And what about Hunter? He's looking pretty pale." This from Skye, who'd joined their conversation. "I can take him down on the sled."

"No," Ty said, as if reading Gage's mind.

Skye had the good sense not to argue.

However, "Skye, you have climbing experience, right? Can you run the rappler?" Gage asked.

She nodded.

"Ty, you lower him down, Skye can brace against the pole and make sure the slack doesn't go out too fast. I'll take Hunter down to the bottom."

Ty glanced at the sled, up to Adam. "You sure you can handle the sled alone? Technically we're above the snow guns—it's too steep. You sure you won't get yourself—and this kid—hurt?"

Maybe it was the bright blue sky, the onlookers, the taste of adrenaline, but in Ty's question, Gage heard the past rise. Heard the voice, quiet, pleading. Female. *"Please, Gage, don't do this. You're going to get somebody hurt."*

It jarred him.

Then, Hunter groaned, and Gage came back to himself.

"Yes," he said. He hiked over to his board, glancing up at Adam. "My friends are going to get you down. Don't worry, kid!"

He happened to look at the onlookers just then. Yes, cell phones were tracking his movements.

Once upon a time, he would have waved; even now he felt the old habit stir inside him.

Then, three chairs down he spotted the T. rex.

And behind him, the buddy with the GoPro.

"You've got to be kidding me."

Ty glanced at him, but Gage shook his head. His rant would have to wait.

Skye was climbing into the belay harness when Gage snapped his boots into his board. He stepped between the brake handles of the sled, and Ty helped him out with a push.

Don't lose control. Don't overcorrect.

Don't get anyone killed.

He glanced up again at the T. rex and shook his head. "Hang in there, Hunter. We'll be down in no time."

The colder it got up here on top of the mountain, stalled on the Timber Bowl chair, the more the T. rex next to her threatened to jump.

19

"I could make it. The only reason that punk missed was because he didn't have enough launch."

"Are you kidding me?" Ella Blair curled her fingers into a ball inside her mittens. She already couldn't feel her toes, and she'd snugged her nose into her neck gaiter, a film of fog covering her goggles.

Three chairs ahead, at the tower, the two ski patrollers had anchored themselves around the pole and were using a kind of belay system to lower the skier. She still couldn't believe the bravery of the first responder—climbing up four stories on the pole to fix the kid into the sling. For a second there, she thought the terrified teenager might just leap into the patrol's arms.

She turned, looking down behind her, and spied him, attached to the bright red sled, sliding through the powder and down the bowl toward the base.

His thighs had to be on fire, shredding the hill at first one angle, then the next.

Now that was the kind of hero she wanted to be—someone who actually helped people with real problems.

Not tracking down her delinquent brother.

Now her fingers had gone numb, and save for the adrenaline of watching the ski patrol lower the idiot teenager hanging from the lift, she would be a frozen, hypothermic ball.

20

She wanted to get off this mountain, and fast. The bright, sunny day had deceived her into believing that heading west to hijack her brother's ski vacation was a brilliant stratagem for getting him turned around and headed back to Vermont, and more specifically, his sophomore year at Middlebury. She still didn't understand why her parents seemed okay with his ski-bum sabbatical.

But the longer they sat here, the longer she despaired of having a real conversation with Oliver. After all, clearly he wasn't taking anything she said seriously. Not dressed in that ridiculous costume.

More, he hardly seemed rattled that his sister had flown across the country, tracked him down, and boarded a ski lift with him nearly out of the blue.

Not so much out of the blue, because she'd been watching him, trying to figure out how to pin him down for a come-to-Jesus chat since arriving at their parents' resort condo this morning. No, actually since she'd gotten the semi-drunk pocket call from him three nights ago. Slurred speech and muffled raucous laughter in the bar around him, something about Montana and skiing down Heaven's Peak.

She'd yelled into the phone at the top of her lungs before finally giving up.

And booking a flight.

21

"No, really, it's not that far," Ollie said, clearly still fixed on his ludicrous stunt. "I can reach it."

He reached out, swinging the chair, and she screamed and grabbed the bar. "Stop! You're going to push me off."

"Look, I can almost reach the pole." He strained toward the rungs on the tower, trying to hook one.

"Stop it, Ollie!"

But he turned around in the chair and shouted to the pair behind them. "Bradley! If I make it, be sure to get it on video!"

She didn't have to look to know that his stupid friend probably gave him a thumbs-up.

"You're not—stop it." She grabbed his jacket and pulled him back, her other hand in an iron grip on the bar.

He laughed. "Calm down. I was just kidding. I just like our little game." He gave her a wink.

"That wasn't funny. I'm having a flashback of when you were six and I was—"

"Ninety-three?" Oliver glanced at her, grinning. Only his face stuck out of the hole right under the inflatable costume's head. He'd shoved the legs into his snowboarder boots.

"Can you even move in that thing?"

"Sure. It's a little tight, but I'm going to get so many hits once we post this on YouTube. I'll be nearly as famous as you."

"Funny."

22

Under that ridiculous costume was a good kid. He couldn't help it that he'd experienced a completely different childhood than hers. Grown up with different parents, different expectations.

Wealth and security.

"I just have to know—why the T. rex outfit?"

"Are you kidding me? T. rex videos are killing it. When we put this up—"

"Stop. I can't hear this. Let me get this straight. You dropped out of your very prestigious private college so you could become a ski bum in a Tyrannosaurus rex costume? This is why you broke your parents' hearts?"

"I didn't break their hearts." His smile dimmed. "And they're your parents too."

She'd forgotten how the wind off Blackbear could slither inside her jacket, find her bones, rattle them. "Legally. But you know they love you the best—and for good reason. Even though we were both adopted, I was just their ward. You are their *son*. You're everything to them, and now you're not only going to get hurt but you'll look ridiculous doing it."

Oliver's mouth tightened. "I won't get hurt."

"Maybe not, but what's next, Ollie? BASE jumping?"

"I dunno. Maybe I'll go to Outlaw."

She stilled. Took a breath, dug deep, and this time hung on to her inner attorney, refusing to let Ollie undo her. No, she grabbed for the woman

23

who'd been a state senator for two years, one of the youngest in the nation. She'd stood her ground in front of tougher opponents than her kid brother.

Still, just the name—Outlaw Mountain—and the memory behind it left wounds.

"If you did, I'd know you were really stupid," she said crisply and looked away, a little unnerved at the gloss filming her eyes. She blinked before they iced over.

The patrol had lowered the kid to the snow and pulled the rope free of the lift. He seemed unhurt but shaken.

Oliver fell silent as they watched. Then, "I'm sorry."

She nodded.

"You didn't have to come all the way out here. I know what I'm doing."

"Which is?"

"I'm not cut out for school, okay? I failed nearly every class last semester—"

"Because you were partying! Don't tell me you weren't smoking pot, Ollie. You couldn't hide it from me in high school, and you can't hide it now—"

"I wasn't high, Ella. I was . . . not smart. I studied. I went to class. I want to be—I wanted Mom and Dad to be as proud of me as they are of you."

She could hardly take him seriously in that

24

inane costume. "Mansfield and Marj love you—"

"But they're *proud* of you." He looked down at his hands. "I'm never going to be a lawyer or . . ." He looked over at her. "A state senator."

"You might—"

"I don't want to be that. I'm sorry, sis, but your idea of fun is a bowl of popcorn and a political debate. Sorry, I know I should care, but I don't. I like powder boarding. I just need some breathing room, okay? I'll figure it out. You'll see. I'll do something amazing and it'll blow you all away. So you can pack up and go back to Vermont and save somebody else."

And, with a jolt, the lift started.

"Too bad," Ollie murmured. "I could've made that jump."

She closed her eyes.

They rode in silence, and she averted her eyes as they passed the bloody smudge in the snow. The ski patrollers skied on either side of the rescued snowboarder; the kid clearly looked rattled as he rode down the bowl. She couldn't see the other patroller anymore. Maybe he'd reached the bottom.

Or fallen.

She didn't want to think about that—the danger that could occur on a mountain.

Outlaw. The name pressed in, leaving bruises. Maybe she didn't know how to have fun. Not anymore.

25

But really, who could blame her? She'd blown her chance at happily ever after—even self-respect—after the tragedy at Outlaw Mountain.

Or more specifically, after Gage Watson.

The top of the lift came into view.

"Life is more than fun, Ollie. And we're not done with this conversation."

The T. rex lifted his board to disembark. "Roar," he said.

"Ollie—"

"Meet you at the bottom, sis." He slid off the chair and away from her, then bent to clip his boot back into his board. She too slid off, remounted her board, and parked herself away from the lift, waiting for Brette and Bradley on the chair behind them.

Bradley rode his board over and high-fived his dinosaur friend. "Let's shred this gnar!" He adjusted his GoPro and gave his subject a thumbs-up.

Ollie, in costume, headed to the edge of the bowl. He gave her one last look, wiggled his backside, and slipped off the lip and down the hill.

Oh, for Pete's sake. But Ella couldn't help a smile. Her brother, despite everything, always knew how to make her laugh.

He disappeared from view, and her attention turned to the breathtaking scope of Glacier National Park, the jagged horizon glistening white and glorious. Below her, miles away, she

26

could just make out Whitefish Lake, the tiny town of Whitefish, and the run of high-end condos, including the one that belonged to her family, just off the slope.

She took a deep breath, filling her lungs with the smell of pine and crisp air.

Maybe it was time she *did* have some fun. After all, she'd managed to sneak away from the maddening swarm of the press after the passing of Proposal 241, a bill she'd worn out her voice trying to defeat.

A clear indication that maybe she shouldn't run again, if 80 percent of Vermont supported the use of marijuana for recreational purposes.

Crazy.

Brette slid over, clipped her boot in, then stood up and adjusted her goggles. She glanced over at the view. "I don't know, Ella. I've never ridden powder this deep. And this is pretty steep."

Ella glanced at her. "Thanks for coming along. I know I roped you into this."

"No, I'm glad to be here. I haven't been skiing in years—since we came out that time with Sofia." Brette's wheat-white hair hung out of her helmet in two thick braids. Athletic and petite, Brette was a deceiving package of curves and brains, her journalist mind always on the hunt for a good story. Ella was glad her former housemate was, and always had been, on her side. "I'm just not sure I'm not going to end up taking my own toboggan ride down the hill. Although, if I could get that cute ski patrol to save me . . .”

Brette grinned at Ella and pulled out her phone. “I got a few close-ups.” She thumbed open her app and began to scroll through the pictures. “Here’s a good one. Handsome, huh?”

She handed the phone over to Ella. The glare on the phone made it hard to see, so she took off her glasses, cupped her hand over the phone, and turned away from the sun.

Everything inside her froze. Wait—*no*. She angled for a better view. He wore his helmet, his face intense and straining as he reached out to fit the sling over the head of the dangling snowboarder. But that set of his jaw under a layer of brown whiskers, the curly brown hair peeking out of his black ski helmet . . .

It simply couldn’t be. “Yeah, he’s handsome,” she managed, her voice barely hitching.

“I think I’m going to fall, just so he can rescue me.” Brette winked at her, tucking the phone back in her jacket.

Ella offered a weak smile.

She tried to remember—had the voice sounded familiar as he called up to the boy?

Maybe.

Yes. She possessed a nearly photographic memory when it came to the regretful moments of her past, and a news article flashed in her mind: *Gage Watson, from Mercy Falls, Montana.*

28

He'd returned home to hide.

Or survive.

Maybe restart his life.

Whatever. It didn't matter. Really, not at all.

Except . . . She'd told herself for years that she *didn't* have to see him, track him down, talk to him.

Let her heart remember.

But she'd also told herself that someday she'd face Gage Watson and explain everything.

Maybe it wasn't him.

She wasn't going to let Brette crash and find out. "Listen, Brette, just keep your arms open and wide, like you're reading a newspaper."

"I'm sorry, what is that? A news— *what?*"

"I know, old-school term. Try this—pretend you saw, oh, I don't know, Kit Harrington at the top of the hill, riding your direction, and only you could save him."

"Kit is your type. Maybe . . . Matthew Goode?"

"Okay, *Downton Abbey*. I don't know why you always go for the fancy boys, but whatever works."

"Not anymore—I learned my lesson. No more rich party boys for me. But I do love a good English accent."

Ella grinned. "Okay, well, the key to riding powder is to hold your arms out and lean back. But not too far or you'll go over. But you want to lift your tip."

Brette held her arms out, settling her hips. "Like this?"

"You look like a duck, but yeah."

"Better than a T. rex."

Ella shook her head. "Keep an even rhythm, don't cut too hard—make a nice smooth line. And don't rush."

"Oh, fear not." Brette headed over to the edge of the bowl. "And you owe me."

Ella laughed. "I'll ski behind you."

But Brette didn't move, just kept staring at the thick, powdery snow, now bumbled and tossed by a day of skiing and shredding. But still soft, still whisper-light in the crisp air.

"How did you learn to do this? I mean, I know the M&M's have a condo here, but—"

"I spent some time in BC, at Fernie. And Whistler. And . . ." She swallowed, forced out the word. "Outlaw. Best powder on the planet."

There, she said it without flinching. And someday, she'd manage it without feeling claws inside, hollowing her out, leaving a burn where her heart should be.

"Hey, isn't that where that guy died? Your family knew him."

Brette, proving she'd done her journalistic homework.

Ella nodded. "Dylan McMahon. You ready?"

"Were you there that day?"

"I'm really cold, Brette. Sitting on that chair didn't help."

Brette's mouth closed in a tight line, and Ella

hated that she'd hurt her. But she couldn't—really couldn't—talk about it.

At least not the entire story.

Not without losing her law license.

But she couldn't stand Brette's face, so, "Yeah, I was there. I saw Dylan die." And Gage Watson's brilliant future end in a devastating crash.

Brette nodded and thankfully turned back to the bowl.

"No one is going to die today," she said, and Ella could have hugged her for it.

"Let's do this!" Brette yelled. She pushed off, leaning back, arms wide as she flew down the slope.

No one is going to die today.

Ella pushed off behind her, praying her words were true.

2

Maybe he would never do that again. In fact, if pushed, Gage could admit he could have used a tail. Ty, or even maybe Skye, helping to control the sled.

"You're okay, kid," Gage said as he slid to a stop near the ski patrol shack.

Hunter appeared a bit whitened, and even Gage's pulse pounded in his throat at their descent. His thighs burned with the strain of slowing them down through the powder.

Worse, twice the sled overtook him, and he'd had to rally around it, pull it back into submission.

His entire body trembled, and sweat filmed down his back as he unhooked his helmet, pulled it off, and guided the rescue toboggan onto the platform near the ski patrol shack.

Late afternoon shadows draped the receiving area in gray, and he pulled off his sunglasses as he unbuckled his bindings from his board. The après-ski aroma of grilled steaks and the sound of raucous music lifted from the nearby Blackbear Base Camp Saloon.

"Hunter!"

Gage turned at the voice and saw a middle-aged woman in a purple ski outfit, white Sorel boots, and short dark hair running toward him.

"Mom," Hunter said, his voice shaky. Maybe he'd been holding it in, but the fifteen-year-old hotshot blinked back tears, his jaw tight as his mom rushed over.

"How could you do this?" she said, bending over him. "They told me you jumped! What were you thinking?"

Gage turned away, just for a second, the words ringing in his ears.

"What were you thinking?"

The Great Question, for every idiotic move. Had Hunter not gotten hurt, the comments on the YouTube videos would be more akin to "stellar, dude!"

Kids.

No, kids who didn't think, who only wanted to show off, or worse, prove themselves to the world.

And kids with iPhones. The little red record button made everyone stupid.

"You made it down in record time!"

Gage glanced around and spied Jess Tagg, EMT from PEAK Rescue, jogging up to him. She wore her blue jumpsuit uniform, and her blonde hair was in a singular braid down her back.

He said nothing, hoping she didn't see the truth in his eyes.

Stupid, bravado decisions got people killed. He should have known better than to take the run on his own.

"Excuse me, ma'am," Jess said and eased past Hunter's mom to unzip Hunter from the sled.

The woman turned to Gage. "Trudy Corbin. We can't thank you enough."

"It's my job, ma'am," Gage said, but her words landed on soft soil. See, what he did mattered.

Pete Brooks came up behind him, pushing a litter to transfer Hunter into their pretty blue Bell 429 chopper. "Ty called in the evac—said you'd need to get this one to the Kalispell Medical Center, pronto." Pete, also in his PEAK jumpsuit, wore his dark blond hair pulled back in a man bun.

"Yes. Call ahead to my dad, see if he'll meet you in the ER. I think he'll want this case." Gage looked at Trudy. "My father is an orthopedic surgeon at the hospital. He'll know what to do to get Hunter back on his board."

"Yeah, well, I don't think we'll be taking any more trips out West anytime soon." Her mouth made a dark line as she turned back to Hunter.

Gage knew the look of a disapproving parent too well.

"I thought you were on avalanche control today," Pete said to Gage as he examined Hunter's splint.

"I was—came out at 6:00 this morning. We bombed along the backside of Timber Bowl. But the snow is still pretty unstable. We'll probably be back in the morning, if the forecast is right."

"Come over to the ranch when you get off. We're all watching *America's Missing* tonight. They're showing the episode about the girl we found this summer."

The body PEAK Rescue found last summer in the Avalanche River had been reconstructed with the hope that her identification might unearth leads to the missing niece of local billionaire Ian Shaw. His niece, Esme, had vanished in Glacier National Park three-plus years ago. Only recently had they discovered that she was, indeed, alive, confirmed by a cryptic phone call Ian received from her last summer. But not even a backtrace of the call and all of Ian's best sleuthing efforts had unearthed the origin. The missing girl might have nothing to do with Esme's disappearance, but identifying her made Ian feel like he was doing something to help someone else find answers.

It didn't mean he wasn't also holding on to the wild hope that it would lead to answers for himself as well.

"I'm going to take one more run from the top, along the perimeter, make sure we don't have any more renegades," Gage said. "I caught a couple of teenagers skiing in the undesignated area today."

A muscle pulled in Pete's jaw, and it took a second for Gage to connect the dots, all the way back to the death of Pete's father over a decade earlier, in an off-run ski accident.

He had no words, so he glanced up the mountain, saw it covered in shadow. He'd have to hurry if he wanted to make it back up on top.

Pete said nothing as he tested for a pulse in Hunter's leg. Meanwhile, Jess radioed in his vitals to Kalispell ER. "We gotta get moving," he said to Jess, who shot him a look, a nod, all business.

Whatever had gone down between Pete and Jess last summer had clearly cooled, not even a simmer remaining. Maybe it had something to do with Jess's extra-friendly relationship with Ty. It seemed that the guy had been putting in more than average hours remodeling her money pit house, helping her paint her bedrooms and most recently gut her kitchen.

However, whatever had happened between Pete and Jess, they could still get the job done and now they worked together to get Hunter onto the litter and gurney.

"Need help getting him to the chopper?" Gage asked.

"No. But you'd better steer around the Base Camp Saloon. I saw Tallie in there, and you know how she loves a great hero story."

"I leave all the hero stuff to you, Brooks," Gage said, grinning, and hiked up to grab his board. He radioed in and confirmed his last trek up the mountain to resume his patrol.

The last hours on the mountain were always

36

the most dangerous, with shadows masking the hollows and the bumps and runnels in the hill that could unweight a skier, send him airborne, only to land in a heap of broken skies, poles, and bones. And, with the lifts closing, some of the hotshots jumped off trail into the undesignated areas, took their last ride down through the trees and deep powder.

It was the patrols' job to make sure everyone got down the mountain safely.

Gage skated over to the express lift and caught the last chair up. He clipped on his helmet and watched the skiers and snowboarders as they finished their runs. He didn't see the T. rex.

The wind had whipped up, and Gage tucked his chin into his gaiter, the chill welcome after the heat radiating off his body.

"I leave all the hero stuff to you, Brooks." Yeah, well, the last thing he needed was Tallie Kennedy, their local reporter, showing up with a microphone and a cameraman. Although it wasn't so long ago he knew exactly how to schmooze a reporter into giving him air time or to strike a pose that might end up on the cover of *Snowboarder* magazine.

But that had been back when he'd been young and stupid and thought he could do something amazing with his life. Thought, really, that he *was* amazing. *Gage "Watts" Watson, lightin' it up on Verbier.*

Echoes. He shook them out of his head.

Wind caught the snow lying in packed layers over the cornice of the bowl, dusted it into the air. He pulled on his goggles and slid off the lift, clicking his boot into the binding of his board. The patrols were calling in, making their last runs of the day.

Shadows covered the back of the bowl, and he stood, staring at the layers of white and gray, the dangers hidden under the frosted, creamy layers. They'd bomb again tomorrow morning and maybe by then get the last of the crust off, open it to powder hounds.

"Ski patrol, Watson. I'm skiing down the perimeter of Timber Bowl—"

His finger paused on the walkie as he spied a form moving down the bowl and into the shadows.

He pulled out his binoculars, found the skier. "You've got to be kidding me."

"Come again, Watson?" He recognized Ty's voice on the other end.

"I've got a snowboarder outside the perimeter," he said. "I'm after him."

"Gage—"

But he cut off Ty's voice and clipped the radio to his chest harness.

Pulled on his goggles.

And breathed in the last of the sunny day, letting it find his lungs, his pores, his bones.

Time to fly.

Gage pushed off and leaned back. The powder drifted up around him, whisper soft, fairy dust on his face as he held out his arms and floated through the snow. He scanned his route, remembering it well from the maps, eased up, and turned on his inner edge and shredded the hill. Powder flew out like a fan behind him. He leaned back and rode the white, catching the boys now in view.

Oh, they had nothing on Watts Watson, two-time freeride world tour champion, record setter, and gold-medal winner of the Xtreme Verbier, the biggest mountain event on the planet.

He edged down a narrow gully, soared over a cliff, catching big air, and while he was at it, added a flip during the forty-foot fall. He stomped it clean and sweet on the snowfield and could now see the T. rex in detail, its head bobbing wildly as the rider took a sweeping turn, caught air, and added a heli-move before landing in a puff of powder.

Gage would give the kid props—he could pick a line. Graceful and smooth, with a little bit of snow poetry as he picked an aggressive line, over cornices, down a nasty couloir, flying off cliff faces as if he had wings.

The kid rode like he'd been born on a board.

Not unlike himself, Gage supposed.

Gage excelled in picking the most creative route down the mountain; it was almost an art, with the powder his canvas. He would study the route, find the one that utilized the rolls, the ridges and drops, see it in his mind as he slashed and carved the mountain into his own masterpiece. He could handle any terrain, from fresh groom to half-pipe, but freeriding allowed him to let go and enjoy the God-given majesty of the mountains.

How he loved the hot sluice of blood in his veins, the scrape of frozen breath in his lungs. Even the clench of his chest when he scared himself and caught air off a hundred-foot drop, leaving his stomach in the heavens. Flying. Then he'd land on a pillow of white only to attack his next big cliff, all the way to the final snow field. His body sore, the wind chafing his ears. Every cell inside him bursting with life.

And he didn't mind the roar of the crowd, either, on and off the slope.

He'd lost himself to it once, and now felt the tug of old habits as he chased down the T. rex.

Gage recognized where he was heading even before the kid hit the cliff.

He pulled up, not wanting to land on him, then saw him further down the hill and let himself go. He found the rock, sighted the fall line, sent himself over.

Let the wind take him.

And for a long second, Gage cut free of his legacy, the guy with tragedy in his wake.

Just clear blue sky ahead of him.

He landed in a puff and followed the trail down the mountain.

The chalet came into view, just over another rise. Gage watched T. rex and pal fly over it, catching easy air.

He couldn't stop himself from grabbing an edge as he followed.

He nearly came down on top of them, but they weren't looking back. He stayed in their blind spot until they hit the chalet.

They had their gear off and were fist bumping on their way inside when he rode up and showered them with snow.

"Hey!"

Oh, he'd give them *hey*.

They turned away then, probably seeing his ski patrol jacket, and hustled inside.

That's right, you should run. Gage unbuckled his bindings, hot on their trail.

He propped his board up, unhooked his helmet strap, and strode inside.

T. rex and pal were making a getaway into the packed Base Camp Saloon.

"You!" he said, pushing past families seated on the vinyl chairs of the luncheon area. The smell of burgers and onion rings lifted off the grills, and the familiar thump of heavy ski boots thundered around the room. Exhausted skiers looked up, their mittens and helmets scattered across tables, as he stormed through the room.

"You, Mr. Dinosaur!"

T. rex didn't turn and disappeared into the saloon.

Gage reached the door four strides later and yanked it open.

The après-ski crowd rocked the room. A country singer crooned on stage, ski bunnies dressed in leggings, turtlenecks, vests, and UGGs sang along while bums in jeans and flannel shirts danced in the middle of the room, frothy beers held high.

Gage knew the party too well and set his jaw, looking for the duo.

He found the pair scooted into a booth with a group of ladies. T. rex was busy deflating his suit.

The kid looked like an escapee from a prep school out East, with short red hair, a smattering of cedar whiskers, mischief and youth in his eyes. He lifted a beer—probably an illegal one—and toasted his partner in crime.

Said partner looked about his age, dark hair, narrow nose, wide cheeks—he looked English, or at least high bred.

Both of them reeked of too much money, too little sense.

Gage had met the type before, and the memory dug under his skin and lodged there like a burr.

"This is where the fun ends," Gage said, stepping up to the table. "Show me your passes."

T. rex jumped up and out of the booth. "Dude! We were just havin' fun."

His buddy edged up next to him, GoPro in hand.

Gage palmed it and yanked it out of the kid's grip. "Sorry, this isn't going on YouTube." He tossed it onto the table. "Your passes. Now."

He spied one of the dinosaur's mittens on the table, with a pass attached, and grabbed it. "I just scored me a season pass," he said and glanced at the picture. "Oliver Blair."

T. rex was peeling off his costume, no more fun and games in his eyes.

Gage spied GoPro's pass on a lanyard tucked inside his jacket. He yanked it over Pro's head.

"Hey!"

"And Bradley Van Dosen." Yeah, the kid looked like a Van-something.

A small crowd had formed around them.

"Leave them alone," said one of the ski bunnies in the booth. She'd scooped up the camera.

"No," Gage said and swiped it away from her. The last thing he needed were pictures of him on the internet. "You think I'm just wrecking their good time, but if they got hurt, we'd have to send our crew out there in the night trying to track them down in an avalanche zone. And every second we're out there, the temperature drops and suddenly it's *our* lives in jeopardy because you guys thought it would be fun to break a few rules."

"It was for the powder," Bradley snapped. Gage wondered if there were a few hash marks after

43

his name. Maybe a Jr., Tripp, or Iver variation.

"I get it—I do. I love riding powder as much as the next guy. But you're not doing it here."

"You've got to be kidding me," Oliver said. "*You* are kicking us off the hill?"

It was the change of tone, dropping a few pitches away from anger or outrage to something that gave Gage one second of warning before the kid continued. "Of all people—seriously? Gage 'Watts' Watson?"

And, despite the warning, for a long, clear second, Gage couldn't move. Just blinked at Oliver as the kid stepped back, a crooked smile forming on his face, half disbelief, half awe.

"Guys, do you know who this is?"

"Stop," Gage growled.

"I saw you this morning, and I couldn't place it—that feeling like I'd seen you before. And of course—*dude!* I have all your videos, that descent down the Broken River face off Craigieburn— that . . . that was over the top. He did a 1080 front flip off a 150-foot face—"

"Please, stop." He glanced over Oliver's shoulder and noticed one of the girls thumb-tapping on her phone.

Maybe texting.

But probably googling him.

Perfect. He had no doubt what might pop up first. Hopefully it would be his world championships. Or maybe that North Face commercial shoot.

But most likely—

"Wait, Gage Watson, that guy from Outlaw?" said one of the girls.

And *bingo,* there it was.

Gage's jaw tightened. He took off his helmet, aware that his hair was matted and thick with sweat as he turned to Oliver. "Yeah, it's me," he said quietly, dark and lethal.

And, frankly, he might as well make the most of it.

That was what cautionary tales were for, right? "So hear me when I say, that kind of stupid behavior gets people killed. I should know, right?"

Oliver's mouth clamped shut, a bloom of red on his face.

At least he'd gotten the kid's attention. He held up the passes, a little show-and-tell that reinforced his words. "Get off my mountain. Stay off my mountain." He pinned a dark look on Bradley, sending his words home while he handed them back the camera. Then he turned and pushed through the crowd, not even wincing at the flash of the camera phones.

Clearly, Gage would never escape the limelight.

She'd found her ski legs again. Ella's entire body burned, a refreshing ache that meant she'd worked hard on the slope, forcing herself to find again the rhythm, the courage, leaning into the

45

adrenaline that had the ability to set her free from herself, her rules. Her relentless ambition.

Snowboarding made her step outside of herself, take risks.

Live.

Yes, maybe Ollie had been right. She had forgotten how to let go, have fun.

Politics and the law did that to a person. The ever-present press of responsibility, the knowledge that constituents' eyes always watched.

The frustration of seeing *nothing* accomplished after two years in office. So much for making an impact on her world. She didn't know how Brette was going to spin her recent epic failure into a campaign plus, but . . .

"Here you go—two hot cocoas," Brette said and slid into the booth across from her. "I have to admit, I did better than I thought. Last time I was skiing, it was with you and Sofia, nearly three years ago."

A white headband held back Brette's two braids, which, along with her white one-piece snowsuit, turned her into a Norwegian ski bunny. She'd unzipped it and pushed the top down to her waist, revealing a purple turtleneck underneath.

"I remember," Ella said. "Sofia fell in love with that guy—I thought he was going to follow us back east."

"What was his name—Richard? Or Randy?"

"Something like that. I thought he was too old

and creepy for her, but she always did have a thing for older men." Ella sipped the cocoa. "I haven't heard from her since she went back to Spain."

"Me either." Brette stretched her legs along the seat of the booth. "Thanks for talking me into coming along." She blew on her cocoa. "I can't really afford it, but it's still good to get away from the dog-eat-dog world of a freelance writer. Please, please let me work on your campaign."

"I don't know if I'm even going to run," Ella said.

"Well, if you do, we need to get working on your biography. You're the walking American success story." Brette took a sip of her cocoa. "Serbian refugee to state senator? How your hard work landed you in Yale Law School?"

"It wasn't my hard work—it was my parents' sacrifice, not to mention my adoptive parents' money. Besides, I don't need a political biography to run for office for a second term."

"In today's world, you do. And I'm sorry, but a girl doesn't graduate from law school at twenty-three without some pretty hard work," Brette said. "I remember those days when you'd spend the weekend doing homework while Sofia and I got into trouble."

"Which is why I stayed at home, studying," Ella said, laughing. "But my mother always said, to whom much is given, much is expected, and I was given a lot."

"Yeah, well, you were a good influence, even if I hate to admit it," Brette said.

"I wish I were a good influence on my brother." Ella signaled the waitress. She came over, looking frazzled. "Can we get a basket of cheesy fries?"

The woman nodded before Ella even finished speaking.

"He'll come around. Not everyone can be as focused and brilliant as you." Brette's eyes seemed to follow a tall cowboy with dark hair threading his way through the crowd. "But if you don't run, then I need myself a hot new story. And what are you going to do? Should we be practicing saying 'Yes, your honor'?"

"No. I have no desire to be a judge." Although if she had her druthers, she'd rather find a way to make things truly fair instead of the legal wrangling that went on behind the scenes. Sometimes the law felt more like a game of poker, with the smartest legal whiz at the table taking home the prize instead of true justice winning out.

She'd seen that up close and personal.

"Then you *have* decided to run again?"

"Put the microphone away. I don't know. Maybe. I don't want to think about it." She took another sip of cocoa, her stomach cheering when the waitress zipped by and dropped off a basket of fries. "I think I've lost my edge, anyway."

"What edge? Oh, you mean your ability to talk anyone into anything?"

Ella gave her a look.

"What? You're incredibly good at getting people to see your point of view." Brette untangled a fry from the gooey cheese.

"That's another way of saying I pester people until they give in."

Brette grinned. "That's *my* superpower—spin."

The country crooner on stage ended his song, and as the cheering died, she heard voices lift from the end of the room.

"Leave them alone!"

It piqued her lawyer ears, and she couldn't help but glance around, find the source.

Her breath wheezed out in a sigh when she spotted her brother, his dinosaur hood pushed back and his red hair on end as he stood up to some ski patroller.

"What has he done now?" She let the words escape even as she found her feet. Brette slid out of the booth beside her.

The crowd around them stood two and three people thick, but her brother was tall and animated, his face betraying surprise as he talked with the local law.

The ski patrol had his back to her and now pulled off his helmet.

Brown curly hair hanging behind his ears to the scruff of his neck.

49

Wide shoulders, a stance that said he didn't back down from trouble.

Oh no.

She froze. Drew back from the altercation.

But the crowd had stilled, apparently listening to the confrontation. And then she heard it.

"Gage Watson, that guy from Outlaw."

She pressed a hand to her stomach. Ground her jaw to Gage's words about people getting killed. About him knowing that better than anyone.

She wanted to cringe.

Yes, yes he did.

But she could have cheered when he ordered Ollie and Bradley off the slopes.

Then he turned, ready to charge through the crowd.

She whirled around, her back to him. Just in case he hadn't forgotten her.

The thought took her by the throat. Like he ever would.

Hard to forget the woman who betrayed you.

"You okay?" Brette said. "You look—"

"Is he gone?"

"Is who—"

"The ski patrol."

Brette glanced in Gage's exit direction. "Yeah. He's gone. He's standing by the door with his other ski patrol pal. Now they're leaving."

"Good." Ella turned back around and headed for Ollie.

"Ella, what's going on?"

But she didn't stop to explain. Could barely speak past the fist in her throat. Still, she muscled past it and managed to find words for her reckless brother.

"Ollie!"

Her voice arrested his attention, and he winced as he spied her pushing through the crowd toward him.

"Just calm down, sis. It's no biggie. I'll get another pass—"

"What did you do this time?"

"Nothing—he's just—I mean, he's one to talk." Ollie picked up one of the beers and brought it to his mouth, and Ella grabbed it away.

"Last time I checked, you weren't old enough to drink."

She said it loudly enough that the girls in the booth snickered.

Ollie turned red. "Thanks for that."

"No problem."

"What's the deal with the whole world turning to hypocrites? Hello, I remember you chasing your own powder a few years ago. You're the one who introduced me to freeriding. In fact— wait, did you see who that was?"

Ella didn't answer him.

"Who *who* was?" Brette said behind him.

"That ski patrol," Bradley said, "Ollie recognized him. It was Gage Watson. Don't you remember—the guy who skied Terminator Wall on the backside of Outlaw three years ago? His partner was killed following his line?"

"It wasn't his partner," Ella said and instantly regretted it. But she was already too far in. "It was a punk kid from Vermont named Dylan McMahon. And he should have never been up there in the first place."

And now she'd said way too much because Brette turned to her, investigator's eyes shining. "Really?"

"I can't say anything else, except that Dylan didn't have the experience to freeride the Terminator. And Gage knew it."

Brette raised an eyebrow. Ella could practically hear her journalist mind ignite.

"Which was why the press took him apart," Ollie said. "He was sued by the family and pretty much ousted from all freeriding competitions. Lost his sponsorships and everything. Brutal."

And that wasn't the half of it. But the law kept her from saying more.

Instead, she turned to Ollie. "What you call hypocrisy is me saying 'learn from your elders.' Gage Watson is right—freeriding is dangerous, and you could get someone killed out there. So yeah, you're done, bro. Time to go home."

Ollie's mouth closed, but Ella wasn't moving.

"I'll grab our cheesy fries," Brette said quietly.

Ollie's jaw tightened. Ella glanced at the girls in the booth.

Okay, so maybe she shouldn't just grab him by the ear and march him home like she once had.

"I'll see you back at the condo, Ollie," Ella said finally. She left him there and headed over to the booth. Brette was boxing up the fries. She glanced up at Ella, eyes narrowed, then looked back to the fries.

"What?"

"I'm digging through my memories, but . . . didn't you have a poster of Gage Watson once upon a time in your room at college?"

"Let's go." She reached for her jacket and helmet.

"You did!"

"I did. It was just a crush."

"Wait a second. I remember—"

"Brette, don't—"

"That's why you went to Outlaw. You were hoping to meet him."

"I went because of Dylan. To stop him from skiing Terminator Wall."

"Did you actually end up meeting Watson?"

Ella sifted her way through the crowd, Brette hot on her trail. They emerged into the lobby. Thankfully, no ski patrol jackets to be seen.

"Wait—didn't you work on Dylan's lawsuit? I thought that name sounded familiar."

"Yeah. Sort of. I was an associate, and his case came to us."

"Right." Brette fell into step with her as they

53

pushed through the doors to the outside. The lights gleamed on their snowboards propped in the snow. "It was one of your first big cases."

"I don't want to talk about this, Brette." Ella pulled her board from the snow.

"Why?"

Ella rounded on her. "Because I'm the reason Gage Watson lost everything, okay? It's my fault he's a has-been, working ski patrol, chasing down hooligans like my brother instead of winning national championships." Her voice dropped. "I wrecked his life."

She turned and headed toward the bridge that led to their on-slope condos. The floodlights lit the night an eerie yellow.

Brette caught up, her boots crunching through the snow. "Hardly. If I remember correctly, he took a novice snowboarder up on one of the most dangerous runs in the world with the promise he'd get him down safely."

"Dylan wasn't a novice by any stretch of the imagination." And she wasn't giving anything away—anyone who watched the tapes could plainly see that Dylan knew how to cut, carve, shred, and follow Gage's line. "He just shouldn't have been out there that day."

But see, now she was treading too close to the border.

"Why?"

Especially with Brette.

Ella sighed, came out to the path that led to the back door to their condo, and found an easy truth. "Dylan was a party animal. I'd seen him out a couple nights before that, good and soused, bragging about the double flip he was going to do off a cliff on Terminator Wall."

The cliff that got him killed.

"If he was drunk, Watson shouldn't have taken him out."

"He wasn't drunk. Listen, all I know is that maybe we shouldn't point fingers at an accident in a sport that has a painfully high mortality rate. If not from jumps and cliffs, then avalanches."

They reached the condo, and Ella set her board on the rack and unlocked the door. Brette followed her into the warmth of the entryway and sat beside Ella, taking off her boots.

"Sounds like you're on his side."

"I'm not on anyone's side."

"Not even Dylan's family?"

Ella got up and walked in her stocking feet to the stairway to the main floor. "Not anymore. Now I'm a politician." She flashed her a wan smile.

Brette beat her to the stairs and braced her arm on the railing, cutting her off. "Ella, what aren't you telling me?"

Ella closed her eyes.

But Brette was like a bulldog when she sniffed out a story.

"Fine. But you can't tell anyone. Promise me."

Brette held up three fingers, Girl-Scout style.

"Okay. C'mon." She headed up the stairs, to the kitchen for some warm milk.

"I'll order some pizza," Brette said. "You talk."

Ella opened the refrigerator. "It all started when I heard that Gage was going to attempt Terminator Wall, and I mentioned it at our family's annual New Year's Eve party. Dylan and his family were there, of course, and I knew he was a snowboarder, so I thought he'd be interested. I never dreamed that three weeks later he'd call me from British Columbia with his crazy plan to get Gage to take him with him. I felt like it was my fault, and that someone had to talk him out of it, so . . . I hopped on a plane . . ."

3

THREE YEARS AGO

Ella had three days to find Gage Watson and talk him into saving Dylan's life.

All he had to do was say no. She might be overreacting, underestimating Dylan's freeriding abilities, but she knew in her gut that if the kid died on the mountain, she would be at least partly to blame.

Her and her big mouth, waxing on about Gage Watson and his freeriding fame. Not that anyone would truly blame her if Dylan got hurt—after all, he made his own impulsive decisions. But she'd been a little unimpressed by Dylan's bragging, so she'd sort of put him in his place.

Which she realized had completely backfired when he told her he was road-tripping to Canada.

She should have predicted it—after all, she'd seen the look in Dylan's eyes when she'd pulled up one of Watson's YouTube videos.

Even she felt the tug of adrenaline, the hot whirr of danger stirring inside when Watson aimed his board downhill, off the lip of a treacherous, powder-fresh mountain face, a tail of snow, not unlike that of a peacock, flaring behind him.

Gage Watson had style and sheer guts.

Whereas Dylan possessed more wannabe than brains or skill, and she dearly hoped her freshly minted trial lawyer skills could convince Gage to walk away from Dylan's no doubt financially enticing offer.

That's what happened when your family ran one of the largest maple-syrup plantations in all of Vermont. All that sugar went straight to the maple prince's head.

Probably her own too, because what on earth had possessed her to think she could don a swimsuit in the middle of January, hang out by the steaming pool at the Outlaw Resort, at the base of the best powder in Canada, and somehow attract Gage's attention?

Yes, she'd left a message for him at the desk, described herself, and asked him to meet her by the pool. But she hadn't counted on the level of spring break crazy.

The resort had built a long chute of snow, and now the snowboarders and skiers alike, dressed in board shorts and stocking caps, wearing their ski gear, raced down the slope and onto the two-story ramp, executing flips and twists before splashing down into the massive pool. Spectators packed three and four deep cheered them on. Country music thrummed against the twilight, girls and guys alike dancing on top of tables, wearing swimsuits, UGGs, and stocking caps. Barbecue ribs sizzling on two huge pits set up in the snow stirred the area with the aroma of celebration.

The pre-party to the Outlaw Freeriding Championships.

Ella stood next to the pool, scanning the crowd, then the jumpers, for any sign of Gage Watson.

Occasionally, her gaze landed on the door. She'd worn a flannel shirt over her one-piece, along with a pair of fuzzy sheepskin UGGs, and had never felt more ridiculous.

A boarder dressed in a furry Russian-style shopka and long johns bumped into her, sloshing his beverage over her. The liquid, cold and bracing on her skin, made her jump away.

"Sorry, sweetie," he said and actually looked like he might lift his hand and wipe it across her legs.

She caught his reach. "Not your sweetie."

He rolled his eyes, bounced away.

Even if Gage were here, she could bet he wouldn't be in the mood to have a serious conversation with her. She should simply call up the front desk, maybe order a pizza sent to his room with an offer to meet her, platonically, in the lounge for a conversation.

She was very good at conversations. This party angle—not her best strategy.

She started to move through the crowd, working her way out of traffic, when she heard the yell.

Off to her left, a scream, more like a war whoop, raised the hairs on her neck as she turned to find the source.

A mass of boarders fresh out of the giant hot tub, dashing for the pool.

The sound gave her a millisecond of warning, however, enough to lift her arms in protection before the horde hit.

They rushed past her, turned her around, and she stumbled.

"Hey!"

An elbow smashed into her face, and in a flash of pain she fell back, arms windmilling.

She hit the water on her back. Her feet crested over her head, and suddenly she was head-down in the water.

Feet kicked her, bodies trapped her, hands pushed her under.

Breathe!

She punched out, connected with a body, and managed to get her feet under her.

Clawed for the surface.

A foot bashed her in the side and she gasped, her mouth opening.

She sucked water, hard, into her lungs. She doubled over, the world turning white even as she fought, pushing—

She found the surface, began to cough, trying to sight the edge of the pool, but another random kick pushed her under.

Panic made her rabid. She fought for air amidst the bodies.

At once, an arm curled around her waist like

a vise. She clawed at it, but her rescuer kicked hard, lifting her.

Her face broke the surface, and she hauled in air. But she coughed it out, retching as her rescuer hauled her to the edge of the pool.

Hands pulled her up and out, and she sat on the deck, gulping air.

"Give her room!" someone yelled a second before a man crouched in front of her. He cut his voice low. "You're okay. Just breathe."

Water dripped from his brown, curly hair, which was nearly shoulder length and pushed back from his forehead. He was in his jeans and wore a dark shirt that was now plastered to his lean torso, outlining his sculpted shoulders. A platinum snowboarder pendant hung gleaming from his neck, the Freeriding World Championship logo imprinted on the front.

And if that wasn't the first clue, the layer of brown whiskers that outlined those enticing lips, the dark brown eyes, filled with mystery and danger, and the tiny cut over his left eyebrow told her exactly who'd rescued her.

Gage Watson.

She couldn't speak, and Gage took her hands in his. "You're shaking."

More than that, her entire body trembled, so violently it shook her grip right out of his.

He somehow procured a towel, wrapped it around her.

Then, he didn't even ask before he bent down and simply picked her up.

Just like that. Holding her against his sopping chest as he headed through the deck doors toward the two-story fireplace of the Outlaw lounge.

Now, she *really* couldn't breathe. Because she'd harbored a crazy fan crush on Gage Watson since he'd taken that run down Heaven's Peak, posted it on YouTube, landed on the cover of *Snowboarder* magazine, and with those brown eyes and renegade smile pretty much cajoled her heart right out of her chest and around his little finger.

He set her down on a worn leather sofa, tucked the towel in around her, and motioned to someone nearby. "Can we get some hot cocoa here?"

Then he turned back to her and smiled. "Are you going to live?"

With the warmth igniting inside her? Um, probably. She swallowed, her hand on her chest, finally able to nod.

"I was looking for you when I saw you go in the water," he said. "I'm sorry I was late. I got your note but had a little trouble finding you in the crowd."

A waitress arrived with the cocoa, and he took it, then handed it to her. He wrapped her hands around the mug, holding his on top. "Take it slow."

She took a sip of the cocoa, let it soothe her raw throat.

"Better?"

She nodded, and he let go of her hands and rested one muscular arm along the top of the sofa, his wet jeans dripping onto the leather. Every once in a while, a shiver rippled through him, although he didn't in the least acknowledge it. But she felt like an idiot now, remembering the panic that took her, the way she'd thrashed. In fact . . .

She spied a welt on his cheek. "Did I hit you?"

"I've had worse," he said, and winked. "But you did pack a wallop."

"I panicked."

"Yes. Yes, you did." He grinned, though, a pretty smirk. He had such enchanting eyes, and for a second she simply forgot where she was.

Until.

"So, what did you want to see me about? It seemed like a pretty desperate note—something about life or death?" His gaze trailed over her. "I'm hoping that wasn't a suicide attempt."

"No—no." And now she just wanted to crawl away. Why was she always so dramatic? "I was . . . I'm here to ask you for a favor."

"A favor. Really." He raised a shoulder. "Okay, I'm game. Shoot it at me."

"Please don't ski Terminator Wall."

His smile dimmed. A frown dipped across

63

his forehead. "Uh . . . you know that's why I'm here, right? There'd be a horde of disappointed people, not to mention my sponsors, a few magazines, and a couple hundred thousand YouTube subscribers if I didn't shred the Terminator. So, maybe you could give me a good reason why I should decimate my entire career?"

When he put it like that . . .

"Because you want to save a life?"

He considered her a long moment, his lips curling up one side.

"Whose life? Because if it's yours—"

"Dylan McMahon."

His smile dimmed. "Oh. Him." He scraped his hair back from his head. "Don't tell me he's your boyfriend."

"What—no! *No.* He's just a friend. Actually . . . I put the stupid idea in his head, and now . . . I just know that if you go, he'll go and—"

He held up his hand. "Pump the brakes. I'm not letting Dylan McMahon follow me down the T-wall, so just take a breath, okay? He's not ready. And I don't need anyone getting killed following my line."

She probably blew out a breath of visible relief because another smile lit his face, his eyes.

Oh, those eyes.

"Thank you. Thank you so much. You can't believe what this means to me." She knew she sounded over the top. But she'd just nearly drowned, and sitting here, wrapped up in Gage Watson's presence—yes, she might have lost her mind a little.

"Okay. Anytime. What was your name again?"

"Ella. Ella Blair."

"Okay, Ella Blair. Gage Watson."

"Uh-huh," she said.

"I'm sort of curious," he said, leaning toward her. "How *much* does it mean to you?"

Oh. Um . . .

He raised an eyebrow.

She stared at her cocoa. "I don't think—"

"Oh no. Wait. That sort of came out wrong," he said suddenly, and for a second, when she looked up, all the suave had vanished, leaving behind someone real, someone not quite as polished.

Someone endearing. And slightly reddening at his awkward statement.

"I just meant, well, I was trying to figure out a smooth way to ask you if you might want to hit the slopes with me tomorrow. I mean, you are a skier, right?"

The way he bobbled around his words, it made his invitation sound sweet and innocent and had her heart doing all sorts of leaps.

"Actually, a snowboarder."

"Really," he said, warmth in his eyes.

"Yeah. And I'd love to ski with you tomorrow.

65

If you promise not to take me anywhere I could get killed."

Her towel had loosened, and he reached out and tucked it back around her, his hands strong as he cocooned her in heat.

"I promise to keep you safe." He gave her a wink. "Because, you know, I'm all about saving lives."

4

Gage had some epic falls in his career, the kind that made viewers wince, the yard sale crashes that became six-second Vines on the net. He'd broken a leg, dislocated his shoulder, emerged with his face so bloody the sports networks attached a viewer warning to it before the replay. He still bore the bump of his broken nose, a sort of freeriding badge of honor.

And while he longed to rewind the tape, maybe choose a different line, none of his mayhem crashes made him wish to go back to the beginning and throw his snowboard across the room. Wish all of it away—his fame, his laurels, the joy of carving his own trail.

Until a punk teenager in a dinosaur costume looked at him with stars in his eyes. *"I have all your videos, that descent down the Broken River face off Craigieburn—that . . . that was over the top."* Gage wanted to smack his hand over Oliver's mouth, keep the memories from surfacing. Keep his exploits from finding root in his brain and tearing open the wounds of regret.

Just when he thought he might carve out a new line for his life.

Gage threw his board on the rack on top of his Mustang, then opened the door.

"You missed a call," Ty said from the passenger seat. He already had his board latched on top, his boots off and cowboy boots on.

Gage slid onto the driver's bucket seat, his feet still outside the door, and started unlatching his boots. He slid one off, slipped his foot into a hiking boot, then picked up his phone from the dash and took a look.

"Two missed calls from my mom." He dropped the phone into the cup holder, then unlatched his other boot. He laced on his hiking boot, then threw the two snowboard boots into the back seat.

His mom. He checked his watch. Maybe he should stop by . . . especially if her voicemail betrayed a slur in her voice.

Gage headed out of the parking lot, the itch of the fight with Oliver still under his skin. *"He did a 1080 front flip off a 150-foot face—"*

He should write to Xtreme Energy, ask them to take his videos down. After all, they'd dropped *him.*

Keeping them up just inspired more idiocy from kids like Oliver Blair.

Or Dylan McMahon.

Gage loosened his whitened hold on the steering wheel as he reached a light and turned on his radio.

Of course, Ben King's sultry country voice crooned through the speakers—it seemed he was the only artist playing on their local country station. The entire town had a love affair going with Ben King and the fact that he'd moved his studio here, healed his past, and restarted his life to the wild applause of his fans.

Yeah, well, it didn't happen that way for everyone. And too many people paid the price when it didn't. They'd all be better off if the fame of "Watts" Watson were wiped from all memory.

"Maybe I'll swing by and see what my mom wants." He glanced at Ty. "Do you mind?"

"I'll order us a couple pizzas to pick up," Ty said, already pulling out his phone. "Although my bet is that Sierra will have fresh-baked cookies at HQ. Everyone's getting together for the show tonight."

Sierra Rose, their dispatcher, PEAK team administrator, and all-around big sister. Although, he had to wonder if Sierra would be there, especially if Ian planned to show up. It seemed that the gulf between them had widened after the mysterious call from Esme Shaw, Ian's missing niece, confirming she was still alive. Sierra seemed to think that Ian should heed his niece's request not to look for her.

Ian never heeded anyone's request. Maybe his billions of dollars told him he didn't have to.

That's what money did—made people belligerent. Stupid.

Reckless.

If the entire team was there, it also meant

that Jess and Pete would be in the same room, playacting the too-bright courtesy between them. Gage still remembered the cryptic conversation with Pete from last summer, when Pete had asked Gage's advice about women.

Or, as Gage deduced later, one woman.

"So, what if," Pete had asked, "hypothetically—you had a friend who you liked, but you weren't sure she liked you back—what would you do? Go for it?"

Gage had guessed, only *after* he advised Pete to go out with Tallie Kennedy—not their coworker, Jess Tagg—that Pete had wanted a different answer. Or rather, maybe *Jess* wanted a different answer, found out about Tallie, and put the kibosh on anything they had going between them.

Then again, maybe Pete had gone for it and . . .

Naw. Jess wasn't the type of girl to be wooed by Pete Brooks and his lazy smile, that country-boy charm.

Whatever the case, spending the evening with his less-than-bonded team seemed only slightly better than watching reruns on Ty's extra-large flat screen he'd purchased for their duplex. No, er, Ty's duplex, one in which he so generously let Gage rent a room at a reduced cost.

Ty was ordering a couple large supreme pizzas, and Gage didn't bother to remind him to keep off the mushrooms. He wasn't hungry anyway.

He turned through the little town of Whitefish,

past the quaint shops, then out to the highway, before looping back along Whitefish Lake to his parents' home, one that the two doctors rarely spent time in.

They'd barely missed him when Gage started spending every hour on the slopes. Then again, they were probably thankful he wasn't getting into trouble with "that crowd," a group of people his orthopedic surgeon father had met plenty of. But Gage had never been on the slopes to party.

"Do something with your life. Make it matter." Only, his dad had probably meant that he should follow in the family footsteps and go to medical school. Spend summers working with Doctors Without Borders or donating his hours in some small-town clinic.

Not becoming the poster boy for harrowing mountain runs.

"I'll wait in the car," Ty said as Gage pulled up to his parents' home, a beautiful yet not ostentatious rambler set back under towering lodgepole pines overlooking the lake.

Gage nodded, got out, and headed through the garage inside.

"Ma?" He stood in the kitchen. Granite countertops, stainless steel, hardwood flooring, and the two-story attached great room that opened to a view of not only Whitefish Lake but also the glittering lights of Blackbear Mountain.

Gage turned away from it. Called again.

The silence had his gut clenching, and he headed for his mother's office, located at the end of the hall in one of the former bedrooms and across from his own.

A light shone out from the bottom of the door, and he knocked.

"It's open," his mother said, and he pushed the door in to see her sitting at her desk, her laptop computer open, her reading glasses down on her nose. She'd freshly dyed her dark hair, washing away the white, and still wore her hospital administrator attire of a pair of soft wool pants and a cashmere sweater, looking every inch the award-winning neurosurgeon she'd once been.

Still could be, if she found the right case. But she'd seemed to lose her fire back when he'd returned home, defeat in his wake.

Now, she only took the most selective of cases, and aside from a few consults, she sat on the board of the hospital and tried to keep it in the black.

His gaze fell on a glass, mostly drained, of her daily cognac, and he hoped it was just the first.

She looked up from her work. "Gage," she said, and he noticed a softening around the consonants. That, and her smile, not forced but a little wobbly. Nope, not her first glass.

"I was on the mountain. Sorry I missed your call—thought I'd check in on my way home."

"So nice of you," she said and pushed her chair

away from the desk. "I wanted to ask you if you'd stop by the hospital."

Gage's eyes darted to a bottle of acetaminophen near the computer. Must have been a rough day fighting bureaucracy.

"Why?"

His mother picked up her drink. "That boy you brought in, Hunter? Guess what—he's a fan. Couldn't stop talking about the fact that you saved him." Her eyes shone, and Gage wished he could attribute it to the drink.

Oh Mom, please don't live in the past.

"I came down to check on your father's schedule, and he was just prepping the boy for surgery. I told him you'd stop by later, cheer him up."

Gage winced. "He's going to be out of it for a while—"

"Tomorrow then. Think of how happy he'll be to meet his hero!"

"I'm hardly his hero—"

"Gage. Of course you are." She got up then, and he noticed her hand steadying herself on her desk.

He grabbed her elbow.

"You're still an inspiration."

"Maybe you should lie down for a bit, Ma." He eased the near-empty glass from her hand.

"I do have a little headache." She pressed her hand to her head.

He led her to her sofa. "I'll get you a drink of

73

water," he said and scooped the acetaminophen into his pocket as he walked away.

Only as he walked past his old room did he see the door ajar, and on his old desk, his scrapbook open.

He went inside and instantly regretted it. No matter how many times he packed away his trophies, his medals, even that stupid Xtreme Energy poster, they still migrated back to his shelves, freshly dusted, the poster repinned to the wall.

He backed out, shut the door.

Headed to the kitchen for a glass of water.

His mother was asleep by the time he returned. He put the glass down on her desk, kissed her forehead. She roused at his touch. Caught his hand. "Thanks for stopping by."

"Anytime, Ma."

Ty was scanning stations when Gage returned to the Mustang. "If I have to listen to one more Ben King song . . ."

Gage laughed and queued up his iPod. Justin Timberlake's "Can't Stop the Feeling" coursed through the speakers.

"Okay, I surrender. Ben King it is," Ty said. He flipped back to the station. "What did your mom want?"

Gage shook his head as he pulled out. "Hunter, that kid who fell from the chair today, wants an autograph."

"From the ski patrol who saved him?"

Gage shot Ty a look.

"What?"

"I'm still a thing to fifteen-year-old wannabe freeriders, apparently."

Ty grinned. "I'm in the presence of snowboard royalty."

"You can walk home."

"No, really, Gage. Stop by the hospital. Cheer the kid up."

"The last thing he needs is to be encouraged by a guy who screwed up." Gage turned on 40, bypassing the hospital. "And the last thing *I* need is to revisit the guy I used to be. He's gone, and I'm trying to put it behind me." He shook his head. "It would help if my mother stopped living in the past."

"What, and join ranks with your father? 'Gage, get a real job. Do something with your life.'" Ty's imitation felt too raw, and Gage clenched his jaw.

"Maybe just leave me alone along with the rest of the world. Let the past die. The last thing I need to do is resurrect some version of that stupid, cocky kid and parade him around to offer false inspiration. What I should be doing is wearing a sign that says 'cautionary tale.'"

Now Ty went quiet, as if embarrassed by Gage's tirade.

Well, nobody liked the truth anymore, it seemed.

75

"Sorry. I'm just in a rotten mood after chasing down that stupid kid in the dinosaur costume."

"Dude. You wear your mistakes like a brand on your forehead. You need to get over it."

"You're one to talk. I don't see you getting back in the simulator. Are you ever going to fly a chopper again?"

Ty drew in a long breath, his jaw tight as he looked away.

Gage probably shouldn't have said that. "Ty, I'm—"

"Leave it, Gage," Ty said quietly. He stared out the window. "Don't forget to stop by the pizza place."

"Please don't tell me you ordered from the Griz—last time we ordered from there, we all got sick."

"Fear not. I put an order in at Glacier Pizza."

They rode in silence until they pulled up to the pizza place. Ty ran in.

He returned in a moment with a couple of steaming pizzas and set them on his lap.

"No mushrooms?"

"I remembered," Ty said.

"Thanks," Gage said. But see, that was the problem. When it came to Gage Watson, they all remembered.

In all the years Ty had known Gage, and even admired him a little from afar, he'd never agreed with the press, the destruction of his career, or the rumors that said Gage had possessed an ego that led the way to his destruction.

Until tonight. *"Are you ever going to fly a chopper again?"*

The question, more defense than actual inquiry, replayed in Ty's ears as he got out of the silent Mustang and headed up to the two-story ranch house that formed the headquarters for the PEAK Rescue team. Their eleven-person team consisted of three EMTs—Gage, Pete, and Jess—their chopper pilot Kacey Fairing, their administrative assistant Sierra Rose, team incident commander Miles Dafoe, country crooner Ben King, and his father, Chet, who started the team way back with its founder, Ian Shaw, and their sheriff department liaison, Sam Brooks. Only Ty was the one without any formal duties. A former helicopter pilot, he now did his rescue duty as a dispatcher, sometimes searcher, all-around pizza delivery guy.

A real asset to the team.

Not that his busted knee didn't give him legitimate excuse to cut back his hours, but frankly, if he wasn't going to sit in the copilot's seat or at the helm, he might as well make coffee and run inventory on the supplies. He didn't have a medical degree like Jess, didn't understand the logistic operations like Sam, couldn't helm a search like Miles or even Pete, who'd recently gotten certified in the government's FEMA rescue services. He couldn't even make cookies like Sierra.

Frankly, he felt about as useful as Jubal, Chet's lab. Maybe less so—at least Jubal knew when to plop down at a guy's feet with a sigh and make him feel like he belonged.

The truth was, Ty stood on the outskirts of the team since the accident. And if they really knew the details, he'd probably be booted off the crew altogether.

He should probably thank Chet for keeping that part secret. But it was starting to raise eyebrows that the old chief wasn't hassling him about getting back in the cockpit.

Instead, Ty honed his pizza-ordering talents. A skill met with cheers as he came in and found the team gathered in the kitchen of the small main room, watching the flat screen on the wall. Miles and Ben sat on the sofa in the middle of the room; Ben held a harmonica and was showing his daughter, Audrey, how to cup it in her hand. Miles bounced Huck, his two-year-old, on his knee, and his wife, Jenni, held their baby girl in a front pack, a seven-pound, one-month-old bundle of time-to-get-serious for Miles. He'd hung up his bull-riding spurs for Jenni and little Gracie May.

Ty slid the boxes of pizza onto the counter. "Two large pepperoni and sausage pizzas, no mushrooms."

Gage had walked in behind him, slid onto a stool at the counter.

Sierra stood in the kitchen, opening a bag of plastic cups. She was dressed in a pair of track pants and a sweatshirt, her short dark hair tucked behind her ears. "Awesome. I was hoping someone would bring pizza."

Kacey Fairing, with her wild red hair held back in a ponytail, was cutting up a pan of lasagna, something that looked homemade. Probably Sierra's doing. Or Willow's, Sierra's younger sister, who was taking a batch of chocolate chip cookies from the stove. She wore her long brown hair in two braids.

"Thanks for sending the chopper today, Chet," Gage said as he reached for a red Solo cup and filled it with cola.

Chet King, their former chopper pilot. The guy who still hobbled around on two crutches as his hips mended from the crash that had nearly ended their lives last spring.

The crash Ty had caused. He still couldn't look at Chet without wincing.

"Did your dad patch the kid up?" Chet asked.

"Yeah," Gage said to him. "My mom saw him in recovery, said he was doing okay."

"My favorite surgeon," Chet said.

Ty picked up the remote. "What channel is this thing on?"

"Channel eleven." The voice came from the

man seated at the computer. Ian Shaw. "But it's going to run numerous times over the weekend, so hopefully we'll get the right leads."

Next to Ian sat Sam Brooks, deputy sheriff and liaison to the PEAK team from the Mercy Falls EMS department, headphones around his neck. He was out of uniform tonight in a pair of jeans and a button-down shirt. "The call center will route all calls here, allow us to vet the callers, interview them, and piece together leads."

Ty still couldn't quite figure out why Ian had spent the past eight months, and who knew how much money, helping to identify the remains of the woman who'd been found by their team in the Avalanche River last summer. Clearly, it wasn't his niece, but the man could spend his billions how he wanted.

"Shh, the show is coming on," Ben said.

Ty popped up the volume with the remote. Only then did he realize that Pete and Jess were missing.

Pete and Jess. Who had nearly become a couple last summer. And, except for Jess's secrets, might be living happily ever after today.

A concept Ty still had to get his brain around, because Pete had never-settle-down written all over him. Until Jess, apparently.

However, their romance was a well-kept secret, as were all things Jess.

Including the reason she went running into Ty's

embrace when Pete tried to turn the limelight on her after their recovery of a group of missing kids last summer.

Only Ty knew why she'd dodged the interview with Tallie Kennedy and channel 11, a secret he couldn't share with anyone, not if he didn't want to betray Jess and her painful secret.

Besides, Ty wasn't all that sure that Jess *didn't* have feelings for him lately. Not with the way she sat next to him during team muster or occasionally called him up, asking him over to her fixer-upper. Sure, usually the invitation accompanied a request to sand or paint something, but still. She didn't seem in any rush to clear up the rumors . . . which meant what? That she wanted him to go from showing up at her house with his DYI tool belt on to asking her out on a real date?

Sure, she was pretty, with her long blonde hair, and around her he almost felt normal, as if he wasn't the team joke. But he wasn't a fool.

Jess pined for Pete so much that any other man would have to pry his way into her heart and jockey for space. Thankfully, Ty had never seen Jess as more than a sister.

Still, as a pseudo brother to her, he had a responsibility to keep her secrets—and according to Jess, that meant keeping her away from Pete. Which meant playing the game, for now.

"Do you know where Pete and Jess are?" Ty

asked, keeping it casual as he dished himself up a piece of pizza.

"I dropped her at her house."

The voice came from behind him, and Ty turned and caught sight of Pete coming in the door. He wore his blond hair pulled back in a man bun, and he eyed Ty as he shucked off his jacket. "Why?"

Pete put just a little too much snap in his voice, and Ty chose to ignore it. "Is she coming over?"

Pete's eyes glinted, his mouth tight as he considered Ty. "I don't know. She didn't tell me." He brushed past him and headed for a plate of lasagna.

Ty couldn't exactly blame him. All of Pete's efforts to patch his mistakes with Jess fell on deaf ears. According to Jess, she simply couldn't risk Pete finding out what had happened back in New York.

Then again, given Pete's history with betrayal, yeah, maybe Jess had a point.

Leave well enough alone.

Ty walked over to the sofa, stood behind it, and folded his pizza in half like a sandwich as he ate it.

The show had started, and the host was giving a rundown of the facts of the case. The girl found in the creek, her approximate age, estimated date of death, and then, the likeness of her created by the forensic artist.

For a second, the room went quiet, perfectly still.

Long dark hair, a regal nose, high cheekbones, the woman looked almost European, maybe Spanish or Portuguese. Dark brown eyes and full lips, although that was just the sketcher's interpretation.

"She was pretty," Pete said.

The announcer gave her height, weight, and what she'd been wearing the day of her disappearance. Shorts, hiking boots, a T-shirt.

She'd also been found wearing a gold necklace, identical to the one Ian gave his niece Esme on her eighteenth birthday.

Either that, or somehow the woman ended up with Esme's necklace in her possession. That mystery, perhaps, was the precise thing that fueled Ian's search. The gut feeling that the necklace connected the two, something that would lead to Esme's return.

Hence deputy Sam, listening for calls on his headset.

A number flashed on the screen, and everyone jumped when a phone buzzed.

"It's mine," Gage said and pulled it out. "Sorry."

He got up from the stool and walked over to the window, cutting his voice low, under the volume of the television.

Still, Ty could hear him, especially as his voice raised.

"Are you kidding me? Oliver—no. It's not safe!"

Ty glanced at Gage. He had his eyes closed, his finger and thumb rubbing the stress—or perhaps disbelief—out of them.

Ty perked up, listening.

"Listen—people get killed trying to ski down Heaven's Peak. It's not—yeah, I know I did it but—what? No, that's insane. It's a two-day trip at best and—"

Ty wasn't sure when he'd taken the step toward Gage, but he found himself near the counter, standing closer to Gage than the group.

Which meant he heard him loud and clear when Gage's voice dropped. "Please don't do this. There's a weather front coming in tomorrow, and with the recent snowfall, the avalanche danger is extreme, plus—I'm sure you're an amazing boarder, but—"

And then Gage let out a word of frustration between his teeth, pulling the phone from his ear. "What an idiot." He set the phone down on the table and then reached out as if to strangle someone.

"Who was that?"

Gage looked at him, shaking his head. "Oliver Blair."

Ty frowned, lifted a shoulder.

"The T. rex guy."

Oh. He didn't exactly understand Gage's ire

84

over the kid in a dinosaur suit who'd broken the rules and skied down the back bowl in an undesignated area. It wasn't like Gage hadn't done that plenty of times. Practically made a career out of it.

"How'd he get your number? And why would this guy call you?"

"I don't know. Maybe from dispatch—I'll have to talk to them about giving out my number. I tracked him down during the last run of the day and chased him into the lodge. I took his ski pass—and all the time he's saying"—Gage changed his voice, turned it incredulous, even silly—" 'Are you Gage Watson, dude? Like, the super awesome snowboarder?' "

Ty couldn't help a smile at Gage's surfer impression. "Ah. That was what tonight's sour mood was really about. This guy recognized you—"

"And announced it to the entire bar."

Oh. That was rough.

"And now, this idiot wants to ski down Heaven's Peak. Follow my line." Gage winced, then shook his head and looked away. "He's going to get himself killed."

"Why? You did it, right? And you said he's a great boarder."

"You have to be more than great for Heaven's Peak. I planned that route for months. And practiced. There's a sixty-foot stomp off a waterfall on the way down that, if you don't take

85

it right, will get you killed. And, a couloir that is nearly straight down. Not to mention the fact that it can't be run in one day. You have to take it in spurts. It took me two days—which meant I had to camp on the mountain . . ."

"And there's a storm front heading toward Montana."

"Exactly." Gage reached for his phone. Pressed redial. Made a face. "Voicemail." He sighed, looked at Ty, then at the team. Pocketed his phone.

"I gotta go over to the resort and see if I can find him. Talk some sense into him."

Ty put his hand on his shoulder.

Gage stopped. "Don't try and talk me out of it, Ty. I know it's not my responsibility, but really, it sort of is. It always will be, as long as my name is associated with freeriding."

"I was going to say that I'm going with you."

Gage led the way out the door. He said nothing as Ty climbed into the Mustang.

They were halfway back to the ski hill when, "Sorry for what I said about the sim, bro. This has been a . . . well, not my favorite day."

Ty lifted a shoulder. "So, how are you going to find this guy?"

"I have his ski pass. I'll ask the lift office for his lodging information."

The place was closed when Gage arrived, but Ty found the resort manager and they dug around in the computer files and found Oliver's name and his local lodging information.

Thirty minutes later, Ty and Gage drove through the snowy drifts to one of the grand lodge-style four-plexes that edged Moose Run. Cedar siding, a thick layer of snow frosting the roof, pine trees flanking the walkway. The place had money embedded in every cranny.

Ty's parents owned two, which they rented out all year long.

He didn't mention that as Gage parked, got out, and crunched up to the front door. A front porch hosted Adirondack chairs, and a porch light glimmered out welcome.

Gage knocked on the door. "If I have to, I'll call Sam, tell him that this kid is drinking underage, get him thrown into the Mercy Falls drunk tank—"

The door opened.

And for a second, Ty's world stopped, stilled on the sight of the woman in the doorway. She wore a pair of baggy gray sweat pants, a tank top, and a pair of fuzzy UGG slippers. With her long blonde hair, gray-green eyes, all curves and a sweet smile, she looked the girl next door. The lilt to her smile suggested curiosity at the two men on her front porch.

"Gentlemen? Can I help you?"

"I'm looking for Oliver Blair," Gage said darkly, clearly not as taken with the woman as Ty.

Then again, Gage was apparently immune to women—hadn't had a date since he moved back to Mercy Falls, it seemed. Definitely not as long as Ty had lived with him.

"I'm not sure if he's back yet." She ducked her head inside. "Ella! Um . . . you'd better come here. *Someone* is here to see your brother!"

Weird, the way she said that. As if, oddly, they were expected.

It was then he felt something shift in Gage. A flushing of the anger, just for a moment, a capture of breath, a quick glance at Ty.

It had Ty frowning. What . . . ?

And then the door opened wide and a second woman appeared. Ella, he supposed.

He wouldn't necessarily call her breathtaking, but she had a unique beauty about her. Pale blue eyes, copper red hair. She wore a pair of pink pajama bottoms printed with penguins and an oversized sweatshirt and was carrying a half pint of ice cream, the spoon just sliding out of her mouth.

Her gaze fixed on Gage, and her spoon stilled mid-escape.

"You," Gage said quietly, his voice almost strained.

Ty looked at him, the way Gage's chest rose and fell, the way his hands curled tight at his sides. Okay, this was weird.

"I should have guessed that the idiot in the bar

was the brother of Ella Blair. And now I know how he got my number. You just can't stop wrecking my life, can you?"

Huh? As Ty watched, the spoon slid out of her mouth, and for a long moment, she stared at him, her jaw tight.

While Gage could be abrupt, even a jerk, Ty had never seen him quite so rude.

Especially to a woman.

Quietly, Ella spoke. "Nice to see you too, Gage."

Her words, her soft tone, didn't seem to dent his ire. "Is your brother here? Because he's about to do something stupid, and I'm going to have to stop him."

5

Oh, Ella turned into such a mess when Gage Watson entered her airspace. What was it about him that even three years later, and with the advance warning of seeing him earlier in the day, the sight of the amazing "Watts" Watson standing on her doorstep still turned her nearly mute.

Nice to see you too, Gage? What was she thinking? That he might, after three years, have forgotten the way they parted?

Clearly not, given the grim slash of his mouth, the pulsing of muscle in his jaw.

It didn't help that she could still so easily remember the *sweet* Gage Watson, the one who'd spent three glorious days snowboarding with her. He'd been a gentleman, too, not even trying to make a pass at her until she began to wonder if he liked her at all or if she'd simply wished it into her vivid imagination.

Then, on day three, it all changed. Dinner, candlelight . . . the most romantic evening she'd ever experienced.

And the darkest heartbreak.

Now, Mr. Heartbreak stood on her doorstep. Up close and personal, he looked every inch the sizzling hot snowboarder she remembered. Maybe more, because age had filled out his shoulders, broadened them. He hadn't lost any of his stun power either, with that long curly hair now held back with a stocking cap, enough grizzle on his chin to turn his whiskers dark and tempting, his eyes just as deep, dark chocolate brown.

He wore his black snowboard pants, the suspenders hanging down to his knees, and a silver fleece that clung to his lean torso and his muscled arms.

How she remembered those arms.

She'd sort of dreamed of this moment, really, for three years. That second—or rather third—chance to talk to him, preferably privately, and apologize.

Tell him that things had simply spiraled out of control. Or, perhaps, dig deeper and admit the truth.

He'd broken her heart when he took Dylan up to Terminator Wall. And that feeling had darkened all her decisions right up to nearly the end. When it became too late to pull back, change the outcome.

"My brother isn't here."

"Are you sure?" Gage snapped.

Another man stood beside him. Taller than Gage, he had shorter dark hair and was attempting a sort of crooked smile, as if to ease the tension stringing out between them. He wore ski pants also, as well as a pullover and open-zipped jacket. She recognized him as the other ski patrol who'd joined Gage in the Saloon.

"Hey, back off, dude." This from Brette, who'd suddenly come alive after Gage's retort. "He's not here, okay?"

"What stupid thing?" Ella asked, referring to his statement. She settled her spoon back into her ice cream. The carton froze her fingers, and she set it down and wiped her hand on her pajama pants. Oh, so sexy, Ella. Worse, she remembered the pattern of her pajamas featured tiny penguins in stocking caps.

"He called me and sounded drunk," Gage was saying.

Or maybe high. Ella tightened her lips against the addition.

"And told me he was going to ski down Heaven's Peak tomorrow, following my route."

He didn't need to elaborate. She knew exactly what he meant.

He'd only traced the route from her fingers down to her open palm, telling her in exquisite, perfect detail every moment of the run, how he'd chosen his line, the perilous moments when he thought he'd skim over the edge, the burn in his legs right before he did a flip off the Weeping Wall.

He'd kissed her palm where he'd spent the night in the cave and then finished the route, curling over her hand, and up her arm until he reached the inside of her upper wrist.

Kissed her there too, and now heat flooded her face, a repeat from when she'd pulled her arm away in the middle of the restaurant, too aware that people might be watching. *With* their phone cameras.

He probably saw her embarrassment, maybe even remembered the past, because he swallowed and looked away.

"Come in," Ella said, and Brette looked at her as if to say "Have you lost your mind?"

Maybe. But she'd been waiting three years for this moment. No, not her brother's crazy assertion that he planned on repeating Gage's legendary run, but the one that included Gage in her living room, away from reporters and lawyers and Dylan McMahon's family.

A moment when Gage couldn't hang up on her. Delete her emails, ignore her texts. "You're right, Gage, my brother is an idiot. Sometimes. Lately." She kept her voice easy, soft.

No fight in it.

Gage stepped over the threshold and into her condo. "This is my friend Ty. He's on the ski patrol."

"Nice to meet you." She turned to Gage. "I don't think he's here, but you can look around. We used the back entrance when we came in, so maybe he's here and we didn't see him."

Brette had her by the arm, tightened her hold. She pulled out of it. "But why did he call you?"

Ty followed him in. The guys tugged off their boots, a courtesy they probably did on reflex.

"I took his ski pass away today after he skied out of bounds," Gage said. "We were in the Base Camp and he recognized me. Maybe it ignited the idea."

"Oh, hardly. He's been talking about skiing your line for a few years now."

Maybe she shouldn't have said that, because Gage glanced up as he set his boots on a nearby mat.

"So, he's serious." Gage shook his head. "Ella, you of all people should tell him how dangerous—"

"I don't understand—what's Heaven's Peak?" Brette said.

"It's a mountain in Glacier National Park," Ella said. "Gage was the first to freeride down the face. He posted his self-made video explaining how he did it, and it's had over a million views. He even made the national news—it sort of jump-started his career."

Gage held up a hand as if to stop her explanation. "It's one of the most dangerous rides in North America," he said simply. "I got lucky."

For a second, with that statement, she glimpsed him, the easygoing, self-deprecating, sweet boarder who didn't deserve to get mauled by the press.

Or by her law firm.

"And Ollie wants to ski it?" Brette said, looking at Ella.

"He's sort of had this fascination with the big freeride champs over the years, thinks he wants to be one," Ella said. "He has this dream of doing something . . . well, carving out fame for himself."

"Fame is an empty dream," Gage said.

And that shut everyone down. Ho-kay.

His friend Ty finally spoke up. "Can we check downstairs? Maybe he came in after you did."

"Maybe," Ella said. She picked up the soggy ice cream carton and brought it to the kitchen.

"I'll go check," Brette said and left, Gage's friend Ty on her heels.

Which left Ella finally, providentially, alone with Gage. She put the ice cream in the freezer.

Gage had walked over to the stairs, as if contemplating taking the spiral staircase up to check the second floor.

"Gage . . . I really am glad to see you."

A fire flickered in the stacked stone hearth, and the place smelled of the uneaten pepperoni pizza recently delivered from the Griz.

The makings of romance if things were different. Much, *much* different.

He glanced at her now. "You are?"

"Because . . ." She walked over. "I wanted to . . . I wanted to talk to you about what happened."

His expression didn't change, just the smallest narrowing of his eyes.

"I wanted to explain."

"No explanation needed, Ella. You were just doing your job." He leaned over the stairway to the basement. "Is he down there?"

"Yeah, I was, but you need to know that—"

And that's where her words hitched. Because he couldn't know the details. Not without her career crashing in around her.

Like his had.

"It wasn't personal."

And that wasn't what she wanted to say at all, but she had nothing else.

"Really." His mouth closed, and he shook his head. "It felt very personal. Especially when you put Ramon on the stand."

"That wasn't my call."

"But it was your examination."

Her mouth closed. She blinked, heat in her eyes, and for a second she was back in court, feeling his eyes burn her as she declared Ramon, his friend and manager, a hostile witness. As she slowly pried out the incriminating conversation from him that sealed Gage's fate.

"I . . . I wish I had recused myself. I should have—"

He held up his hand as Ty came up the stairs.

"He's not here," Ty said. "But I did find this in his room."

He handed Gage a folded map. She came over and took a look at it as he unfolded it.

96

"Oh no. It's a map of Heaven's Peak, with my route traced down it." Gage folded it back up, shoved the map into his pocket. "I have to find him before he does something stupid."

"Thank you, Gage." She touched his arm almost without thinking. "But I can find him."

He jerked his arm away as if her touch might contain an electric spark. It rattled her, but she found the politician in her and schooled her voice. "You've done enough. I'll stop him."

She wasn't sure why so much surety came out of her mouth.

People simply did what they wanted, regardless of common sense.

But Gage just looked so . . . well, wrung out. As if, with Ollie's words, he saw the past flashing before his eyes, same song, second verse. She couldn't let him feel responsible. Or take the blame.

Not when it wasn't his fault.

Had *never* really been his fault.

And maybe only she and two other people in the world truly knew that, but if she could, she'd let him walk away from this one unscathed. So, she kept her voice low and even. "He's my brother. I'll find him, and I'll talk him out of it. Coerce him if I have to. I won't let him go up Heaven's Peak."

Gage's mouth was a tight bud of doubt.

"Thanks for coming over, but you've done

97

enough. Thank you for helping my brother. It was nice of you. You're a good guy, Gage. I've always known that."

It wasn't much, especially when she wanted to say so much more.

He blinked then, as if perplexed, his brow dipping into a frown.

Swallowed.

She offered a smile.

He didn't return it. But he did give her a quick nod, as if willing to hear her words.

Her tiny, pitiful peace offering to the gigantic wound she'd inflicted on his life.

"You let me know if you have trouble with him," he said, proving her words about him being a good guy. He walked over then, shoved his feet into his boots. His friend pulled on his cowboy boots.

"Nice to meet you, Ty," Brette said and held out her hand.

"You too." He shook it, glanced at Ella. "I also work for PEAK Rescue with Gage."

PEAK Rescue. Well, of course Gage would have joined a rescue team. That thought wrapped around her heart, offered her some healing as he opened the door.

So he *had* put his life back together.

He walked out, and just when she thought he wouldn't turn, he did. Looking back at her, and for a long moment holding her gaze.

I'm sorry.

He swallowed. Opened his mouth as if to say something. Then abruptly turned away and walked down the steps to his car.

Brette's hand tugged on her arm, pulling her away from the door. "Let him go."

She took a breath at Brette's words.

If only she could.

Then Brette shut the door and turned to her. "Let's go find your idiot brother."

Ella Blair could still dismantle him. First, simply from the shock of seeing her as she opened the door. Gage thought his heart had stopped, right there, banging to a halt in his chest. She looked— well, almost like the first version of Ella Blair, the one who'd wooed him with her smile, her laughter on the ski slope. Her amazing hair might be shorter but was just as tangled, just as pretty. A sunburn on her nose, those cherry lips, and she wore pajamas.

He nearly didn't recognize the woman who'd later dismantled his life. Buttoned up. Lethal.

Seeing her in those penguin-printed bottoms, the tank top and sweater, reminded him that he'd known a different side to Ella Blair.

A kinder, sweeter side.

Yeah, seeing her unsettled him, but it was her words that nearly took him apart. Because sometime after his heart started beating again, *after* he'd grabbed ahold of his emotions, she'd become the woman that, once upon a time, he'd fallen in love with.

"You're a good guy, Gage. I've always known that."

And that nearly had him unraveling the tight fist of control he had over his words, his hurt, to hurtle at her the one question he still hadn't found the answer to.

Why?

He pulled up to the duplex and into the garage, got out, and headed inside, not waiting for Ty.

Who hustled in on his tail anyway.

"Okay, I let you simmer on the way home, but clearly that just built up a head of steam."

Gage wrenched off his boots, pulled his fleece over his head, hung it on the entry hook, shucked off his snow pants, and headed up the stairs to their main floor.

"You can run, but you can't hide!"

"Leave me alone." Gage headed to the kitchen, opened the fridge. Stared inside, for what, he hadn't a clue.

Mostly for the cool air that wafted over him.

He could nearly feel the way her hair sifted through his fingers, heard her tiny moan when he kissed her—

He slammed the fridge door.

"Dude—take a step back from the appliances," Ty said, now coming up the stairs in his stocking feet. "Who was that girl? Because, I'm sorry, but you were a royal jerk."

Gage's mouth pressed tight, and he grabbed a bag of chips off the top of the fridge and headed into the family room, where he flopped onto the sofa. He picked up the remote. Maybe he'd find a decent western, something that might lull him to sleep without memories of Ella.

In his arms.

Block out the sound of her laughter. The shine in her eyes when he told her stories about the many peaks he'd torn up.

The taste of her lips on his.

He settled on a rerun of *The Fugitive*.

Ty opened the freezer and pulled out an ice pack, one of the many he kept frozen for his off-duty recuperation. He'd probably spend the evening with his leg up, the pack wrapped around his knee. Gage had noticed him starting to limp as they'd come out of Ella's condo.

Ty retrieved a can of soda from the fridge, came over, and leaned against the edge of the other sofa. "She knew you, back—"

"Yeah." Gage reached out, turned up the volume.

"Did you guys . . . ?"

"We barely knew each other. Skied together a few times. It was nothing."

"So, how terrible would it be if I follow you back to Vermont?" His voice, soft over the

101

flickering candlelight of their dinner table, a private space in the Outlaw resort.

"It didn't *look* like nothing. She went white, you looked like you'd been hit by a truck."

"She prosecuted the McMahon case against me." He kept his voice light and stared at the screen as Harrison Ford did a header into a waterfall. Not unlike how he'd felt when he'd walked into the hearing to see Ella Blair, the girl he hadn't forgotten, sitting in the counsel for the plaintiff's side of the table.

"What?"

"She was a junior lawyer, but . . . yeah. She worked the case, got my manager to testify against me."

He didn't take his eyes off the screen as Ty slid into the sofa. "How?"

Gage glanced at him. "You just can't let this go."

Ty glanced at the television. "Can you?"

Gage took a long breath, saying nothing, not trusting himself with the emotion roiling through him.

Not when the woman could still take his heart from his chest and grind it into pieces.

Ty finally got up and headed upstairs to his bedroom.

Gage stared at the screen, watching a relentless Tommy Lee Jones drag the river for the body.

He cleaned out the bag of chips until he got

only crumbs, then he got up and went to the fridge. After considering the beverage supply, he grabbed a bottled water and returned to the sofa.

On-screen, Harrison Ford was tracking down his friend, the one who would betray him.

Run away, dude.

Gage finally picked up the remote and flicked off the television, then stood in the darkness of the room.

No, maybe he couldn't let it go. But it wasn't his fault.

A guy just didn't forget a girl like Ella Blair, no matter how hard he tried . . .

6

THREE YEARS AGO

Gage wasn't sure how he'd gotten so lucky. One minute he'd been walking out to the pool deck, thinking he was meeting a fan for a quick autograph, and the next, he'd pulled beautiful Ella Blair out of the pool and into his life.

Yeah, he'd gone into the pool to rescue her, but being around her for the past three days made him feel as if he might still be gasping for breath.

First, the woman could shred the slope with her board. From tricks on the half-pipe to carving the snow to riding the powder, Ella strapped on and stayed in his line like nobody's business.

She could compete on the freeriding tour if she wanted it enough. He couldn't believe the way she'd carved her own line down the back bowl of Outlaw, even taking on the twenty-foot drop off Purgatory Ridge.

She belonged in competition instead of behind a law desk, but when they slowed down, rode up the chair lifts, or surrendered the hill for lunch and dinner, he could get lost in her stories of cases, her dream of fighting for the underdog. Apparently, although her family had money, she wanted to do something to help the downtrodden, the lost, the overwhelmed.

He could hardly believe that she'd traveled all the way from Vermont to make sure some distant friend didn't do something stupid.

Namely, follow him down the mountain.

As if he'd let a punk chase him down the biggest ride of his career.

But telling her that had seemed to contain some magic. Turned him into some kind of hero in her eyes.

Gage wasn't that guy who encouraged a flock of snow bunnies, so he made a point of keeping things casual. Friendly.

But he longed to capture that pretty mouth, taste her laughter.

Especially after she'd dried off and lost the bedraggled, drowned expression. Her hair turned out to be a rich copper, and he found himself watching the light bounce off it at night when they sat by the firelight in the lodge.

Her beautiful pale blue eyes could hold him captive, make him forget his tricks, the route he hoped to carve. He was even more drawn by the deep note of compassion embedded in them, as if she could weave through his layers with a look. Not that he had much to hide—but around her, he didn't have to be someone he wasn't. Didn't have to pose, scrawl out an autograph, or be the persona that the public wanted.

With Ella, he was just a guy who loved to snowboard.

"Table for two, near the fireplace," he said to the maître d' of the Gaddy Room, the five-star steakhouse attached to the Outlaw Resort. A tall river stone fireplace soared two stories, past the stripped beams and rustic ridgepoles. The massive picture window boasted a view of Outlaw Mountain as the sun was falling in a crimson glow over the western ridge.

The restaurant smelled of the fresh grill and the flickering fire, and a Brad Paisley tune played from the band in the bar off the main dining room.

"She's everything I ever wanted . . ." And how. Gage had finally, on this last night before his big run, asked her out for dinner. A date.

An evening to test if this might be real. If everything went well, he'd ask her if he could chase her back to Vermont, maybe see her between his freeriding events . . .

Or take her with him.

A thought that latched on with a fury when she showed up for dinner in a little sleeveless black dress, a sweater, a pair of shaggy sheepskin UGGs, and black tights that showed off the shape of her legs. Her deep copper hair hung down in tousled curls, long and tantalizing, and he just barely stopped himself from reaching out.

"You . . . where did you get that dress?"

"The gift shop," she said, smiling.

He felt like a slug in his jeans, a gray T-shirt, and a sports jacket. He hadn't even shaved, because he'd been going over the final arrangements with the camera crew from Xtreme Energy sports for his epic run.

"Let me know if you get cold," he said then.

Ella blushed at his words, and he wanted to wince and hit his head against something hard. He was *so* not a charmer—hence his decision to keep a wide berth between him and the female fans of his sport. More, he still had a few morals left over from his parents, despite the fame, the social media feeds, the magazine covers, the awards and parties.

And, of course, Ramon's ambitions. His publicist had chased him down after he'd won the first world championship as a rookie free-rider and instantly saw a future for Gage he hadn't envisioned for himself.

In a way, he owed everything he was to Ramon Castillo.

Gage managed to help Ella into her chair and settled down beside her.

He eyed her hand, trying to figure out a way to hold it . . .

"I love this song," she said, glancing at the bar crowd. "Have you heard of them—Montgomery-King? They have the most amazing ballads. I love Ben King's voice."

She started humming along.

Are you dreaming of me, out on your own
Are you thinking of us, and our own song

It couldn't be just that easy, could it? "Would you . . . like to dance?"

"Oh—no, I mean—"

He got up, held out his hand. "Please?"

He must have said something right, because she smiled and his entire world lit on fire. Especially when, after he found them an edge of dance floor, she lifted her arms and settled them around his shoulders. He put his arms around her, pulled her against himself, and swayed to the music.

She smelled so good, a hint of the wild outdoors on her skin, the floral scent of shampoo still lingering in her hair. And the way she was looking up at him . . .

"You're amazing on the slopes," he said.

She smiled. "No, you are. And you're going to be spectacular tomorrow." Her mouth curled up in a smile. He wanted to press his lips against hers and taste them. "Thank you for the last few days. They were really fun."

He leaned his head down, touched his forehead to hers. "It's going to get crazy after the run. Media and lots of press—I don't know when I'll be able to see you . . ."

"I have to go back to Vermont anyway." She wrinkled her nose. "My brother is turning sixteen, and my parents have turned it into a big family event. My parents are a little too doting."

Maybe I could come with you . . .

He wanted to say it—but the words wouldn't come. Not when she looked up at him, her eyes catching the lights.

He just couldn't stop himself. It was like when he spotted the perfect line midway through a run and just had to take it. The wild impulsiveness that had put him on the map.

And now, that impulsiveness made him kiss her.

He leaned down and pressed his lips to hers, right there on the dance floor. And he didn't care who saw him, who might be taking pictures and loading them on Twitter or Instagram or even sending them off to TMZ.

Just pulled her close and lost himself for a long moment in her touch. The smell of her skin. The fresh taste of her mouth, the sense of finding something he hadn't realized he'd been searching for.

Her hair tangled in his fingers, whisper soft and thick, and he felt her tremble, a sweet sigh of surrender as she kissed him back.

He could have stayed there forever had the song not ended, had the clapping around them—hopefully for the band—not brought them up for air.

Then, she smiled, and he knew forever had just started.

7

As he soared over the great expanse of the back bowls of Blackbear Mountain, hanging out of the door of the Bell 429 PEAK Rescue chopper, Gage just barely reined in the desire to leap.

To land waist deep in the white, feathery cascade of champagne powder, swim to the surface, and then ride the wave down the mountain, leaving his mark, a thin scar upon the face as he hurtled—no, flew—down the mountain.

The urge filled his lungs, nearly pulled him out of the open door, and save for the ANFO bomb in his lap, he might have taken flight. He blamed it on the rush of adrenaline after a night of reliving his mistakes.

Or maybe, what had been his wild hopes. Whatever. The what-ifs and yesterdays didn't matter anymore, and seeing Ella had only picked at the ache he'd thought had long scabbed over. So, when his patrol boss alerted the team with an early morning text, asking for bomb volunteers to take out the ledge at the top of Timber Bowl, he'd texted back his answer and hopped in his Mustang.

"Ready?" Ty sat beside him, holding the second fifty-pound bag of ANFO—ammonium nitrate mixed with fuel oil—attached to a ninety-second fuse. Enough to light up the entire ridge and send the thick, four-foot layer of fresh snow sitting on a slick foundation of surface hoar down the backside of the mountain and out of the danger areas.

Normally, they'd throw the explosives by hand by trekking up the ridges, traversing the slopes on their boards, and catching all that beautiful sun-kissed powder. But today, with the addition of last night's snow, the piles needed unleashing from above.

"Iggie on!" Gage shouted over the thwapping of the blades as he slipped the igniter over the fuse.

Ty started the countdown.

"Fire!" Gage pulled the igniter string. He couldn't hear the fuse sputter, the spit that evidenced a live wire, so he pulled off the iggie, took a look.

Lit and ready.

He turned, glanced at his safety tether that attached him to the chopper, then stepped one foot out of the chopper onto the skid.

The urge nearly took him again to leap, to fly, land in a puff of powder, then let the silence, the freedom of the run take him.

Let him, at least for the space of the run, escape the whirr of regret, of mistakes that kept him grounded.

Indeed, he might have if he'd been wearing his board. And not been a hundred feet above the earth.

"Throw it, Gage!" Ty yelled, and Gage jerked himself out of the moment and hurled the bag of ammo like a chest pass, out into the white.

"She's out!"

Kacey Fairing, the pilot at the controls, veered the chopper away and to the right, hovering away to watch the explosion.

Ninety seconds felt like a century as he watched.

And in that space, Ella tiptoed in, sat down across from him at a table, dressed in a crisp white shirt and pencil skirt, her beautiful copper hair pulled back and up. *"Hello, Mr. Watson. I'm here as representative for the family of Dylan McMahon."*

The explosion discharged with a puff of white, like a breath in the massive expanse of the slope. The concussion of it, however, rocked the chopper, the window bowing just a fraction.

Then the trickle of release and the snow started to run. The slab at the top broke away slowly, as if resisting the tear from its moorings. It moved en masse, gaining speed, then broke into pieces as it slammed against boulders, cliffs, and, lower into the bowl, tree trunks. On the way, the run of snow triggered smaller slides, trickles of snow rivers that took out pine trees and saplings on its

112

way to the bottom. A cloud of powder lifted from the chaos, obscuring the tumble of snow, but Gage didn't have to see it to know the power of it.

He knew what it felt like to feel the rumble of the avalanche in your bones a second before it cascaded over you. The fight to ride it, stay on top, avoiding trees, boulders, your heart caught in your throat as you struggled to stay upright. Then, the taste of your own blood in your mouth as you fell, catapulted into the flood, swimming to stay above the current until the tumult slowed.

The snow pressing in, encasing your arms, your legs into icy cement, the cold filling every pore. The real fear now was suffocation and the battle against panic as you fought to build an air pocket, praying your beacon wasn't dislodged or lying forty feet downhill.

You prayed for a rescue dog while you dug for the surface, hoping desperately that you weren't in fact upside-down. And you counted down the precious fifteen minutes of the golden zone, the highest chance of survival.

In truth, once an avalanche took you, there was little hope of escaping.

Unless, of course, someone found you.

"I think we're clear," Ty said into his mic. He shoved his bag into the cargo area behind the seat. "Take us in, Kacey."

Kacey affirmed his assessment, and soon they

were banking, heading over the ski area, which was just now coming to life with cars in the lot and a few early morning enthusiasts hiking up to the chalet.

She put them down in a controlled area near the ski patrol hut and turned off the chopper. "Chet said we should probably sit tight in case we have any calls today," she said as she got out. As the only SAR chopper in the area, PEAK Rescue hired out for all sorts of jobs to help fund their SAR efforts. The budget from Mercy Falls EMS just didn't stretch far enough. Thankfully, they'd scraped up enough to buy a pair of late-model Polaris snowmobiles, perfect for backcountry rescues.

Hopefully, however, they'd stay locked up, pristine and unused this season.

Gage followed Kacey and Ty into the ski patrol headquarters, located in an outbuilding not far from the main compound.

The patrols had already been deployed to ski the slopes, check the runs. A few probably also headed to the ridge to rope off the back slope.

By tomorrow, the avalanche pack would settle and they could reopen the slope.

He walked past the empty front office— probably Emmett, his boss, was out on the slope, gathering snow conditions. He'd call everyone in for a briefing before the resort opened.

The main area housed four padded picnic

114

tables, first-aid gear, and a few thermoses and lunch boxes piled in the middle. A television tuned to the weather channel displayed the low-pressure system coming in from the west.

Another storm front, and this one might hit them by tonight.

Hopefully Ella had talked some sense into her brother.

Gage pulled off his gloves and helmet and wandered over to the kitchen area to pour himself a cup of coffee. Jess stood in her black ski pants and a purple fleece, her golden hair caught back into a braid. She shoved a bag lunch into the ancient yellow fridge.

"Hey," she said. Her gaze ran back, behind him, and landed on Ty. She smiled, and Gage knew it wasn't just for him. Or perhaps not for him at all.

He didn't know what exactly was going on between Ty and Jess, but it seemed, from Jess's smile, that Pete was a distant memory. At least at the moment.

"Hey, Jess. I didn't know you were on patrol today."

"I asked Emmett to give me a few more hours. I need to buy some carpet for the upstairs bedrooms."

Every penny she earned went to fixing up her 1902 Victorian fixer-upper in Mercy Falls.

Ty poured himself a cup of coffee and followed Gage back to the main area. Jess stayed in the kitchen with Kacey, and Gage took the opportunity to glance at Ty and raise an eyebrow.

"What?"

"So, I don't get it. Do you or don't you have something going with Jess? Ever since last summer, you two seem to be hanging out more, much to Pete's ire. You should see the way he looks at you."

Ty's mouth tightened around the edges. He looked away.

"See, that's what I mean. Are you two dating or—"

"Jess and I are just friends."

His tone, quiet and dark, cut Gage off. He glanced at Jess. "Why? Jess is a knockout. And she's perfect for you. Solid, down to earth. She likes you, which . . . no offense, but you're not exactly Casanova."

"I'll leave the lineup of women to Pete," Ty said. He got up, glanced at Jess, then back at Gage. "Let's just say that Jess needs me, and if that means you and the team think we're dating, then . . . well, that's what teammates are for. Standing beside each other even if it doesn't make sense. Now it's your turn. Tell me about Ella."

Gage was about to answer something along the lines that there was nothing to talk about when his cell phone vibrated in his pocket.

He pulled the phone out. The area code looked familiar.

Recognition slid into him a moment before he answered. He dove right in. "Oliver, you'd better be calling me to tell me you've called off—"

"It's Ella."

Her voice came through the line wobbly, and it was the tiny gasp of breath that made him stop, slow down.

Listen.

"Oliver is gone."

His tirade had alerted Ty, who turned around, listening.

"What do you mean, Oliver is gone?" Gage asked. He sent Ty a look, a shake of his head.

"We went out looking for him, but we didn't find him. When we got home, he was already in his room. I know he took the semester off to be a ski bum, but I thought for sure he was just kidding about skiing Heaven's Peak." She paused, and her breath caught. "Oh, Gage, I think he did it."

He closed his eyes, her voice tunneling through him, finding root. He imagined her pacing, wrapping a finger around that beautiful red hair, staring out the window at the mountain.

He found himself walking to the window and also staring at the mountain. The skies overhead arched blue, but in the western horizon, dark, gunmetal-gray clouds hovered, slowly rolling in.

"All his gear is gone, and Bradley's is gone too," Ella was saying.

"Maybe he's come over to Blackbear?" Gage said.

"You took his ski pass."

"He could go over to Big Mountain."

"There are no bowls there. No powder."

In other words, no danger.

"Calm down, Ella. Just take a breath here. In order to get up to Heaven's Peak, they'd have to get a chopper ride. Going-to-the-Sun Road is closed past McDonald Lodge. And there just aren't that many heli-ski pilots around. I'll get on the horn and see what I can find out."

"Seriously? Oh, Gage, thank you so much! I know"—she swallowed—"I know this isn't your problem, and I appreciate it." Her voice pitched low. "Thank you. I meant it when I said you were a good man."

He didn't have any response to that, feeling suddenly raw, wounded. He took a breath, kept his voice cool, unaffected. "I'll get back to you, Ella. Don't panic yet."

He clicked off.

Ty had sat on the picnic table. "That kid is gone?"

"According to Ella, she woke up and found her brother missing."

"Who's missing?" Jess asked, coming to sit beside Ty.

"This kid who Gage chased down yesterday. Gage had to take away his ski pass, and that's when the kid recognized him. Apparently Gage is his hero."

The way Ty said *hero,* with a little singsong lilt, sent a smile up Jess's face. See, Ty was a charmer—he just didn't know it.

But a guy didn't have to be a charmer with the right girl. No, the right girl made him say the right things, feel like he could stand on top of the world. The right girl laughed at his jokes and met his eyes with a smile that said he could do no wrong.

The right girl turned a guy into a bona fide hero.

"I'm no hero," Gage said. "And if this kid follows in my tracks, he'll get himself—and his buddy—killed."

"What tracks?" Kacey said and stuck a spoonful of yogurt in her mouth.

"Gage's epic run down Heaven's Peak. Some kid he met yesterday wants to duplicate it," Ty said, neatly leaving out their visit to the kid's condo last night and Gage's connection to his sister.

"I saw that run on YouTube, Gage." Kacey raised an eyebrow. "Scared the air out of me."

Gage allowed himself a smile. "I was younger, dumber, and braver. It's a bad combination."

"And exactly the combination of this Gage wannabe," Ty said. He slid off the table. "But before we jump to conclusions, let's check the lodge, see if he's simply slunk back here and tried to get his hands on a new ski pass." He thumped toward the door.

Gage followed him and pulled out his phone to scroll through his local heli-pilot contacts. All three of them.

Because he'd once been Oliver Blair. And without a doubt, Gage knew the kid was up on the mountain.

Brette Arnold could spot a great story. Especially when it appeared in the lip-biting, pacing, muttering form of her former housemate and best friend, state senator Eloise Zorich Blair.

"Are you okay?" Brette said as she poured herself a cup of coffee.

Ella glanced at her, her lips a tight, grim line.

Yep, there was a story behind those tired eyes, that wan look. And it most likely had a great deal to do with a handsome, long-haired ski patrol. *It's my fault he's a has-been, working ski patrol, chasing down hooligans like my brother instead of winning national championships. I wrecked his life.*

Those words sat in Brette's head like bait. She simply couldn't shake them, despite her hope of letting it go.

And she hated that it all tasted like a juicy filet mignon of a story, something she desperately needed if she wanted to put juice back into her writing career.

A career that seemed a little like the deflated T. rex she'd found this morning on Ollie's floor. Sure, she could go back to writing speeches for Ella, and if Ella decided to run for reelection, she would put together a set of cover articles— or yes, even a biography—that would have Ella winning favor the likes of Duchess Kate. And it wouldn't be lies—Ella had a heart of true compassion. But if Ella didn't run, well . . .

Ever since Brette had lost the contract on her biography for Senator Carlyn Lynch, a woman intending to run for president, she hadn't found one decent story, and especially nothing that would be worthy of a *Time* magazine or *National Geographic* spread.

It wasn't Brette's fault—the minute she'd unearthed proof that Carlyn had creatively diverted election funds to her personal account, Brette had been forced to confront Caryln. The woman had the good sense to withdraw from the race.

She took with her Brette's faith in the honor and integrity of those in public office, not that she had much to begin with. If it weren't for Ella, she might give up on politicians indefinitely.

Thankfully, Ella was one of the good ones. And not just with politics but with her inheritance too. She defied the odds that money corrupted.

But maybe Ella was exempt, having not been born into it. She could vividly remember the cost of food, clothing, a home.

Memories Oliver clearly didn't share.

Ella was one of the few people who still possessed integrity. Who believed in and fought for justice. A true hero, someone who put others ahead of herself.

A rare find in today's world.

Which was why her words about being the cause of Gage's downfall wedged into Brette's brain and wouldn't shake free.

She came over to Ella, blowing on her coffee.

"What did you mean when you said you're the reason he lost everything? That Dylan shouldn't have been out there that day?"

Ella shot a look at her. "Wow, you don't forget anything, do you?" Her bloodshot eyes betrayed a long night, and she'd bitten her nails down nearly to the nailbed, a habit she'd fought to break for years. She wore yoga pants and a long brown sweater. She sighed and added softly, "I probably shouldn't have said anything . . ."

Brette pointed at her forehead. "Iron trap up here. I don't forget faces, events, or details. And I have a gut sense when someone's not telling me everything, especially you, El. Sure, Oliver might be missing—but let's be honest. He probably sneaked back into Blackbear, went early to hike up some slope, and is probably sitting at the top of Timber Bowl, eating a power bar."

Her words made Ella blink, and she let a faint smile curl up her face. "You're probably right."

"Of course I am. And I'm also right about the fact that it's Gage Watson that has you so rattled. I didn't even have to know your history with him, the fact you fell for him hard three years ago, to know that seeing him last night nearly blew you over. What I don't know is what happened *after* he kissed you on the dance floor. After he asked if he could see you in Vermont after he skied Terminator. And why you prosecuting him wrecked his life. Sure, that had to hurt, but c'mon, he should have known he'd have to face up to his mistakes."

And that's when Ella took a long breath. She caught her lower lip in her teeth as she exhaled.

"Oh my gosh, there's more. You're wearing the look you did when you caught Sofia with that TA. Like you have a terrible secret you don't want to tell."

Ella's eyes widened.

"You'd make a terrible poker player. Sit down."

Ella considered her a long moment. Then she tucked her hands in the sleeves of her sweater. "You can't tell this story, Brette. Ever. To anyone. I could get disbarred. People's lives would be destroyed . . . or *more* people's lives."

"The things you ask of me—"

"I mean it. You're not an ace biographer right now. You're my friend. My *dearest* friend from college, and don't forget that I know what you did your freshman year during the homecoming game."

"Wow, you are a politician. Okay. This is serious."

Ella raised an eyebrow, and Brette sank down on the sofa. Held up three fingers. "Girl Scout honor."

"You weren't a Girl Scout. Just give me your word. This is just between you and me. Forever."

Brette nodded. "I promise."

Ella sank down on the sofa, wearing such a forlorn look that Brette wanted to give her a hug. But Ella knew how to gather herself, knew how to hold her ground, to pop out a speech. Putting on a brave face for the hard stuff was practically her specialty.

"That last night at Outlaw Resort, before the run off Terminator Wall, I knew I had completely fallen for Gage, in three days. He was the perfect gentleman, a great snowboarder, and I loved the way he laughed and listened to me. He wasn't anything like the cocky snowboarder I thought he'd be—he was genuine and honest and grew up in a Christian home, and frankly, I was ready to give him my heart, right there. And then he kissed me, and . . ." She closed her eyes, pressed her hands to her mouth. "Yeah, there was no going back after I kissed Gage Watson."

A smile tweaked up her face at that, and as she opened her eyes, Brette could practically see it. The shine of hope, the way she must have looked up at Gage as she danced in his arms.

For a moment, Brette longed to look at a man that way, to trust him, believe in his love.

But that meant she'd probably have to let him close, risk letting him see the real Brette Arnold. Risk letting him hurt her.

Nope. Not again.

"So what happened?" she asked, cutting through Ella's memories.

"We went back to the table, and he was holding my hand, telling me about his run at Heaven's Peak, when his friend Ramon came in. He wanted to talk to him. Ramon was his manager at the time, and with the big run coming up—well, I told Gage to talk to him while I went to the ladies' room. I was sort of freaking out anyway."

She blew out a breath, looked away. "The bathroom was located across the foyer of the chalet, and I didn't realize they'd stepped outside the restaurant, or that when I came back, I'd be able to hear them. But I did."

She met Brette's eyes. "They were arguing about Dylan McMahon. He had apparently offered Gage a lot of money to take him on the run—and Ramon was pressuring him to take Dylan with him. Gage told Ramon that Dylan wasn't ready, that he'd just get himself killed. I didn't hear any more, but I wasn't worried— Gage had promised me, after all, that he wouldn't take him. I went back to the table . . . but Gage never showed up. He just left me there. I got home on my own."

"He just left you?"

"Yeah." She stared down at her hands. "During the deposition, I found out that Dylan McMahon showed up during the conversation, and he and Gage got into a little altercation outside. Ramon got in the middle and ended up with a bloody nose. Gage said that Dylan swore to go down the mountain by himself if Gage didn't go with him, and that he had, in fact, already paid the chopper pilot, but no one heard him. And Ramon had actually taken Dylan's money, so it looked bad for Gage, and . . ."

"So, you didn't believe him?"

"I didn't know what to believe. I was so shocked—I watched in horror the next morning when Dylan stepped into that chopper with Gage. He'd *promised* me. And then, I watched the accident happen on live feed. Dylan, skiing off the trail, over the cliff. Then the avalanche that Dylan triggered crashing over Gage as he chased Dylan down, trying to find him. I just stood there in disbelief."

"Was Gage hurt?"

"Yeah. He rode the slide, had his beacon on, and they were able to pull him out fast. He broke his shoulder, I think. I'm not sure—they took him to the hospital, and I never got a chance to talk to him. Once Dylan's family showed up, distraught, and . . . it was a bad time. I went home to Vermont and tried to forget it all."

She got up, walked over to the counter, and

opened the cabinet. Took down a mug. "The next thing I knew, the McMahons were plaintiffs and our law firm was filing a lawsuit and I was assigned to the case. I did disclose that I knew Gage, but because I was just an associate and since the fight between he and Ramon was confirmed by other witnesses, I didn't have to disqualify myself. So, I didn't. Nine months later, I faced him in the hearing."

She didn't speak as she poured herself a cup of coffee. Then she turned, her voice thin. "You should have seen him, Brette. He'd lost weight, and he looked completely wiped out. He'd written to Dylan's parents and even tried to come to the funeral, but Harry and Jane were so angry. I think maybe, if he hadn't shown up at the graveside, they might have left it alone, but . . ." She took her coffee back to the sofa, cupped her hands around the warmth as she sat down.

She took another sip, but Brette noticed her hand shaking.

"I should have stepped aside, just the fact that I was so angry. I wanted to face Gage. Until I did. Seeing him like that . . . it took me apart. I wanted to run from the room. And then, the lead lawyer asked me to question Ramon. Oh, Ramon was mad—he didn't want to reveal that Gage had his hesitations about Dylan's abilities or that Dylan had paid him. I listed him as a hostile witness, and . . . I pulled it out of him."

She closed her eyes again, and Brette wanted to reach out, touch her arm. "I couldn't look at him as I did it. I knew he felt like I'd just shoved a knife through him. My own chest hurt."

"Oh, Ella."

"Gage didn't even defend himself. Ramon's testimony sealed the case. Gage's lawyer settled, and Gage lost everything—his sponsorships, his earnings, and his sport." She wiped her fingers across her cheek. "It was only after we'd settled, when I was going over the final papers of the case, that I discovered the truth."

The truth?

She looked up at Brette again, this time her eyes clear, her face solemn. "And this can never be repeated, because it's part of the sealed case. But . . . the family had a private autopsy done on Dylan. I'm not sure why—it was clear he died of suffocation and massive trauma. But the toxicology report was in the file, so I read it." She swallowed. Took a breath.

"Dylan McMahon had THC in his system. Marijuana."

Brette couldn't move. Ella just stared at her, meeting her gaze. Then, she nodded. "Whether or not he was accomplished enough to ride that mountain didn't matter. Dylan was high when he went down that mountain."

"Gage should have been exonerated," Brette said.

"Maybe. It was a civil case, so there may still have been damages awarded . . . but maybe not. It might have all gone away. I was horrified, but we'd settled, and I didn't have the authority to open it back up. And I was on the side of the plaintiff."

"Not to mention sworn to silence."

Ella nodded. "Yeah. And that's when things turned ugly. I confronted my boss, as well as the family, and he told me that I was required to keep quiet. I was so angry, I quit. I walked away from my law firm."

"I remember that. I couldn't believe you did that—especially since you were on your way to being a junior partner. I thought it was because of your mother—her cancer."

"That was all about timing. She needed to step down, and she offered me her seat. Of course the governor endorsed me, and it was such a small election, I'm not sure anyone even really knew, but . . . by then I was just trying to fill her shoes."

"And trying to forget Gage Watson," Brette said softly.

Ella tugged a tissue from a nearby box, blew her nose. "But it wasn't as if I could ever forget him. I'd always hoped for a chance to . . . I don't know, fix it, maybe. Silly, I know, but—"

"Not silly. Because you're still in love with him, aren't you?" Brette asked quietly.

Ella sighed. "It doesn't matter. Because there's

129

no way he'd ever love me. In fact, I'm the last person he would ever help. I can't believe he actually took my phone call or that I still had the right number."

A knock at the door jerked them both out of the conversation. Brette got up, walked to the door, glancing back at Ella.

She'd found her feet. Wrapped her arms around herself, looking as if a stiff wind might knock her over.

Brette opened the door.

Gage's hot friend, Ty Remington, stood in the frame. Tall, with wind-tousled dark hair and amazing green eyes, he wore his black ski pants and red ski patrol jacket. "Uh . . . Gage sent me by to tell you . . ." He glanced past her, to Ella, then back to Brette. "It's not good news. He found the chopper pilot who Oliver paid to bring them into the park."

Brette hooked his arm, tugged him inside. He stepped into the foyer. Brette closed the door.

He looked over at Ella, kept his voice even. "He dropped your brother off on top of Heaven's Peak over two hours ago."

The replay of Dylan McMahon's tragic tumble off Terminator Wall and the avalanche that followed him down looped in Ella's mind as she pulled up to the Blackbear Mountain ski patrol shack.

Ty pulled in next to her in a shiny blue Mustang.

"Nice car," Brette commented to Ella as she slid out of Ella's rental SUV.

Ella had noticed Brette's gaze lingering on Ty just a little longer than necessary as he'd explained how Gage had called his chopper pals and finally tracked down Deke Curry at AirCurry. He'd confirmed dropping off Bradley and Oliver at the top of Heaven's Peak.

Which meant that right now, her brother could be flying off a cliff at a lethal rate of speed. Or buried in an avalanche.

Or maybe, hopefully, still on top, having found a smidgen of general good sense.

Probably not.

She followed Brette and Ty into the patrol shack—aka headquarters. The slope at Blackbear had opened an hour ago, and only a couple patrollers' skis and a snowboard were parked in the rack outside the door.

She opened the door and stepped into an expansive room filled with picnic tables, the smell of coffee and sense of adventure embedded in the wooden walls. Ski equipment—helmets, gloves, snow-crusted neck gaiters— lay scattered on the tables. A couple patrolmen were snapping the buckles of their boots, ready to head back out.

Across the room, Gage bent over a map. He wore black ski pants, his red suspenders up over his thick shoulders, and a gray pullover turtleneck. His long hair was down and tucked behind his ears, and the slightest stubble of whiskers along his chin suggested he hadn't stopped to shave this morning.

Still every millimeter the freeriding poster boy that she'd made space for on her wall.

She didn't deserve for him to say yes to what she was about to ask. That part she knew, deep in her gut. She had no business driving down here, marching into the shack with her dangerous request.

But it was Ollie, and . . .

Well, Ollie was all she had of her biological family.

Gage looked up.

She stilled as his beautiful brown eyes fixed on her. His jaw tightened, and he looked back down.

"C'mon," Brette said and tugged her arm.

Yes. Right. Gage, after all, was a rescuer now. Of course he'd help her.

Her heart gave a little jump of hope when she saw, open on the table, a colored topographical map of Glacier National Park, and most specifically, Heaven's Peak.

Gage held it open with his wide, strong hands. Didn't acknowledge her as she came up.

Instead, "There's a storm rolling in," he said quietly. He handed her a piece of paper with the weather report, a printed picture of the current storm front still over the far western tip of Montana.

She set it down, hating the look of it.

Ty leaned over one end of the map. "Where are they?"

Gage ran a finger along an area in the middle, clearly indicated by the four ridge points running toward the peak. To the west of the mountain, a lake sat in a groove at about six thousand feet. Tiny circles radiated out from the apex at wider and wider intervals, giving the elevations.

"If they follow my route, they'll take the northern route. They start by skiing along the spine, then dropping into this nice wide bowl to the north." He spread his hand over the three-thousand-foot drop filled with gullies and streams and plenty of thick forest. "They'll camp on the mountain overnight, then they'll head over to the far eastern ridge and ski down that eastern face to Going-to-the-Sun Road. I camped here, about halfway down the face, then the next day skied through the bowl, then I took the chute on the backside of Heavens Peak down to the base. It's about forty miles of skiing. But here"—he pointed to a dip between the mountains—"is called Weeping Wall. It's a waterfall, frozen in the winter, with a fall of about sixty feet. I thought I could jump off it, but once I got there, I deviated from my plan and couldn't take it head on—there was too much ice accumulation at the bottom to land safely."

"Would Oliver know that?"

"I don't know. I talked about it in the video I

shot, and there's a picture, but the plan I posted online included the waterfall jump, so . . . maybe not." Gage stood up, his jaw tight. "I should have taken that stupid video down."

She didn't say anything. But she'd seen his helmet-cam footage dozens of times—maybe more. Could still hear his breathing, his calm voice as he tackled each part of the slope.

Still taste the rush of awe as he sprayed powder in the field he'd dubbed the Great White Throne. And sped down the couloir called Angel's Wings. She had held her breath through the Cathedral Forest, where he'd cut a trail through thick pine trees, his body quick and lithe, and finally down the last section, a sheer drop into a bowl called Bishop's Cap. She would have loved to see the entire run from a distance instead of up close, but that would have meant a friend traveling with him.

And back then, just like now probably, Gage skied alone. He could have died on that mountain if he'd fallen into a tree well or landed wrong off a cliff.

At least Oliver had Bradley.

After a moment of silence, Gage picked up the weather report. Studied it.

"Just be honest," Brette said, speaking Ella's thoughts. "What chance do they have?"

Gage sighed. And this time he met Ella's eyes.

She couldn't move, couldn't breathe, with the

sense of his gaze reaching in, taking ahold of the shaking inside. He'd always had that power—the crazy calm aura that seemed to suggest, given the chance, he could tame the world. Make the elements surrender, smooth out the rough edges of a mountain, and even teach the sky to call his name. Fearless. Confident.

And even as he seemed to weigh his answer, Brette's accusation hit her. *"You're still in love with him, aren't you?"*

No. Or, probably not—Ella didn't want to take a good look to figure out the answer. But she *did* respect him.

Even trusted him, although he couldn't know that, not after their history.

"Oliver and Bradley are both decent boarders," Gage started. "I saw them yesterday when I chased them down through the trees. Oliver can handle his board, knows how to move in the trees. Good instincts. He can cut a line."

"But . . ." Ella said and drew in her breath.

"I trained for months—a year, really—before I took that ride. And even then . . . well, it was pretty—it was intense."

He glanced at Ty, then back to Ella. "There's a reason I haven't repeated it."

Ella swallowed. "He's in trouble, isn't he?"

Gage lifted a shoulder, his mouth a grim line.

And she couldn't stop herself. "Please, Gage, you have to go after him." She didn't even realize she'd narrowed the space between them. Had reached out, touched his arm.

She felt his muscle twitch under her hand. But she didn't care. "You're on a rescue team, aren't you? That must be your chopper outside. Just go up there and find them, bring them home."

She still had her hand on his arm, and he reached up, put his hand on hers.

For a second she thought he might wrap his fingers through hers, a tender gesture, meant to calm her, assure her.

But he drew her hand off him. Then he stepped back. "Ella—"

"Please, Gage!"

"We can't." The voice came from behind her, and Ella turned and saw a tall woman, her auburn hair pulled back in a ponytail. She wore a blue jumpsuit and a pair of aviator sunglasses perched on the brim of her baseball cap. Pretty, with freckles and high cheekbones, she didn't smile as she walked up holding a tablet.

"The storm gives us about a four-hour window. Just to get into the park will take an hour, maybe longer. Then, to search the mountain—that's hours, not to mention the time to airlift them out. We simply don't have the window. I'm sorry."

But Ella was doing the math. "But you have time to go in, drop someone off, right?"

The woman glanced at Gage, back to Ella. Gave a slight nod. "But in order to do that, we'd

136

need the Mercy Falls sheriff's department to issue a formal callout. Otherwise, we don't have the funding—"

"I'll pay for it." Ella turned to Gage. "Please." This time she didn't care if he pushed her away. "Please, go up and get them. Ollie—or Bradley—could be injured right now on the mountain. And if they're not, then you could find them, help them get down the mountain—"

"Ella . . ." Gage started, his voice low, almost a growl.

"I know that I shouldn't be asking you this, but Ollie is my only flesh and blood." She took a breath, closed her eyes, swallowed her voice back into submission. Then, "He's young. And he thinks he's doing something that will make him famous—"

"Like his big sister," Gage said, a little derision in his voice.

She tried not to wince. "I know I don't deserve your help. You have every right to walk away—"

"That's not why I can't go up there." Gage's voice was tight. "Of course I'll help you, but—"

"Only you can ski this ridge. Only you understand it, only you can get them down safely."

She hadn't even realized she'd put her hand on his chest, and now he put his hand on hers. This time he closed his over it. "Ella, just calm down. I haven't skied terrain like this for three years—"

"Oh, c'mon! You're the best freeriding snow-

137

boarder in the entire world, and we all know it!"

He drew in a breath as her voice echoed in the silence of the room.

Gage let her hand go, stepped back from her. "Even if I did go up there, with the storm coming, it's too dangerous, especially alone." He glanced at Ty, then back to Ella. "And you're right. I'm the only one who can get down that mountain." He shook his head, turned away, and reached out to roll up the map. "If they don't show up at the bottom in a day, then we'll assemble a rescue team and go in after the storm passes."

"He'll be dead by then! And you'll be back to regretting your choices all over again."

He stilled. And with everything inside her, she wanted to yank back her words. Especially when his mouth tightened. His chest rose and fell as if he might be trying not to flinch.

"I'm sorry—"

He held up his hand to ward off her words. "Leave it, Ella."

"No, I'm sorry, but it's the truth. You're not the guy everyone accused you of being—arrogant and reckless. I know you regret what happened with everything inside you."

He rounded on her, his voice desperately low, his eyes sharp. "Of course you do. And you used it to destroy my life."

She didn't care who was looking. "Yeah, I did. And I regret that too, but I doubt that guy I knew can live with himself any better now if my brother dies on the mountain than he did when he chased Dylan McMahon down an avalanche to save his life."

"Dylan died because of me," Gage growled. "And now, your stupid brother is out there—again, because of me."

"No, he made his own choice, just like Dylan did. But that doesn't mean his sorry hide doesn't need saving. Please, go after him." She wanted to add "for me," but that wouldn't do her any good at all. So, "I know you're a good guy, Gage."

He gripped the map in his fist. "You don't know anything of the kind." He stalked away from her.

But she scrambled after him, ignoring Brette's hand on her arm. "Yes, I do. The guy—the guy I fell in love with was generous and protective, and he wouldn't let some stupid kid lose his life if he could save him."

And that's when Gage stopped short. Whirled around. She nearly plowed into him and put a hand out to his chest to stop herself.

He didn't move, but the look in his eyes turned her cold.

"First—that guy, the one you met three years ago? He's gone. Why? Because he tried to do something right, and the world, not to mention the woman I . . ." He cut his words off. "That guy was idealistic and thought he could save someone who really didn't want saving. Because

139

of it, my career, my entire life was eviscerated. And I learned a few things about trusting people and doing the *smart* thing instead of the right thing. So I don't think you know me at all, Ella. And . . . as for falling in love with me? You have a pretty interesting definition of love."

Her eyes filled, but she didn't move, her jaw tight, as she fought to pull words from her aching chest. "Okay then, what about the rescuer I met last night? The guy who showed up on my doorstep hoping to stop my brother from making an epic mistake? Where is he, because I want to talk to *him*."

Gage glanced behind her, probably at his friend Ty. And she could see him thinking, practically wearing that same expression as when he'd been asked why he'd taken Dylan McMahon onto a mountain that would take his life. *"Because I thought I could keep him alive."*

"Yes. You probably could have if you had just stopped him." Her words from the past nearly tripped out.

Instead, she added, "That guy could save my brother's life, if he wanted to."

Gage closed his eyes, almost as if in pain. Then he took a long breath and turned to his chopper pilot. "How soon can we leave?"

8

"Listen, Gage. You get on the mountain, find this kid's trail, if the wind hasn't scraped it clean, grab these kids, and get off the mountain." Chet King hadn't been thrilled with the prospect of sending his only chopper up the mountain. Gage sat on a table in the lunchroom, his feet on the bench, listening to his instruction through the phone while Jess and Ty assembled his gear.

"And I don't like you going alone. It's dangerous. Can't you take Pete? Or Jess?"

Gage knew the dangers, too well, having skied alone the first time. He ran a hand across his forehead. "Sorry, boss, but no one can ski the big stuff." If Ty didn't have a busted knee, maybe . . .

Of course, there *was* one other person who could keep up, but really, that was out of the question.

Gage could nearly see the old man standing in his office, probably staring at the mountain range, even see his grim expression as he sighed.

"Okay, but remember, you aren't alone out there."

"Yeah, I know. PEAK will track me—"

"Yes, but no, I meant God is with you."

Gage drew in a breath.

Chet must have read his silence. "I know you

141

have a history with God, Gage. Once upon a time, you trusted him."

"That was before I . . ." Gage looked around, cut his voice low. "Listen, I made some bad decisions, and they backfired. Since then, God and I have agreed to stay out of each other's way."

Gage glanced over at Ty assembling his navigational gear—GPS, compass, map.

"Don't for a minute think that God has forgotten about you or doesn't have your back. And don't base God's love or desire to help you on your opinion of yourself. Base it on who God says he is."

Gage said nothing, and thankfully, Chet didn't press him. Instead, "Now listen, you stay safe and come back."

In other words, live.

"Roger, Boss."

The simple objective ticked off in the back of his brain as Gage hung up and took inventory of his gear.

Ty added the navigation equipment to the table. "You've got skins, an avi beacon, a probe, a signaling mirror, a whistle, an ice ax, and a two-way radio."

"Grab me another set of batteries," Gage said. He added a head lamp, a first aid kit, matches, a lighter, a camp stove, a knife, a two-man bivvy, and a sleeping bag to the pile.

"I really hope I can find these kids in the next

couple hours. I don't want to spend the night on the mountain." He grabbed his pack and began to tuck in the supplies.

"I don't want you to either." This from Jess, who came over with rations—energy bars, a dehydrated pack of chili mac, and some beef stroganoff. "I'm still trying to decide if I think you're crazy or brave."

"He's in love with the girl," Ty said, bringing over an emergency blanket. "Ella."

Gage looked up at him. "What?"

Ty handed Jess the blanket. "I figured it out." He turned to Jess. "Last night, when he saw Ella Blair, he went white and turned grouchy."

"I was trying to find her brother before he did something stupid. Like this," Gage growled. To the back of the pack he attached his folding ski poles and tucked his skins into a side pocket.

"And then we got back to the condo, and he went into hiding. Turned on *The Fugitive*."

"Wow, yeah, that's bad," Jess said.

Gage frowned at them. "*The Fugitive* is a classic."

"I'm just saying—when you want to think and pretend you're not brooding, you watch classics." Jess folded her arms. "Usually westerns, but I can see the draw of *The Fugitive*. All that running."

"Whatever."

"He knows Ella, from *before*," Ty said. And then he turned to Gage. "And that's where it gets

143

complicated. I kept thinking, the entire time she was talking today, why would Gage even talk to the woman who'd prosecuted him in civil court, stripped away everything he had—"

"Her brother is missing!"

"And then I went back to what he said last night about knowing her—he went skiing with her *a few times.*"

"Gage went skiing with her?" Jess looked up at him.

Gage held up his hand. "Enough."

"Oh, Gage. Dude." Jess stood up. "Now you're really busted because we know you—you ski alone. Always."

Ty walked up and handed Jess toilet paper, an extra pair of socks, and binoculars. "Exactly. And the rest isn't hard to figure out. The way I see it, Gage fell for Ella, somehow, and then she broke his heart."

Gage stood up. "Quit analyzing my life."

"And he hasn't gotten over her," Ty finished.

Jess gave him a sad look, and he wanted to punch Ty in the mouth. "Thanks for that." He nearly said something about the torrid nonaffair these two were having, trying to fool everyone, but he had more important things to worry about.

Still. "We had one date, nothing more. She only liked me because I was famous in that corner of the world." He knelt and shoved his sleeping bag into the top of his pack. Then he added an insulated hydration bottle to the outside pocket.

"Let's go." He hoisted the pack onto one shoulder and grabbed his helmet. "I'll keep in contact with PEAK once I get to the top. Hopefully I'll be back for pizza tonight at the ranch."

Ty sobered now, clamped him on the shoulder. "And here's where I say I wish I were going with you."

"Your knee still isn't what it should be and we both know it. The stress of the powder would make you the third person I have to carry off the mountain. There's plenty of things you can do that I can't, Ty. It just so happens that backcountry skiing is in my wheelhouse. I'll be fine. You show up at the bottom, okay?"

Ty nodded, and both Ty and Jess followed him out into the lunchroom. He'd opted out of his red ski patrol jacket and now grabbed his gray down ski jacket. He picked up a smaller terrain map, folded it, and shoved it into his zippered pocket. Then he pulled his gaiter over his neck, zipped up his jacket.

"He's in love with the girl."

Maybe, once upon a time. But that was before she'd walked into his life and then proceeded to dismantle it. But despite their one date, as he'd put it, she still knew how to lay his heart open with her words, make him see something in himself he didn't know he possessed.

"That guy could save my brother's life, if he wanted to."

He wished she hadn't said that because looking at her, so much confidence in her beautiful blue-gray eyes, well, for a second, he *did* want to. Wanted to be the hero he'd been, the one who'd pulled her from the pool, held her in his arms, who'd watched her eyes light up when he suggested he find her in Vermont.

That guy had risen from the dead and volunteered, like a love-sick teen, to risk his sorry neck on some nearly unskiable mountai in Glacier National Park.

But he wasn't doing this for her. He was doing it because, for all his mistakes, he still couldn't get past the fact that it was the right thing to do.

Oh, this was going to be fun.

The sky still shone blue and bright, just the finest hint of gray cumulus to the west as he stepped out onto the patrol shack porch. He pulled on his pack, put on his helmet, and grabbed his board. His gloves dangled from the clip on his jacket, and he'd shoved a headband into his pocket for the high-altitude winds.

Then he tucked his board under his arm and headed out toward the chopper.

Kacey met him as he approached the gated area. She wore a down jacket over her jumpsuit and her helmet.

"She won't leave."

146

Huh?

Kacey turned, walking with him as he headed toward the chopper. "That girl, Ella Blair. She's sitting in the chopper. She was there when I came out, wearing a backpack, dressed for Siberia, and holding her board. It looks like she's going with you."

He stared at her, the words sliding through him, latching on. Then, "Oh, no, she's not."

Ella was sitting in the second row of seats, already strapped in, as if that meant something. She was wearing an orange ski jacket and had her helmet on, her pack stowed between her feet.

He opened the door.

She glanced at him, then looked straight ahead. "I'm going."

"No," he said, climbing aboard. He shoved his board into the back of the chopper. "You're leaving. Right now."

"I'm going. You know I can keep up with you, and it's my brother."

Gage drew in a breath. "I know you can keep up with me—on tamed powder. This isn't that—this is backcountry skiing down a steep face—"

"I've been backcountry skiing. With you." She turned, her mouth in a tight bud of defiance. "Redemption Ridge?"

"That was different. It was practically a highway—"

"I went off a cliff. I followed your line perfectly.

147

I'll do it again—I'll stay right in your line, do everything you—"

"Ella, you're not going!" He reached over then, frustrated, and grabbed her buckle.

She shot him an elbow in his chest. "Get off me!"

He fell back in his seat, his chest burning. "Please. You're just making this harder. Don't be so stubborn."

She rounded on him. "Do you even remember anything about me? The reason we met in the first place? I came a thousand miles for a guy who was a friend of the family. This is my *brother* we're talking about."

He stared at her, the flash in those devastating blue-gray eyes, the pout of her lips, the way she met his gaze, unflinching. "Oh yeah, I remember," he said quietly.

She sucked in a breath, and he wondered which part she thought he might be referring to. Then she nodded. "Good."

"But that doesn't mean I'm going to let you go. This is dangerous enough for me. I'm not going to let you get hurt."

"I won't get hurt. You'll keep me safe."

Oh. And what was he supposed to do with that? "No."

She sighed. "Fine. Then I'll just hire this Curry guy and ask him to—"

"Stop it, Ella! I'm not playing this game with

you. If you want to risk your neck, alone, then fine—but I'm not giving in to threats. Not again."

That took the fire out of her. She looked at him, then away. "Sorry. You're right. That was . . . a desperate attempt."

"Or a low blow."

She closed her eyes then. Nodded. "I'm sorry."

Her soft answer knocked some of the edge off his anger. "No—I get it. I know you want to go. And yeah, you're a good skier, Ella. Probably one of the best amateurs I've ever met. But it's . . . dangerous. And there's a storm coming in, so I have to ski fast. Find them, lead them off the mountain."

"I know. And I'll stay right on your trail. I went to the ski store—I bought everything. A pack, sleeping bag, extra clothes, food, and my own avalanche beacon. I'm ready."

Kacey had climbed into the front cockpit and now glanced back at Gage.

"Do your preflight, Kacey," he said. She put on her helmet, raised an eyebrow, but nodded. He heard her on the radio, calling PEAK HQ.

"Listen to me, Gage," Ella said. "You're right—it is dangerous. But you might as well not go at all than go alone. What if you do find my brother, and he's hurt? Are you going to ski him down alone? Even my brother brought a buddy."

He looked out the window. Ty stood beside

149

Jess at the edge of the gate, and Gage heard his friend's words twine through his head. *"Let's just say that Jess needs me . . . that's what teammates are for. Standing beside each other even if it doesn't make sense."*

Brette, Ella's friend, walked up, stood next to Ty.

Gage turned to Ella. "Let me see that backpack."

She handed it over. As he sifted through it, he had to admit that she'd thought of everything, and quickly, including hand and foot warmer packets and even a folding snow shovel. He'd forgotten that.

"I'm ready," she said, as if confirming his thoughts.

"You promise to stay in my line? Trust everything I do, even if it doesn't make sense?"

"I promise."

"And you have to promise me, Ella, that if I say we need to get off the mountain, and we haven't found your brother, you won't freak out. You'll obey me, even if it hurts."

She swallowed. Nodded.

"And then, after this is over, you leave. And I never have to see you again."

She hitched her breath, as if he'd slapped her. But nodded.

"Fine." He tightened his jaw and turned to Kacey. "Take us in."

• • •

God, please bring them home.

Ty let the prayer free from where it gathered in his chest, let it follow the chopper as Kacey fired it up.

If there was one thing he'd learned last spring, while trying not to die as the pieces of the chopper scattered in the snow around him, as Chet's groans bruised the air, was that prayer kept people alive.

At least, it had kept *him* alive. Him and Chet. And frankly, that prayer had reignited something inside Ty he hadn't realized he'd needed.

Faith. It was a story he couldn't quite tell yet. Not with him still floundering, unable to find his feet. Like now—he should be in the pilot's seat.

Ty stood back as the chopper's blades churned the snow around them, powder spitting into the wind. He held up his hand and watched Kacey ease them into the air, lifting them out, away.

The blue bird headed into the sunlight, toward the Flathead mountain range of Glacier National Park.

Ty could nearly feel the vibrations through the gear stick, the drop of his stomach as the machine slid into the sky, his right hand controlling the lift.

Once upon a time, flying a chopper felt like an extension of himself.

He missed the view, the soaring over the pine-

151

laden hills, the snow-frosted granite cliffs of the park.

Back when life made sense. He had a job, a reason for being here.

Didn't stand on the sidelines.

At the very least, he could sit in the copilot's seat. It wasn't as if Kacey hadn't invited him.

Someday, hopefully, he'd figure out what kept him from stepping into the simulator. Maybe even find the words to talk about the accident.

Why it happened.

How they'd lived.

Only Kacey had read the accident report, only she really knew the specifics of the crash. And no one knew the story of how he'd dragged himself to help.

He planned to keep it that way.

No use reliving what he couldn't change.

"Ella wanted me to ask if I could go back to PEAK Rescue with you and monitor their progress on the radio." Brette had come up to him and Jess just before the chopper lifted off. She wore a ski jacket, a pair of leggings, utilitarian Sorels, and a headband that held back her mane of pale blonde hair. Short and cute, she'd peppered him with questions about how Gage had tracked down Curry, asking for details on when and where the chopper pilot had dropped Ollie off.

"Sure. You can ride with me," Ty said. "Gage

left his Mustang here. Or you can ride with Jess."

Jess turned to her, stuck out her hand. "Jess Tagg," she said. "I'm an EMT for the PEAK team."

"Brette Arnold. Journalist."

Only Ty noticed the slight twitch at the sides of Jess's smile. "Glad to meet you," Jess said, just a hint too brightly.

"Why don't you ride with me?" Ty said, and for a fraction of a second, he met Jess's eyes.

But Brette hadn't even blinked at Jess's name, hadn't given her a second look, hadn't in the least suggested she might know her from somewhere.

Didn't realize that she was standing in front of a juicy story—"Missing Heiress Finally Located."

Not that Jess was in hiding, but she certainly wasn't alerting the media to her change of address. Or name. Or overall identity.

So maybe she *was* in hiding. Ty hadn't really thought about it in that way before. But people like Brette could blow Jess's world to pieces with a headline. And Jess, despite her mistakes, didn't deserve that.

He glanced at Jess, who was heading into the patrol shack, then back to Brette. She was still watching the chopper disappear over the mountains.

So maybe he was overreacting; maybe Jess's paranoia was starting to affect his common sense. "If you leave your car here," he said to

153

Brette, who turned to him, shading her eyes against the sun, "Ella will have something to drive when she and Gage get back." Sooner than later, he hoped.

He'd checked the radio reception and thrown extra batteries into Gage's bag. He shouldn't worry—if anyone knew how to get down the mountain safely, it was Gage. For all Ty's years on the slopes, he'd never managed to acquire the brazen, powder-hound skills of Gage "Watts" Watson.

Frankly, watching Gage fly off a cliff or flip in the air took the breath out of Ty's chest. Just thinking about sticking the landing made his leg ache.

He just wasn't the hero that Gage was—his one skill had been flying. And with that off the radar, he was relegated to . . . well, currently, babysitting.

Although, as Brette looked up at him, her pretty eyes betraying worry, maybe he could be a friend. "Gage knows what he's doing," he said. "He knows these mountains, and how to survive. He's probably part mountain goat. If anyone can bring Oliver and his friend—and Ella—back safely, it's Gage Watson."

She nodded. "I know—I read up on him. Two freeriding world championships and a couple dozen epic descents that have over a million views on YouTube. A real hero."

"What makes him a hero is the fact that he spends every day keeping kids like Oliver safe, rescuing the hurt or lost." He took out Gage's key, clicked the Mustang open.

"Aren't you on the team too?" Brette went around and climbed in.

"Mmmhmm." Ty got in, adjusted the seat back, and in the rearview mirror spied Jess climbing into her Jeep.

"How many people are on the PEAK team?" Brette asked.

"There's nine of us—three EMTs, including Gage. We have a couple brothers on the team— Pete is our rock-climbing and swift water rescue specialist. Sam, his brother, is a deputy sheriff and liaison to the sheriff's department. Then there's Kacey, our chopper pilot, and Miles, our incident commander, and Ben King—"

"The country singer?"

Ty looked over, nodded. "He actually moved here last summer. Was involved in the rescue of flood victims. His fiancé was in a house that collapsed."

"You're kidding. And he rescued her?"

"Him and our team. PEAK was started by Ian Shaw, who owns a ranch—"

"Ian Shaw, the billionaire?"

"You know who he is?"

"Of course. He's on the board of a big charity in New York City I wrote a feature on a couple years ago. It's a charity that helps children with autism and Asperger's. His son that he lost in Katrina was autistic."

Ty didn't know that part. "He's been single as long as I've known him. He did have a niece who went missing a few years ago in the park, but they found out she's alive—"

"She went missing in the park? Wow, that sounds like quite the story."

"Maybe. I wasn't involved back then."

"And what do you do?"

"I'm the backup chopper pilot." Not a lie. Just not current.

"You fly helicopters?"

The way she said it, a little breathlessness in her voice, stirred something inside him. A long-dormant feeling he couldn't quite place.

"Yeah. I was the main pilot before Kacey got here. She used to be a search and rescue chopper pilot for the military, in Afghanistan."

"A war hero."

"Yes. She has a bronze star."

Brette looked out the window. They were passing through main street Whitefish, past the quaint shops, the cafes. She glanced at her watch. "Think they're on the mountain yet?"

"Soon, probably. We'll get an update when we get back to the ranch."

"I can't believe this happened. But I'm not surprised. Oliver grew up entitled, was told he could do anything . . . and believed it. That's what happens when your parents give you everything you want, when you need nothing in life. You go looking for adventure, hoping to fill up the empty places that only hard work and accomplishment can give you. Ever since I've known Ella, she's been worried about Ollie. She didn't grow up the same way he did."

"Really, how's that?"

"Ella and Oliver are immigrants from Serbia. They came over in the early nineties with their parents. The Blairs sponsored them and took them in, gave them jobs. Ella was about eleven and Ollie four when both their parents died in a car crash. The Blairs adopted them, but Ella never forgot how her parents scraped together a life for them. Ollie, however, never really knew them. He can't remember any parents but Mansfield and Marjorie Blair. They own half of Vermont's maple syrup production, and Mrs. Blair was a state senator. To say that Ollie and Ella made a giant economic jump is an understatement. But I think that's why Ella is so grounded. Now Ollie, he grew up getting anything he wanted, but also in the shadow of giants. With such high-performing adopted parents and Ella setting the pace, I guess he decided he had to do something epic. I'm hoping that this experience teaches him that he's not invincible. That is, if they make it home in one piece."

She fell silent then, and he heard a low muttered "please."

But her words had clung to him. *"He grew up getting anything he wanted. I'm hoping that this experience teaches him that he's not invincible."*

Yes, tragedy and mistakes and being in over your head did that to a person.

"So, you're saying you have a country singer who moonlights as a rescuer, a billionaire cowboy hiding out in Montana after the tragic loss of his family, a snowboarder rewriting his life as a rescuer, and a war hero dedicating her life to saving civilians?"

Ty hadn't thought about his team in that way, but . . . "Yes."

"This is definitely the right place for me to hang out."

He glanced at her. Brette had taken her phone out, was typing. "Who are you texting?"

"A note to my agent, asking what she thinks about a story about a team of heroes."

Oh. "What kind of journalist are you?"

She finished her note, tucked her phone away. "I write inspirational pieces for *Time* and *Nat Geo* online, as well as biographies and other bio-pieces about larger-than-life heroes. Actually, it's harder than you think to find a true hero. Everyone has secrets, and if you look hard enough, we're all just hiding behind how we hope people view us."

How we hope people view us. Yeah, he'd had that persona firmly in place, trying to be a hero, keep up with the rest of the PEAK team.

"You need to meet Pete. He's our local celebrity. Saved a couple kids from a grizzly last summer and brought home a group of teenagers who went over a cliff in their van."

Her eyes widened. "Now you're talking. Where do I meet this Pete?"

He didn't know why, but the question, the little lilt of curiosity in her voice, had his stomach tightening. "He'll probably be back at the ranch."

She was silent for a moment, then turned to him. "And what about Jess? What does she do?"

"She's an EMT."

"How long has she been with the team?"

"A couple years, why?"

Brette had taken out her phone again. "I don't know. There's just something about her. She looks so familiar, like we've met before. It's just outside my brain, and I'm trying to grab it."

He swallowed, said nothing.

"But don't worry. I never forget a face, or name, or details. I just have to place her, and I'll remember her story. No one hides from me."

One look at Heaven's Peak, its white-capped spine cutting through the wispy clouds to soar magnificent and deadly above the mountain scape of the Livingstone Range, told Ella that maybe she should have kept her mouth shut.

Listened to Brette as she followed her into the mountain ski shop, arguing for sanity.

"You can't go down that mountain—you'll only end up in pieces, like Ollie."

No, she wouldn't. Because she'd skied with Gage before and knew he'd pick a safe route, one that she could ski.

And she'd been a backcountry skier for years—where did Brette think Ollie got his inspiration?

Now, watching the wind lift the top layer of snow from the cornice that capped the mountain, and then following the narrow ridge that wound down toward the bowl, a sheer drop intersected only by steep cliffs and channels of deep powder, Ella had to bite her lip to keep herself from glancing at Gage, letting him see that he might have been right.

It was dangerous. And yeah, she might be in way over her head.

But she also meant her words—if he got injured, just who would save him? He could perish up here just as easily as anyone else. Gage needed a partner, and she could do this. And he *would* keep her safe, to the best of his abilities.

She just had to stay in his track.

She took a long breath and tried to appreciate the view. They'd flown into the park, over a frozen Lake McDonald, then up the river toward

Logan Pass. White-capped mountains littered the horizon, jagged peaks of glacial ice and razor-edge granite, tufted with deep, crystalline, heavenly powder. Unblemished, frozen, perfect.

Pine trees laden with snow jutted up through the white, a postcard beauty, but lethal if they didn't measure their turns, cut too close, and ended upside down in a tree well.

This was why she was here—in case even legendary Gage Watson made a mistake. Besides, her brother needed her, even if he wouldn't admit it.

She finally hazarded a glance at Gage. He had the map out, was studying the mountain. She leaned over, and without asking he traced their trail along the map, starting along the ridge. He pointed out a cliff face maybe two hundred feet down, then another, even lower. Then down the face, not quite perpendicular, but veering off to the east.

Then lower, to a cave in the cliff wall.

"We'll camp here tonight!" he said into his mic.

She nodded.

Kacey rose along the front face of the peak, which was too steep for snow to cling to, a barren gray granite. An icing of snowy, thick frosting covered the ridgeline, a cornice of ice maybe twenty feet thick. And, as they got closer to the top, she could almost taste the fresh powder

161

stinging her tongue and cheeks as she surfed over it.

Big mountain skiing felt a lot like flying, as if through weighty, powdery clouds, with the occasional drop into thin air, the breath of heaven in her lungs.

She never felt as though she could abandon herself, dive into the moment, like she did when she rode powder.

As if sensing her thoughts, Gage glanced over at her then, and for a second grinned. It stirred up so much memory she had to swallow, fast.

Then, as if he'd forgotten himself, the grin vanished and he returned to the view.

They reached the peak, and Kacey hovered over the ridgeline, a forty-foot expanse that dropped off two thousand feet on either side. Creamy, untouched powder deceived as it hid gullies and drop-offs, lethal spires of granite and ice floes that could break off in layers and chase them down the hill.

Rotor wash skimmed a surface layer of powder into the crisp air like fairy dust.

"I can't actually set down on the mountain, but I can hover and you can jump out, okay?" Kacey's voice came through her headphones.

"Got it," Ella said.

"I'll go first," Gage said, but she shook her head. No way was he getting down there only for Kacey to fly away with her still in tow.

"I'll go—you hand me the gear," she said. Besides, the snow pack on her side of the chopper looked more stable.

His mouth tightened in a grim, acquiescing line.

She took off her headphones, put on her helmet, and opened the door. The wash of the rotors nearly sucked her out. Kacey hovered maybe five feet from the base of the hill, and it didn't take much for Ella to step out onto a skid and jump off.

She landed in the powder, soft as pudding, and had to dig herself out. When she found her feet, Gage was leaning out of the chopper, handing her down her board, then the two packs.

She set them in the snow, then took his board.

In a moment, he landed in the snow next to her. Then he stood up and waved, and Kacey veered away. Gage checked in his radio, and Kacey confirmed.

Ella stood on top of the world. For as far as she could see, mountains pressed up against the vault of blue sky. To the west, gunmetal-gray clouds shadowed the peaks, evidence of the encroaching storm. And standing here on the cornice, the air turned whisper thin.

She examined their route—the thick spine, then the bowl below, the cliffs and bushy green pines, so far below they seemed like toys. Wind swirled around them, dusting up from the pristine snowpack. "I don't see any tracks," she said.

"Could be the wind sheer scraping it away. Or maybe they put down somewhere else," Gage said. He had put on his pack and now held hers up for her to back into.

Apparently, he simply couldn't help the gentleman part of him. She snapped on the waist belt, hitched down the shoulder straps.

He locked his boots into his board. "Good to go?"

She did the same, pulled her goggles down, and the world lost the sharp glare. "Let's do this."

"Just keep it easy, and stay behind me." He bounced himself forward, added an adjustment in weight, and began to slide down the thick wide spine.

For a long moment, her heart simply slammed against her ribs, watching him. Seeing his grace on the snow, making it look effortless. As he slid, snow cascaded from the top in a shower, sending bullets and a wave of powder in his wake.

Follow my line.

She eased herself forward with a shift in her hips, bounced along to start movement, then found his trail, a beautiful thick crease in the snow. She spread her arms, found her balance, took a full breath.

She refused to glance down, but kept her gaze on the line, glancing at him, some thirty feet ahead. He seemed to be taking it slow, glancing back at her occasionally but setting a steady pace.

His course was easy, wide, no sharp turns, a

164

beautiful rhythm as they rode down the spine into the wild blue yonder. Heat suffused her body as it warmed up to the dance, the swish of the snow like a whisper under her board.

He finally paused in a spray of white when they reached the first chute. She caught up to him, breathing harder than she wanted to admit.

She stared at the chute, trying not to let her breath catch.

The chute spanned maybe twenty feet but dropped down two hundred feet between two thick runnels of granite. It ended at an outcropping of granite, where it disappeared into white space.

She knew from looking at the map and his video that the first fall was nearly forty feet.

"Why are you stopping?"

"There's another chute, a little further down the ridge. It's wider, and longer, and no jump."

She glanced at him, wished she could read his eyes through his goggles. "Won't that take us off course?"

His mouth tightened in an affirmative nonverbal.

"Why would we do that?"

He looked at her then, a little bit of "really?" in his expression.

And that just added a swirl of heat to her chest. "No. I can do this, Gage. Don't go slower, don't pull back because of me."

His mouth tightened in a tight bud of frustration. "Fine. We'll stop right above the ledge, just ski under control."

"In your line," she said.

His jaw clenched, but he edged forward, the tip of his board over the edge, into air. Seemed to consider his route.

She held her breath. It felt a little like waiting for the needle in a doctor's office.

With a hop, he lifted off the edge and into the chute.

She watched him go, powder curling up behind his turns like a wave. He moved as if he were dancing, smooth, no hesitation as he caught air off a rise, circling his arms for balance, then landed in a graceful puff of snow. He continued down, and she couldn't move, caught in the sight of him.

Gage Watson belonged to freeriding. Or rather, freeriding belonged to him. He flew down angles most men—and women—would cling to, terrified.

He caught another jump and this time tucked for a second, and she knew he'd let a part of himself hearken back to the days before the fame. Back to the time when he simply rode powder for the fun of it.

He stopped above the ledge, a tiny prick of gray against the vast white.

She still didn't move. Because although he'd

carved a wide, easy route—probably the easiest through the chute's jagged rocks—all of a sudden, the what-ifs paralyzed her.

Not unlike the moment when she saw Gage sitting in the hearing and she knew that someone's life was about to be dismantled. But by then it had gone too far for her to step away.

Please, God, don't let anyone get hurt.

With a cry that echoed through the chambers of the mountain, she eased forward and launched herself into the white.

He'd made a nice wide arc down the mountain, but she adjusted a little too late, took her leading turn too wide. The next, a countering turn, she anticipated too early, cut it shallow.

Following a line meant staying in the safe zone. Especially on a mountain like Heaven's Peak that obscured drop-offs and crevasses. And Gage was an artist when it came to creating a line. He looked for ridges and rises, the flow of the snow around landmarks, the chutes that led to air. And air led to flair.

But today, his art was all about staying in the safety zone, and she adjusted her speed as she came up to the first jump. She made the turn, shifted her weight back, then centered it above the board as she lifted off.

Her stomach stayed, but her body soared, and she held her arms out for balance. She hit too soon, surprising herself that she stayed up, found her balance, and curved into the next turn.

She didn't look at Gage, simply the thick, beautiful line he'd created for her to follow. She squatted into the next turn, rising fast to unweight herself, and turned. His familiar technique rushed back to her. Easy carving in the heavy powder, with pumping turns in the tighter, rolling sections of the run, a quick dart up to a jump, air, and then a sweet, tufted landing.

She took the next jump, and for the fun of it tucked a second before setting down on the thick powder.

She didn't want to stop when she met Gage. Her breaths caught in puffs of air as she leaned over, grabbed her knees.

"Having fun or something?" Gage said, and she looked up to see his mouth twitch on one side.

"Last time I skied this hard, I was . . ." *Oh. With you.*

She stood up, tried to find something to fill in her gap. "It's just been a while since I lost myself like this. I don't know why, but snowboarding makes me center into the moment, forget about everything else but the powder. It's distracting. And relaxing, even though I haven't forgotten why we're here. But maybe I remember the urge that pulled my brother in."

"Yeah," he said. "Out here, you can feel so small and yet sort of invincible. And that's how people get in over their heads." His smile fell, and she could hear in his words the echoes from the past.

She imagined that it might be hard for him to ski without the shadow of his mistakes following him down the mountain.

He pointed toward the cliff's edge. "I think if you take off the left edge, it's a little less steep, the drop shorter."

"Which one did you take last time?"

He pointed to the right.

"Then that's what we should take. Ollie will want to do everything you did."

"Oh, I hope not," Gage said quietly.

She felt for him, the fact that his fame caused others to follow in his footsteps, get hurt. "Gage, this isn't your fault. Not in the least. My brother makes his own decisions, and you're not to blame if people get in over their heads and get hurt."

He stared at her. "What?"

"I'm just saying, you're not to blame—"

"Are you kidding me? You took me to court precisely because you blamed me for Dylan's death."

His words bruised.

"I've had a little distance since then."

He drew in a breath, and his jaw tightened. He looked away. "That must be nice. I can't seem to put it behind me."

Her mouth opened then, but he pushed off, heading for the left side.

He looked back at her. "It's easier over here!"

"Gage, stop protecting me! I don't want to go the easy way. I can do this—watch!"

She pushed off toward the edge, the jagged wall on the right side that dropped forty feet into steep, thick, dense powder.

She didn't stop. She took a breath and sailed right off the edge into the clear, bright air.

Then she looked down, the world so far she thought it had fallen away.

She began to scream.

9

Ella's scream as she went over the edge found Gage's bones and turned them to liquid. He stood at the edge of the cliff as she disappeared, and couldn't move.

For a second he was caught inside the memory of watching Dylan simply miss the turn and fly off the cliff, soaring over the jagged edge of the mountain. Then falling more than two hundred feet below into a catastrophe of broken bones and crushed vertebrae.

"Ella!" Gage bounced himself forward and went straight over the edge, dropping fast and landing in a poof of snow. If he'd had more momentum going over the cliff, he might have remained aloft, but his body weight implanted him in the powder and he found himself stuck, having to wiggle himself free. He rolled out of the hole his body made in the deep powder, unbuckled his boots from his board, and scrambled to Ella's crash site, a tumult of snow and fine dust still caught in the wind. "Ella!"

She lay in the hole, her board just peeking out of the crevasse, with just the orange arms of her jacket and her gray helmet showing. She waved at him, trying to wiggle out of the hole.

He dropped to his knees beside her. "Are you okay?"

"Not much of a graceful landing, but—yeah." She even smiled at him, as if her scream hadn't ripped him open, baring something he'd been trying to ignore for the past two days.

He missed her. Missed the straight-shooter, no-nonsense way she didn't dance around her words, said the truth as she saw it.

Or, he hoped it was the truth.

"You're a good guy, Gage. I've always known that." Her words had stuck around, latching on, growing inside him, casting forth too many memories. Like the way she could keep up with him on a mountain. And that time, after their first night of skiing, she'd talked him into singing karaoke with her. *I got you, babe.* He could still hear her pitiful impression of Cher. Feel his chest expanding with unnamed emotion, a little off balance with the sense that he didn't have to impress her.

But he'd wanted to. And as he knelt down beside her now, unsnapping her boots from her board to free her, he realized he *still* wanted to.

And that gnawed at him. Because he couldn't get past the fact that she'd destroyed his life and still she'd managed to crawl under his skin. Seeing her again had awakened him to the fact that no, he'd never forgotten Ella Blair. He should have been furious with her. Instead, he could barely catch his breath with the relief that she'd survived.

She'd never been nothing or just a date.

He'd loved her. Or wanted to.

He put his arms around her and tugged, pulling her free of her landing hole. She tumbled over into his arms, her helmet bumping against his.

It wasn't hard to remember how perfectly she'd fit into his arms.

To make it worse, she held on, her gloves fisted into his jacket.

He'd never forgotten, either, how pretty she was. The kind of pretty that slid into a man, that deepened more inside him a little each day. He couldn't take his eyes off her, the way her blue-gray eyes shone, the way her deep copper hair curled from the back of her helmet.

He held on to her just a second longer than necessary, perhaps, until she pushed herself off him and rolled onto her back.

Only then did he realize, with a painful start, that he was in very real danger of Ella Blair carving her way into his life again.

She was staring at the sky. "I thought I left my stomach up on that ridge."

"You pretty much scared the life out of me when you screamed."

"Sorry I screamed—it was just a reflex. But wow, that was fun."

"It is fun. I feel like screaming sometimes too." He looked over at her, gave her a smile.

But she must have related his comment to something in their past because she sat up, pulled her goggles up, and looked at him with so much raw pain in her eyes that he longed to grab back his words.

"I know it must tear you apart. You had so much, and then . . . but you've become a rescue skier. That's so . . . heroic."

He lifted an eyebrow.

"I'm trying too hard, aren't I?" She made a face. "I just can't stop talking, can't stop trying to figure out how to . . . I don't know, maybe make things better."

He sat up. "Why don't we just forget the past and ride? Dropping off a cliff into chin-deep powder *is* amazing and worthy of a scream."

Slowly she smiled, and for a moment all the anger, all the hurt he'd stewed in for the last three years drained away, leaving only one brilliant thought.

He was on a mountain again with beautiful Ella Blair. Surrounded by champagne powder and the delicious smile of a girl who once thought he hung the moon.

Maybe she still did.

"We're going to find your brother, Ella. I promise."

She nodded, as if blinking back tears, and

he had the urge to reach up, touch her cheek.

"Oh!" she said. "Did you see—I wasn't the only one who made a dent in the hill." She pointed to two more landing zones, disturbances in the snow not far away. And from them led tracks, now half-swept with snow. "Ollie and Bradley were here."

If they'd taken his way, they would have missed the trail.

"Good job, Ella," Gage said, a little chagrined. "But we'd better hurry." He pointed to the swell of dark storm clouds closing in on the park. More, the wind had whipped up, stirring the snow into whirlwinds of crystalline white. Overhead, too, the cloud cover had thickened, stretching long shadows over the mountain.

He could smell storm in the air, the makings of a blizzard.

"We need to find them before this storm hits and get us all off the mountain," he said. "You promise that you *really* didn't hurt anything?"

"I'm fine."

"Good—so I promise, no more taking the slow route. But no more going off cliffs before I do, okay?"

She nodded and reached for her board.

He hiked back to his, strapped it on, and slid back to her. It seemed that Oliver knew his trail well, which meant he'd continue down this bowl for the rest of the day, hopefully stopping

175

tonight above Angel's Wings and Cathedral Canyon.

"Stay right in my path. If they're below us, we don't want to set off an avalanche."

"I'm right behind you."

He didn't know why her words filled him up with heat, but it charged through him as he leaned into the slope.

It could be that it wasn't only Oliver and Bradley who were in over their heads.

Brette had landed in the middle of a journalist's jackpot. Pure gold surrounded her; every one of the members of the PEAK team was heroic to the bone, evidenced by the team's current conversation about heading into Glacier National Park to look for missing Oliver, Bradley, and now Gage and Ella.

No one had been able to rouse them on the radio, and apparently that had chopper pilot Kacey Fairing and her boss, Chet King, worried.

The two stood in front of a computer, watching the weather map refresh every few seconds as the low pressure front from the west closed in on the mountains. Kacey, tall, lean, and pretty with her long auburn hair, looked every inch the former military pilot Ty had described on their drive over.

Chet, maybe in his early sixties, leaned on a cane, his body still strong despite what Ty said were two new hips after a chopper accident. She made a mental note to add Chet to her list of heroes. The boss greeted her with a firm handshake and a crooked smile. Reminded her a little of Harrison Ford.

Kacey and the chopper hadn't returned by the time Ty pulled up to the PEAK ranch, an actual former ranch with the old house reconstructed for their headquarters, including bunk rooms, a kitchen, an office, and a main meeting area. It didn't take long, however, for Kacey to arrive and land the blue and white rescue chopper on the pad outside, in front of a two-story white barn that had the words *PEAK Rescue* written in red on the front.

Ty had given Brette a quick tour of that too, in his explanation of the PEAK resources and activities. "We do everything from search and rescue in the park, including climbing rescues and swift water rescues, to emergency medical evacuations, and we even help with avalanche control for the nearby ski areas, as well as the backcountry."

He'd pointed out their wilderness ambulance, a Land Rover converted into a medivac unit. "We have a 4Runner and a couple Polaris snowmobiles for off-road needs. And of course, the dual-engine Bell 429 chopper." He'd said it with such warmth in his voice she couldn't help but remember his words.

"I'm the backup chopper pilot. I was the main pilot before Kacey got here."

Interesting.

Ty had brought her in the house then, and introduced her to the team, at least the ones at the base. Chet, of course, then Sierra Rose, the team administrator. Petite, with short dark hair and hazel-green eyes, she greeted Brette by inviting her to grab a piece of leftover pizza, some soup, or one of the cookies in the jar in the kitchen. What had Ty said—the big sister of the team?

Sierra had assembled an hour-by-hour weather forecast for Heaven's Peak, as well as satellite images of the area, and spread them out on a massive table in front of a map of the park affixed to the wall. A flat-screen against the back wall played the local weather and news.

Brette nearly fell over when country singer Ben King appeared from some back office and greeted Kacey Fairing with a quick kiss. She must have been staring because Ben turned to her, held out his hand. "Ben King."

His album covers and posters didn't do him justice. With blue eyes that she could lose herself in, just like his songs, he wore a baseball cap backward, faded jeans, and cowboy boots.

And, here he was, a bona fide hero, working on a rescue team. Blow her socks off.

"Brette Arnold. I'm a friend of Senator Ella

Blair. She's out with Gage on Heaven's Peak, trying to track down her brother and his friend."

"Right," Ben said and glanced at Kacey.

And now she felt a little silly, because he probably knew all that.

"It's an honor to meet you. I have all your albums . . ." Please, now she must sound like a rabid fan.

Which she was—at least a mildly rabid fan. Not the kind to stalk him to Montana.

"Thanks," he said, a warmth in his smile that made her disbelieve everything his former bandmate Holly Montgomery had said about him in her interview about their breakup. *Cold and difficult to work with.*

That's what bad journalism did—showed only the one-sided perspective. She liked to dig inside a person's life, find the truth, show the world the full person, good and bad.

Let the public decide.

"I'm sure Gage will find them," Ben said. "If anyone knows how to handle a mountain, it's Gage. He'll get them all down safely."

Brette nodded, believing every word that came from his golden, mountain-twangy voice.

"The weather is closing in fast," Kacey had said, giving her a smile, then headed over to Chet, where she huddled up, strategizing.

Meanwhile, Brette helped herself to a cookie. She hadn't eaten since breakfast. Now, her stomach was starting to curl into a fist over the emptiness. She actually felt a little nauseated.

Ty must have noticed, because he pulled out a container of vegetable soup, ladled some into a bowl, and heated it in the microwave.

"Sit," he said, putting the bowl on the counter and setting a spoon next to it.

She slid onto a high-top stool. "Thanks."

Ty washed his hands, then grabbed a towel, turning to her. "It'll be a long night, I'm guessing. And they'll probably have to spend the night on the mountain."

"Why?"

He parked the towel over his shoulder and reached in a nearby bread bin for a half loaf of French bread. Pulled out a knife. "The storm is rolling in. Even if they find Ollie and Bradley, Kacey can't fly them off the mountain in this weather."

Brette glanced out the window and noticed the beginning of flurries. The sky had turned a dark pewter. "That was fast."

"Weather moves in quickly in the valley. It'll take a little longer once it hits the mountains, but still, my guess is that by late this afternoon, they'll be battling some winds and snow."

She pressed a hand to her stomach.

"Worried?"

She sighed. Nodded. "Ella is a good snowboarder, there's no doubt. She and her family used to come out West every year. They bought a place here at Blackbear just a few years ago, and she's skied all the big mountain country—even went off Corbet's Couloir at Jackson Hole. If anybody can keep up with Gage, it's Ella. But . . ." She looked out the window. "I should call their parents."

"That's a good idea," Ty said.

"Yeah, maybe, except . . . this could go south, fast."

"They're going to be okay. Gage is a good skier, and he prepared for a storm."

"I was more talking about . . ." She sighed. "Well, Gage has a reputation, and if her parents find out she's with him . . . well, not to mention that Gage and Ella have a past. And then Ella did something that really hurt Gage—"

"I know about their past. They'll work it out. Gage isn't going to let his mistakes—or his wounds—stand in the way of saving Ella's brother."

She might have given him a dubious look, because he frowned. "What?"

"He won't let her get physically hurt, if he can, but Ella still holds a little torch for him, and . . . well, I just don't want her getting her heart broken. She's my best friend—probably only friend, actually—and she hasn't exactly dated a plethora of men. None, actually, since Gage, I think. So . . ."

Ty set a glass of water in front of her. She reached for it, touched his fingers. He had nice hands, strong, long fingers. In fact, all of Ty Remington seemed sturdy and solid, from his wry smile and pale green eyes to his wide shoulders, firm torso, and fit legs. She had the sense that there was much more to know about Ty than he suggested.

Backup chopper pilot. From her perspective, the guy seemed more like the hero behind the lines, keeping everything running.

"So, I just hope they all come home in one piece," she finished softly.

To her surprise, Ty reached over and cupped his hand over hers. Gave a little squeeze.

When he let go, little eddies of warmth sank into her skin.

Yeah, he had nice hands.

"So, you mentioned that billionaire Ian Shaw started PEAK Rescue?"

Ty nodded, wiping the outside of the soup container. He put it back in the fridge. "When his niece went missing in the park, he discovered that Mercy Falls just didn't have the resources it needed to wage a full-scale search. So he invested in our first chopper and used it to search the park, and then later let the local Mercy Falls EMS department use it for their needs. He funded the entire thing until last summer, when he handed it over to Mercy Falls."

"Wow, that's generous."

"That's Ian," said Sierra, who came up beside her and slid onto a stool. "He doesn't want anyone else to go through what he did, searching for Esme." She reached for the cookie jar. Pulled out a cookie. "Thankfully, she's alive, although we still don't know where she is."

"Really?" And Brette thought of her editor's reply text to her suggestion of writing a stor of these local heroes. *Dig around, work it up. Could be a good human interest piece.*

"Yeah," Sierra was saying, "she called about five months ago and left a message on Ian's cell phone. Told him to stop looking for her. Which, of course, he can't."

"Is it because of his wife and son—and the fact they went missing and died in Katrina?"

The room went silent, and Brette looked at Ty, then back to Sierra.

Sierra had gone a little white. "How did you know that?"

"Uh, because Ian is . . . well, he's on the board of a charity I did a profile on not long ago. He had a terrible allergic attack last summer that put him in the hospital—"

"I know," Sierra said. She slid off the stool. "I was there."

She didn't offer more, just walked away, and Brette looked at Ty. He pursed his lips, then

183

leaned down, pitching his voice low. "Sierra used to be his personal assistant."

Oh. Interesting. Brette turned back to her soup. "So, besides the flood rescue, the grizzly attacks, and the search for lost kids in the park, what other epic adventures has this team had?"

Ty just kept wiping the counter and didn't answer her.

"Ty?"

He glanced over at her, shook his head. "I can't think of any more."

She frowned. His tone was just . . . off.

And that's when the door opened, sweeping the weather into the room along with a wide-shouldered blond, his hair in strings around his face. He wore a gray jacket, a pair of snow-crusted pants.

"Hey, guys. I just got a call from Jess. We have a family whose Caravan went off the road. She was driving by when she saw it and is wondering if we can get them out of the ditch. Jess is already there—it's not far from the ski hill."

He stood in the doorway, just a little larger than life. Thor, in the flesh. And he had the grim, one-sided smile to go with it.

"That's Pete Brooks," Ty said quietly.

Pete Brooks. The guy who had rescued the kids from a grizzly bear—she remembered Ty mentioning that.

Here, maybe, was a man with a story.

184

"I'll go. We can take my truck," Ben offered and got up and pushed past Pete, heading outside.

"You need more help?" Ty asked.

"We got this," Pete said, glancing at him. Something in his expression . . . Brette couldn't read it, but it was definitely there. A chill, perhaps. A glancing blow of dismissal.

"Stay here and wait to hear from Gage," Kacey said to Ty. She got up and followed Ben out.

Ty nodded, glanced away. And something in his expression definitely said he'd been benched.

"I was the main pilot before Kacey got here."

She couldn't erase the sense that the greatest story of all had something to do with handsome yet quiet Ty Remington. The only question was . . . how to get him to tell it.

The sky had turned pewter gray, and the clouds were low and oppressive as icy snow flew from the sky and whirled into the back of Ella's jacket and down her neck as she fought to stay in Gage's line.

Two hard hours of skiing and she wanted to weep with the pain in her legs, the way they trembled. Sweat lined her helmet, and when she spied Gage waiting for her in the alcove of a wall of granite, she wanted to cry out in relief.

Collapse in a heap.

She'd never skied so hard in her entire life. She

185

couldn't bear to ask if Gage was pulling back or going easy on her.

She pulled up to him, breathing hard, the snow falling so thick around him that it accumulated on his jacket collar, turning his dark whiskers into a fine film of ice.

"The tracks are disappearing and it's starting to get dangerous," he said as he pulled off his goggles. Snowflakes caught in his lashes. "Even if I flick on my head lamp, I can't find a good line. I need to see farther down the hill. I think we need to stop."

"But we're not at the cave."

"I know. We're still a good hour away, probably. And between us and the cave is the Weeping Wall. We can't take that in the dead of night. The day is dropping away fast—I need to set up camp."

She looked at him, then around. "Where, here?"

"We're on a little ledge, protected from the wind. This is a good place."

"Did you bring a tent?"

"I have a two-man bivvy. It'll be cozy, but it's an expedition tent, made for high-altitude camping. And I'll anchor us into the rock."

She'd promised to trust him, but oh, how she'd hoped to spend the night in a cozy cave instead of anchored to the side of a cliff. "What do you want me to do?"

"Hold my pack while I pitch camp." Gage took it off as she clicked out of her bindings, set up her board, and hunkered down to hold his pack. He put on a headlamp and shined light on his progress as he used her shovel to dig out a foundation for them. Then he pulled out the tent contained in a tiny five-pound pack. It snapped open as he released it, and he set it in to the area, tacking down the snow stakes deep into the pack. Then he zipped open the door.

"I'll secure our boards and the tent, you get inside, unpack, and get some snow melting. There's a stove in my pack."

She threw his pack in, then sat at the edge of the tent and pulled off her boots, bringing them inside with her. Her feet ached, and she rubbed them as he closed the door.

The wind shook the tent, and she tried not to think of where they were perched, the flimsy fabric and thin Kevlar wires that anchored them to the rock and ice. She found a Maglite and held it in her mouth between her teeth as she unlatched his sleeping bag, then rolled it out. She did the same with hers.

For a long moment she considered just what her mother would say about sharing her tent with Gage. But they'd sleep fully clothed, and, well . . .

Gage Watson was so angry at her, he was probably the last person who would entertain thoughts of romance.

Although, today, for a moment after she'd dropped off the cliff, he'd almost seemed . . .

well, had seemed actually friendly. *"Why don't we just forget the past and ride?"*

Wouldn't that be nice? To just start over, meet each other anew? Discover the people they'd been before the accident, the civil suit, the betrayal.

Before her secrets.

Ella unzipped her jacket and pulled off her helmet. Then she slid into her sleeping bag as she rooted around in his pack for the stove. She found the attachable mug and unzipped the tent and packed the mug with snow. Gage had secured the snowboards to the rock and brought them up under the vestibule that he'd attached to the entrance. He then followed her into the tent and closed the door behind him, leaving on his headlamp for illumination.

"The sun is dropping like a rock—it's getting black out there. And the snow is really coming down," he said. He'd taken off his gloves and now blew on his reddened hands. "Must be twenty below out there."

"And in here," she said, lighting the stove.

"Not for long. The tent will warm up with our body heat."

She didn't look at him, not sure exactly what he meant. But she shouldn't have worried, because Gage took off his boots, then climbed into his sleeping bag fully clothed. He worked off his helmet and his wet gaiter and clipped them to a hanging loft loop. Then he pulled out his walkie and stored it in a pocket on the wall.

The snow began to melt.

"I think Jess packed a dehydrated meal or two in there," he said.

Ella dug through the pack and unearthed two meals.

"Beef stroganoff or chili mac?"

"Stroganoff. Hopefully we'll get back before we have to dig into the chili mac. It's more like chili paste." He unzipped his jacket, pulled it off, and wadded it behind him for a pillow.

Underneath he wore a gray fleece pullover that shaped to his wide shoulders, his thick arms. He'd captured his trademark shoulder-length brown hair back into a low bun and now freed it, ran his fingers fast through it to untangle the snarls.

Then he pulled out his walkie and tried to call in to base. "Watson to PEAK, come back."

He'd placed a call earlier today, shortly after they'd tracked Ollie's trail off the cliff. Ella couldn't help but wonder how Brette was faring with his PEAK friends. She had no doubt that within twenty-four hours, she'd have some brilliant story dug up about a daring rescue.

Brette did that—found the stories hidden inside people, dragged them out into the light.

Static answered Gage, and he tried a few more times to no avail.

"Probably the weather."

"They'll be worried," Ella said as the water came to a boil. She poured it into the open pouch of stroganoff. Then she stirred the meal with a plastic spoon she'd found in a bag of essentials—salt, pepper, wipes. Thoughtful, that Jess.

"Maybe. We'll get ahold of them first thing in the morning."

"I hope Ollie's found the cave." She glanced at Gage, hoping for some reassurance.

"From his tracks, he's handling the mountain better than I thought. If he's following my line, he'll be in the cave. He had a five-hour start on us. My guess is that they're already hunkered down, asleep."

Ella nodded, wishing she had his confidence. "I can't help but feel like this is my fault. I came out here hoping to talk him into going back to school. Maybe he's trying to prove something to me." She handed the pouch to Gage. "There's no plates."

He took the pouch and the proffered spoon and dug in. "It's good."

"That's my specialty—adding water to food. You should taste my hot cocoa."

"Yes, please," he said and grinned at her.

Yeah, he was right. The temperature in the tent had warmed.

She opened the door again, retrieved more snow in the mug, and set it on the stove to melt.

He passed the pouch over to her, keeping his spoon, and she dug in with a fresh utensil. "Thanks."

"You did well today. I . . . I'd forgotten how well you handle the powder, Ella."

She couldn't look at him. "I'm pretty sore."

"Well, me too. I haven't been freeriding . . . well, not since Outlaw, really."

Oh. She didn't know where to go with that. "You came home, though, and started working on the rescue team?"

"No. I came home and my dad wanted me to go to college. I think he thought that snowboarding was a well-funded hobby. But I never wanted what he saw for me—medicine. Becoming a doctor. It was his fault—he started me snowboarding when I was three. I was never meant for college." He shook his head, reached for the pack, and rummaged around.

"I hooked up with PEAK Rescue about two years ago because of Ty. He was flying the chopper for them at the time and told me they needed an EMT. I went to classes at the local community college, got my basic EMT, and started working rescues. The ski patrol was an easy jump from there."

He'd found the cocoa and now poured two packets into the hot water, stirred it with a knife. "Sorry, only one mug." He turned off the stove.

"It's fine," she said and handed him back the

pouch, now empty. The stroganoff had heated her core, and when she chased it with the hot cocoa, yeah, she might live.

Especially with her and Gage finding new footing. Maybe he was right—they should put the past behind them, just stay focused on their goal.

"How about you? Still working at your law firm?"

She shook her head. "No. I resigned, nearly right after . . ."

He looked up at her, frowned. "Why?"

He had such pretty eyes, the kind that could hold her fast, drag truths from her. She looked away. "Uh, well, my mom got sick."

"Oh, Ella, I'm so sorry."

"Thanks. Breast cancer. She's doing okay now, but she was a state senator, in our Vermont congress."

"I remember that." He took the cocoa she offered and took a sip. "Mmm."

"I know, right?" She folded up the garbage, put it in the plastic bag. "Anyway, Mom suggested I fill her shoes, so I stepped in, got elected by a special call election, and served out her term. It ends this year."

"Seriously? You're a state senator?"

"It's not that exciting. I mostly give speeches and sit in meetings." She made a face. "Actually, I'm trying to decide if I want to run for reelection. I don't know."

"But you always wanted to do something to help people—I remember that part. You were going to defend the weak and save the world."

"Yeah. Well, the world doesn't want to be saved, I don't think. I recently tried to filibuster to block a bill vote on the recreational use of marijuana, but it didn't work."

"I'm sorry."

"Sometimes I feel like I'm spinning my wheels, working hard for something that doesn't matter. No one is listening, no one cares."

He handed her the cocoa. "Finish it."

She took it, and felt the heat of his hand lingering on the container.

"Sort of like your brother?" Gage said softly.

She looked up at him. "Yeah. I can't believe he would do this—risk lives. Ours, his, Bradley's. But now I'm wondering if I worried for nothing—he's clearly fine. I shouldn't have dragged you out here."

"You were worried. I get that—we panic when we're worried. And that emotion clouds our judgment." He dismantled the stove. "Like when I saw Dylan go off that cliff—I couldn't think of anything but getting to him. I'd seen other people live, despite the fall, landing in thirty feet of spongy powder. So I cleared the cliff as fast as I could, saw where Dylan landed, and then . . . that's when I heard it. The thunder of the avalanche that Dylan had dragged from the cornice when he went off. It unlatched and then . . ."

"I know. I watched it on live feed," she said quietly.

He looked up, met her eyes, and for a second, silence fell between them.

"Yeah. Right, well . . ." He shoved the stove into his pack.

"I watched you try to out-ski it, and you were amazing. The way you kept riding it, even when it caught you . . . and then you vanished." She pressed her hand to her mouth.

"It was pretty terrifying," he said, drawing in a breath. "It just swept me up like a wave, and I was just . . . helpless. The snow washed over me, and I couldn't breathe. And then, just like that, it stopped. Everything went eerily quiet. And that's when I realized I was stuck. Entombed."

She held her breath. *Entombed.*

He wasn't looking at her now; he was someplace distant even as he spoke. "I've never been so alone as I was then. Truly buried alive." He drew in a shuddered breath. "Even though I wore an avalanche detector, I had to tell myself not to panic, to slow my breathing. Had to believe that they would find me."

He glanced over at her, offered a wry smile. "Sorry, I'm not sure where that came from."

But she wasn't going to let him go, this glimpse

of the Gage she'd known. "I couldn't move, couldn't breathe until they found you."

He met her eyes, nodded, his mouth a tight line. "That's pretty much how I felt, except my world was black and frozen. And brutally quiet. I tried yelling but it just bounced back at me." He blew out a breath. "And the cold . . . I've been cold before, but this cold—there was no escape. At least it helped mask my dislocated shoulder."

"I remember the rescue team pulling you out. I wanted to go to the hospital, but . . ."

"Dylan." He was quiet for so long she wasn't sure he wasn't done. Then . . . "I had something, you know? A life I loved, respect, a future. And you took that away—or at least I blamed you. I've spent the last three years, however, taking it apart. Replaying what people said in the hearing. Thinking about that night when Dylan and I fought. The fact is, I did tell Ramon that Dylan wasn't good enough. And I realize that to you, it looked like I'd been reckless with Dylan's life. But Dylan had already paid the chopper pilot, and he was going to ride Terminator Wall. I thought I could keep him from killing himself, and maybe that was arrogant, but the truth is, I was trying to help."

"I know that now."

His mouth tightened. "But I do know that I screwed everything up. I thought by doing the

195

right thing, it would protect me, and him. But life doesn't work that way. Doing what's right comes at a cost. I just wasn't ready for it."

He looked at her then, and she had the unsettled feeling that he didn't just mean his career.

As if he could read her mind, he swallowed, kept his gaze in hers. "Sometimes I go back to that night and think, what if I hadn't gotten into that fight with Dylan? What if when I came back you were still there, and we had talked . . . I don't know. Maybe it would have turned out differently."

Huh? She stared at him in the light of his head lamp. "What are you talking about?"

He was sitting there, not looking at her, closing up his pack. "I'm not blaming anyone but myself, but I was a mess that night, and I thought we were friends."

She couldn't move. Hardly breathe. "Gage—I waited for you, but *you're* the one who didn't come back. We were friends," she said softly. *We could be again. Please.*

His chest rose and fell. "Well, anyway. Just so you know, I didn't leave you at the restaurant. I went back for you. I'm sorry it was too late."

It's not too late. The thought rose, filled her head, her chest. But it didn't matter. It wasn't up to her anymore.

"Get some sleep. Tomorrow we have to take

Weeping Wall, then the Great White Throne. If we get up early enough—"

A great screech tore through the tent as the wind sheared down from the peak. It caught their enclave, shuddering the walls with gale-force winds. Ella screamed and hit the floor of the tent.

It began to slide.

She only barely sensed Gage rolling over, on top of her, pinning her down, his sleeping bag covering hers as he dug his knees into the snow foundation alongside of her. The wind roared, but his head came close to hers, his voice in her ear. "Shh. We're fine. The tent will hold. Trust me."

She *did* trust him. It was the world outside that had her coming unglued. She closed her eyes and didn't even hesitate as she reached out and wrapped her hands around his wrists, burying her face in her jacket as the tent shuddered around them.

10

No call from Gage or Ella had Ty and the entire team on edge. Especially as the storm closed in around Mercy Falls and blew through the Flathead Valley just west of the park. And not just the team, but Brette, too, who curled up on the sofa, her hands around her waist, as if holding herself together.

Ty couldn't help but feel sorry for her as the evening drew out. She watched the weather reports and jumped at every squawk of the EMS box that kept the team rotating out to help drivers out of ditches.

Kacey and Ben were still out on a call, this one involving a semi that had slid off the road. Pete had returned earlier, grabbed some soup, then headed back out to help his brother, Sam, on another call.

Only Jess had returned and stayed, joining Sierra and Chet, who were manning dispatch and occasionally trying to connect with Gage and Ella.

The storm howled around them outside, as well as in Ty's head as he watched Jess talking to Brette, answering questions about the team.

No, she was mostly talking about Pete and his epic saves this summer.

The woman fairly glowed when she talked about Pete Brooks. Jess's blue eyes alight, her entire body animated as she gestured with her hands. Ty didn't have to be the team psychologist to see that away from Pete Brooks's presence, Jess had no problem waxing glorious about him.

Not that Ty was jealous, but . . .

She should just tell Pete about her connection to the Great Scandal and the fact she wasn't who she claimed to be. Stop using Ty as the defensive line to keep Pete away from her.

Judging from Pete's glacial shoulder toward him —especially tonight—he'd probably be so relieved that Jess and Ty weren't dating he wouldn't care that she was the daughter of the most notorious white-collar thief in recent decades.

Most of all, Jess should stop talking to Brette. Because Ty, again, didn't have to be that intuitive to see Brette's wheels turning. *"No one hides from me."*

He got up from where he sat at the computer watching the weather report, intending to run interference of some kind, when Sierra did an end run and sat down beside Jess.

"It's getting late, and my guess is that Gage and Ella are holed up somewhere, probably getting warm and strategizing about how they're going to get down the mountain tomorrow. They're probably drinking hot cocoa right now, right, Jess?"

Jess nodded. "I packed them a few packs, along with some chili mac, and Gage knows what he's doing. Don't worry." She glanced at Sierra, then back to Brette. "In fact, I think you should come home with us. I have real beds at my place now, and—"

"I think she should stay here."

Ty didn't know why those words emerged from his mouth, but he blamed his "protect Jess" reflex, the one he had seemed to be honing for the past five months.

All three women looked at him as if surprised he was still in the room. Yeah, well, Pete hadn't assigned him to any impromptu callouts. In fact, if they had a *real* callout, their official incident commander, Miles Dafoe, would be here, taking the helm. Pete wasn't even in charge.

"What if Gage calls in—Brette will want to know, right?" he added, for logical reinforcement.

Brette looked at him, nodded.

"She can stay in the bunkhouse," he said, seeing Brette warm to the idea. "Kacey is staying too—she mentioned it to me earlier. Just in case the storm abates and she needs to take the chopper out early. And Ben will probably stay too, then. I'll stick around . . ."

Jess was frowning at him, and he wanted to send her a silent message. *Trust me.* After

Brette's initial introduction, it seemed that Jess had shrugged off any danger.

In fact, she turned back to Brette. "We're about fifteen minutes from here, and they can call us if Gage calls in . . ."

Sheesh, he wanted to wave semaphores. Did she not hear the word *journalist* earlier? See the way Brette probed her about Pete? The woman was just warming up for the kill.

Thankfully, Brette shook her head. "I guess if there's a place for me to sleep here, I'll stay. Especially if Ty is staying."

Huh. He didn't know why, but those words sent warmth through him.

"I'm staying."

She smiled up at him, and for a second, he didn't care that Pete had sideswiped his offer to go out tonight.

Apparently, tonight, the pretty girl chose Ty. Take that, Pete I-own-the-world Brooks.

"Okay, but if you need to escape, you know who to call," Jess said. She got up and grabbed her coat from the hook, and Sierra followed her.

Chet walked back to his office.

"C'mon," Ty said. "I'll show you the bunk rooms." He led the way upstairs to the two rooms —one for women, one for men. Tiny rooms, with four bunk beds in each, along with their own bathrooms. "It's cozy but warm."

Brette sank down on one of the beds. "Thanks,

201

Ty. I'm feeling a little nauseous, so I think I'll lie down."

Oh. He didn't know why he expected . . . apparently he'd read too much into her statement, "especially if Ty is staying," like she might want to spend time with him. He gave her a smile. "Let me know if you need anything." He closed the door behind her, tiptoed down the stairs.

The room was quiet, empty, only the occasional noise from the squawk box. He fished a cookie from the jar, went to sit down at the computer.

C'mon, Gage, call in.

Ty sat listening to the computers hum, the static on the box, the wind rattling the windows.

And for a second, he imagined it had been exactly this way the night he'd crashed. The team on edge, not knowing where to look, how to help. And Ty alone, on the other end of the static, knowing he and Chet would freeze to death if he didn't get help.

He reached out, rubbed his knee, kneading the swollen ligaments. He probably needed some ice.

The door opened, and snow swished in on the tail of Pete, who closed it fast, then stamped out his boots on the mat. "It's cold out there," he said as he pulled off his gloves. He looked up, around the room, back to Ty. "Where is everyone?"

"If by everyone you mean Jess, she went home with Sierra."

Pete just looked at him, a muscle pulling in his

jaw. Then he sighed, sat on a nearby stool, and pulled off his boots. "Is there any coffee left?"

"Yeah," Ty said and got up, almost on reflex, to fetch it.

"I got it, Ty." Pete beat him to the counter and poured himself a cup, then stuck it in the microwave to warm.

"There's some soup too," Ty said.

"Listen," Pete said as he stared at the microwave. "We need to just . . ." He turned and pinned Ty with a look, something of desperation in it. "What's the deal between you and Jess? I've sat back for five months, watching, wondering if you were going to make a move, and every time I think you're not dating, every time I think maybe I could get close enough to talk to her, suddenly you show up at her house, or offer to drive her home, or even volunteer to team up with her on a callout, and frankly, I'm starting to think it's not that you like Jess, it's just—you don't want me to date her."

Ty looked at him, kept his voice casual. "You want to date Jess?"

Pete stared at him. "Oh, c'mon. Are you kidding me? What do I have to do—wear a sign? Yes! With everything inside me. Jess and I—we had this thing this summer, and it was great. And then suddenly, she just blew up at me and ran into *your* arms. And I wasn't in the least okay with that, but you're my teammate

203

and I'm not going to call you out. I figured this thing between you two would blow over, or if it didn't, then, well—okay. But I can't figure it out . . ."

Ty closed his eyes, ran a hand along his forehead. "Pete, listen, you and Jess have to talk. I can't tell you what's going on in her head—"

The microwave beeped, and Ty looked up. Pete was just staring at him, his jaw tight.

"She won't talk to me. Every time I try, she dodges me. Runs to you."

Yeah, she did. Because in her head, telling Pete who she really was felt akin to standing naked in the middle of Times Square.

"She has her reasons."

"Tell me what they are!" Pete ignored the beep of his coffee, palming the counter. "It's about Tallie, isn't it? Jess thinks I'm still dating that reporter, but I'm not—and I wasn't. And that's the old me. The new me—"

The microwave beeped again. Pete turned and hit the open button with more force than necessary. He yanked out his coffee and it splashed over him. He stifled a word, set the coffee down, and grabbed the paper towels.

Ty didn't move to help him, pretty sure he didn't want to get in Pete's way. But apparently, Pete wasn't finished, because as he attacked the stain on his thermal shirt, he looked up at Ty.

"So, are you in or are you going to get out of the way?"

So what, Pete could trample over Jess's feelings? Because Ty agreed with her—Pete could be unpredictable, and the fewer people who knew her secret, the better.

"No," Ty said quietly. "I'm not getting out of the way."

Pete's jaw tightened, and he drew in a breath. "Fine." He glanced at the weather report on the screen behind Ty. "Any news of Gage?"

Ty shook his head. Pete threw the paper towels in the garbage. "Let me know if any calls come in. I'm going to get some shut-eye."

He didn't look behind him as he climbed the stairs.

Ty got up, drained the coffee cup, rinsed it, and loaded it in the dishwasher. Braced his hands on the counter.

He didn't like lying to Pete. Or pretending in front of the team. But if it meant giving Jess some time to figure out how to tell Pete the truth . . .

Ty picked up a towel, started wiping his hands. If only he had feelings for Jess, then maybe this wouldn't be so awkward.

Or if she had feelings for him. But any idea that she might harbor a spark for him had died tonight listening to her extol Pete's accomplishments.

Maybe he *should* have told Pete the truth— he did seem different over the past five months.

The old Pete would still be here, arguing. This Pete seemed kinder. Gentler.

As if he really had feelings for Jess, the kind that went beyond the usual Pete Brooks charmer persona.

A creak on the stairs made him look up. Brette appeared, looking pale. Ty met her on the landing. "Are you okay?"

"Yeah. My stomach is upset. I think it's just worry, but . . ." She made a face.

"How about some hot cocoa?"

She nodded and walked over to the counter, then slid onto a stool. "I'll be fine. I've always had a weak stomach. I had a tradition—I'd go out for pizza late Friday night, then be up in the wee hours of the morning with a twisted stomach."

He turned on the kettle to boil. "That doesn't sound like a very awesome tradition."

"I couldn't help it. I liked hanging around Ella and her friends, and one of her friends, Greg, ran a pizza joint just off campus. We'd show up after hours, ready to study, and he'd give us all the unsold pizzas. I was so poor, I needed the food."

"Where did you go to college?"

"Middlebury, with Ella. I was on a scholarship, however. Didn't even have enough money to live in the dorm. I answered an ad on campus to rent a room, and it was in Ella's house. But when I didn't make rent the third month, Ella figured it out. I paid her back, but she never raised my

206

rent, and covered for me when I was late. She would have probably let me live rent free."

"Wow." Ty fixed her cup of cocoa, pouring out the chocolate from the package, adding a few mini marshmallows from the supply. "That was nice of her."

"Ella's like that. Always looking out for the people around her. She defies every stereotype about the rich."

"Which are?" The kettle whistled, and he poured the boiling water into the mug.

She lifted a shoulder. "Oh, you know. Entitled. Selfish. The world revolves around them, and they'll take anyone down to keep it that way."

"Ouch."

She grinned at him. "Oh, c'mon. You live with Gage. He drives that fancy Mustang. Don't tell me that he isn't just a *little* about himself? After all that fame? And how about Ian Shaw? He started an entire rescue team to search for his niece."

"Wouldn't you?"

"Maybe. I can't even contemplate that kind of wealth. I'm here on Ella's dime, and frankly I'm not sure I'll be able to pay the rent on my tiny one-bedroom when I get home."

He handed her the cocoa. "Why?"

"Oh, I had a contract to write a book on this senator who wanted to run for president. Turns out she was dirty and she dropped out of the race, and I lost my contract."

"You didn't expose her?"

She looked up at him. Brought the mug to her mouth. "I write inspiring pieces, not dirt. Although, right now, I might be desperate enough to print an exposé on a Kardashian if I got wind of it." She winked at him and took a sip.

Oh. He managed a smile, but . . .

"Thankfully, I met you guys. And I'm thinking there are plenty of feel-good stories here. My agent says she thinks a positive story, with pictures of heroes skiing down mountainsides, might land me a delicious spread in *Nat Geo* or even their online mag. That will generate enough cash to keep me out of sleeping in my car for at least a month."

He was afraid to ask if she was serious. "Unfortunately, you just missed Pete—"

"Actually"—she put her mug down—"I'm more interested in *your* story, Ty."

He stilled. "My story? I don't have a story."

But her eyebrow quirked up. "Really. The 'main pilot, before Kacey got here'? Why aren't you the main pilot now?"

He considered her. Pretty, and too smart, really. She had pulled out her blonde hair, and it cascaded down in pale gold strands around her face. She smiled at him, as if she hadn't just tried to blow his world apart.

But he had her number. "Did I mention that Kacey won a bronze star? In Afghanistan?"

She frowned, one quick draw of her eyebrow, then set her cocoa down. "Really?"

"Yep. Saved a unit of rangers or something. You should ask her about it."

"Just like I should ask Pete about his exploits, and Ian, and Ben, and probably Gage, but definitely not you, huh, Ty?"

He shook his head. "There's nothing to tell. I hurt my knee in an accident, and it's not easy to use the anti-torque pedals with a bum knee." He lifted a shoulder, kept it casual.

Her smile fell. "Oh."

"Yeah. Sorry. I'm not the hero of the team. But I do make good cocoa, huh?"

She smiled. "Sorry. I guess I read into things."

"I'm sure it's a hazard of the job," he said, keeping his voice light.

At that moment, he felt utterly grateful he'd sent Jess and Sierra home without little miss Katie Couric to dig around and ask the wrong—or right—questions.

He came around the counter. "C'mon over to the sofa. We'll see if we can find a Western instead of the weather channel, huh?"

She slid off the stool, walked over, and curled up on the sofa.

But when he handed her a blanket, she turned to him and said softly, "But as for you not being the hero of the team, I completely disagree."

Oh. He had no words as he picked up the

remote, letting her smile warm him through as the blizzard turned the world to ice.

Please, God, don't let us die. The thought, maybe a prayer, thrummed through the back of Gage's brain as the tent convulsed around them at the mercy of the blizzard winds.

He lay awake thinking through today's route, watching the light change from pitch to shades of faint amber, the wan light of dawn pressing through the orange fabric of the tent.

He hoped, desperately, that he hadn't led Ella to her death.

The temperature had dropped, but inside his glacier bag, and with Ella huddled against him in hers, they were in no danger of freezing.

Still, they might be encased under three feet of snow by morning. And if the snow didn't abate, he'd be trapped with her on the mountain.

Which would be lethal to his resolve of keeping her from wheedling her way back inside to those places that hadn't forgotten. He still remembered, too well, what it felt like to hold her in his arms, to feel like, with her, he could be himself.

Although, frankly, that would mean letting her see the wounds she'd left.

Maybe even letting her inflict more.

"I couldn't move, couldn't breathe until they found you."

He didn't quite know what to believe, but her

soft words had nearly undone him. Tempered the residual anger, made him revisit that night.

"We were friends."

Yes, maybe they were. Which meant that really, probably, they *were* just two old acquaintances catching up.

And weathering a storm. Still, it wouldn't do Gage, or his heart, any good to spend another night huddled next to her. Not if he hoped to keep from repeating his mistakes.

No doubt she only clung to him because of her sheer terror at sliding down the mountain.

"Gage, are you awake?"

He looked over, and her eyes were open. She wore a stocking cap, her curly penny red hair spilling out of it, and had her sleeping bag up to her chin.

"Mmmhmm," he said.

"What are you thinking about?"

He rolled over onto his side. "Just trying to figure out the right line down the rest of the mountain. And hoping your brother is at the snow cave, and . . ." And how devastatingly pretty she looked in the press of dawn, her eyes more gray than blue in this light. "Wishing life had turned out differently."

She blinked at that. "Like . . . us?"

He didn't allow his face to betray anything.

She caught her lower lip in her teeth. Sighed.

"What?"

She opened her mouth, then closed it fast. Sighed again. Then, "I know you're probably wondering why I . . . well, why I didn't recuse myself."

He couldn't help it—he nodded. "I figured I'd hurt you, and it was payback."

His blunt words reflected in her eyes; she flinched. He hadn't said it with malice, just a fact, softly.

Because, really, they were just acquaintances catching up, clearing the air.

She drew in a breath then, as if fortifying herself. "I was hurt, yeah. But, the truth is, it was ambition. When the senior lawyer decided to take the case, I was assigned it. Since it was so high profile, he suggested that I would be offered a junior partnership if we won." She closed her eyes, as if in pain. "I thought maybe I could do the legwork and that you'd settle out of court. Then I wouldn't have to actually see you . . . but . . . why did you wait so long to settle? I never dreamed you'd let it go to a hearing."

His jaw tightened; this was why he shouldn't spend another day with her, because Ella seemed to find new and more lethal ways to hurt him. "I *wanted* to settle. But then I was angry too. And hurt. I dislocated my shoulder and even cracked a couple ribs—I nearly *died* in the avalanche that Dylan started. I wanted to talk to his parents, help them understand that he

212

was . . . he was reckless and belligerent and—"

She drew in a breath, as if she was going to add something, but when he looked at her, she shook her head.

So he continued. "I wrote to them, but they responded with a lawsuit, and I was angry. My entire career hinged on defeating them . . . but then I got to the hearing and I took one look at them and I told my lawyer to just let them have what they wanted. But by then it was too late."

She stared at him. "Oh. Now I know why your lawyer barely defended you."

"And you had me for lunch."

She closed her eyes, and he instantly regretted his words. "Sorry—it's fine. It's over. I've started over, and I like my life—"

"But you were famous. A champion—"

"And look where it got me. Where it got *you*." He made a face. "Stuck in the middle of a blizzard, chasing your brother down the face of a mountain."

"That's not your fault, Gage."

He lifted a shoulder.

She was just looking at him. "Can I tell you something?" she said softly. The wind seemed to have died with the rising of the sun, although it still shook the tent. "It's incredibly hard to follow a line perfectly."

"You did great yesterday."

"No, I didn't. But I tried. And I also found that if I looked too far ahead, I lost where I was. But if you looked back, you would see that I was all over the mountain."

"As long as you made it safely down," he said.

"That's the point. You gave me a line. A safe one. It was my job to ride it. And if I didn't, it wasn't your fault."

He knew she was trying to make a point, but it was too late. "In the end, any way you cut it, it *was* my fault that Dylan died, and we both know that, Ella. You were right to help Dylan's family—I should have thrown him off the chopper that morning. I know that. So please, listen to me. It's in the past, so let's just leave it, okay?"

She shook her head. "Not if you keep blaming yourself."

"There's no one else to blame. And if I don't get you off this mountain safely, then we're right back there, aren't we?"

Her eyes were glistening, and she reached up, wiped her cheek. "I hope not. Because I don't want to go back. And I know I can't say it enough, but I'm so sorry. I was ambitious and hurt and I should have walked away from the case."

He stared at her, wishing she might add, *"But not from you."*

Aw, shoot.

"I understand ambition, Ella. I lived it, breathed it. It's what made me a champion."

"No—you don't understand!" She blew out

a breath. "Fine. Listen," she said, her voice shaking. "It wasn't just ambition. My parents asked me to help the McMahons, and I wanted to prove to my parents that I was worth all the energy and all they'd sacrificed to give me a future. But . . . ." Her expression turned so forlorn. "I just managed to destroy the life of someone I cared deeply about."

He frowned.

Cared. Past tense. But really, what did he expect? That she'd pine for him? "What did you mean, you wanted to prove to your parents you were worth it?"

She sighed. "I'm adopted, Gage. I should have told you that—or I would have, if we'd gotten further into our relationship. My parents are . . . well, the Blairs are my adoptive parents. I'm a Slovakian refugee. Me and Ollie."

He frowned. "What are you talking about?"

She swallowed, made a face. "I lived in Serbia with my parents—my Slovakian parents— until I was eleven years old. My father was a philosophy professor at Belgrade University and a pastor. My mother was a physician. We lived in Belgrade with my older brother, Jovan, who was seventeen, and Ollie, who was four."

She took a breath. He didn't move.

"We were refugees from the war between Serbia and Kosovo."

He stared at her, trying to reconcile her words

with the composed, preppy lawyer he'd met at Outlaw.

"We came to America under refugee status, and my parents started working for the Blairs. My parents died in a car crash a couple years later, and that's when the Blairs adopted Ollie and me."

She met his eyes. "Jovan died in the NATO bombing of Belgrade. It happened right outside our apartment, actually. By then, most of us who were left in the city were living in ruins, and Father was working in the underground, getting fellow Slovaks out of the country. I'll never forget the day Jovan died. We were getting ready to leave, and he went out. I never knew why. Father was standing at the window, watching for him when he saw him come home. It was early in the morning, and Jovan was simply crossing the street . . . and then, the world exploded."

He could almost see it in her eyes, the grief flashing there.

"Ella—"

"It was so senseless." She clenched her eyes closed, and he wanted to stop her from reliving whatever she was about to say.

"The bomb destroyed part of our building." She opened her eyes, her gaze far from him. "I was in bed with Ollie, and we woke up to the explosion, our room raining debris, the wall in our room shattering open to the world. Mama was screaming—Papa had been blown back into the kitchen." She looked at him then. "There was nothing left of Jovan. Papa looked . . . and then we fled. Papa had already connected us with a church in Vermont, and the Blairs sponsored us, brought us into their home. They were good people. Had no kids of their own, so . . ."

He had the terrible urge to reach out, thumb away the tear sliding down her nose.

"Anyway, Ollie never really remembered our parents. The Blairs are the only parents he knows. But I remember everyone. It's my job to keep Ollie safe. He's the only real family I have left. And I have to make my parents proud—all of them. They've given me so much. And I need to—"

"Save the world, apparently."

Her mouth tightened, and he guessed he wasn't too far off. So he softened his voice. "I'm so sorry, Ella. I didn't know."

"I should have told you. I wanted to . . . but I didn't know how, and then . . . well, it doesn't matter anymore."

There was something so painfully honest about her sigh.

"You're right, it doesn't matter. Not now."

But she shook her head. "I've been so fortunate. And I'm so grateful. And when my parents came to me with the McMahons' lawsuit, I told them we'd help them. I didn't think about what would happen. And then, suddenly, I was being given the case, and . . . well, my hurt and ambition took over. Until I saw you . . . and then, I just wanted to run. I felt caught between two worlds, and I chose . . ."

"You chose your family." And now he couldn't help it—he touched her face, caressed his thumb over her nose. Rested his hand on her cheek. "I get it."

She touched her hand to his, and for a long moment, he stared at her, caught in her beautiful blue-gray eyes, watching the dawn turn her hair to fire and highlight the freckles on her nose.

Wow, she could take his breath away. His voice emerged low. "Okay, so we both have baggage. And made some mistakes. And are pretty good at blaming ourselves, apparently."

She slid her hand from his. "But that's the thing, you really shouldn't blame yourself—"

A gust of wind raked the tent. She gasped and closed her eyes.

"Shh, we're going to be okay." He tugged on her stocking cap. "Close your eyes. We need our sleep if we want to get down this mountain alive, okay?"

He felt her nod.

Exhale.

And he finally said the words building up in his chest, freeing them in a soft whisper. "You said you know you don't deserve my help—but that's the thing. No one in trouble should be worried about whether they deserve help. They need help, and that's the point. I'm glad you called me."

He wanted to say more, but when she backed away and looked at him, tears in her eyes, maybe that was enough.

For now.

Brette opened her eyes and tried to get her bearings. Right, the PEAK ranch house.

The last time Brette had woken up in a public place, she'd been following the early presidential campaign of Michelle Bachman, a senator out of Minnesota, vying for a private meeting to pitch her biography.

But even at the Hilton, she'd woken up on the sofa, alone, and *not* cuddled up to the very safe presence of Ty Remington.

This was much better. She wouldn't exactly call it cuddling, maybe, because he sat, his long legs propped on a pillow on a straight back chair, his head to the side while she curled in a ball on the rest of the sofa, her head on a pillow next to him. But he had let his other arm drop and settle on her shoulder, as if checking to see if she might be okay.

Maybe she'd been groaning in her sleep, because her stomach still ached.

But not so much that she'd turn down whatever was cooking in the kitchen. She pushed herself up with a moan.

"Are you okay?"

Ty had come alive beside her and was scrubbing a hand down his face. He leaned up.

"Yeah. I think so. How did the movie end?"

He looked up at her, and for a moment, it struck her how incredibly handsome he was. Wavy black hair, dark whiskers, beautiful green eyes. And a little smirk to his mouth that only added that sense of some personal humor, a kind of secret behind his eyes.

She might just be dreaming that part, but she liked it all the same.

"The cowboy saved the day, got the girl, and they lived happily ever after. Just the way it's supposed to happen," he said in an easy Montana twang.

She hadn't realized how much she liked cowboys, really, until this moment.

A bang sounded in the kitchen as the microwave door slammed shut.

She glanced over, a little surprised to see Pete at the helm, holding a flat spatula, his back to them. The microwave hummed. And if she wasn't mistaken, coffee gurgled in the pot.

"Hey, Pete," Ty said.

Pete didn't turn, and when Brette glanced at Ty, he was frowning.

Outside, dawn had barely begun to dent the night. She got up and headed to the window.

Light scraped across the freshly fallen snow, and the wind lifted it in soft layers and drifted it up against the house and fencing in white waves. But it seemed the worst of the storm had abated.

She headed to the kitchen and slid onto a stool. Pete still had his back to her and was now pulling bacon from a cast-iron pan onto a plate with paper towels. "That looks good," she said.

He glanced over his shoulder at her, then at Ty, who'd risen and was walking upstairs.

"What kind of eggs do you like?" Pete said, looking back at her. He didn't smile.

"Over easy?"

He nodded and reached for a couple eggs in the nearby carton. Cracked them into the cast-iron pan.

Maybe coffee would help her stomach. She got up and helped herself to a mug from the cupboard, then poured herself a cup. She leaned her hip against the side of the counter. "Jess told me a little of your exploits this summer."

He glanced at her. "She did?"

His voice held a little shock, even an edge of delight.

Huh.

"Yeah. Told me about how you saved the team from a grizzly. And then how you tracked down a bunch of kids. Said you helped with the flood victims this summer too. Apparently you have your FEMA certification and work as an incident commander for the PEAK team?"

He made a funny noise, turned back to the stove. "Yeah. Sometimes."

She stole a piece of bacon. "I'd love to interview you, if I could. I write inspirational stories for *Nat Geo* and sometimes other national publications—"

"I don't think so," he said. He reached up into the cupboard and pulled out a plate. Set it on the counter.

"Why not?"

The stairs creaked, and she looked over to see Ty emerge. He'd run a comb through his hair, changed his shirt to a thermal gray pullover with the PEAK team logo on the breast.

Pete turned back to the eggs.

"I don't give interviews anymore. I'm not about the limelight—I'm just trying to get the job done."

He scooped out her eggs, slid them onto the plate. "Here you go."

She couldn't help but be a little taken aback by his demeanor. This was not the Pete both Ty and Jess had bragged about. She brought the plate to the counter, slid onto a stool.

"You making breakfast, Pete?" Ty asked.

Pete turned off the stove. "Eggs are in the carton and there's some bacon left." He took his plate of fried eggs and a mug of coffee to a nearby table.

He didn't look at them as he sat, didn't invite them to join him, just stared out the window.

Okay. She glanced at Ty, who frowned, then cast a look at her.

Smiled.

Ty had such a nice smile, it warmed up the entire room.

Oh, for crying out loud. She must be really tired.

Besides, the last man she'd let in her heart had left so many scars on her pride and psyche, not to mention her body, she'd be a fool to trust any man again.

She tamped down her renegade heartbeat and cut up her eggs. The coffee hadn't set well, and the bacon was setting her stomach on edge.

Ty fired up the stove and cracked a couple eggs in the pan. The door opened, and Brette turned to see Sierra and Jess come into the room. Sierra stamped off her feet on the mat.

It was just a flash, a snapshot of memory, but for some reason as Jess came in the door, as she flicked her hair back and grabbed the frame and waited for Sierra to move over, something flickered in Brette's memory.

The snapshot fled her recall before she could wrap her fingers around it, but in that second, she knew.

She *had* seen Jess before.

"Hey, everyone," Sierra said as she pulled off her coat. She headed over to the coffeepot and poured herself a mug of java before going to the communications station.

Jess shut the door behind her, hung up her coat, then looked at Pete. "Hey."

"Hey," he answered softly and gave her a small smile.

Look at that. For a second, something passed between them, and Brette wanted to slow it down, take it apart.

Regret? Longing?

Then Pete glanced away, looking back toward the snowy landscape.

He was a handsome man when he smiled, Brette would give Pete that.

Jess headed over to the kitchen. Brette watched her, the way she moved, the tiny touch she gave Ty on his shoulder, another flick of her long blonde hair. She was pretty, with high cheekbones, a tall, lean body. She wore a pair of jeans, a sweater, no makeup.

"Can I order two eggs, sunny-side up?" she asked Ty.

Jess carried herself like a woman used to getting what she wanted. Or at least used to being in charge.

Ty plated the eggs he was cooking and handed the plate to her, and she carried it to the counter. She slid onto a stool beside Brette.

Then Jess reached for a napkin and put it in her lap. Interesting.

It was right there, the answer, floating around in the back of Brette's mind, almost tangible. She must have been staring, because she didn't hear Sierra until she raised her voice.

"Ty! It's Gage calling in."

Ty turned off the heat on the stove while Brette slid off her stool and followed the rest of the team over to the radio.

"PEAK HQ, PEAK HQ, this is Watson, come in, over," came the voice again.

"Watson, this is PEAK HQ. What's your position? Over," Sierra said.

The noise brought Chet out of his office, where he must have spent the night.

"We're still on the face of Heaven's Peak. We didn't make it to the snow cave, but we're okay. Heading down the face this morning, and we'll keep you posted. Over."

"Roger. No sign of the boys?" Sierra asked, voicing Brette's question.

"No," Gage said. "But we'll find them."

Brette glanced at Ty then. The sunlight illuminated his profile—strong, with an intensity about it that slid under her skin and into her heart.

Yeah, she very much liked cowboys.

He nodded in the wake of Gage's words, as if agreeing. Then he turned, met her gaze, and held it.

And Brette forgot all about the mysterious Jess Tagg.

II

Ella had awoken to Gage's voice as he finished his call to headquarters.

"They know we're alive?"

"Yeah. We need to get going."

Dawn crested into the tent. The wind still rattled the poles, but no more torrential gusts, the kind that could blow them right off the mountainside.

For a second, she simply stayed tucked into her sleeping bag, her gaze on Gage as he pulled his hair back and scratched his fingers through his dark whiskers.

She had the urge to do the same, feel his whiskers between her fingers as she ran her hand along his jawline.

His earlier words caught in her head. *"No one in trouble should be worried about whether they deserve help. They need help, and that's the point."*

But see, it *wasn't* that easy. It seemed, to her, there needed to be some sort of payment, some penance, some *reason* for him to want to help her.

He stretched, moving his arms side to side, then behind his back, and she watched with a greedy eye, a little mesmerized at those snowboarder muscles.

But she averted her eyes when he looked at her. "Are you getting up?"

"My muscles are sludge," she muttered.

He gave her a tight smile. "C'mon. Let's see if I can dig us out. By tonight, you and your brother will be back at your resort, drinking cocoa."

"Oh, I know you're just trying to make me feel better, but when I find him, I'm going to kill him with my bare hands. Right after I weep with joy."

"How about if I make you coffee?"

"I'll trade it for my birthright."

He raised an eyebrow.

"That was a Jacob-Esau joke my mother used to say." She wrinkled her nose. "Sorry."

He laughed and reached for the pack. "So, your parents are Christians? I mean, the Blairs?"

"Oh yeah. Mansfield and Marjorie never missed a Sunday or Wednesday night at church. And my parents too—Jozef and Alena Laska. I still have my father's Bible. And my mother's prayer covering. She was Orthodox until she married my Protestant father—*quite* the uproar."

Gage had pulled out the stove, and now he cleared a space for it, then opened the back door. Snow had piled up against it, and he took the shovel, knocked it away. "It's just a drift. We're not snowed in." He leaned out then, and for a second she thought he was getting snow for the container. Then, "C'mere, Ella, you have to see this."

He came back inside, the finest frosting on his hair, his eyelashes.

He had such pretty dark brown eyes. They bore flecks of gold near the center in the early morning. A new day, fresh starts.

Oh no. Because that thought found her heart. Nope—forgiveness was one thing. Romance, a different story.

They couldn't go back there. But they *could* be friends, and she leaned up toward the door in response to his request. He scooted out of the way and she looked out.

A glorious sunrise just barely tipped the eastern ridges, gilding the fresh snow on the peaks an impossible molten gold while striations of deep crimson and fiery orange burned into the deep indigo sky.

"Gorgeous," she said.

"I know."

Farther down, in the valley, ragged magenta shadows draped over the crisp white snow, so thick and fluffy it seemed the world had been frosted with one giant dollop of heavenly meringue. Perfect. Unblemished. And probably lethal.

"Can you get us safely down?" she asked as she slid back into the tent.

"Yeah. I got this." His eyes sparked, just for a second. "As long as . . ."

"I follow you and don't fly off a cliff."

"I was going to say as long as your brother is okay. But that too."

She managed a wry smile, and he didn't waver from her gaze. He suddenly reached out and touched her hand, squeezed.

His expression turned solemn. "I'm going to get you down this mountain in one piece. And you might even have fun doing it."

His touch on her hand sent warmth through her entire body. Not unlike the effect it had last night, when he cupped her cheek, thumbed away her tear.

She'd nearly kissed him when he told her that they'd be okay. In that moment, she'd believed him.

Now, she squeezed his hand back, wanting to believe him again. "Okay."

"That's the girl I remember." Then he let her go and turned back to the stove to light it.

But his words had ignited something inside, and if he kept it up, there was no way she would make it down the mountain in one piece. Not if, at the end, he walked away with her heart.

He boiled water while she packed up her sleeping bag, zipped up her jacket, pulled on her boots, and took a hygiene trip outside. He had a tidy breakfast assembled when she returned, including power bars and instant coffee. He'd also packed his gear.

"So, how's it looking out there?" he asked as he pulled on his boots.

"White," she said.

He grinned, and all of a sudden, it was the kind of grin he gave the cameras after a triumphant run, something that would grace magazine covers and posters and not a few sponsor webpages. Only this one was better—it included a twinkle in his brown eyes, the tiny huff of laughter, deep and low in his chest.

Oh my, 3-D Gage Watson was worth the trip up the mountain. Exactly what she'd told herself three years ago.

"I'll dig us out," he said. "Let me know when you're ready for the tent to come down." He pulled his pack out with him.

He climbed out, and she finished her power bar and the coffee, then capped the canister, packed the rest of her gear, and set her pack outside the tent. She zipped up her jacket and added her helmet. "Coming out!"

His gloved hand appeared to pull her from the tent. She scooted out and let him help her up.

The wind hit her hard, and she grabbed his arms.

"It's still a bit gusty!" he yelled. He wore his helmet and his goggles, and she pulled her goggles down and nudged her neck gaiter to her nose.

Despite the cold, the glory of the world

dropping at her feet could steal her breath. "Great is the Lord and worthy of praise," she said.

Gage was taking down the tent, but he looked over at her. Smiled. "You said that before. Right before we skied Redemption Ridge." He leaned toward her. "And killed it."

"It is pretty mind-blowing," she said, trying to tamp down the adrenaline raking through her.

From her perch, the mountain looked like it dropped straight down into nothing.

He tucked the tent into the tiny bag. "We'll take it one section at a time. Just like I did. Nothing fancy."

She looked at him. "Oh, please, Gage. You have fancy in your soul. And I know it's itching to come out."

He raised an eyebrow, but one side of his mouth ticked up.

She retrieved her snowboard. "Help me get this pack on."

He had tucked the tent into his pack and now lifted hers, and she climbed into the shoulder straps, then connected the straps at her waist.

He hiked his on and strapped it tight around him.

Then they stood together at the top of the mountain. "I sort of feel like we should pray or something," she said.

He glanced at her, held her gaze. Then he held out his hand.

Really? She met his grasp.

"God. You know we're here. You know what we have to do. Make us smart. Brave. Sensible. And keep us safe. Help us find Oliver and Bradley. Amen."

She hadn't even closed her eyes; she just watched Gage, listened to his words.

Bold as he approached the throne of the Almighty.

Huh.

She dropped her board, strapped in, and he did the same.

"Okay, we're going to follow this wedge down into a nice bowl. It's steep, so we want to take it slow, but we'll work our way down to the Weeping Wall. And then, from there, the Great White Throne. We'll hit the cave by lunch, probably."

"Got it."

He held up his fist for a bump, and she met it. However, a line of sweat formed at the back of her neck as she watched Gage traverse the hill, slowly, warming up. He cut a beautiful, arching line through the fresh powder, and it bloomed up behind him, a crystalline plume of light and color.

The master at work. If only she had a GoPro.

She hopped in place, trying to get the blood flowing, then eased down after him, her arms out.

He had such a beautiful rhythm that her heartbeat settled down, and she took in the view, the pine-furred valley, the frozen waterfalls. Powder slicked her goggles, crusted on her neck gaiter, sprayed up over her board as she dug in. He stopped every hundred yards, maybe more, just to let her catch up, point out their next destination. Then, they'd hit it again.

The sun rose, shortening the shadows as they worked their way down across the bowl toward the granite face known as the Weeping Wall.

She recalled what she knew of it—a sixty-foot drop, nice soft landing zone, thick powder—at least that's how Gage described it in his video. But he hadn't taken his planned route. To the right, a frozen waterfall added drama, but the landing would be treacherous, mostly because of the ice forming below the powder.

He'd changed his line at the last moment and had probably saved his own life with the impulse.

Hopefully her brother had watched that part of the video, listened to Gage's explanation of how he'd survived.

She'd done plenty of cliff jumping in her life— mostly ten- or twenty-foot drops. She could almost hear Gage in her head, from one of his many instructional videos put out by Xtreme Energy.

"Square up before you take your ride off. You have to be balanced before you launch or you'll flip in the air."

Unless, of course, like Gage, you *wanted* to do a flip.

"And don't forget forward momentum—a little speed helps with your landing momentum. But you don't want to fly into the cliff—too much and you'll do a superman, probably into a tree or off a cliff."

Those words, spoken before the Dylan McMahon accident.

"Finally, keep your eyes on your landing."

That, she'd never accomplished. The world always turned to a blur the minute she launched.

Gage stopped on the mountain, this time in the gap above the Weeping Wall.

When she reached him, he handed her his water bottle and she took a drink.

"So, here's what we're going to do. We're going to edge down to the left, through this channel, keeping clear of the waterfall. The ice is probably thick, but we'll want to watch for crevasses."

He couldn't know, probably, how her eyes widened.

"Slide down until you're right above the cliff, about twenty feet. You won't want more of a run than that. But you need enough to clear the outcropping at the bottom, so don't cut it too close."

Her breath must have hitched, because he looked at her. "Ella?"

She didn't move.

He grabbed her jacket. "Ella. Listen, you got this? Can you do this?"

She nodded, but it was more of a wobble of her head.

He reached down and clicked out of his board.

"What are you doing?"

"Getting into your head."

She stared at him as he stepped in front of her and grabbed her helmet in his hands to center his gaze on hers.

"You're only scared because you've built this up bigger than it is. We're not dropping from a sixty-foot cliff, we're suddenly dropping from Freedom Tower, right?"

She nodded.

"You probably saw my video—"

"A couple hundred times."

His mouth tweaked up in a smile, just for a second, then he nodded. "Okay, then you know, first, we're jumping into a pillow of powder. Second, I'll go first. You just have to launch off, keep your eyes on me, and you'll land right where you need to be."

She nodded, trying to take in his words.

"Ella. Breathe. One full breath."

Oh. She breathed out. In. Swallowed.

"Again."

She repeated it.

He grabbed her shoulders. "Stop looking at

what you can't do and look ahead, to your safe landing. Visualize it."

She gave him a wan smile.

He put his arm around her, turned her. "Look at what you've already done."

There, above her, stretching nearly straight up into the clouds, the peak betrayed a beautiful curving S down the hill, a line so perfect it could have been made by one person.

"We did that," he said. "And it's because you let go, stopped looking at your feet, and just trusted the line."

Huh. She had, actually. Started to feel it, believe in Gage's rhythm, his ability to choose the right path.

He turned her back to him, and this time he lifted his goggles onto his helmet. "Listen, Ella. Remember what I said about trusting me? Even if it doesn't make sense?"

She nodded.

"This is now."

He didn't smile, didn't blink, just met her gaze with his.

"Okay," she said.

"Atta girl."

And then, he pressed a kiss to her nose, quick and fast, a cute gesture probably meant to reassure but which instead left her just a little weak.

"Ready?"

She nodded and watched as he stepped into

his bindings. Then he reached out and took her hand.

She held on as they slid down, her heart a fist in her chest. Overhead, the blue sky arched over the mountains.

"Remember, stay balanced, flex your knees, and keep your eyes on me."

She nodded.

He considered her one last moment, then squeezed her hand and jerked his board forward.

In a second, he'd cleared the cliff, arms out. She heard a shout, something like a whoop, and couldn't help but move forward a little to peer over the edge.

"Are you okay?" she shouted.

"I'm down and it's perfect."

She couldn't see him from here.

"C'mon, Ella, let yourself fly!"

Right, yes.

She slid down the mountain, her breath caught, and—

Just before the edge, she tried to pull up. *Wait, no!*

But despite the fact that she'd cut hard, her momentum kept going.

She flew off the cliff. Soaring, her arms wind-milling.

Look for Gage.

She saw him below, waving and hollering, and somehow she found her feet below her. She landed in a poof of snow, bounced, and found herself up on her board, fighting for balance.

Headed straight for Gage.

"Whoa, slow down—"

She edged hard to cut out of it, and he leaped out of the way a second before she would have taken him out.

The momentum tossed her into the snow.

Gage landed beside her, on his back.

And then, he was laughing. His voice low and sweet as the sound bubbled out of him. "Oh, El," he said, sitting up on his elbows. "I wouldn't exactly say that you stomped that landing, but— well, I'm proud of you."

"Thanks."

He looked over at her. "All right, now we just have the Great White Throne—"

A shot reverberated in the air, and Ella looked up, trying to locate the sound. Gage sat up.

The entire cornice cap above Weeping Wall, right where she'd cut hard above the cliff trying to stop herself, was cracking.

"Get up!"

Gage nearly vaulted to his feet, reached over, and somehow grabbed her by the waist. "The wall is coming down!" His hand was on her back, pushing.

"What?"

"It's a slide—get moving!"

The wall gave way and dropped.

• • •

Get off the mountain. Get off the mountain.

The words thundered in Gage's head as he pushed Ella in front of him. "Sideways—we need to ski out of the track of the slide!"

He didn't look back—the roar of the snow crashing toward him had his heart slamming against his ribs.

Ella cut downhill, and he raced after her, grabbing her arm.

"This way!" He angled right, because to go left would be to cross in front of the slide.

But right led them over the ravine. A ten-foot fissure in the snow cut by frozen river and razor-edged granite walls.

However, they could sail right over it if they worked up enough speed.

"Faster! Stay on your edge but keep your weight centered—don't carve!"

He probably didn't need to tell her that—Ella possessed enough board skills to teach fast-gliding. Instinct, really, kept him shouting.

That and the sheer panic of knowing what it felt like to get caught in a slide. The pressure of the snow as it crushed your ribs, wrenched your shoulder out of socket. The suffocating cold—

"Don't slow down!"

He hazarded a glance uphill. The slide careened down, gathering momentum, taking out spindly, high-altitude pines, tumbling over rocks. And while they'd slid mostly out of the zone—

"No! Gage, are you serious?"

She'd spotted the gully.

"Take it fast—we'll launch off—it's a sweet landing on the other side, I promise." Although, in reality, he'd never taken it, only studied this route. Instead he'd opted for the nearly straight drop of the Great White Throne, a series of cliff drops, each about three to five feet down a face of nearly a hundred feet.

"Gage!"

Just in time and with the lead snowballs overtaking them, the edge of the ravine came up at them.

"It's all about the speed, Ella. Spring off the top, get lots of boost. Let's hit this!" He hunkered down, hit the lip, and sprang off, riding the air.

Next to him, out of his peripheral vision, he saw Ella mimic him.

He didn't know if he'd call what emerged from her mouth a scream, but it definitely lit some-thing inside him. Adrenaline, a little goofy fear, and a whole lot of pure crazy panic that bubbled out in unexpected terror-filled fun. He landed, cut hard to slow his speed, and saw her stomp her landing just a little behind him.

He glanced behind, further back.

The slide had turned, slowed at the ravine,

but it had enough momentum to make the leap.

"We have to keep moving!" But here, they had more slope to work with. He rode his edge and traversed the hill, cutting hard right, along a ridge.

She followed him, her jaw set.

Gage shot a look back again just as the slide swept past them. It careened into pine trees, off a cliff, and dumped into the valley below.

He angled upslope, slowed, and found a notch in the mountain where he could stop.

He leaned over and grabbed his knees, breathing hard.

Ella slipped up beside him, unclipped her pack, dropped it in the soft snow, then collapsed next to it with her arms out. "Seriously."

He unsnapped his boots and freed himself from the board. He secured it into the snow, slid off his pack, and plopped down next to her. "You okay?"

"Give me five minutes."

He reached over and unbuckled her bindings. Set her board next to his.

"Okay, I never want to do that again."

He offered a smile. "Me either."

She looked over at him. "I had no idea—I mean, I saw you live through that other slide, but . . . Gage. That was terrifying."

His smile fell. "Yeah." He unbuckled his helmet, pulled it off. Underneath, a line of sweat had formed. He wiped his glove across his forehead, noticed that his hand shook.

Okay, so maybe he wasn't quite as put together as he thought.

Next to him, she sat up. Lifted off her goggles, then unbuckled and pulled off her helmet. She wore a white headband, her hair caught back. She pulled her gaiter down and unbuckled her backpack. "I need a drink."

"Whiskey?"

She looked at him, and he finally got a smile. "Funny."

He retrieved his water bottle and handed it to her.

They sat in silence.

Finally, softly, "I'm sorry, Gage. I . . . I'm in over my head here."

He didn't want to admit it, but, well . . . "Me too."

She glanced at him, and he let one side of his mouth tweak up.

"What do you mean? You could ski this with your eyes closed."

He looked at her then, his gaze roaming her face. Then he pulled off his glove and touched his warm fingers to her face. "That's not what I mean."

Her mouth opened, her eyes widened.

Maybe it was the adrenaline, the near-death experience, but all his feelings bubbled up, without the reserve to save him. His voice shook. "You scared me. You always scare me a little, Ella. I never have been able to take a full breath around you."

He didn't know how he'd gotten here, suddenly, the inside of his heart spilling out into the cold, windy air. But he seemed unable to stop. "I'm . . . I'm so afraid you're going to get hurt. And if that happened, I could . . . that would be the end." He fixed his gaze into hers, unmoving. "I could not bear to have you hurt because I couldn't keep you safe."

He dropped his hand but couldn't take his gaze from hers.

She blinked at him, as if trying to assimilate his words.

Oh, where were red flags, waving him off?

Then, whisper soft, "Gage—I trust you."

Oh no . . . that's not . . . "You shouldn't."

She frowned, and he cut his voice low, serious.

"Ella, you should not trust someone who's made the mistakes I've made." He shook his head. "I mean, frankly, I had no business praying like I did today. I have no doubt God is up there laughing."

"Gage, God doesn't laugh at our prayers."

"Trust me, he's thinking, you've got a lot of guts, pal." He sighed. "And to remind me of that, thanks, God sent an avalanche. Believe me when I say that I am not your good luck charm here."

"Whatever! You only got us to safety. And I have a feeling God put us exactly where we needed to be to get away, so—no, I don't hear any laughter. I hear God saying, 'You messed up, but that doesn't mean I did. Trust me.' "

He let her words in but couldn't feel them. "Oh, El, you don't get it. I'm not the hero you think I am. But around you, I forget that. You make me think that I am more than who I am."

"You are more—"

"No. That's the whole problem. I used to think I was, and it went to my head. And then I was this guy who strapped on a video camera and risked his life for a living, and somehow thought that was brave or honorable when it was just plain stupid. Then my luck ran out. And people got hurt."

"Gage, you inspired—"

"Crazy. I inspire crazy. I'm not a hero, Ella. I'm just a guy who keeps trying to do the right thing, hoping desperately he doesn't get somebody killed in the process."

And then, because they were alone, here, right now, in the glorious ethereal wake of near disaster and heady triumph . . . "And I know I should be angry with you, but . . . I can't stop thinking about how it was before, and how much I still want you. So desperately I can taste it. Because when I'm with you, you make me cut past all the debris of the past three years to that guy I used to be—only maybe less arrogant. Less reckless. Being with you just might make me into the guy I actually *want* to be . . ." He swallowed, pretty sure he'd lost his mind back there in the slide. "You're . . . you're good for me," he said, sighing. "But if I can't get you down this mountain, I'll be disastrous for you."

"Gage."

"No. We shouldn't be here. This is no good." He closed his eyes, shook his head.

And that was why he didn't see her roll to her knees and grab the front of his jacket. But, a second before she kissed him, he opened his eyes and saw her intent.

"Ella—"

She pressed her lips against his, sweetly, her gloves fisted in his jacket.

He didn't move, so shocked by her touch . . .

And then, he found his bearing, the place he wanted to be. The place he'd wanted to be for three long years.

With Ella.

Right here in her embrace.

She tasted of the morning coffee, the sense of adrenaline and fear and adventure, her kiss so fresh and crisp and alive, he lost himself a little.

She slid her arms around him, and he wove his fingers in her hair, put his arm around her shoulders as he leaned her back, cradling her in the snow.

She relaxed, moved her arms up to rest on his shoulders. He felt a smile curve her lips.

And it only made him deepen his kiss, his heartbeat slowing, finally. The world stopped around him, and the moment cocooned him, blotting out the avalanche, the gusting wind, the worry for Oliver.

Yes, here he belonged.

He finally leaned up and found her beautiful eyes. "Wow, I missed you."

She smiled, her eyes a pale blue to match the sky. "I never stopped thinking about you, Gage. Never."

He leaned back in, covered her mouth with his.

He could stay here all day, all year, until the thaw found them on top of the mountain.

And then they could simply hike down. Instead of risking Ella's pretty neck on yet another cliff, another avalanche, a run through the trees that could impale her.

He winced and pulled away from her, rolling over.

"What is it?" She sat up. "Are you hurt?"

"We have to find your brother and get off this mountain." He met her eyes. "Alive, preferably."

"We will, Gage. I don't believe in luck. I believe in courage. And loyalty. And you. I believe in you. And I want to believe that God is on our side, despite our mistakes. Don't you?"

He looked up at her, swallowed. Nodded.

"Okay, then, get up and figure out our line."

He stared at her, and she raised an eyebrow.

"You're a little bossy, you know."

"Mmmhmm." She reached for her backpack. "Want a power bar?"

He probably didn't need one, since, at the moment, he felt downright invincible. But he nodded as he stood up to study the hill. They could ride the ridge down, drop down a wall of cascading cliffs smaller than the Great White Throne, then down what looked like a chute of white, between two walls of granite and . . . "Ella, you're not going to believe this, but we're right above the cave. This is a shortcut."

She handed him a power bar. "Well done, champ."

He grinned at her and sat down in the snow, tearing open the snack. Then he reached into his jacket and pulled out his walkie.

"What are you doing?"

"Checking in with PEAK, telling them we're okay. And that we *are* going to get off this mountain alive."

Someone needed to get out into the backcountry and start searching from the bottom. The thought came to Ty as he listened to Gage's second transmission, an update about the avalanche they'd narrowly escaped.

No, it came to him as he watched Brette push

away Sierra's homemade tomato soup and ignore the grilled cheese sandwiches. She sat on the sofa, her arms around her stomach, gritting her teeth, looking pained, probably at the thought of her best friend outrunning a slide.

Not to mention all the other perils awaiting them as they headed further down Heaven's Peak. Like Angel's Wings, a thin couloir in the rock that ran two hundred yards straight down through two towering granite cliffs, so close together that if he and Ella deviated one foot, they'd crash into the side. Or Cathedral Canyon, the vast pine forest that littered the backside of the peak near the final descent.

Ty had watched Gage's video a few hundred times back in the day when he realized the guy came from Mercy Falls. Back then, however, Ty's life had been full of trips to Vail or Steamboat Springs—no backcountry skiing for his family.

No, he'd been too busy keeping up with Selene Taggert and her brother, Barron, and their circle of New York friends. Ty Remington, the wealthy rancher's kid from Montana, hobnobbing with the page six crowd.

Brette's words from last night hung in his head. *"Entitled. Selfish. The world revolves around them, and they'll take anyone down to keep it that way."* Her comments about the class of people that he came from.

He'd kept his mouth shut.

After all, he wasn't that guy anymore. Not since the accident, really.

Nearly dying had a way of teaching a guy who he was. And wasn't.

And who he wanted to be.

Now, Ty got up from the table, brought his bowl to the sink, rinsed it, and loaded it in the dishwasher. Then he grabbed his coat, slipped on his boots, and hunkered down into the cold, heading to the barn.

Last night's storm had sculpted the land, drifted the snow against the house, the fence, the barn, leaving bare patches in the heli-pad and in the yard. Overhead, the sky had cleared, a perfect powder blue. The air contained a bite, and a faint wind bullied its way down the back of his jacket as he scurried out to the barn.

He opened the door and flicked on the lights. The chopper sat in the relative warmth of the heated barn, having been brought in on the hydraulic pad. Beyond that was the gear room, and in the back of the barn, their various vehicles—the medivac truck, the 4Runner, and the two Polaris sleds. Ty might have lived the life of a playboy, but his father also taught him the workings of the ranch. Including how to repair the vehicles.

He opened the cover, pulled out the dipstick, and checked the oil.

"So you've decided to make a run for it?"

He found the voice, saw that Pete had followed him out. "What?"

Pete had his hands shoved into his pockets, as if trying to look casual, but with his hair pulled back, it only accentuated the sharp planes of his face and his dark expression. "Caught between Jess and Brette?" Pete shook his head. "I'd run too."

Huh? "I'm not running. There's nothing between . . ." Him and Jess. But he opted for the version that Pete knew. "Me and Brette."

"Then why did I find you two all cozy this morning on the sofa?"

"She couldn't sleep. We watched a movie."

Pete had come up to him, his face unmoving. "Watched a movie."

"Yeah. She's upset and worried."

"And you decided to comfort her." Pete took another step toward him. Too close.

"Yeah. Now back off, Pete."

Pete didn't move. "I can't believe I'm saying this, but I swear to you, Ty, if you break Jess's heart, I'll run you back to that fancy ranch of yours so fast—"

"Step. *Back*." Ty had put the dipstick back and now pitched his voice low and turned to Pete. "I'm not afraid of you, Pete. Sure, I might have grown up with a few more advantages, but I promise you, I'm not who you think I am."

"Clearly. Because I thought only I was stupid

250

enough to date two women at the same time."

"I'm not dating—" He sucked in a breath. "I am just being Brette's friend. She needs one."

"Really. Maybe *I* should be her friend," Pete said.

Ty had never really understood men who got instantly riled when other men talked about their girlfriends, but suddenly he had the very real image of slamming his fist into Pete's smug face. Maybe rock him back from his righteous perch, remind him that Jess had chosen to walk away from *him,* into Ty's embrace. And yeah, it might be a platonic embrace, but she'd still chosen the safety of Ty's arms over the warmth of Pete's.

He managed not to say that, or let the thought tip a smile to his lips. Instead, he took a breath. He schooled his voice. "Pete. You're so jealous you're not thinking straight."

The air went out of Pete at Ty's words. He swallowed.

"Brette is just a friend. I promise I won't hurt Jess."

Pete's jaw tightened.

Ty met his gaze.

Silence passed between them until Ty heard the door open behind Pete. He looked over his shoulder.

Jess had walked into the barn, her timing impeccable.

"Pete? Miles just came in. He wants to talk

to you about the possible evac off the mountain over land."

Pete didn't move for a long heartbeat. Then, finally, he turned and must have smiled at Jess because she smiled back as she passed him.

Polite. But she wore so much longing in her face as Pete walked by, Ty wanted to shake them both.

She came up to him, and Ty waited until Pete closed the door behind him.

"Jess, this has gone on long enough. You have to tell him. The poor guy is completely in love with you and nearly took my head off just now because he thinks I'm cheating on you with Brette."

Jess swallowed, looked away. "I know."

"You *know?* Good. Yay. Because I'm tired of Pete being furious with me, and frankly . . ." He didn't want to say the rest. The part about him watching Brette as she fell asleep, the way her blonde hair swept over her shoulders, the very real urge to twine her hair between his fingers.

"I just need you to settle this thing with you and Pete. For the good of all of us. Trust him, Jess. Tell him the truth. No one is going to betray you here—your secret is safe with us. At least it is with Pete, just as much as it is with me."

Jess nodded, wiped a hand across her cheek.

"You're right. I'm being silly. After all, what could happen? So he finds out that I'm actually the missing whistle-blower of the Taggert Financial scandal. You're right—I'm blowing this out of proportion."

"Yes."

"Because he won't care that I testified against my father, put him in jail."

He frowned at her. "No, I don't think he will."

"Even though his own father died in an accident his brother blamed him for. "

"Jess, where are you going with this?"

"And it won't matter at all that he felt betrayed and rejected—"

"Okay, just take a breath." Ty took her by the shoulders. "It's not the same thing."

Her eyes glistened, her breath falling. "I betrayed and rejected my entire family. And, most recently, Pete."

"You were scared. And trust me, he'll be so glad we're not dating he won't hear anything else, I promise."

Her mouth lifted up. "I hope so."

"Trust me, Jess. Everything is going to be fine."

Please, let everything be fine.

12

Ella could hardly believe that twenty-four hours ago, she'd practically had to chain herself to the chopper to make Gage take her with him.

Now he rode as if he hadn't a doubt she could keep up.

Across the tufted ridge, down a narrow chute, into open country, dodging a few pine trees, then a stair-step drop down a cliffside that left her stomach somewhere on top.

He stopped at the bottom, and she pulled up beside him, breathing hard.

"Look at what you just did," he said and pointed behind her.

She didn't want to look, but . . .

Even from the bottom, it took her breath away. Five ledges, no more than five-feet deep, iced with powder, and she'd skipped down them without doing a header or crashing, mostly in control the entire way.

But she definitely wasn't in control of her heart when Gage turned back to her and held out his gloved hand for a fist bump, his incredibly brown eyes alight with pride. "Pretty good there, Senator," he said. "I shouldn't have been so worried about the Great White Throne. That was just as steep and you handled it no problem."

She grinned, and her heart gave an extra bang in her chest.

Really, she didn't know how she'd managed to put herself together after their embrace in the snow.

Gage Watson could still turn her world inside out with his touch.

Not to mention his words. *"Being with you just might make me into the guy I actually want to be."*

She liked who he was now. Today. The man he'd become despite her.

Gage studied the terrain below, choosing his path. "We're going to come around the cave from the back side. It's easier access to go along the ridge and approach it from the flank than to drop down on top of it and hike back up the way I did before."

He reached for his water bottle, uncapped it, and took a drink. When he offered it to Ella, she shook her head. He took another drink, then capped it.

"I actually found the cave by accident the first time. I had read about it from a backpacker's guide to Heaven's Peak but didn't know if I'd find it—wasn't even planning to, really. And then I came over the top of the roof and landed in the field just below the entrance. I was catching my breath when I spotted it, and since I was losing daylight, I climbed up. Couldn't believe how big it was on the inside—the entrance is barely visible, the way the snow curves over it, but inside it's dry and out of the wind. I wish we'd made it last night."

Except then she wouldn't have had a good reason to curl up next to him. "I hope my brother is there."

"Me too," Gage said. "Ready?"

She nodded, and he eased himself forward, down the ridgeline. It seemed like he rode with a new confidence.

Knowing that maybe he could trust her.

She urged her board forward, following him.

Frankly, she was beginning to trust herself. Because with Gage pushing her, challenging her, she saw a side to herself that so rarely emerged. With him, she let go, found herself actually enjoying herself.

It made her believe what she'd said to Gage— the hope that God was on their side. That she didn't have to prove anything. That she could let the past go.

Except, well, she couldn't. Not with the last terrible secret remaining between them.

Dylan's drug usage. It was possible that, had he not been high, he wouldn't have skied off that cliff.

Would have lived. More, Gage could stop blaming himself.

She needed to tell him.

But what if it made Gage only blame himself more, regretting that he hadn't seen it? Maybe it would only add to the pile of mistakes that kept him from truly breaking free. Trusting.

Her. Himself. God.

"I had no business praying like I did today."

His words rattled through her.

She understood Gage better than he thought. Because one look at herself told her that she had some audacity to think God would listen to her, let alone grant her requests.

Gage made some quick cuts down the ridgeline to slow them, his body smooth as liquid.

She fell into the rhythm, nearly on his track but not quite.

Her own words came back to her about God, *you messed up, but that doesn't mean I did. Trust me.* She wasn't sure where they'd come from, but they lingered, hung on.

Maybe that was the key—just because she'd made a mistake with her life didn't mean that God had, and it hopefully didn't change the way God saw her.

Still flawed but worth loving anyway.

And if God loved her despite her failures, maybe she could let go of trying to control everything, start trusting him.

Please, God, let my brother be okay.

Gage paused at the top of the chute, the right flank of the cave. "We'll just slide our way down this—it's pretty steep at the bottom, and we don't want to overshoot the cave."

She had a feeling that if he were alone, he might just ride straight down, but she didn't argue with him. He angled his board parallel to the fall line and skidded down the nearly vertical chute, following it down to a steep white field at the base.

"Hey! There are tracks down here!"

She followed him down, maybe too fast because she nearly flew by him. Powder flumed as she skidded to a stop.

He raised an eyebrow but didn't say anything about her wild descent. Then he pointed to a thick white line leading out of the cave and down the mountain.

"Is that one track or two?"

"I don't know." But he was unbuckling his boots from the bindings. "Let's check the cave."

She unclipped her bindings, settled her board in the snow, and hiked up.

Facing eastward, the cave was, indeed, difficult to see, especially from their route. The sun gilded the ice around the edges and cast light into the opening, a small oval that she had to drop to her knees to crawl into.

Gage had already climbed inside and turned on his head lamp, illuminating the cave's interior. Maybe it had once been filled with water, because the edges were grooved with lines and the floor was a smooth, polished granite.

Dry and tall enough for her to stand, the cave tunneled back into the rock. The main cavern rose around her and dipped into a dry pool before it narrowed into small tunnels in the back.

In the middle of the pool sat an orange two-man tent. A snowboard lay beside the tent, a pair of boots outside the door.

"Ollie!"

Ella scrambled over to the tent, right behind Gage, who'd knelt to open the door.

He grabbed her arm a moment before she barreled inside.

The figure lay on his unrolled sleeping bag, one arm flung up over his eyes. He was dressed in a thermal shirt and fleece pants. Nearby lay the debris of his gear—snow pants, jacket, and a helmet smashed in on one side.

His right leg lay elevated on a rolled-up sleeping bag.

His knee looked the size of a soccer ball. The fleece pants had been ripped open to accommodate the swelling, but judging by the redness and the swelling at his ankle, he'd landed wrong, and hard.

Worse, the leg had taken on a dark purple hue.

"Oh my gosh, Ollie!"

With a start, the man moved his arm down. Lifted his head. He had dark hair and was a little taller than Ollie, which her brain had skipped right over.

"Bradley," Gage said. "What happened?"

She couldn't move, not sure what she felt. Relief? Horror? Disappointment?

Maybe all of it as she watched Gage move into the tent. "When did this happen?"

Bradley looked dehydrated, and he moaned as he lifted himself up on his elbows. He stared at them as if he didn't recognize them.

"It's me, Ella. And you've met my friend Gage. He's an EMT."

Gage was already slinging down his pack, reaching for the water. He held Bradley's head, gave him a sip.

Bradley grabbed the water and drank until Gage pulled it away. "Ease up, pal. Not too much, too fast."

Bradley wiped his mouth, his eyes thick with pain. "I fell coming down the Great White Throne. Bounced all the way down, landed . . . well, you can see. I think my knee might be out of socket. I can't move it at all. And my ankle is probably busted. I turned it inside my boot."

Gage was probing, very gently, the mass that was his knee. "How'd you get here?"

"Ollie carried me on his back. Rode most of the way, and then when it got too hard, he made me get on my board and we slid down together."

"Where is Ollie?" Ella asked. She noticed that Ollie had left Bradley their stove, food supplies, even a bottle of water, now empty. And that gave her the clues she needed, even before Bradley answered.

"He left early this morning to get help. I thought maybe—you haven't seen him?"

Ella shook her head. She glanced at Gage. "The track outside—it's his."

Gage nodded, then scooted out of the tent and touched her arm to urge her away from Bradley.

He pitched his voice low.

"Whatever he did, he's not getting enough blood flow to his foot. We need to get him out of here, but the mountain is too treacherous to sled him out. We need to call Kacey and ask her to bring in the chopper and airlift him out."

Ella nodded, but he'd taken off his glove and now found her own ungloved hand.

"We'll go after Ollie as soon as we get Bradley out, okay?" Gage gave her hand a squeeze.

"You need to go after Ollie now," came a voice from inside the tent. She frowned and followed Gage back to the tent entrance.

"Why?" Gage said.

"Because I'm not the only one who fell going down the Great White Throne." He reached over and gripped the destroyed helmet. "This is Ollie's."

Brette couldn't blame her upset stomach on watching Jess and Ty walk out of the barn together—but she wanted to.

261

That was silly—she barely knew the guy beyond his ability to make eggs and pick a good cowboy movie. But the way he smiled down at Jess, warmth in his eyes, the way he held the door open for her, even the way he stood beside her, almost protectively, as they mapped a route into Heaven's Peak by snowmobile, made Brette want to know Ty Remington better.

Want to know what it felt like to *really* wake up in his muscled arms, his low baritone sliding through her as he whispered good morning.

The thought took her up, made her draw in her breath. She hadn't had a thought like that since—well, since she knew better.

Besides, Ty was probably already taken. Probably by Jess, if she read things correctly. Except, since he'd returned from his excursion, he kept looking over at her, a warm, almost worried smile tipping his mouth, as if checking on her. She sat on the stairs, her hand to her roiling, spasming stomach.

"We could take the snowmobiles in through Haystack Creek, toward Crystal Point, around the backside of Heaven's Peak, then follow this tributary along the base," Pete was saying as he and Ty, founder Ian Shaw, and a guy named Miles, who'd come in earlier, studied a map.

Miles had a military look about him, his dark hair shaved short, his body lean and tough. He wore a solemn take-no-prisoners look in his eyes.

"We could catch up with them here, below Bishops Cap," Pete said, finishing his suggestion.

What a disappointment Pete the so-called epic rescuer had turned out to be. Sure, he'd said the right thing—"I'm not about the limelight—I'm just trying to get the job done"—but it came out surly and a little hard-bitten.

Which left her hoping for an interview with billionaire Ian Shaw.

He'd shown up about a half hour prior, pulling up in a mud-splattered pickup. She might not have even recognized him if Sierra hadn't greeted him when he came in. He wore a stocking cap, dark hair curling from the back, a down parka, work pants, and snow boots as if he'd been shoveling his own walk like a normal human being.

He shucked off the parka, hung it on the hooks by the door, and stepped out of his boots. "How's the search going?" he asked as he took the cup of coffee Sierra offered.

Chet, sitting at the computer and watching the radar, gave him an update on the two call-ins from Gage. Ian actually leaned forward, looking at the weather maps, rolling up the sleeves on his flannel shirt as if he might actually dive in, go after Gage and Ella himself.

Interesting. When he wasn't dressed in a tux and being auctioned off as an eligible bachelor for charity, Moneybags helped run rescue missions.

Apparently, no one here cared about the rumor that suggested he'd left his wife and son behind in Katrina to die. Or that he'd made his billions off the catastrophes that caused the BP Gulf oil spill.

She had just been gathering the fortitude to introduce herself when he came over. "Ian Shaw. I hear you're a friend of the victim?"

"And Senator Ella Blair, one of the rescuers. I'm her . . . I'm a journalist."

"Really," Ian said. His eyebrow quirked up. "And you just happened to be *here,* at this opportune moment, when a senator's brother gets lost?"

"I'm her friend. Oliver just happened to pull this stunt while I was here."

"So, you're not looking for a good story?" He added a confusing smile to the end of his words.

Which made her bold. "Of course I am. But, actually, I was hoping I could interview you." She ignored the pain in her side and stood up. "I heard you were the one who started PEAK Rescue, and I thought maybe you could tell me about what led—"

"Nope." His smile had vanished.

And suddenly, the room went very quiet. She glanced around, saw Sierra standing in the kitchen, making another pot of coffee. Sierra glanced at Ian with a pained expression.

Out of the corner of Brette's eye, she saw Ty stand up, start to move toward her.

"I'd be happy to talk about the achievements of the team, but the disappearance of my niece is still an open case. I don't want to discuss it."

Oh. She winced as the pain in her side convulsed.

Ian's tone changed. "Are you okay?"

"Yeah. I just—I ate something yesterday that doesn't seem to want to get out of my system."

"Probably the pizza from the Griz," Ty said now, miraculously beside her. He had her by the arm and led her over to the sofa.

She thought she heard a groan from someone, and then Jess crouched in front of her. "You look a little flushed. Can I take your temperature, maybe get a blood pressure?"

Brette nodded.

Ty handed her a pillow and helped her lie down, put her feet on the sofa. Then he crouched next to her. "Can I get you something to drink?"

She shook her head, and Jess returned with a medical bag. She sheathed a thermometer, and Brette stuck it under her tongue while Jess took her blood pressure.

"It's a little low," she said, then removed the thermometer. "And you have a low-grade fever."

"It's just food poisoning," she said.

But Jess stood up, shaking her head. "I don't like it."

265

"I'll be okay."

Jess took a breath, then pursed her lips, as if thinking. She stood there, her arms folded over her chest, her blonde hair pulled back in a ponytail, and suddenly Brette had another flash of memory.

Jess, or someone who resembled her, standing in front of reporters, her face tight, almost angry as she fielded questions.

In another moment, the image blinked away, and it left Brette staring up at Jess, grasping for it.

Jess Tagg had been someone famous. Someone even influential. Or notorious?

"I'll keep an eye on her," Ty said quietly and reached for a chair.

Brette closed her eyes, thinking. Where . . . she knew . . .

Court steps. A throng of press.

She pressed harder, searching—

"Are you sure I can't get you something? Acetaminophen? Ibuprofen?"

She opened her eyes to see Ty standing over her, his brow furrowed. Sweet. "No, I'm fine. I just need to rest and—"

That was it. *I need to rest and get away . . .*"

She could nearly hear her, in echo, part of a sound bite the news played over and over after the sentencing of Damien B. Taggert.

One of the biggest swindlers in history.

A man whose Ponzi scheme had bilked thousands of investors out of billions.

The words had been spoken by his daughter, Selene Taggert.

No. She stared at Ty, then at Jess. "Selene *Jessica* Taggert," she said quietly, just under her breath.

She'd found the missing piece to the mystery of the Taggert Investment scandal, the heiress who'd vanished the day her father was sentenced to 150 years in prison.

The woman who'd turned him in and testified against him—or so the rumors went. Because no one had ever landed her side of the story.

Yet. Brette drew in a breath, looked at sweet, kind Ty. "Yeah. Could you get my phone? It's on the counter in the kitchen."

He nodded, his frown deepening, and got up.

Poor man. He probably had no idea.

Right?

And that's when her stomach decided it had had enough. Bile rose in her throat even as she pushed herself to a sitting position. The pain moved from her stomach, down to her right side, as if a fist had punched in, grabbed ahold of her intestines, and squeezed. She cried out, grabbed her side, doubling over.

"Brette!" She heard Ty's voice even as she hit the floor, landing hard on her hands and knees.

Suddenly a trash can appeared in front of her and she lost her meager breakfast in it. Sweat pooled on her forehead as the emptying of her stomach turned her weak.

Then Ty was there, crouched beside her, holding a wet washcloth. She pressed it over her face and leaned back against the sofa.

"I'm okay," she whispered, her body shaking.

Jess had crouched beside her, was snapping on gloves. "I'm just going to palpate your stomach, okay?"

Brette took the washcloth off her face and stared at Jess as she touched her stomach, moving down from the center to her lower right abdomen. "Does this—"

"Ow! Stop!" Brette grabbed her hand away.

"It could be her appendix," Jess said to Ty as she took off her gloves. "Maybe you should bring her into Kalispell Regional to get an ultrasound." She reached for the garbage can. "I'll clean this up."

When Jess stood up, she gave Brette such a look of compassion, all her accusations screeched to a halt.

No. She couldn't be Selene Taggert. Selene was a high-brow Wharton grad who'd lived the life of a fashionista. A pampered rich-and-famous who wouldn't think of cleaning up vomit, unless maybe it had come from a night of partying. No—even then she would have summoned her hired help.

Someone like Brette's mother.

Jess looked at Ty. "I'll call you if we hear anything from Gage."

Ty nodded.

And then, suddenly, and without asking, he scooped Brette into his arms.

His amazingly strong arms, because she was no lightweight.

"No—wait. Ty. I can't go to the hospital."

"Yes, you can. I'll drive you—"

"No!" She wanted to push against him and wiggle out of his embrace, but he was so solid, so strong, she couldn't help but sink against him. "I can't—I don't have insurance."

A blink, and something shifted in his eyes. And she wanted to look away, a sort of shame creeping through her.

"I can't afford it. It's cheaper to pay the penalty."

"It's okay, Brette. We'll figure out something—"

"No, I can't! I don't want to be a charity case. Please."

"Shh. You're shaking, you have a fever, and even though I'm not a doctor, I can see you're in bad shape."

She cringed.

"It'll be okay," he said quietly and wore such a look of worry on his face that she looked away before he could see the tears glaze her eyes. Then pain wrapped around her body like tentacles and she could barely speak, let alone protest as Pete wrapped a blanket around her and Ty carried her out to his truck and settled her inside. He closed her door and went around to the driver's side.

Apparently, she'd let her sickness separate her from her common sense. And her flimsy checkbook. She leaned her head against the cool window. Saw Jess come out, stand on the porch, also wearing an expression of worry.

"Don't worry, Brette, everything is going to be fine," Ty said as he pulled out.

And despite her better sense, she wanted to believe him.

Time was of the essence, and Gage saw it fading the longer it took Jess and Pete to stabilize Bradley's leg, move him onto the stretcher, and pack him up for delivery to the PEAK chopper hovering outside.

Four hours—Gage checked his watch again, just to confirm—but yeah, it had taken nearly four hours from the time he'd called HQ, waited for Kacey to arrive and the EMTs to descend and then assess Bradley's condition. They'd even called his dad over in Whitefish for a heads-up and to ask if they should relocate the knee on scene.

In the end, they packed it with an inflatable splint, did the same for his ankle, administered an IV of fluids, then tucked him into a litter.

Gage helped the team carry Bradley out to the

snowfield and attach the litter to the suspended lines. Jess attached her harness to another line, and Pete radioed up to Kacey to start the lift. Jess rode it up, and while she got Bradley settled, Pete pulled Gage aside, back into the cave, out of the wind. Ella was packing up the tent, and when Pete pitched his voice low, Gage suspected trouble.

"Ella's friend Brette collapsed just before we got your call. Ty took her to the hospital."

"What? Why?"

"We don't know. Could be appendicitis. Maybe just stress . . ." He glanced at Ella. "We could make room in the chopper for her."

Gage glanced at Ella, who'd said little since Bradley's revelation of Oliver's fall. Her lips pressed together in a tight line of worry.

He should send her back with Pete. It was the logical, safe thing to do. With the day on the backside of lunch, he had maybe two, possibly three hours of daylight left. He'd have to ski fast to catch Ollie.

Gage thought the slide would have rattled her, slowed her down, or turned her timid. Instead, she seemed to bloom, staying on his tread, hot on his neck as he skied down.

She had even nearly overtaken him as they'd barreled down the flank of the cave wall.

"How's she doing?" Pete asked, as if reading his thoughts.

"She's good. She's . . . really good. But, yeah, we have Angel's Wings and Cathedral Canyon coming up, and . . ."

"It's not going to get any easier," Pete said.

Ella was tucking the tent into the case, and if she heard them, she didn't make a move to glance his direction. Still, she radiated worry in her tight, fast movements.

He could just imagine the fight she'd wage against him if he suggested her leaving.

Still . . .

"I don't know. If I find him, I might need her help. Especially if we have to ski him down."

A voice cut through the radio. "Brooks, this is Chopper One, we're ready for you. Better hurry, the wind's picking up again."

"Do we have another storm front heading in?" Gage asked.

"Winds, maybe some snow, but nothing like last night," Pete said. "Hopefully, however, you won't have to spend another night in the rough." He picked up his walkie, looked at Gage. "Should I request a ride for two?"

"It's up to Gage." Ella had come up, her backpack over her shoulder.

Gage stared at her. "Did you hear us?"

"We're in a cave. Acoustics are amazing." She looked at Gage. "I trust you. I trust your decision, and I trust the fact that if you want me to go home, then you'll get Ollie out."

But he saw the red around her eyes, what it cost her to say that.

And for a second, he saw her waving from the chopper, leaving him alone on the hill.

He hated to admit it, but he liked her *with* him, following him, occasionally whooping when she took a cliff, or stopping next to him to marvel at the scenery. And yeah, while urgency pressed a hand to his back, he'd felt something loosen inside him as they'd ridden down. Since she'd looked at him with those beautiful blue gray eyes and said, *"I won't get hurt. You'll keep me safe."*

"We have a couple pretty intense areas coming up," he said to her.

"I know. I saw the video of Angel's Wings, but . . . I can do it. I promise. But only if . . . only if you want me to come with you."

When she put it like that . . . "I want you to come with me," he said softly. "But we're going to ski fast and hard—"

"I know. And I don't want to be in your way."

"You're not in my way, you're . . ." *The reason I'm here.* In fact, knowing he was cutting her a line made him ski better, the responsibility of keeping her safe making him more cautious.

He probably should have had her in his life from the beginning. Because, with the exception of the slide, this might be the best line he'd ever carved.

For the first time in three years, he didn't look backward and see his failures.

Now Gage looked at her standing there, holding the pack, her beautiful hair curling out from her headband, her eyes in his, trusting him.

He took a breath. "You should know—your friend Brette? She collapsed. Ty took her to the hospital."

So maybe Ella *hadn't* heard everything. Her mouth opened, and she turned to Pete. "What's wrong with her?"

"Upset stomach."

She breathed out, nodding. "She has that a lot. Had an ulcer a few years ago in college. She'll be okay." She looked at Gage. "It's up to you. I'll go back if you think I should."

Huh. "I admit, I thought you'd put up more of a fight."

She took a breath, then shook her head. "As much as I want to go with you—you know that—I trust you, Gage. I trust you to find my brother and bring him home."

He nearly pulled her into his arms and kissed her again. However, if he did, he might never stop.

Instead, he looked at Pete. "That's a ride for one."

13

It took Gage a moment to center upon the feeling, to give it a name and let the realization find his bones.

Fear.

Gage stood at the apex of Angel's Wings, listening to his pulse pump in his ears, trying not to betray the sweat that beaded along his neck, the fact his hard breathing might be because he'd forgotten the deep terror this section of the mountain induced.

He'd been young and oh so stupid the first time he'd run this. Hadn't given a thought to broken bones or his body smashing against granite—

"It's nearly straight down," said Ella next to him. She was standing a few feet away, balanced back from the edge.

"I named it Angel's Wings because the two granite slabs look like wings jutting out from the rock." He pointed to the tiny prick of light almost two hundred yards down the trail between the wings. "That's about five feet across. The wings narrow on the way down, and by then you have so much speed you simply fly out of the opening into this great white shelf."

A slick, sudden memory of careening out of the space, so much air between him and the ground that he'd actually felt like he was flying. Only by God's grace did he not end up on his face. Or going over the cliff. His line had him cutting hard, slowing, then curving around the ridgeline and dropping into a beautiful, spongy white field before he hit Cathedral Canyon.

He must have been caught in the memory too long because he suddenly felt a hand on his arm. "Gage? Are you okay?"

He nodded, his mouth dry.

More than any of the other perils, this run had his number. He wasn't exactly afraid of heights, but the sheer drop, the speed . . .

But he'd negotiated it before, and Ella was right. If they found her brother, and his friend, hurt, he'd need her help.

He wanted to take his helmet off, wipe away the sweat trickling down his temple.

They were losing sun. An hour of hard skiing over drops, along ridges, into mini-bowls, and around stands of pine, and Ella had stayed right with him.

In fact, she'd nearly beat him here, pulling up right on his tail.

Probably worried about Oliver. Which he was too. He couldn't imagine what kind of injury the kid had sustained to destroy his helmet. The fact that he went for help suggested Oliver had the stuff of real heroism, not just the reckless-ness of a big mountain snowboarder.

Now to find him before night fell.

Ella still had her hand on his arm, and now gave a squeeze. "Take your time."

Sadly, he didn't need any time to find a line—there was no line here. Just a straight drop into speed, and one wrong shift of weight would careen them into the side of the wall.

A spectacular and fatal crash. Oh, why had he brought them this way? He looked at Ella, and she smiled at him.

He should have sent her home. To safety. His words from this morning shuddered through him. *"I'll be disastrous for you."* Never did that feel more true as she stood there, grinning, poised at the edge of a cliff.

More, he was very much in danger of losing his heart to her, careening full speed into something he'd been trying to forget, trying to deny, for three years. Just twenty-four hours with her had him right back where he'd been at the Outlaw resort, longing to figure out a way to see her after they got down off the mountain. The words had been forming inside him all day. *"So, how terrible is it if I follow you back to Vermont? I'd like to see you when this craziness is over. In Vermont, or wherever."*

"Gage—"

"I'm just . . ."

"Are you freaking out?"

He looked at her, a little afraid she could read his

mind, maybe see right through him to his heart.

"Because if you are, it's okay. It's . . . well, if I didn't have you with me, I'd be trying to figure out a way to walk down. But we don't have time. And I know you can get me down safely."

He stared back at the run. Right.

He closed his eyes. *God, I could use a little help.* The prayer emerged, unbidden, but he latched on to it. *I want to believe that you're on my side, just like Ella said, despite my mistakes.*

The wind lifted a gust of snow, swirled it at his feet and down the gully.

"What if we slarve the line?" Gage said, the thought coming to him fast. *Of course.* "Not a slide, but not carving our way either. It'll keep us going slower, and we'll weave our way down. And we'll just stay on the fall line, closed turns all the way until it narrows up. "

She was silent beside him. For so long, in fact, that he looked at her.

"What aren't you telling me, Gage?"

He pulled his goggles off then, wanting her to see his eyes. "Yeah," he said softly. "I'm freaked out. And not just about the run or your brother, but maybe what happens when we get back to base. But we don't have time to talk about it right now. Right now, I'm just trying to figure out how to not get our necks broken. Because last time I barely made it out alive. And this time—"

"Yeah, let's slarve it," she said. "There's no

278

GoPros, no circling choppers watching us. We take it at our speed, okay?"

He nodded.

"How about if I go first," she said. "That way, if I fall, you can pick up the litter."

"That's not funny," he said. "But yeah. Good idea."

She could take her time, inch her way down.

Ella took off, scooting over the edge before he was ready. Arms out, she traversed the hill, leaning back, keeping her board flat, the nose out of the powder as she traversed the fall line, then cut hard, a thick carve the other direction.

Nothing epic, but yeah, at their pace.

He edged over the lip and headed down, following her wide, easy, beautiful line.

The weave shortened as she descended, as the gully narrowed, until she finally opened it up and glided down the last forty yards, through the five-foot slit out into the open.

He followed, taking his time, his heartbeat slowing, his thighs burning as he skidded down the hill. He broke free near the bottom and sailed through the crack at a speed that might still break his neck but didn't tear his heart from his chest. He emerged into the bright white, carving hard on her trail, pulling up behind her.

She had stopped and was breathing hard. "My legs are on fire."

His too, but his heartbeat had settled into

something reasonable. Or slightly so, because as he looked at her, he just wanted to pull her to himself, kiss her.

Tell her that they didn't have to take it too slow.

"Never thought I'd have Gage Watson following my line," she said.

Baby, I'll follow you anywhere. The words were almost on his lips when he saw her smile dim. She bent down and unclipped her bindings, then took off, up the snowfield, back toward the base of the chute.

He followed her, a few steps behind. "What do you see?"

But he answered his own question as he came up beside her.

A puddle, where someone, after racing down that chute, might drop to their knees and lose it. Yellow bile and a pool of dark red blood stained the whitened snow.

"Oh no," Ella said.

Gage grabbed her hand and pulled her up. "It might be internal bleeding. Let's get going."

Ella simply didn't care if she got impaled by a pine tree. She should have taken Angel's Wings faster, maybe.

Her fears, holding her back.

In fact, she probably should have gotten on that chopper. She still couldn't believe that Gage had agreed to let her keep going.

But she planned on keeping up. Gage had located Ollie's trail and now led them into the clutter of the thick piney forest, moving carefully but steadily.

She tried to keep his words in her head.

"Don't focus on the trees, or you'll hug wood. Watch for the white spaces."

"Stay low, crouched, and your knees loose."

"Point your board downhill, and remember, speed is your friend. You need momentum to turn."

"Keep your weight on your back leg, nose pointed up, like a surfer."

"And stay close to me. Very close."

No problem. She kept his jacket in sight. However, the falling sun made the trees cast lethal shadows, hiding gullies and rock, turning the maze of forest treacherous.

And exhausting. Twice, she'd gotten stuck, slamming into a tree, hugging it for a long second before shouting.

Gage had stopped, waited for her.

Once, he'd bent down to unsnap his bindings, but she wiggled free and dialed back into the line.

The danger of skiing in the trees was the tree wells, the deep powder that fell around the tree but not to the trunk, leaving a deep cavern around it. She'd heard of skiers falling headfirst into these traps and, unable to get out, freezing to death.

Not unlike being caught in a slide. Both left the skier entombed in snow.

Gage stopped in a clearing and kneeled in the snow, breathing hard. She pulled up beside him.

"How could he go through this with internal injuries?"

Gage said nothing, his mouth a dark line. But he pulled off his backpack, dug through it, and pulled out his head lamp.

"We're not stopping, okay? So I'm going to slow down and you're going to stay right behind me. Like, ten feet, okay?"

She nodded, and he affixed the light to his helmet and flicked it on. The daylight was still enough to diffuse the wan light. But she imagined the shadows would thicken when they reentered the forest.

"I have to admit, your brother has stamina and not a little raw courage to make it this far."

She nodded. "He grew up on stories of Jovan. He would help Father smuggle Christians out of the country."

"And you're not exactly a couch potato."

Heat pressed through her at his words. "I grew up remembering Jovan too. And, of course, my parents."

He was putting his pack back on. "My parents always wanted me to follow in their footsteps into the medical field. They couldn't quite understand how much I hated school. I admit, I preferred adrenaline to grades." He adjusted his head lamp. "But when I started landing on magazine covers, they got on board. Sadly, after the accident, they didn't know what to do with me. Dad kept trying to get me to go to school. My mom . . . she built a little shrine in my room. Won't take it down." He rolled his shoulders. "Ready?"

She nodded, and he moved away. She watched him go, arms out, perfectly balanced, so comfortable, so capable, so in his element.

And he'd lost it all. Certainly he could figure out a way to get it back. He was different now—there was something wiser, more controlled about him.

Before, he'd been a phenom. Now he would be a real-life role model for kids like Ollie.

Fame didn't have to be a bad thing, did it?

She pushed off, right behind him, ignoring her aching body as he dove into the forest, following Ollie's line. The wind had followed them into the canyon, shaking the trees. Snow drifted down and sprinkled her face as Gage pushed away branches.

"We're not stopping, okay?"

She could have kissed him for that. But if they didn't find Ollie soon, they'd be following him in the inky folds of night, and—

"Ella!"

She looked up, saw Gage pointing. The forest had thinned, and despite the shadows and the clutter of trees, she spied a form in the snow.

Lying on his stomach, arms out, sprawled on the ground, his board still attached to his boots, as if he'd simply fallen over.

"Ollie!"

Gage reached him first, had his board off in a second, and dropped to his knees beside Ollie's prone form. Gage pulled off his goggles, took off his gloves, and reached for Ollie.

He'd already found his pulse by the time she caught up.

"Is he—"

"He's alive," he said. "Unbuckle his boots."

She lifted off her goggles, then snapped Ollie's boots off the bindings and helped Gage roll him over.

Ollie's cheeks were white. "Oh, Ollie!" She pressed her hand to her mouth, fighting tears.

Gage put his hands on Ollie's cheeks, then opened his jacket and placed a hand on his chest.

"We need to get him warm and call in the PEAK chopper for help." He got up, scrambled for his pack, and pulled out his walkie.

"PEAK HQ, PEAK HQ, this is Watson, come in. Over."

Ella knelt next to Ollie. Despite the layer of patchy whiskers, he still looked impossibly young, terribly innocent. She took off his goggles, leaned down, and kissed him on the forehead. "You're going to be okay."

"PEAK, this is Gage. Come in!"

She looked over at him, and he shook his head. "I think the trees are disrupting the signal. Too much clutter. We need to be higher, or at least in a clear space. There's a final ridge once we clear the forest, but that's . . . that could be hours away if we have to carry him."

"I could go—"

"No, Ella. You have no idea where you are." He came back over, knelt down next to Ollie. "But I could go . . ."

"Really? Because it's going to be dark soon, and even you—"

"I'll be okay."

She swallowed. Nodded.

"I don't want to leave you here."

She hated the hot tears that flushed her eyes. "But Ollie needs help, and I can do this. I'll pitch the tent, make a fire . . . I can do this."

He reached up, cupped his hand against her cheek. "I'll come back—as soon as I get a signal, I'll be back."

"I know," she said, trying to keep her voice from wobbling.

And that's when he kissed her. Just grabbed her by her jacket and pulled her to himself. Not a sweet, champagne powder kiss, but hard and solid, the kind of desperate kiss that said what she needed to hear.

He really didn't want to leave her. And yeah, he might be a little scared too.

So she kissed him back exactly the same way, tasting salt on her lips as he backed away. He got up then, walked over, and snapped on his snowboard. "Get the tent up, get him inside it, and build a fire. There are matches in my pack."

"You need your pack."

"No. I just need this." He held his walkie in his hand. "And these." He dropped to his knees, opened an outer zipper, and pulled out what looked like thick ribbons. Then he grabbed his compact ski poles, which were folded down and secured with Velcro on the back of his pack. "My skins and poles. So I can hike back to you."

She nearly wept at his words. Especially when he stood up and pointed to his head. "I remember every inch of this mountain. And I'm going to figure out how to get us out of here."

Then he pushed off.

And if she'd forgotten how amazing he was on his board, if she thought she'd been keeping up with him, she saw the truth as he arrowed through the trees.

She watched him until he disappeared into the fold of shadow and branches.

Please hurry.

She wiped her cheek, then turned back to Ollie. He hadn't moved. She stumbled over to Gage's pack, opened it, and dug out the tent, and in a second, she'd shaken it out of the case.

It snapped together automatically, and she used the shovel to dig out a base, just like Gage had done last night.

She set up the tent and unzipped the door. Then she pulled out her sleeping bag and Gage's and unrolled them.

Despite her fear of breaking something else in his body, she took Ollie by the collar and tugged him toward the tent. Night was falling fast, the shadows thick. She would need her Maglite to start the fire. "C'mon, Ollie, work with me."

He woke up to her exertions and groaned. "What's going on?"

She hit her knees beside him. "Ollie, it's me, Ella."

His eyes focused on her. "Are you kidding me? What are you doing here?" He ended his question on a wince. "My stomach hurts. And I fell and hit my head. I have a raging headache."

She wanted to get his helmet off, take a look at his head wound, but she was suddenly more concerned with the way he held his side.

"Let me get you into the tent," she said. "Gage is getting help."

"Gage Watson? Whoa—seriously?" He was inching his way backward toward the tent, helping her as she eased him inside. He settled onto Gage's bag, moaning.

"Yeah, seriously," she said as she took off his helmet.

She found a matting of blood, a little softness on the side of his head, but nothing that seemed devastating. She wanted to weep with relief.

"What's the face for?"

"I saw your helmet earlier."

"You found Bradley!" He leaned back. "How did you even know we were up here?"

"I'm your sister, you idiot." She pulled up his shirt then, searching for bruising. Sure enough, a purpling along his lower right side. She pressed it gently, but he grabbed her hand.

"What are you doing?"

"Seeing if you have a broken rib."

"I probably do, but that's not why I'm sick. I caught something—maybe food poisoning. I've been feeling sick for the last day. I was fine when we started down the mountain—it just caught up with me."

She sat back. Stared at him. "Food poisoning? I saw blood in the snow after Angel's Wings."

"You did Angel's Wings? Whoa."

"The blood, Ollie. What's with the *blood?*"

"Yeah, I sort of, well, that was pretty freakin' scary and . . . I sort of lost it. And, like I said, I wasn't feeling well, so I was drinking cherry Powerade—"

"Oh, I think I hate you right now." She had a terrible urge to get up, strap on her board, go after Gage.

Because right now, he was risking his life for her not-so-injured brother. She sat back. Stared at him. Shook her head.

"I can't believe you did Angel's Wings."

She got up and pulled the other pack into the tent. Sat on the sleeping bag, unzipped her coat, and hoped with everything inside her that Gage wasn't impaled on a tree.

Outside, with the night falling, the wind picked up, shuddering the tent. And in its wake, she heard the faintest howl.

It lifted the tiny hairs on her neck.

Ollie pushed up on his elbows, then winced and fell back to the bag. "Is that a wolf?"

She looked at him. "Probably an entire pack. I hope they eat you."

Then she pulled out the stove, set it on the ground. "All we have is chili mac. So I hope that's okay."

"That sounds delicious. I'm totally starved. I could eat a moose."

She lit the stove and stared out into the darkness, listening again to the wolves howl.

Oh God, please keep Gage safe.

How Ty hated hospitals. The hurry up and wait of the emergency room. The expression of desperation and worry of family and friends in the surgical waiting area. And the helplessness of waiting for Brette to wake up from her emergency appendectomy.

Ty stood at the window, staring at his reflection against the black night. He needed a shave, a change of clothes, and a decent night's sleep.

From behind him, Brette stirred and he turned, caught her moaning. She lifted her hand to the oxygen mask.

"Hey there—ease up," he said as he moved to her bedside and caught her hand. "You had emergency surgery."

She seemed to be trying to grasp her surroundings. A furrow crested her brow.

"Shh," he said and slipped his hand into hers, smoothing back her hair with his other hand. "Your appendix burst in the emergency room— they had to put you out."

She nodded, as if the memory was coming back to her. Frankly, he'd like to forget the entire episode, her howl of pain, the sudden frenzy of the ER doc, the way a nurse barred him from following their dash into surgery.

Not that he could have helped. He just wanted . . . maybe to tell her everything would be okay.

Again. *"I don't want to be a charity case. Please."*

Her face had flashed with such an expression

of desperation he couldn't take it. Which was why he'd talked personally with the billing department while she'd been in surgery.

Had settled up her account in advance. It made him feel a smidgen less helpless.

Now he leaned over her, gave her a smile. "You're going to be fine."

But to his horror, her expression crumpled, and she looked away. Closed her eyes.

"Brette?"

"Go away, Ty—please. I can't . . ."

Then she lifted her hand to her face, hiding her eyes as her shoulders began to shake.

What?

"Brette, what's the matter—should I call the doctor?"

She shook her head, her breath hiccupping.

"Please don't cry."

She moved her hand away, looked up at him then, and the expression she gave him—fear? shame? vulnerability?—seemed miles away from the woman he'd met two nights ago. That woman seemed confident, bold. Unafraid.

Then again, he knew how injury could turn someone inside out, strip away everything they thought they were, leaving only the instinct for survival.

"What's going on?"

She pressed her hand to her cheek, wiped away the wetness there. "I just . . . I didn't want surgery." She pulled the oxygen mask away from her mouth.

"I think you're supposed to keep that on," Ty said, but she was already removing it from behind her ears. And now, reaching to sit up.

"Settle down, Brette—you just had surgery."

"I don't want to rack up any more bills—"

"Calm down! It's paid for!"

She looked at him with such a stark expression of shock he didn't know what to say.

Definitely not the truth, so . . . "I talked to billing. They were able to get you into a . . . uh, special program. For those without insurance. It's all covered."

She stared at him, as if testing him, and then, suddenly, her body seemed to surrender into his words. "Really?"

So much hope in her voice, he couldn't help it. He lied again. Sort of. Because it *was* covered. And that was all that really mattered. "Yes. So stay put, please."

She sighed, closed her eyes. Turned her face away.

And then another tear raked down her cheek.

He'd heard of people being overly emotional after surgery, so maybe this was just a side effect. "Um, by the way, Gage and Ella found Bradley. He was injured, but he's on his way to the hospital now."

She just nodded.

And that response had him even more unsettled.

"Brette, talk to me. What's the matter?"

Silence, and her breath drew in, shaky. But he noticed she hadn't let go of his hand. In fact, her grip tightened around his.

Finally, she looked at him, her eyes wet, tears glistening on her cheeks. "Thank you, Ty."

"For what?"

"Taking me to the hospital. And staying here with me. Being so nice to me."

"I told you right before you went into surgery that I'd be here waiting." Maybe she didn't remember.

"I know. But you didn't have to." She offered a small, chagrined smile.

"Of course I did. I said I would. Besides, you're all alone here and . . . well, nobody likes to wake up alone, right?"

Oh. He hadn't meant that in a lewd way, so he amended. "I mean, I didn't know who to call, family or friends, so . . . you got me."

Her gaze didn't fall away as she took a breath. "Actually, I don't have family."

He frowned. And now she sighed.

"My parents have both passed away. I'm an only child."

"I'm sorry, Brette."

"It's okay. I'm used to being alone. But . . . I am glad you stayed."

And now her smile touched her eyes, and he

felt the warmth of it reach out and twine through him. She looked so fragile connected to an IV, dressed in her hospital gown, her blonde hair in a nest on the pillow, that something inside him just wanted to scoop her back up into his arms.

He hadn't minded that part in the least—carrying her out to the car, her body sinking against his, her silky hair falling down over his arm. He'd tucked her under his chin in an effort to protect her from the frigid postblizzard wind.

And that urge hadn't died in the least.

"I'll stay longer, if you want." He wasn't sure what possessed him to say that. But she nodded, and he hooked a chair with his foot and pulled it over.

He sat down, still holding her hand.

"That's good, about Bradley," she said, rolling onto her side. Wincing.

"Easy there, champ. You're not supposed to be doing a lot of moving around. You'll be on your feet in a day or so."

She sighed. "I hate hospitals. The last time I was in one . . . well, it's just a place people go to die. Or at least for me it is. My mom spent the last week of her life in a hospital, and before that, I had to go to the hospital to identify my dad, so . . ."

"Brette, I'm so sorry. How did they die?"

"My mom had cancer. My dad . . ." She swallowed. "He took his life."

He stilled, his throat suddenly thick.

She seemed to sense his discomfort. "He lost everything in the Taggert fraud."

Oh no. *That,* he didn't see coming. Because, yes, he knew about the Taggert scandal, but only from Jess's point of view.

And of course, from the conversation around the Remington dinner table, the words of his father, who was grateful he'd never invested with any of his friend Damien's companies.

Brette might have mistaken Ty's silence for confusion, however, because she went on. "It was a big Ponzi scheme out east with an international investment firm—Taggert Financial, run by Damien B. Taggert. Basically, Damien rooked hardworking people like my parents out of everything they had by getting them to invest with his fraudulent company."

She eased herself onto her back. "My dad was a plumber, my mom a housekeeper. Damien Taggert was a friend of one of my mother's employers, and they entrusted him with their entire retirement savings. When the scheme was discovered, it was right after my mother was diagnosed with breast cancer. My dad tried to pull the funds out, but it was too late. There was nothing—it was all just on paper. I'm not sure if it was panic or just despair, but we found my dad in the car in the garage one Sunday night, not long after."

She wiped her cheek. "Maybe he thought the life insurance would see it as an accident. But they didn't . . . My mom declared bankruptcy when she got the medical bills. She lost their home and moved into my tiny apartment. But by then, the cancer had progressed so far, it didn't matter." She sighed again. "At least I got to be with her at the end."

The story slid into Ty, found his bones, and turned him cold.

"I'm so sorry," he whispered.

"I can't help but wonder if she'd had better medical care . . . or if my dad had been around . . . Anyway, I'm glad Damien Taggert got 150 years in prison, even if he'll only live to do a fraction of that."

Ty simply nodded, a fist closing around his chest.

Because, in that moment, her words at the house rushed back to him. *Selene Jessica Taggert.*

Oh no. But he didn't move, didn't let his face betray him. Maybe he'd imagined it . . .

"The thing is, Taggert was supposedly turned in by his own daughter, Selene. She even testified against him in a closed hearing. She joined him in court on the day of his sentencing, and then she vanished. Just walked away from her entire life—left her brother and mother to fend off the press. There's a rumor out there that she testified

296

to save herself from jail, but she ran before anyone could dig the evidence up."

Ty had to clench his teeth to bite back a defense, an explanation. But that was for Jess to unravel.

"I can't get it out of my head that if I could just corner her, ask her why, maybe even get an apology . . . I don't know. Maybe I could let go of this darkness inside, find some peace."

If that was all it took . . . a confession? An apology? This wasn't exactly Jess's fault, but Brette didn't seem to think that way.

"You know what's crazy?" Brette said then, finally looking at him again. "I thought, for a while there, that Jess Tagg was Selene Taggert, the missing heiress. I mean, she just looked so familiar to me. Long blonde hair, a sort of regal confidence about her, the look of someone raised in wealth." She lifted a shoulder. "I think probably it was the pain going to my head."

He raised an eyebrow, offered a nod, as if in agreement.

Let out a breath.

She had ahold of his hand, ran her thumb over it. "So, you see, Ella is all I have."

"Not all you have," Ty said quietly.

She smiled, and it made him ache. He reached out, pushed her hair from her face, let it fall, silky between his fingers. "You're not alone. I'm not leaving you."

She wrapped her hands around his, cradling it on her chest. "Thank you, Ty."

Her tears welled again, and he touched his other hand to her cheek, wiping the wetness away with his thumb.

"I'm sorry," she whispered. "I don't know why I keep crying."

He shook his head. "It's been a stressful couple of days."

But she'd reached up and curled her hand behind his neck. Met his gaze.

And for a second, he simply stilled, seeing a crazy intention in her eyes.

One he harbored right now too. For no other reason than just the need to sort through the clutter and listen to the tug of his heart.

And then she pulled him, gently, down to her. And he didn't resist, didn't even think, really, just gave in to the soft nudge of her hand, leaned down and kissed her. A feathery press of his lips to hers, sweetly, almost in comfort.

She sighed and kissed him back, just a whisper of desire in her touch.

But it lit something deep inside him, something he hadn't felt in—well, never, really. Brette was steel over velvet, taken down by life and circumstances, brave and loyal, and still willing to let someone past the broken edges of her heart.

Tyler Remington could too easily fall in love with Brette Arnold.

He let his caress linger for a moment. When he eased back, he felt her smile even before it touched her eyes.

Such beautiful eyes.

"Well," she said. "Here I was afraid you were already taken."

He could barely hear over the thunder in his chest. "Taken?" he managed.

"Yeah. It looked like you and Jess . . ." Brette made a face. "I was reading into a lot of things today."

He managed a feeble laugh. "No, Jess and I are just friends." But the words burned in his throat.

"Good. Because I'm not a man-stealer," she said. "Even if you, Ty, are a man worth stealing."

He smiled at that, not sure how to respond. Because it might be that she was well on her way to stealing his heart.

14

Gage had really lost his mind now because no snowboarder with all his working faculties, no matter how accomplished, rode through a steep, deeply powdered, pine-cluttered mountainside in the dark of night.

Lost. His. Mind.

The light from his head lamp cut through the darkness at sharp angles, and he just hoped he was heading toward the eastern ridge, the closest clear point to call in a rescue.

Which, most likely, PEAK couldn't manage, not with the winds picking up, the night closing in. But he had to try.

And after he connected with PEAK, he'd hike his way back to Ella.

He couldn't erase Ella's distraught expression from his brain—*of course* he'd go for help. In fact, the one thing he could do right was find his way through these trees.

He ducked a low-hanging branch, angled his board toward a clearing in the trees, shot through them, and—

He emerged into a clear white field that ended in a nearly thousand-foot drop-off of sheer granite.

He skidded to a stop, breathing hard, sweat

300

trickling down his back despite the howl of the wind. Below the cornice that capped the rocky edge, the world fell away into a rugged valley of granite, pine, and unridable terrain.

In his original descent, he hadn't gone this way for those exact reasons—the lethal drop-off. But tonight, this position provided a clear view to the VHF antenna at Crystal Point. It was just the boost he needed for his radio reception to clear the mountains and reach PEAK HQ communications.

Overhead, a half moon had risen, the stars just starting to wink awake. The luminosity shone enough for him to trace the razorback peaks to the east. It would be a glorious, even romantic night under the stars if Ella's brother wasn't fighting for his life.

He worked out his walkie. "PEAK HQ, PEAK HQ, this is Watson. Come in!"

Static, and he pressed the unit to his helmet, wincing. *Please.*

The wind stirred up eddies of powder around him, and the temps had dropped drastically with the disappearance of the sun. His cheeks burned with cold, and as his heartbeat slowed, he knew it wouldn't be long until the cold found his bones.

"Ty! Pete! Someone pick up!"

Please let someone be there at HQ. But he couldn't imagine that anyone would have left. Not with him and Ella out on a search.

"Watson, this is PEAK HQ. Go ahead. Over."

Jess. Thank you. He wanted to weep with the sudden rush of relief. "We're just east of Cathedral Canyon, about a mile or more west of the final ridge. We found Oliver."

"Roger, Watson. What is his condition?"

"He might have internal bleeding—we need an extraction ASAP."

"Stand by," Jess said, and he imagined she was conferring with Miles or maybe Pete. The wind ruffled his jacket, pressed him toward the edge, and he fell to his knees, just to ground himself.

The last thing he needed was to take a header off the ridge wall.

"Watson, Miles here. We're watching the wind off the mountain, and it's gusting up to forty miles per hour. In the darkness and that complexity of flying in, it's a no-go right now. We might be able to get in at first light."

Gage closed his eyes, wincing.

"And that's pretty tight tree cover down there. We might be able to drop in a litter, but there's no guarantee we can pull him out. Over."

"If you drop it in, I can ski him out." Maybe. But with the thicket of trees, the ridgeline cordoning them off . . .

No, of course he'd ski Oliver, and Ella, out. Safely.

"Wilco," Miles said. "Repeat your position."

"We're in the Cathedral Forest, about another mile to the ridge. Heading down along the ridge into the center of the canyon."

"Roger. We'll leave at first light and radio when we get close. And we'll map a route in on snowmobile. Ty and Pete will head out as soon as they can. Best we can do."

It would have to be good enough. "Roger. Wilco. Watson out."

He stood there a moment, just watching the stars breach the dark blue canopy of night. The jagged, glistening outline of the mountains against the indigo heavens.

And rising above them all, Heaven's Peak.

He stared up, seeing in his mind the trek they'd taken down the mountain, that first jump, where they'd camped last night, Weeping Wall, the cave where they found Bradley, Angel's Wings . . .

This is where it had started, all of it—the epic YouTube video, the freestyle championships, meeting Ella . . .

The rise before his colossal fall.

And God had led him right back here. As if he might be trying to tell Gage something.

Ty's words to him, only a few days old, drifted back to him. *"Dude. You wear your mistakes like a brand on your forehead. You need to get over it."*

Maybe God brought him back here to give

303

him a reset. A do-over. Gage didn't have to be a cautionary tale, not anymore.

He should go see that kid—Hunter—when they got out of this. Maybe his fame could come to some good.

In fact, maybe everything could change if he did this right. Restart with Ella in his life—yeah, he'd figure it out. Move to Vermont.

Maybe start freeriding again.

Gage sat, unlatched his boots, and snapped off the bindings from the board. Then he stood it up and unhooked the board where it latched at the top, then at the heel. He split the board, then reattached the bindings into touring mode. After standing the skis upright in the snow, he pulled out his skins, took one, and attached it to the tip of his board. He did the same with the other, pressing them tight along the bottoms.

Then he clipped his boots back into the bindings. Took a breath and sighted his line. He'd simply follow it back to Ella and the camp.

"Okay, Ella, here I come."

The howling was just the wind.

Really, it had to be.

Please.

Ella sat at the edge of the tent, shining her light out into the night through the tiny opening, her hair rising as another mournful cry hung on the wind.

Start a fire—right. She hadn't a clue how to find dry firewood in the woods, especially in the thick of night. She did well to get the stove going, melt water, and make supper.

She'd saved a cup of chili mac for Gage. Who would be back any minute.

Any. Minute.

"It's cold out there, sis. Come in and shut the door," Ollie said from behind her.

"I'm trying to keep the wolves away," she snapped. "Someone has to keep us alive, and poor Gage is out there somewhere, alone and . . ." She closed her eyes. Now she simply sounded hysterical.

She didn't do hysterical. Ever. Even when she wanted to fly apart—like watching Gage get swept away in an avalanche, or even after escaping her own avalanche—

"Do you know that I outran an avalanche looking for you today?" She glanced at Ollie. He lay on the sleeping bag, finishing off a power bar. A sheen of sweat slicked his forehead. She frowned—it wasn't that warm in here. In fact, she could still see her breath.

"Cool," Ollie said, and grinned at her.

On second thought, it was probably his own arrogance heating him from the inside. "Glad to see you're feeling better."

"Yeah. I think it was just exhaustion. I stopped

to take a breath, and the next thing I knew, you were slapping me on the face."

"I didn't slap you." She turned back to the door. "And it wasn't cool. It was terrifying. In fact, the last two days I've pretty much lived in terror trying to find you."

"You didn't have to come after me—"

"Are you kidding me? Of course I did. You're my brother, my idiot brother, but—"

"Hey." He sat up, and she noticed the quick intake of breath, as if he was in pain. "I'm not an idiot. I've been studying this route for two years. And this weekend was my chance to go down in history."

Oh. His solemn tone took some wind out of her anger. "I didn't know that. Really, you've been studying for two years?"

"Watching videos, studying the mountain."

"But you were partying the night before you left!"

"No, I wasn't. I was in the bar, yes, but I wasn't drinking. I was meeting with our chopper pilot. And okay, I might have called Gage Watson, but that was just pride talking. I'd been studying his style for so long—and then to have him track me down and take away my ski pass . . . it turned my crank."

Ollie slumped back. "Why'd you have to bring him, of all people? Now he sees me as some hotshot who needed to be rescued."

She was still trying not to see him that way. "Because he knows this mountain. And—oh never mind. Ollie, listen. I know you're angry with me—"

"I'm not ten years old anymore. I'm an adult, and I don't need you to rescue me. Or tell me I'm an idiot."

Her mouth pressed tight. "I'm sorry."

"It's fine—"

"No. I'm sorry that I didn't know you had actually prepared for this. I might not have called out the cavalry."

He nodded. "Well, it's probably good you did. Bradley needed help. And I'm still not feeling well. My head is starting to really hurt."

"How'd you get sick, anyway?"

"I don't know. Maybe the pizza?"

"I didn't have any." But Brette had, and Gage's words about Brette going to the hospital nudged her memory. "I was out looking for you."

He made a face.

"I know you're not a little kid anymore, but . . . you're still my kid brother, and you're all I have."

He opened his eyes, a little incredulity in them. "No, I'm not. You have Mom and Dad."

"They're not my mom and dad—"

"Yes, they *are*. And if you'd just slow down and realize you don't have be so awesome all the time, you'd figure out that they love you just because you're their daughter. Look at me—I spent the better part of my high school years, and yeah, maybe freshman year in college—screwing up. But they still love me."

"I know. You sooo don't deserve it." But she smiled.

"I don't. And, by the way, I know you think I'm still smoking pot, but I'm not. I kicked that six months ago when I went in training for this run. Went home, told Mom and Dad I wanted to do this. I showed them a video of me, showed them I was actually good at this. They finally told me that if that was my passion, that they would support me."

"They so did not. Not after what happened to Dylan."

"They so *did*. Accidents happen, yeah, but I'm not a child, Elle. And they get that. Mom knew I was flying out here. Do they know *you're* here?"

Oh. She shook her head. "I just assumed . . ."

"Yeah, well, you know the saying."

"I'm sorry, Ollie. I jumped to conclusions and . . . now we're out here . . ." Surrounded by wolves. Another cry hung in the air.

Ollie seemed to not hear it. "You've been busy, I get it. It's not like we talk or anything."

She sat down on her sleeping bag. "No, it's not. I'm sorry."

He lifted a shoulder. "Like I said, you're busy saving the world."

"Not saving the world, but yeah, I have people who depend on me."

"Senator."

She frowned at him.

"There you go, assuming I'm mocking you. It could be that I'm proud of you. And maybe someday you'll be proud of me."

Oh, Ollie.

Another howl drifted in on the wind.

"Is that getting closer?" Ollie asked. "Because I have a gun in my pack."

"You have a—you have a *gun?*"

"Yeah, I thought—well, bears and wolves . . . I got my permit about a year ago, right after I turned eighteen, took a bunch of classes—"

"Wow, I really don't know you."

"But you want to, don't you?" He grinned, winked.

Yeah, she sort of did. Because, in that lopsided smile, she saw him. Jovan. Cocky, smart, brave. And a touch of her father.

Here she'd spent her life trying to resemble her amazing parents, and Ollie did it by just being himself.

The howls outside sounded closer.

"Where's that gun?"

"Do you know how to use it?" Ollie asked as he pointed to his backpack. "Outside pocket."

She found a 10mm Glock and pulled it out. "I don't know what to say."

"How about yes, I know how to use this gun, bro?"

She nodded. "I've gone to the firing range a few times with Brette."

"Really?"

"She's into self-defense. She has her reasons." She scooted toward the door, holding her flashlight. She hoped he didn't chase down an explanation.

Instead he ran down a different path. "So, you and Gage spent the last two days together?"

The way Ollie said it . . . but no, he couldn't know the stirring in her heart at just the mention of Gage's name. She kept her voice even. "Like I said, he knows this mountain."

"Hmm . . . does he know you have a wicked crush on him?"

She glanced at Oliver. "What?"

"Hello. Posters? And because you went out to Outlaw three years ago to watch him freeride? Or even the fact that you still have his number in your phone?"

She said nothing.

"Sis—"

"Okay, yeah. He knows I like him. And I think he likes me back. I mean, I'm pretty sure—"

"Describe pretty sure."

She sighed. "He kissed me."

"Whoa." Ollie sat up.

Yeah, whoa, because suddenly the past twenty-four hours felt a little like she had while standing at the apex of Angel's Wings—a fast and dangerous slide into the unknown.

What exactly was she expecting? For Gage to follow her back to Vermont?

For her to stay in Montana?

"So, is this true love?" Ollie said.

"I don't know. Let's just pray he gets back in one piece. Then we can think about—"

This time, the feral moan was joined by a chorus of high-pitched, skin-prickling whines.

She unzipped the tent, shone the light into the darkness.

There, a form, a flicker of light.

What did they say about wolves' eyes in the darkness? She stood up, held the Maglite in her mouth, pointed the gun.

Movement in the woods, just on the outskirts of her light. She wanted to scream, but the light gagged her. She took the light out of her mouth.

"Go away! Shoo!"

And then, just to add emphasis to her words, she lifted the gun over her head and pulled the trigger.

The sound cracked the night, resounded through the forest, echoed against the dark vault above.

In its wake, a terrifying yell came from the woods, and the light flickered through the trees. "Yah! Git!"

Gage?

She grabbed the flashlight, shone it into the woods.

The stream of light fell on a figure running on what looked like skis through the woods, his head lamp illuminating his path.

"Gage!"

"Get in the tent!" He cleared the edge of the clearing, just ten feet away, and that's when she saw the dark form of a wolf dart behind him, into his path, snarling.

She screamed, lifted the gun, and only then realized someone had grabbed it from her.

"Get down!"

Not her voice, but Ollie's, next to her. Gage dove for the entrance of the tent just as Ollie squeezed off a round.

The night exploded with a flash of light, and a dog howled in pain, whining.

"I think I hit it!" Ollie said. He was holding his side, crouched in the snow.

Gage struggled to get his boards off. "Get in the tent right now!"

But Ollie didn't move. "Hurry up, man!" Ollie shouted.

Ella wanted to launch herself into Gage's arms, but really, that was simply adrenaline.

And joy. Because he'd come back for her.

Gage got his boards off and scrambled to his feet. "Get inside!"

Ollie scooted back inside, and Ella felt Gage's hands on her, guiding her in. She let him push her, turned, and saw him plop down beside her, pull his feet in, and zipper the door shut.

Then he just sat there, breathing hard, his chest rising and falling in great thunderous gulps.

She had no words as he unclipped his helmet, dragged it off. Then he turned and looked at Ollie, at Ella, then back to Ollie.

"I thought you were supposed to be dying or something."

Oliver nodded. "I get that sometimes." He looked pointedly at Ella.

But Ella's gaze was on Gage, so much relief coursing through her she could hardly breathe. Ice encrusted his dark beard, the ends of his hair, tendrils around his face, framing his cold-reddened cheeks. He looked like some winter explorer back from the far reaches of the earth.

"You came back," she whispered.

"I told you I would." And for a long moment, his eyes held hers, so much warmth in them she felt it through to the core of her body.

In fact, she just might burst into flames.

Then he smiled. "Got any of that chili mac left?"

Brette eased herself back onto the bed and pulled the cotton blanket up as the nurse finished checking her vitals.

"You should be ready to go home in the morning." A no-nonsense woman with short dark hair and the name Hanson on her badge, she'd come on shift and immediately made Brette get up and walk around. Brette's protests fell on deaf ears. Now, however, nurse Hanson had turned Florence Nightingale, smiling at Brette. "There's a handsome man waiting in the hallway for you. Shall I let him in when we're finished?" She lifted the edge of the blanket to check Brette's laparoscopic incision.

Brette nodded, feeling a smile curl up from inside. She'd finally found a hero worth writing about. A man without secrets, guile, or an agenda.

A man readers would be inspired by, the kind of guy who simply showed up. Loyal, sweet, compassionate. Trustworthy.

Her own words from yesterday rang in her head. *"Actually, it's harder than you think to find a true hero. Everyone has secrets, and if you look hard enough, we're all just hiding behind how we hope people view us."*

Not Ty. He seemed like a man without masks. Finally.

Brette pressed her fingers to her mouth, still feeling Ty's kiss on her lips. So soft she could have imagined it but for the way he looked at her, so much sweet longing on his handsome face.

He hadn't looked at Jess that way—Brette

saw the difference now. *"No, Jess and I are just friends."* His words had ended on a funny, almost incredulous laugh.

Her reporter's brain had simply been working overtime, fetching facts that didn't exist. Like her belief that Jess Tagg could be wealthy investment princess Selene Taggert.

Brette closed her eyes, her body aching from her walk. Ty had excused himself, and she'd suggested a run for ice cream. She didn't want him to see her cry again.

And not just because the nurse made her practically trek the entirety of the Kalispell Regional Hospital but because his words had found soft, pliable soil in her heart. *"I'm not leaving you."*

She knew what he meant. It wasn't a declaration of happily ever after or anything, but still, her empty, lonely heart hung on to his words too much.

Oh, she could get into trouble this way. She could almost hear Ella, tiptoeing into the room, sinking down onto the side of her bed. Handing her a pint of mint chocolate chip ice cream. *"No man is worth this kind of pain."*

Of course, the last time Ella did that, Brette had held the ice cream carton up to her face, her cheekbone still swollen. And then Ella had offered to drive her to the police station.

But Ty wasn't the kind of man who would

315

turn on her, lose control, treat her as if she were worthless.

"How's your pain?" Nurse Hanson asked.

"Manageable," Brette said, almost meaning it.

"You're due for another pain pill in an hour. I'll be back." She squeezed Brette's leg and headed out the door.

Brette sat up and raked her fingers through her tangled hair. She looked disastrous—a glimpse in the bathroom mirror told her that. But Ty hadn't seemed to mind—

A knock, then the door opened.

She smiled.

Pete poked his head around the corner. "Hey."

Oh. She kept her smile, feeling just a hint of a frown.

He came into the room, producing a spray of flowers in a vase. White daises, a few yellow roses. "I just wanted to come by and say I'm sorry for being a jerk earlier today." He set the flowers on a tray near the bed.

Really?

He looked like he meant his apology, the way he turned and shoved his hands into his pockets. He still wore his blond hair back in a bandanna, a grizzle of gold on his chin, and now gave her a wry smile. "I wasn't myself. Or maybe I was, but I'm trying not to be, so much."

She hadn't a clue what he meant, but his self-effacing comment had her warming to him.

316

"That's okay. I know I shouldn't pry—it's the reporter in me."

"If you want to ask about the stuff that happened last summer, I'll tell you. It's just not that exciting. And, frankly, it's not like any one of us wouldn't have done the same thing. My brother, Sam, for example, was really the one who rescued the missing kids this summer. Their van went over a cliff, and he and his girlfriend, Willow, hiked them out to safety. He nearly died doing it too. He'd make a great story."

"Oh. Okay, thanks." But that wasn't the story she was hoping for, really. "Um . . . can I ask you a question?"

He glanced down at the chair Ty had occupied. Picked it up and turned it around, straddling it. He hung his arms over the back. "Go for it."

"What about Ty? He mentioned that he used to be the main pilot before Kacey came on the scene. He was a little dodgy about why Kacey took over."

"She's a decorated pilot," Pete said.

"He said that."

"And we needed someone, especially after the crash," Pete continued. "Ty was pretty shaken up after the accident, and the ordeal—and he's still getting used to his new knee, so . . ." He lifted a shoulder. "I think Chet realized that Ty wasn't going to get back in the cockpit anytime soon. And Chet certainly couldn't do it. He can barely walk. And I'm sure there's some tension there, especially since Chet nearly died. Kacey was coming home anyway to be with her daughter, so I guess Chet saw a chance to get her on the team."

Brette just stared at him, trying to process the information. Accident. Ordeal. New knee. Chet nearly dying. "Oh, wow, uh . . ." And she was trying to figure out where to start when he held up his hand.

"Wait." Pete stood up and pulled his phone from his pocket. He answered it. " 'Sup?"

He glanced at Brette, nodded. Then, "Roger that. I'll track him down. But did you call Jess? He might be at her place." A pause. "Okay, well, I'll look around, then head back." He hung up.

When he turned back to Brette, he wore a grim expression. "We got a call from Gage. He found Oliver, but apparently he's hurt and they need an extraction. They're waiting for the winds to die down, but we might have to go in on snowmobile. Have you seen Ty?"

She was about to shake her head, but his words suddenly registered. "What did you mean, he might be at Jess's place?"

"Oh, they're dating. Let me know if he turns up." He turned to leave, was two paces to the door when he stopped. "If you need anything, consider me a friend. I'll see if I can track down my brother for that interview too."

She managed a nod, but he vanished out the door before his words could register.

She simply couldn't get past "Oh, they're dating."

Dating.

She felt as if a hand had reached in and run claws along her insides. Dating?

She couldn't breathe. Closed her eyes.

She rewound her memory to Ty leaning over the map, standing shoulder to shoulder with Jess. Wow, Brette had read that wrong.

Her memory, for a moment, focused on Jess. What else had she read wrong?

Brette slid out of bed, hobbled over to her personal effects in a plastic bag on the bed tray, and fished out her cell phone.

She climbed back into bed and pulled up her Facebook account. Searched for Selene Taggert.

Nothing.

She pulled up Instagram, did the same, then Tumblr, and finally Twitter.

Nothing.

Selene had been thorough in deleting her accounts.

Brette did a Google search and clicked on images.

Sure enough, Google still stored a few tagged photos of Selene, most of them taken during the allegations and arrest of her father. And these showed a woman with shorter hair and makeup; she was thinner, and for the most part her face was hidden by an arm, or a newspaper, or a jacket.

Inconclusive, but scrolling down she found a grainy old picture of an engagement announcement. *Selene Taggert to marry Felipe St. Augustine.* She clicked on the image, found it attached to a blog post over five years old detailing a lavish engagement party with pictures worthy of a gossip page.

26-year-old Felipe St. Augustine, heir to the 7.2 billion St. Augustine Corporation, celebrated his upcoming nuptials in a style fit for the daughter of American investment tycoon Damien Taggert.

The first shot showed beautiful Selene Taggert wearing a silver sequined dress, waving while standing in the cutout of a stretch limousine, her handsome fiancé beside her with one arm around her neck, the other holding a bottle of frothy champagne.

The second was a Vine that ran over and over of Selene on a dance floor of some New York Club, laughing as she danced with a group of people.

Brette stilled.

Selene stood in the middle of the room, one arm raised. Beside her, her fiancé bobbed, clearly laughing. And behind him, in a shot caught over and over, a man turned and flashed a smile at Selene.

Tall. Dark hair, curly around the ears. A hint of five o'clock shadow.

Brette would recognize that smile anywhere.

Ty Remington.

He wore a printed T-shirt, a suit coat with the collar up, and his sunglasses tucked in the center of his shirt.

Ty knew Selene Taggert.

The realization rushed over her.

Brette's instincts *hadn't* been addled by her appendicitis attack. Jess Tagg was Selene Jessica Taggert. More, Ty knew it.

And was hiding her.

Brette felt suddenly naked and foolish as she recalled telling him her story. He was probably out right now, warning Selene, telling her to run.

Brette leaned her head back and closed her eyes, her heartbeat hammering in her chest. She was a fool. She ached everywhere, and not just because of her surgery.

The door opened. Footsteps. Please let it be Nurse Hanson with my meds.

"I had to go all the way to the Griz, but I scored us ice cream sandwiches."

She opened her eyes and just stared at him.

Ty stood in the wan light of the room, holding two sandwiches, grinning at her.

"Get out." The words surprised even her, but she didn't pull them back.

His smile fell and he frowned, clearly rattled. "What?"

His fake innocence only raked up the hurt. The betrayal. "Get away from me. I can't believe I trusted you. You knew all this time who Jess was, and you just stood there and lied to me."

And if she was wondering if it was true, if she was simply misjudging him, the question died with the ashen hue of his face. "Brette," he said, his voice low, as if trying to calm her.

"No, I don't want to hear it. Please just leave." Her throat burned, her eyes glazed, but she refused to cry in front of him.

He set the ice cream on the table. "No."

15

"Just let me explain." Ty stood at the foot of Brette's bed, her wrecked expression like a fist inside him, punching through the layer of hope he'd constructed around himself.

He'd only known her for a few days, and it wasn't like he was asking her to marry him, but she somehow made him feel like he might be the only hero in the room.

"You, Ty, are a man worth stealing."

He might have grabbed ahold of those words, hung on to them too tightly, because he could feel them unravel in his grip as he stared at Brette. Her eyes filled and his chest tightened.

"Please, Brette—"

"I said get out." Her voice shook, though, and she seemed to have lost her previous venom.

He held up his hand. "Okay—yes, I will. But first, let me explain."

She flicked away the moisture on her face. "I don't know where you're going to start. Maybe with the truth about why you're not flying anymore? Some sort of crash?"

"How—"

"Pete told me. When he brought me flowers." She folded her hands over her chest, then tilted her head. Glanced at the bouquet of flowers on the table.

Pete had brought her flowers.

Ty could kill the man with his bare hands. "Pete was here."

"Yeah. He apologized for being a jerk. Which is a lot easier to forgive than lying."

"Brette, listen, the crash story. I—" He closed his mouth. "I don't like to talk about it."

"Apparently that's epidemic with you. There I sat, pouring out my history with the Taggerts to you, how they'd destroyed my family, practically killed my parents, and you just . . . you *protected* her. You sat there as if you didn't even know who she was. But you do—you were at her engagement party!"

"How did you . . . how do you *know* that?"

"Seriously? Google."

He came over to the chair. Sank down. "Listen, I grew up with her. Jess and I used to ski together. And yeah, I am—was—friends with her brother Barron. And her fiancé and I were roommates at Wharton. Jess's entire life fell apart when she discovered her father's fraud."

"Don't you mean Selene?"

Ty closed his mouth. Blew out a breath. "She's Jess now. Just Jess. Trying to start her life over."

"I don't think she has a right to do that after her father destroyed so many lives."

"She wasn't responsible for her father's

324

actions. She testified against him. Betrayed her entire family. Her mother disowned her, and her brother ripped her apart in the press. Her life was destroyed, and when she left New York, she had nowhere else to go. So she texted me, and I told her to come here. That I'd help her start over."

"Hide."

"Rewrite her life. She lost everything—her family, her home, her fiancé—she just needed to be safe."

"So she came to you." Brette ground her jaw so tight, it looked like she might break a few molars.

"Yes. She came to me. And I told her I'd protect her."

"And now you're dating her. Some protection, Ty."

"No!" He closed his eyes. Blew out another breath. When he opened his eyes, he put as much truth into them as he could. "We're not dating. I told you the truth about that. But Jess needs me to . . . well, she has her reasons."

"Do her reasons have to do with me?"

Ty groaned as he turned and spotted Pete standing in the doorway.

Pete's expression was so dark that Ty found his feet. Not out of fear, but frankly, he was just a little tired of all of Pete's posturing.

"Yeah, it does, Pete," Ty said, pulling no punches. "She doesn't want to date you—or at least—oh man, this is not my story to tell." He glanced at Brette, back at Pete. "I do not want to be in the middle of this."

"Clearly you are," Pete said. "What do you mean, Jess wanted to rewrite her life? That she lost everything, including"—and now he swallowed, as if trying to get the words down—"her fiancé?"

Ty could see how wounded Pete was and wanted to have some compassion for the guy. But Pete made it hard for anyone to feel sorry for him.

"Jess Tagg is really Selene Jessica Taggert," Brette said quietly. "The daughter of Damien B. Taggert."

Pete stared at Brette. "Who?"

"She's the daughter of a billionaire who bilked thousands out of their investments," Ty said.

Pete frowned.

Really? All this trouble, and the guy didn't even know what Ty was talking about. "Pete, she testified against her own father. He was sentenced to 150 years in prison."

Pete's mouth opened then. Just a moment of disbelief before he blew out a breath. "Wow."

"Yeah, and knowing how you felt about being betrayed—"

Pete held up his hand. "Trust me, I feel more betrayed about the fact she acted like you two were dating."

Oh. That. "Sorry—"

"Wait a minute. Pete, did you not hear him?" Brette said. "She *lied* to you."

Pete stared at her. Then, quietly, "I heard him." Then he looked at Ty. "Miles wants us back at HQ. We need to get into Heaven's Peak and pick up Gage and Ella. They found Oliver."

Then he turned and left, leaving Ty standing there, nonplussed.

He looked at Brette.

"He might not care who Jess Tagg is, but I do. And pretty soon, so will the world."

"Brette—"

"No. She owes the world an explanation. She doesn't just get to start over. She . . . she . . ." She was crying again, and he hated that even in her fury, he wanted to reach past it, pull her to himself.

Tell her that if she just took a breath, she might see this from a different perspective. But then again, he understood exactly how it felt o feel bereft, to have life pulled out from beneath you.

Longing to figure out how to find your footing again.

"Please, just wait until we can talk about this—"

"No. I trusted you. I . . . I thought you cared about me."

"I *do* care about you—"

"And I even kissed you. How stupid can I be?"

She shook her head, her voice falling, breaking. "I just never learn."

Never learn? "You're not stupid—"

"Stop." She looked at him then. "Admit it. The minute you saw that I recognized her, you decided to run interference. That's what the ride to PEAK, the babysitting was all about."

He shook his head, but he knew she saw right through him. "Maybe at first, but—"

He could have punched her with less effect. She winced, and he felt it in his own solar plexus.

He pitched his voice low. "Brette, I do care about you. And I know you think I should have told you, but it wasn't my secret to tell. I got caught in the middle, but I promise you—that kiss, for me, meant something. Please, just trust me—"

"Get out."

He took a breath.

"I mean it, Ty. Any trust I had in you died the moment you chose Selene over me. You can't have both."

"I didn't choose—"

"Get. *Out!*"

He froze, then gave her a tight, sad nod. "Okay, Brette, if that's the way you want it."

She drew in a breath, wrapped her arms around her waist. "What other way could it ever be? I'll never be able to trust you again."

Then she rolled over, her back to him.

He walked past his soggy ice cream sand-wiches and out of her room.

Gage needed to get off this mountain and back into his life.

No, into a *new* life. One that included Ella.

He sat at the mouth of the tent, holding a blackened stick, occasionally stirring the fire back to life. Reaching over to his pile of kindling, he added a thick branch that would have to do for a log. His fire wouldn't win any Boy Scout awards, but at least he'd found kindling, enough low-hanging, dry branches to keep a feeble blaze alive.

Sparks spit into the waning night. Already, the dent of morning pressed against the black, a shade of lavender with hints of gold against the jagged horizon to the east.

He felt stupid to have to tell Kacey in the morning that they didn't need to airlift Oliver out, but better that he'd been wrong about Oliver's condition than to have the guy bleeding internally or going into shock. Gage had checked his bruising, and it hadn't seemed to be deepening.

Foolish decision, good outcome. This time.

Behind him, in the tent, Gage heard stirring. Probably Ella tossing in her sleeping bag. He'd dozed off in front of the fire for a while, the heat from the flames melting the snow around the circle he'd built.

Although Oliver's gunshot seemed to have scared the pack away, Gage couldn't be sure the wolves weren't lurking in the ring of forest, watching.

Waiting for Gage to let his guard down, make a mistake.

He ran his hand over his eyes, rubbing the sleep from them. Maybe he should have taken Ella up on her offer to let him sleep in the middle between her and Oliver, but it just felt too awkward. Besides, someone had to make sure they didn't get eaten.

Behind him, the zipper sounded, and he turned to see Ella climbing out. "What are you doing?" he whispered. "Stay in there and get some sleep."

She had pulled her hair back and secured it with a wool headband. She wore her ski pants and jacket and now settled beside him. "I can't sleep."

"I won't let the wolves get you." He meant it playfully, but her eyes widened. "I'm kidding."

"About saving me from the wolves? I hope not." Then she smiled, and he surrendered to the sweet comfort of having her sit beside him. She stared up at the stars, the faintest hint of the Milky Way still foggy in the sky. "So, what's next?"

He lifted a shoulder. "Easy. We wait until morning, get on our boards, and head down. We just have to ski through the rest of the Cathedral,

330

and then there's a final five-hundred-foot drop down to the base. I call it Bishops Cap because there's usually a pretty thick cornice at the top. Avalanche country."

She nodded. "Actually, I meant . . ." She bit her lip. "Well, what's next . . . for us."

Us.

He let the word settle in. A smile tipped his face, and he let it show in his eyes. "Us."

She shrugged, then looked away.

"I like the sound of *us,*" he said quietly.

"You said earlier that you were freaking out."

A log fell, and sparks lit the sky. "Yeah, I know. And if I sit here and think about my mistakes, and how I don't deserve another chance with you, I'll freak out again." He glanced at her, painfully aware of his heart, beating and vulnerable, on his sleeve.

She was looking at him, however, so much emotion in her eyes, it took his breath away. "Kind of like how I felt when you walked back into my life—I longed for a way to tell you I was sorry. I've spent the last three years wishing to rewind time, wishing I could fix the past."

"It's done, Ella. It's over—"

She was shaking her head. "I need to tell . . ." She sighed, and he frowned when she looked up at him, her eyes wet.

"What's the matter?"

"You know why I became a lawyer?"

"To make your parents proud?"

She shook her head. "Because I hate injustice. And recklessness. And the fact that people make selfish decisions that affect the lives of others. That's why I opposed this bill on loosening the regulations on the use of recreational marijuana. People put their personal comfort over the well-being of others and it's . . . wrong. And there's nothing to protect people from the carelessness of others."

She was crying now, and he couldn't help but reach up, thumb a tear away.

"Yeah, it is," he said. "Being on the PEAK team has taught me that."

"I just hate that people like you have to put their lives on the line for . . . people who don't deserve it."

"But it happens every day, and just because people are careless, or even intentional in their recklessness, doesn't change the fact that we have to go out and rescue them. We do it not because they deserve rescue but because that's what we do. That's who we are."

"I know. And that's why . . ." She took a deep breath. "You have to know that I fell in love with you three years ago, Gage, because you were this guy. The kind of guy who tries to do what is right. I just got confused with all the shock of Dylan's death. His parents, and then the case, but . . . I realized today that . . ."

He stilled.

"I'm still in love with you."

Her words rushed over him, taking with them his breath. He could barely scrounge up his voice. *She loved him.*

And yeah, the response forming inside felt like leaping off the Weeping Wall or plummeting down Angel's Wings, a rush of heady adrenaline, even a little fear. But he had come this far. "I never stopped loving you, either."

She gave him the smallest hint of a smile then, and he couldn't help himself. He leaned forward and captured her beautiful lips with his. Hers were still warm from the tent, and he reached up and cupped her soft cheek with his hand.

Ella loved him.

She leaned into his touch, surrendering into him, and he moved his hand behind her neck, scooted closer, and deepened his kiss.

And wow, he loved her back. The fullness of it rushed over him, took hold. Yes, they'd get off this mountain and then . . . then . . .

Kissing Ella tasted like the past he'd lost, the cheers and dreams and epic heights of being a champion, and yet . . . so much more. She was kissing the man he'd been but also the man he *wanted* to be. The man trying to break free of his regrets, reaching out to freedom, forgiveness, a fresh start.

A man who longed for tomorrow.

Suddenly, that old stir of adventure, of abandon ignited inside him. Cascaded through him, caught fire.

He leaned away from her, caught her eyes. "Ella. I don't know what it is about you, but seeing you again has made me wonder if maybe . . . I don't know. I've been stuck. Like I never really escaped that avalanche, but I was afraid to dig myself out because I knew that I didn't have a right to start over, be free. But then you said . . . you said that you wanted to believe in a God who was on our side." His eyes burned, and he blinked away the smoke.

"The thing is, I haven't exactly been on my knees much after Dylan's accident. In fact, I've been pretty mad at God. See, God and I had a deal. I knew the danger and I could handle it. I didn't expect God to rescue me. Then Dylan came along, and I thought that since I was trying to actually protect him that God would have my back. But he didn't—and Dylan died. And it felt like God broke the deal."

"God doesn't make deals."

"I know. But I never thought that doing something I thought was right would backfire . . . and when it did . . ."

"So, what you're saying is that you don't trust God."

He looked away. "Yeah. And why would God

334

help someone who didn't trust him? I don't deserve his help."

He reached out, caught her hand, and laced his fingers through hers.

"But then God saved us from an avalanche, and helped us find Bradley, and even kept your brother alive . . . and maybe we're not alone out here."

He stared at her hand in his.

"I grew up with parents who told me that my life mattered—and to go do something about that. And then I landed inside my own limelight, and it blinded me. I forgot who I was and why I was there. I started to believe that my fame was about me. And then when it began to drown me, I labeled it as evil. But what if—what if it wasn't? What if I was supposed to use it for good?"

"To whom much is given . . ." she said softly.

He frowned at her.

"It's something my parents used to say."

"Hmm. I was thinking . . . Maybe I could start competing again and . . ." He turned to face her. . "You could come with me."

She raised an eyebrow. "Like a groupie?"

"Like . . . a girlfriend. Or . . ." He swallowed.

She caught her breath, and her widened eyes suggested that he might be bombing the hill, picking up too much speed.

Clearly, yes, because she pulled away. "Wait, Gage, you have to know something. I've been trying to figure out a way to tell you . . ."

335

Her tone stilled him. Oh no. "You're not dating anyone, are you?"

"What? No. Just . . ." She closed her eyes. Winced.

Her expression shot a chill through him. "You're scaring me a little here, El. What's going on?"

"Please, let me get this out." Her low tone sounded more like a prayer than a request to him. Then she blew out a breath and looked at the flames of the fire.

And now he *was* freaking out.

"There's something you need to know about the civil case."

He let out a sigh. That was what the fuss was all about? "No, Ella, let's not talk about that. It's behind us—"

"You weren't to blame for Dylan's death."

Huh?

She swallowed, met his gaze. "Dylan McMahon had marijuana in his system when he went down Terminator Wall."

He couldn't breathe; her words were a blow right to the center of his solar plexus.

"What? How do you know that?"

She cringed then. "Oh, Gage, I'm so sorry. You deserved to know, but I wasn't allowed to tell you. Even now, it's in violation of my code of ethics, but I just can't bear you believing you're at fault. You didn't cause Dylan's death."

He frowned at her words. "Yeah, I'm pretty sure I did. I shouldn't have let him go down the Wall."

"He told you himself that he would go without you. What choice did you have?"

He looked away from her.

"Dylan's parents had an autopsy done on him. The lab report came back with evidence of THC."

With her words, her expression turned stricken.

Oh Ella. Always finding a way to blame herself. He took her cold hand. "That doesn't mean he was high that day—THC stays in your urine for days. And if Dylan was a regular user, it could be found in his body up to ten days afterward, sometimes longer."

Gage didn't want to go back to that day, to remember Dylan suited up and waiting for him at the chopper. He hadn't checked, hadn't asked, just warned him to stay on his line.

Gage wasn't unfamiliar with the telltale signs of weed, a guy too stoned to ride. If he'd done more than gotten on the chopper, practically ignoring Dylan, if he'd taken a moment to think past his run, and how he'd make it epic for the cameras . . .

"But here's the important part," she said. "It doesn't matter if he was high or not. The test would have been enough to cause reasonable doubt, get the decision reversed." She swallowed then. "And if I'd had the courage to stand up for

337

what I believe in, you'd still have your career today."

He stared at her, her words hitting home.

"You could have saved me?"

Slowly, she nodded.

"And you didn't."

Her mouth tightened into a bud of grim assent.

He just stared at her. Moved his hand away.

"Gage—"

"Stop. Just . . . I need a minute here." He stared at the fire.

"I had to tell you . . . I thought, how could we start over if—"

"No. How could we start over. Period." He looked at her. "That lawsuit *destroyed* everything I'd worked for, Ella. My career, my awards, my sponsorships, gone. And yes, I made mistakes, but the press eviscerated me. They tore my life apart, some even called me a murderer. My mother practically had a nervous breakdown, started drinking. And I lost everything I loved."

She just stared at him. "I know. I'm sorry."

He had nothing. Then, tightly, "You're *sorry*. Yeah, well, me too."

"Gage—"

He held up his hand, a stiff arm to her words. "Don't."

"Gage! You're not the only one whose life was destroyed over it. I quit my job—"

"You became a senator. I chase down hotshot skiers. Big difference there, honey."

She sucked in a breath, as if he'd slapped her, and he had to look away.

He didn't know why her words skewered him. He'd agreed with the lawsuit, agreed with his own culpability, and if he had to surrender everything to help the McMahon family cope with their loss, it was a small price to pay. He'd practically begged his lawyer to settle the case.

Maybe if he hadn't, his attorney would have pushed harder, found the truth, but Gage agreed to everything the plaintiffs asked for without a blink.

Still, he could way too easily conjure up the image of Ella sitting across the room with the enemy camp, again feel a fist closing over his heart as he watched her betray him.

He couldn't breathe.

"I can only say I'm sorry so many times," she said finally.

"Me too," he said quietly. "The difference is, I'm sorry that I couldn't keep Dylan from killing himself on the slopes. *You're* sorry because you knew the truth but let me burn anyway."

Her quick intake of breath made him want to turn, to push it all away—the hurt, the anger, the way the night had turned crisp and dark, the stars winking out as dawn approached. He wanted to rewind time back five minutes and take her in his arms, forget the past and even the future and hold on to the place where none of it mattered but now.

But it did matter. All of it. He didn't move.

"Yes," she said softly. "Yes, I did."

"Yes, I did."

Her own words sat like a stone in her heart as Ella considered Gage. He sat, his knees drawn up, his arms hanging over them, staring into the fire. Her words seemed to flicker in his eyes.

"You knew the truth but let me burn anyway."

She blinked, hating the rim of tears, and turned back to the tent. "The sun will be up soon. I'll make some breakfast."

He nodded, and she caught her breath when he didn't even look at her.

She should have known this would happen. Of course he'd feel betrayed.

"That lawsuit destroyed my life, Ella."

And she'd dragged him out here, rekindled the past, even hinted at a future, all the time harboring the secret she knew would destroy him all over again.

She glanced back through the doorway. Gage hadn't moved.

Probably thinking about how she'd manipulated him, again.

Or . . . maybe thinking about how he could

reopen the case, maybe get the judgment against him vacated.

Which would mean betraying her to the authorities. Which, probably, she deserved. Still . . .

To whom much is given . . .

She, too, had been given much, and look what she'd accomplished. A useless term in office, the destruction of Gage's livelihood . . . all because she'd been trying to prove something. Take control of her life, make sure it mattered.

That she was worth the effort God made to save her.

Ollie lay on his back, his mouth open, still sunk into slumber. She shucked off her jacket, wiped her hand across her cheek as she reached for the stove. She needed water, so she ducked her head outside and scooped up some nearby snow.

Gage didn't look at her.

She could fix this—she just needed a minute to figure it out, to take it all apart . . .

"Sis?"

She looked up to see Ollie staring at her.

"You look upset."

"I'm fine, Ollie. Go back to sleep. I'm getting breakfast made."

"My head really hurts." He winced.

"I don't see why. It's as hard as granite."

She smiled at him, but he didn't move, his eyes fixed.

"How bad is it?" she asked, leaning over him.

His body jerked, hard, and he started to flail.

"Ollie!"

She grabbed his arm, but it shook out of her grasp. His eyes rolled back. Then his entire body went rigid, arching up.

"Gage! Help! He's having a seizure."

But Gage was already there, appearing by her side. "Help me roll him to his side, in case he vomits," he said, his voice calm. He put his hands on Ollie's shoulders. "Get his head."

She fought to control her breath as she steadied Ollie's head. "What's the matter with him?" She smoothed Ollie's hair back.

"I don't know," Gage said. "Could be from the head injury. Maybe a stroke—"

"A stroke! He was fine! He talked to me just a few seconds ago!"

"I don't know, Ella." Gage pressed his fingers to Oliver's neck, against the carotid artery. Timed it against his watch. "His pulse is a little high."

Ollie's body suddenly went limp.

"Let's roll him onto his back."

She held his head and they rolled him to his back. Gage opened his eyes. "Pupils are reactive, but slow. One is more dilated than the other."

"What does that mean?"

He sat back on his haunches. "It could be a brain bleed."

A brain bleed? Her voice cut low. "He was

fine. He was laughing last night and—he just asked me if I was okay."

Gage looked up at her then, as if registering her words. She looked away.

Silence passed between them.

Then Gage said, "We need to get him to help ASAP."

"How are we going to do that?"

He ran a hand across his forehead. "We can't wait for the PEAK team. I don't know when they'll get here." He looked at her. "We'll have to get creative."

She just stared at him.

"We can make a stretcher out of the sleeping bags, reinforce it with the tent poles. But I'll need help carrying him out."

She nodded.

"We'll take the trail I took last night, get out to the ridge, call PEAK, and get an extraction." He was already moving toward the door. "Let's get him inside the bag. Get his helmet on him. I'll work on creating a litter."

He disappeared out of the tent.

"Oh Ollie, stay with me. Please be okay." Her hands shook as she tucked Ollie into Gage's sleeping bag and zippered it up. His head wound hadn't looked that bad. Still, she had a memory of that destroyed helmet.

She clipped on his helmet, then cinched the sleeping bag drawstring around his face. He looked like a mummy, frail, his skin pale.

Gage came back inside. "Okay, I found a couple long branches that should work."

She hadn't a clue what he was talking about and could only watch as he took her sleeping bag and pulled it back outside.

"Grab my pack, Ella. I need the ropes and carabiners."

She pushed the pack out of the tent, then climbed out and brought it over to him. The sunrise turned the snow to gray shadows tipped in gold. The fire had died down. Gage crouched next to a couple thick branches about the width of her wrist. He had unzipped the bottom of her bag, leaving the rest attached, and now took both poles and shoved them into the bag. "He can lie in the middle, and it'll make a sort of sling for him," Gage said without looking at her.

She handed him her pack, and he set it on the ground, then dug out the rope he'd used to secure their tent to the rock. "We'll strap him in. And then we'll just have to do our best not to jar him."

Much. He didn't add that, but she felt it in the quick, grim look he gave her.

"Help me get him out."

She climbed into the tent, grabbed Ollie's feet as Gage took his shoulders. They grunted, easing Ollie out of the tent.

Only when they had him settled on the makeshift litter did she look up and see the cloud cover. "Is it going to snow?"

"It might. Or it might pass us, but we need to get going." He had strapped Ollie into that stretcher, running the rope around his shoulders, across his body, down to his feet. Roughly three feet of branch length emerged from the top.

Then he took his ski poles and ran them horizontally across the top. Secured them with webbing from his bag.

"Are we going to carry him?" Ella asked, moving her hand over Ollie's nose and mouth to make sure he was still breathing.

"We'll ski him out."

She raised an eyebrow. "How—"

"We'll need his board." He grabbed Ollie's board and set it beneath the lower end of the stretcher, binding the board to the bottom. "It'll flow over the snow better."

Finally, he took her backpack and unclipped the straps. These, he secured to the rope near Ollie's feet. "This is for you to hold on to, to help guide him down in case things go south. We'll have to leave the pack behind, but be sure and grab anything out of it you need. You can add it to my pack."

She stared at the makeshift stretcher, and her brother strapped into it like something out of a survival reality show, and shook her head. "This is crazy, Gage. We can't carry him out on this."

Gage was dismantling the tent in record time.

He shoved it into its tiny carrier, then packed it in his bag.

Now, he stood up, buckled his pack on. "Did you get everything from your pack?"

She nodded and turned to get her board, but he caught her arm.

She looked up, met his eyes.

And whatever hurt, whatever anger he'd held in them before, had vanished. Instead, he wore a look of dark determination. "Trust me, Ella. I'll get him home safely."

She nodded. Because it didn't matter if she deserved it or not, Gage was a hero.

And she trusted him with everything inside her.

That had never been her problem, really. It was getting *him* to trust her.

"I do," she said.

He drew in a breath, nodded.

He tried PEAK one last time before he dropped his board at the head of the stretcher. He clipped in his boots, then picked up the ends of the branches, holding Ollie up in his grip. Ollie's head was raised to nearly waist height.

She stepped up behind him, grabbed the webbing. The sun was just starting to hover over the eastern rim of the earth, gilding the snow.

Tiny flurries swirled in the sunlight, probably whisked up by the wind.

"Let's go," he said. "Just stay in my line and we'll all get down this mountain in one piece."

16

Please, God, let me not be killing Ella's brother.

The prayer simply bubbled up, more like a moan of desperation as Gage wound his way toward the ridge. He'd tried to make the ride as smooth as he could for Oliver, but the trail he'd cut last night was designed for speed, not comfort.

He tried to cushion the jarring of the drops between trees with his knees and arms. Occasionally, Ella, behind him, let out a tiny gasp of terror, but she stayed on his line without a word.

His entire body ached. And not just from the fatigue of staying up most of the night, but . . . he longed to rewind this day, back to last night. To before her revelation of her betrayal.

They came to a clearing, the morning sun turning the snow to crystal, the powder thick, save the groove he'd made through it last night. He skidded to a stop, breathing hard.

Oops, too fast, because Ella slid up behind him, nearly tumbling over into the stretcher, bypassing it with a quick cut, a spray of powder.

"Gage!"

"Sorry, I should have given you warning." He set Oliver down, rolled his shoulders.

She glanced at him. "No, it's fine." She fell

to her knees, scooted over to Oliver. "He's still out. But he's breathing."

He pulled out his walkie and put in a test call. No answer.

She pushed herself up. "How far are we from the ridge?"

"Maybe another hour, at the speed we're going."

He sort of expected her to press him to go faster, but she just nodded, her mouth grim.

He couldn't take it. "Ella, listen, about this morning. I was just . . . you just . . ." What? Because suddenly he ached to put it behind them. Wasn't that his hope in moving home, to Mercy Falls? To break free of his mistakes?

You're not the only one whose life was destroyed over it.

Maybe not like his, but clearly neither of them had emerged unbroken.

And he was tired of looking over his shoulder, of trying to piece together his life.

I don't care. It doesn't matter.

Yes, that's what he wanted to say, wanted to cross the distance to her, pull her into his arms.

Start over, like the pristine grace of a fresh snowfall.

She shook her head. "Let's just get Ollie down, and then I promise I'll never bother you again."

Right. Priorities.

Still. "You're not a bother, Ella," he said, and picked up Oliver.

Her eyes widened. "You've got to be kidding. I'm completely a bother." She picked up the tail end. "Let's go."

He urged his board forward and started down again slowly through the trees. The sun bled through the shaggy pines, fingers of shadow pressing on the powder between glimpses of golden light. Such silence sliding through the trees like this nothing but the swish of their boards. He loved freeriding, getting lost between the trees.

Maybe, someday, he could start over.

Oh, who was he kidding? The accident and the lawsuit shattered his pro career. No sponsor would take him now . . .

And yet, a little voice he couldn't help hearing whispered, *So?* He liked his life with PEAK Rescue. Liked saving lives. No, he couldn't change the past, make Ella break her confidentiality, and resurrect his career. He could only choose what he did next.

What if he just . . . forgave her? No one was forcing him to hold this grudge, to hate her for not sacrificing herself for him.

She cared for him. And just a couple hours ago, he was sure he loved her.

He felt the change in the wind even before they reached the ridge. Sharp and frigid, it thundered up his jacket, turned his overheated body into a shiver.

They came out to the ridge, the snow sweeping

off it into the drop below. This time, Ella came up slowly, as if sensing the danger.

The sun had risen and now turned Crystal Point and the Going-to-the-Sun Range a glorious, snow-capped lavender. But the wind buffeted his helmet, his jacket, raising the collar. No way PEAK would be able to bring the chopper in.

He made the call anyway. "PEAK HQ, this is Watson, come in. Over."

Almost instantly he heard Jess's voice. "Watson, PEAK HQ. We've been trying to reach you. The chopper is a no-go. We've sent Ty and Pete in on snowmobiles. Over."

"When?"

"Two hours ago. They're planning on meeting you at the base of Bishops Cap. Over."

"Wilco. Are you in radio contact?"

"Roger." She gave him the frequency.

"We'll ski along the ridge, then down the northern edge of Bishops Cap. If I can't get ahold of them, tell them to look for us on the eastern wall."

"Wilco. How's Oliver?"

"Not good. He had a seizure. How's Bradley?"

"Your dad operated on him last night. Says he'll be fine."

He glanced at Ella, who was standing away, listening, her arms wrapped around her waist.

"Okay, we'll see you in a few. Watson out."

He slipped the walkie back into his pocket. Met Ella's gaze. "You can do this."

She nodded.

Then he knelt by Ollie, took off his glove, and took his pulse.

Regular, if not a bit fast, but it bothered Gage that Oliver hadn't woken up. Maybe if he had more than EMT training, he'd know what to do.

He put his glove back on. "Let's go. Pete and Ty are on their way on snowmobiles."

She moved over to the back of the stretcher.

"Listen, we'll take it slow along this ridge—it's pretty steep, but we'll skirt the trees. It'll come out on Bishops Cap."

She nodded. "I'm with you."

He hated how much he wished that were true.

He picked up the stretcher, his shoulders burning, but started the slide across the ridge, along the cornice. His thighs burned as gravity and the wind fought to push them over the edge.

He heard Ella breathing hard behind him and realized that she was probably in agony, holding onto the rope as if to slow them down.

This wouldn't work once they reached Bishops Cap. The steep, nearly straight-down face would push the stretcher down on top of Gage, regardless of his strength. And Ella couldn't hold it back.

Unless . . .

He had it worked out by the time they topped

the cornice at the peak of Bishops Cap. A painfully steep drop, edged on one side by runnels of granite, and along the other side by another deep bowl. The snow glistened pure and unblemished, deceptive. When Gage had taken his epic run, he'd run the bowl fast, cutting hard the entire way down. But he'd never manage that with their makeshift stretcher.

"Ella, do you think you can cut a line down this?"

He glanced at her, and she let go of the rope, unbuckled one boot, and skated up next to him. Stared over.

He said nothing, but he hoped she read in his words exactly what he meant.

I trust you.

To cut a line, yeah, but also to help him figure out tomorrow. How to be the guy who made the right choices and didn't let his mistakes take him down, but turned them over to God.

Maybe even to trust God, believe that he had something good for Gage.

So he let his question hang in the air.

She turned to him, finally. "I think so. Why?"

"We're going to go down this backward. I'll turn him around, go behind you. You guide us down."

A flare of panic, or perhaps just doubt, flashed in her eyes. But she turned again to the slope. "Okay, let's do this."

And right then, all the residual anger broke away. Ella might have been the woman who'd stood against him three years ago, but she'd done it because she'd been trapped, just like him.

It was time to set them both free.

"You can do this, Ella. And this time, I'll be right behind *you*."

She blinked at him, then nodded and gave him a whisper of a smile. Then she knelt beside Oliver. "I am believing you can hear me, Ollie. You're going to be okay. Just hang on." Then she pressed a kiss to his forehead.

He frowned, began to squirm.

"Oliver?" Gage knelt beside him, too, raised an eyelid.

Pupils reactive to the light. Oliver groaned. "Leave me alone."

"Not quite, pal," Gage said.

Oliver opened his eyes, looked around, clearly confused.

Ella leaned into his line of vision. "Ollie, it's okay. You had a seizure. But we nearly have you down the mountain—just hang on, okay?"

He frowned again, fear in his eyes.

"You're in good hands," Gage said, meaning Ella, but she nodded.

"Gage will get you down."

He looked over at her, then back to Oliver. "No, *we* will get you down."

Oliver swallowed, and his eyes fluttered closed.

Gage stepped in front of the stretcher, turned, and grabbed the stretcher in a dead lift. Wow, Oliver had gained ten pounds in the last five minutes.

Ella took the front end line.

"Big, sweeping turns, okay?"

She nodded. Then with a smile she said, "Try and stay in my line."

No problem.

Just go slow. Ella kept the words in her head, turning them over and over as she slid down Bishops Cap. Steeper than it looked in the pictures online, the face was more a spoon, dropping fast into a long run at the bottom.

She just had to make it down the face. She gripped the line, guiding the stretcher on the thin board, glancing back now and again at Gage, who braked with everything he possessed, trying not to run her over. He had to be in agony, his legs on fire.

And it was up to her to guide them home. "No, *we* will get you down," he'd said to Ollie.

It was the first time he'd said that—*we,* together, like a team.

She didn't know what to do with the confusion stirring inside her.

The wind whipped off the edge of the bowl, and it caught her, threw her off balance. She held out her arms, fighting for control, her legs shaking. If she went over the edge of the lip, she'd fall into the next bowl.

And that one boasted a cornice just waiting to collapse.

She made her turn, wide and gentle, brought the makeshift sled around, and traversed her way across the bowl, the other direction, toward the ridge.

"You're doing great!"

Gage's voice carried on the wind, and she glanced back at him. He held up the sled as if he'd been lifting weights his entire life. Nodded at her. "But keep your eye on the slope!"

Right. She skidded toward the next turn, took it easy and wide. Gage followed her.

See, this wasn't so hard. Just one turn at a time, not unlike how she'd slarved Angel's Wings.

And maybe that was the key to figuring out how to get Gage to trust her again, to prove to him that she wouldn't betray him.

Just go slow. Keep it easy. Except nothing felt slow or easy with Gage. Theirs had been a whirlwind romance from the beginning. Sure, he hadn't actually asked her out until the third day, but by then they'd spent nearly every waking hour together.

She had already given away her heart to Gage Watson by the time he walked away from their table.

So maybe she couldn't go slow . . . but she wouldn't pressure him. Wouldn't make him feel as if he was stuck with her, just because he'd rescued her brother.

At the bottom, still a few hundred feet down, she spied a couple of snowmobiles emerge from the thick forest. They angled up toward the snowfield at the base of their bowl.

"Pete and Ty!" she yelled.

He didn't answer her, so she looked back. "Pete and Ty are below!" She pointed down.

But he was looking at her. "Turn, Ella! Turn!"

She whirled around and saw the lip of the bowl coming up, too fast. She cut hard, fighting to bring Ollie's feet around, but the action swung the sled around too hard.

Like a whip, Gage flew over the edge, taking Ollie with him.

"Gage!"

Her grip on the backpack strap twisted her around, hard, and in a second she landed on her backside, the strap ripping out of her glove.

But she didn't have time to call out, because the force of it turned her over, and suddenly, she was sliding.

Face first, down the mountain, plowing into the thick powder.

This was how people ended up in tree wells, buried head first, never to be seen again. She rolled her feet up and around in a moment, edged her board hard into the slope.

Too hard. A burn shot into her ankle, lighting it

afire, and she couldn't stop herself from crying out.

But the scream disappeared into the frothy white silence of the powder still drifting down around her.

She lay there a moment, unmoving.

And then, "Ollie!"

She pushed herself up and barely made out the pair of them. Gage had flown into the next bowl, a thick, powdered section riddled with trees and rocks. No doubt that without his charge, Gage could easily handle the terrain, maybe even turn the run into something spectacular.

But not now. Now he flew down the hill backward, dragging Ollie behind him.

Oh Gage. She watched, stranded, her heart thundering as he fought his way down the steep slope, clearly trying to slow them down or even stop. But the board ran with a mind of its own. Gage barely steered them around trees and boulders.

Then, in what seemed a superhuman move, Gage managed to swing the sled around, maneuver himself behind it.

And slow them to a stop.

He bent over, breathing hard, halfway down the slope.

She let out the breath she'd been holding.

Then, suddenly, he looked up as if searching for her.

"I'm over here!" She tried to push to her feet,

357

but her ankle screamed in pain, so she stayed on her knees, waving. "I'm fine!"

Just a little lie, but maybe he'd heard her because he waved back. Gestured her to come to him.

And oh, how she wanted to. Force herself to her feet, fight her way down the hill. Help Gage bring her little brother to safety.

Except for her ankle. And the very real sense that Gage really didn't need her. Had never needed her. Frankly, had been humoring her this entire time. And she'd nearly gotten him and her brother seriously injured.

As she pushed to her feet, the pain shot up her leg, nearly sent her back to her knees.

Below, Gage had clearly spied the guys because he began to inch his way down the slope with Ollie. They angled for him, cutting a line through the snow, the motors from their machines thundering in the air despite the distance.

She gritted her teeth, began to slide down.

Her ankle gave out on her, the pain blinding, and she sat again in the snow. She'd have to scoot down, on her bottom. Except the powder was too thick, and she found herself just digging a hole.

Below, Ty and Pete had reached Gage. They were maneuvering Ollie onto the emergency rescue sled attached to the snowmobile.

For a moment, she dearly wished one of them might see her stranded on the hillside and head her direction. But the powder would bury the sled as they plowed uphill.

She had to get to them.

Ho-kay. This couldn't be harder than delivering a four-hour speech to her fellow senators, a filibuster move that had backfired.

Except, this couldn't backfire.

Now Gage had turned, was looking up at her. She saw him wave.

She waved back. *Yeah, I'm just fine. Enjoying the view.*

Tears filled her eyes as she got up, gritted her teeth. Pointed her snowboard downhill.

Gage was still waving, now both hands in the air.

Huh?

She raised her hands too, held them out, like a giant shrug.

And then, Gage was moving, still waving his arms.

Yeah, she knew she was taking her time but—

And then she heard it. A crack, then a low rumble behind her.

She went cold as she turned.

Just to confirm the truth.

The cornice had unlatched from the top.

The mountain was coming down in waves of thick snow.

She screamed as she aimed her board straight downhill and flew.

17

Ella couldn't outrun the slide.

Gage saw it even before the entire cornice broke off—maybe due to the roar of the snowmobiles, he didn't know—but he did the quick geometry.

Even if she headed straight down, the waves of snow would overtake her, bury her. Entomb her in ice.

Was she wearing her beacon? He couldn't remember—it had been clipped to her backpack, but he'd emptied it when he stripped off the straps, and left it behind at the campsite.

She might have picked the beacon up, but . . .

His was clipped securely to his body.

While she could be lost in a tsunami of snow.

The thought hit him like a fist as he watched her bend low, shoot down the hill, racing the wave of snow.

He shouldn't have let her come with him. Should have stopped her from getting on that chopper.

He'd led her to her death. Just like Dylan—

Unless he got to her first.

God, please make me fast.

Behind him, he heard Pete yelling over the roar of the snowmobiles, where they were packing up Oliver for delivery. Pete had him unwrapped and had been checking his vitals and radioing them into PEAK HQ when Gage saw the cornice start to slip.

Now, as the tumult of snow raged down the mountain, he kept his eyes on Ella, who was bending over her board to increase her speed.

Stay on your edge.

If only he hadn't made her go first, cut the line—but he couldn't go there now.

He set a course to intercept, his board on one slick edge as he cut downhill at a diagonal. He went right up over the lip of the bowl into the path of the slide.

She screamed his name as she shot across his path, and he cut hard, turned his board, and lit out after her.

The forward trickles of the slide swept past him, the full force thundering down just yards behind him. Ella looked back over her shoulder and reached out to him.

He caught her hand. And then in a second had his arms around her, pulling her against him.

But they couldn't ski this way and get out of the path of danger. "Put your board on my feet!"

He lifted her up and she set her board on his boots. Now he could move. "Hang on!"

She didn't argue, just put her arms around his neck, leaning into his movements.

Good girl.

He held her tight against him as he cut hard

361

again and headed out, toward the edge of the flow.

But the swell had reached them. It caught them up in the force of the flow.

"We can't get separated!" Gage fought to stay on his feet, to balance with the tumult of the wave. The powder and debris rose around him, engulfing them, turning the world white.

Ella started to scream.

"I can't hold you—don't let go!" He began to swim with his arms, moving the snow away from them even as he rode the slide down. It crested over his head, a cloud of white, blinding him.

Just stay calm.

The thunder of the force filled his ears, and he wrapped one arm again around Ella as he thrashed to keep upright. He had to stay above the debris of rock, tree—anything the slide had mowed down on its way down the mountain.

He felt the wave lift them, and Ella's arms around him loosened.

"Ella!"

He clamped both arms around her and squeezed, leaning back to keep his feet under him.

But the snow crested over his head, a hand on his back, his shoulders, slamming him forward.

And then they were in the wash, tumbling, their bodies at the mercy of the slide.

He felt his board rip off his boots, a violent twisting of his ankles, and beside him, deep inside the surge of the wave, he could hear Ella's muffled screams.

Boulders of snow slammed his back, his shoulders, and he focused on holding Ella to him, despite the wrath of the slide fighting to rip her from his embrace.

He couldn't breathe, not with the snow filling his mouth, his nose. Still, he arched one arm in front of him, hoping to clear out a pocket of air.

Elle had apparently lost her board too because she clamped one leg around his body, glued to him as the pressure eased.

The roar subsided.

All at once, they jerked to a stop, encased in layers of ice. Silence, abrupt and thick, enfolded them.

Above them, in a bluish wash of light, the final runnels of snow rolled over the top, adding layers to their tomb.

He'd managed to eke out a bare channel of space in front of them, but now he couldn't move.

Eerie quiet descended, and he fought the memories, hearing only the hammer of his heartbeat against his rib cage. And Ella's soft gasps beside him. But he couldn't move; their bodies were cemented in snow.

Their biggest danger, right now, was suffocation.

He began, however, to spit, to breathe out, create a pocket of air before the snow settled and his body shut down with cold. When he'd created a tiny air bubble, he shook Ella.

"Ella—you need to spit. I know it sounds gross, but you need to create a pocket of air for yourself. Spit and blow and breathe and make a hole."

Hypothermia would come later.

Please let my beacon be working.

He could hear her, next to him, obeying, and he widened his own pocket, able now to move his arm. He started digging with his hand, hoping to free it through the layers, to give Pete and Ty a visual.

He had no clue how far they'd slid. It could be five hundred feet, given the clear terrain of the bowl.

Stay calm. He heard his heartbeat pound out the words.

"Honey, how badly are you hurt?"

Ella trembled in his arms.

"El?"

"I hurt my ankle when I fell, and now it really hurts. I think it might be broken."

"Okay." He moved his arm down, into the area behind her, and tried to push up snow, make room for her to lean away from him, but the snow had turned to plaster around them. He managed to press enough away for her to lift her head.

He still wore his helmet light, crazily undamaged in the fall, and now flicked it on. The light bounced against the shadows, bleeding through the white.

He was able to press his helmet to hers, see her expression through her goggles.

Wide-eyed, tear-stained. But she was trying to be brave. Her body trembled, maybe from the cold, probably from the terror.

He might be trembling too.

"It's going to be okay," Gage said. "I'm sure the guys are looking for us. And I have my beacon."

"Oh no. That's why you came after me—I don't have a beacon."

Well, yeah, but . . . "Of course I came after you, Ella. I was following your line, remember?"

But instead of smiling, she shook her head. "Gage! What were you thinking? This is your worst nightmare."

"Being stuck in an avalanche with you? Not hardly."

She shook her head. "No. *You* being stuck in an avalanche. Again. And this time, it was to save me."

"We're going to be fine." *Please.*

"But I messed up—I wasn't paying attention. I cut too sharp and sent you over the edge—"

"Shh." The snow had started to penetrate his layers, especially the wash that had found the collar of his coat. And in his arms, Ella's tremble had turned to all-out shaking.

"I can't believe I talked you into coming out here after everything I did—"

"Ella, stop!" He lifted off his goggles, then hers. Found her eyes. "Listen, trust that I can make my own decisions, okay? Just like I need to trust you!"

She blinked at him, her eyes wide, and he lowered his voice.

"Listen, maybe this isn't about either of us. Maybe God brought us out here because we were supposed to see that accidents happen. And I have to realize that I can't stop them—even if I am at my best. And maybe it's time for you and me both to believe *exactly* what you said—that God is on our side."

She frowned at him. "Yeah, I guess . . . It reminds me of something my dad used to say. That God proved his love for us even before we asked for help, when we were still not only a mess but his enemies. We didn't trust him . . . but he didn't let that stop him from saving us."

Gage made a small, dark noise, from deep inside chest. "Yeah. Chet says the same thing. That we shouldn't base God's desire to help us on our opinions of ourselves. Otherwise we'd always be in over our heads. We need to start *believing* that he wants to help us. Even when we make mistakes."

He lowered his voice, turned it soft. "If I haven't said it yet . . . I forgive you, Ella. I forgive you for everything."

She closed her eyes, and he saw her chin tremble.

And suddenly, despite the cold, a knot began to unravel in his chest. He could almost feel it—the full breath of grace filling his lungs.

He should have said the words years ago.

Ella was sobbing. And he didn't know what to do.

But then, because it just felt right, because he longed to believe his words, to make it better, to give him hope, he closed his eyes. "God, I know you see us. Not because we've earned your eyes on us but because you love us. Because of who you are. Because that is your nature . . . to love the lost and broken and scared and . . . buried. Thank you that we are still alive. Now, out of your great love, please rescue us. We trust you."

He opened his eyes and met Ella's gaze.

"Right?" he asked.

She swallowed, her eyes reddened. Took a long breath.

Nodded.

Then she smiled, and it filled him with warmth and light and the sense that, yes, they might just live through this. "What?"

"I just can't believe you rode into an avalanche to save me."

"And I can't believe you were angry at me for it."

"At least we made it down the mountain."

He laughed then, and right behind it, heard the sound of shouting.

"Gage! Are you down there?" A probe came through the snow, and he grabbed it, gave it a tug.

"We're here!"

Scraping above, and in a moment, daylight found them.

Pete's head appeared over the edge of the hole. "Are we interrupting something?" He grinned, clearing out the snow around them.

And then, because they'd all lived, and because for the first time in three years he could actually breathe, Gage couldn't stop himself from leaning in and kissing her. Just pressing his lips to Ella's, tasting the salt of her tears, and adding just a touch of spark, heat, and the promise of what could be, once they got out of the snow.

"We got you, Ella. You can let go of Gage." Ty lay on his stomach, reaching down into the hole he and Pete had dug into the slide debris.

Ty had stood, watching with cold horror as the slide overran Gage and Ella. Without Gage's beacon, Pete and Ty would have lost Gage and Ella in the massive field of tumbled snow.

And then, in the aftermath, silence descended over the valley, a quiet in the wake of the storm that settled into his bones.

It brought Ty right back to the moment after his crash, nearly a year ago, as he lay there, stunned, his knee shattered.

He was still trying to sort out how it had happened. How, one second he and Chet had been flying, the next, careening to earth.

But that's how it happened—one moment you're flying, the next, an avalanche or a malfunctioning engine cuts out on you.

And you're left trying to dig yourself out of a hole. Or dragging yourself out for miles through a blizzard.

Reaching up for anything that might offer rescue.

Ty took Ella's proffered hand, wrapped it around his neck, reached down, and grabbed the back of her jacket. Pete knelt beside her and grabbed her other arm, and in a moment they'd pulled her out of the snowy tomb and into freedom.

She collapsed on the snow. Scooted back, away from the hole. "Gage!"

"He's next," Ty said and turned back for his friend.

Gage was seated deep. Pete dug out around him, and Ty braced himself on the edges with his feet, reached out to grab Gage's arms. Together they wiggled him out of the hole.

He finally crawled out and fell beside Ella. "She's hurt," he said as he unstrapped his helmet and pulled it off. He sat up, and Ty ignored the shake of his hands. It would help Gage to attend to Ella.

"Brace yourself, honey, this is liable to hurt," Gage said as he worked off her boot.

Honey?

Interesting. Ty glanced at Pete, who clearly heard the endearment but said nothing as he got on the snowmobile, leaning on it with one knee. They'd brought in two litters—Miles's idea—and now he moved the snowmobile up to Ella and Gage.

Oliver still waited, trussed up for his evac, beyond the edge of the slide field where Ty had left him. Ty had jumped on the back of Pete's machine the moment the field solidified.

Now, he hiked back to Oliver, pulling out his walkie.

"PEAK HQ, Remington, come in, over."

Jess answered, and it only made his conversation with her yesterday stir in his mind. That, and Pete's strange response when he discovered Jess's secret.

How he wished Pete hadn't found out that way.

"She owes the world an explanation. She doesn't just get to start over," Brette had said.

Why not?

He had, without an explanation.

In fact, if anyone should be paying for crimes, it was Ty.

He updated Jess on their situation, gave an ETA, and asked Kacey to meet them at the base. They could airlift Oliver from PEAK to the Kalispell Regional Medical Center.

Then Ty checked on Oliver, who seemed to be hovering just below consciousness.

He climbed on the snow machine and headed over to Pete. Gage already had Ella loaded into the litter. He'd splinted her ankle in an inflatable cast, then strapped her in, surrounded by blankets.

Ty noticed the kiss Gage gave Ella before he climbed on behind Pete.

Good for you, Gage.

The gesture only brought to mind the kiss he'd shared with Brette before everything went south.

Pete kept a steady pace, back through their early morning trail, to the medical truck parked on Going-to-the-Sun Road. Ty and Pete loaded in Oliver and Ella while Gage drove the machines onto the trailer.

Then, with a little help and a groan, Gage climbed in back.

Ty took the wheel.

Pete slid into the passenger seat.

Pete hadn't said anything outside the parameters of their evacuation plan on the drive into the park, and even now, he sat silently looking out the window.

His jaw tight.

In the back, Gage sat on the floor between the two litters, taking Oliver's blood pressure.

"Let us know if there's any change," Pete said to Gage.

He nodded.

Ty glanced at Pete. Okay. "Dude, are you going to say *nothing* about Jess?"

Pete glanced at him. "What's there to say? She clearly doesn't trust me. I'm not sure what I did, but I wish she'd given me a chance to prove to her that I could keep her secret." He turned away. "She didn't have to go running to you."

The roads out of the park weren't well plowed, and Ty kept his speed down as they traveled around Red Rock Point.

"She was upset and scared," Ty said. "And we've been friends a long time."

"How long?"

Ty drew in a breath. "My father was friends with her dad and some of his buddies. The Taggerts would come out skiing, sometimes stay with us, or we'd go with them to their condo at Vail. Jess—Selene—and her brother Barron and I would hang out. Later, when she went to Wharton, she started dating my roommate."

"Her fiancé," Pete said softly, but Ty sensed an edge to his words.

"Yeah. But the minute he found out about the scandal, he left her, so . . ."

Pete swallowed, said nothing for a long while. Then, "I suppose she thought I might do that too."

"It's a good bet. She came out here looking for a fresh start. She had nothing. She surrendered all her possessions, her bank account, every-thing when she testified against her father. And imagine for just one second how that felt—to testify against your own father. It wasn't like they had a terrible relationship. She loved him. He came to college to take her out to lunch, or

372

on holiday. He actually told Jess to testify against him as part of a plea deal to save her brother."

"So why the secrets?"

The road had been cleared here, by Lake McDonald, and Ty picked up the pace.

"You heard Brette. There are a lot of people who blame the entire family for Damien's actions. Jess doesn't want to get pulled into that again."

"I wouldn't have broadcasted it—"

"No, but your friend and our local reporter Tallie might have." Ty glanced at him. "Think about it—the night you two broke up was the night you brought in the youth group from their accident last summer. Tallie was there, with a press crew. Jess took one look at that and ran."

Pete was looking at him now. "I thought she was jealous of Tallie. Or at least thought Tallie and I had something going."

"Do you?"

Pete frowned. "No. Of course not."

Ty lifted a shoulder. "It's a fair question."

Pete drew in a breath. "Not anymore. I'm trying to change."

Ty could give him that—he'd seen the change in Pete at the hospital. And maybe in his off- hours, which he spent mostly working out, training, or on the occasional weekend climbing trip.

"I'm in love with her, Ty."

Ty hadn't expected that. He glanced at Pete. "Really?"

"I have been since last summer. I thought it was just a . . . maybe a crush, but I can't get her out of my head. And I tried to tell myself that she was with a better guy—"

"Thanks for that."

"But it didn't help."

Oh.

"So, you're really not dating, then," Pete said. *Sorry, Jess.* "No. She just didn't—"

"Trust me enough to tell me about her past."

Ty had no words.

"The problem with keeping a secret is that you don't give someone a chance to come through for you, to prove to you that they love you unconditionally."

"It was too risky, Pete. Sorry, but it could have gone south and destroyed her world. Although, with Brette in possession of her identity, probably it will anyway."

"We need to stop Brette," Pete said quietly.

Ty had reached Apgar Center, took a left toward the West Glacier entrance. "Yeah, how?"

"Maybe I could talk to her. Offer to tell her my story for Jess's."

"I don't think your feel-good story about saving a bunch of kids—one that's already been told, I might add—is going to top her scoop of the year. She'd need something . . . juicer."

Or at least something just as revealing.

The answer hit Ty like a blow to his chest.

He might have even groaned because Pete looked at him. "What's up?"

Ty sighed. "I could tell her about the crash."

Silence from Pete. Then, "What about the crash?"

See, this was why Ty had never talked about it. Because every time he even thought about it, shame cut off his words. Still, if he was going to tell Brette, maybe he could try it out on Pete first.

"It was my fault we crashed."

Another beat of silence. "Chet said it was weather, a wind shear—"

"Our engine seized up. In midair."

Ty turned onto Highway 2, toward Mercy Falls. "That's not—"

"I was supposed to do the preflight check. We were low on oil, and I would have seen it. But . . ." He forced his words out. "I didn't do it. We were in a hurry to get to the callout—"

"It was just a mistake, Ty."

"No. The reason I didn't check it was because I'd been out partying. I was a little wasted, and I wasn't thinking."

Pete went quiet beside him.

"I hid it from Chet, but I was in no shape to fly that night."

More silence, then finally, "Yeah, I'd probably keep that to myself too."

And Ty felt it again, that hand on his chest telling him to take a step back, into the safety of obscurity.

He forced himself to keep talking. "Except that's not the only thing that happened. While I was dragging myself out of the crash site, trying to get help, I had a weird thing happen. You could call it a spiritual encounter, maybe, but . . ."

He didn't know how else to describe it. A divine presence, a holy moment as he collapsed in the snow, overwhelmed.

Done.

Ty lifted his voice to the back. "Five minutes out, Gage."

"Good," Gage said.

Ty turned back to Pete, took a breath, and tried to frame it. "I guess I realized that I had a choice. I could die with my mistakes or let God save me and start over. Be someone different. And I know that sounds crazy, but that's what happened. One minute I was freezing to death, the next your brother had found me."

"I remember him telling me how he thought he heard you calling out, but when he got to you, you were completely passed out," Pete said.

"So, the thing is, I *do* have a story to tell. About a guy who used to think he was somebody but who had to nearly die in order to figure out how to live."

Pete was just staring at him.

"What?" Ty said.

"I have this terrible feeling that you *are* the better man."

Ty let a grin tug up one side of his face. "Maybe."

"I was kidding."

"Good. Because Jess isn't in love with me."

"Really?"

"No, dude. She has it bad for you. And she'd kill me if she knew I told you that."

"I thought so. I mean, I couldn't put it together, the way she ran to you—"

"Hey. I'm a catch."

Ty pulled up to the PEAK ranch. Kacey was already striding toward them, Jess beside her. Ty put the truck into park and turned to Pete. "I'll talk to Brette. No more secrets, huh?"

Ella hadn't seen Gage since he and Ty had transferred her and Oliver to the chopper. Jess had jumped in beside them and taken the short hop to the hospital.

Ella had, however, met Gage's father, an orthopedic surgeon. He even looked a little like Gage. A handsome man in his late fifties, with dark brown hair cut short, earnest eyes, and a confidence in his work that echoed his son's abilities on the mountain.

"You've got a double break, in both your tibia and fibula. You need surgery to set them." While he'd pointed out the X-ray, Ella kept her eye on the door.

But Gage didn't show up, even in time for Dr. Watson to take her away to surgery.

Her only other thought was for Ollie.

"My wife is looking in on him," Dr. Watson said.

Ella had forgotten that Gage had *two* outstanding parents. Talk about needing to keep up. No wonder he pushed himself into being a champion.

She woke in the quiet late-afternoon shadows of her hospital room, her leg in a cast. Outside, snow had begun to fall, gentle flakes peeling from the sky. The clouds hung low, obscuring the mountains from her view of the park. Someone had come in, left flowers on her tray.

But no Gage.

He hadn't been hurt, had he? She reached for the call box and buzzed for a nurse.

The door opened, and the nurse came in. "Oh good, you're awake."

She walked over, lifted Ella's wrist to take her pulse.

"Do you know anything about my brother? He came in with me—Oliver Blair." The anesthesia still weighted her body, turned it heavy.

The nurse reached for the pitcher of water, poured her a glass, and handed it to her, holding the straw. Ella took a drink, the water soothing on her parched throat.

"He's in surgery. That's all I know."

She sighed. "Have I had any visitors?"

The nurse reached for the blood pressure cuff.

"As a matter of fact, I have someone outside your room, just waiting to come in." She took Ella's blood pressure.

It might have risen a little with the nurse's words.

She sat up, wishing she'd had a chance to comb her hair, maybe pull it back into something that resembled anything but a rat's nest. But that's what two days of backcountry snowboarding did. Messed a woman up, made her forget who she was and what she thought she wanted.

No. She knew what she wanted. Gage.

The door opened and she heard footsteps. She smiled.

"Oh, honey, I'm so relieved."

"Mom?" Ella didn't have time—or presence of mind—to school her disbelief. "What are you doing here?"

"As soon as Brette called us and told us what was happening, we caught a flight. We had to drive up from Missoula—last night's winds wouldn't let us in—but we're here now, and . . . oh, honey. What a terrible ordeal."

Marjorie Blair had never lost her senatorial grace, despite her cancer. Dressed in a pantsuit, her honey blonde hair cut short in a bob, her makeup impeccable, the woman looked ready for a press conference.

"You look nice. Heading up a board meeting down the hall?"

Marjorie sat on the side of her bed. "Yes, well, I did want to talk to you about something." She took her hand. "But not now. I'm just so thankful you made it off that mountain."

"Me and Oliver. Mom, he told me you knew what he was doing."

"Yes, we knew. He talked with us six months ago and told us his plans. Showed us the video of him skiing, as well as one of someone who'd skied it years ago. We finally agreed that if this was his passion, we were behind him—"

"He could have gotten killed. Did you not think of Dylan?"

Her mother's mouth tightened. "Yes. Of course we did. But he's an adult, and I can't wrap him in cotton. He has to live his own life, make his own choices. It was time for us to let him."

She stared at her mother. "If Gage and I hadn't gone after him, he would still be up on that mountain."

"Gage?"

"Watson—yes, the guy who was with Dylan. But before you say anything, he saved Oliver's life. And mine. He rode into an avalanche to save me. I would have been buried alive if it weren't for him."

Her mother took in a long breath as if weighing her words, her opinion of Gage. Her diplomacy apparently won. "Well, we're very proud of you going after your brother the way you did.

You remind me a lot of your mother, you know."

Ella just stared at her. "What?"

"Your mother had such determination. Even when she was dying, she hung on until she made sure you and Oliver were going to be taken care of by Mansfield and me. After all you two had gone through, she didn't want you to be alone."

"I didn't know that."

Marjorie touched her hand. "You know, if you stop trying so hard to take care of everybody, you might find that there are others already looking out for you."

She met Marjorie's gaze. Such warmth in it, the kind of compassion she'd always seen but never let herself embrace.

Thinking, of course, she had to earn it.

"Thanks, Mom," she said softly.

Marjorie leaned forward, pulled Ella into her arms. "I know you're not mine by birth, but your mother gave you to me to love as my own. And I do, precious daughter."

Ella closed her eyes, allowing herself to sink against her mother. "I love you too."

A beat passed, and then Marjorie held her away. "Good. Because I need to ask you if I can have my senate seat back."

Ella raised an eyebrow. "Seriously?"

"I know you took it on because I asked you to. But I've seen the strain, the frustration, and . . . do you still want to be senator?"

381

"I don't . . . I don't know."

"Well, it's not an 'I don't know' job. And if you're not all in—"

"No. I don't want it. I guess I don't know what I want."

"Really?" Her mother regarded her with a smile. "Because now I'm doing the math, and I think I know who that man is who kept asking to see you. Your father sent him away. But he's your boyfriend, isn't he?"

"What?"

"Sorry, honey. We thought he might be one of Oliver's wild friends. That long hair . . ."

"That beautiful, amazing long hair. Mom, that's Gage Watson."

Her mother's mouth opened, closed. She drew in a breath.

"Uh-oh."

"What?"

Her mother drew back, eased up from the bed. "Now I think I understand what had your father in such a kerfuffle." She got up, paced the room.

"What are you talking about?"

"Oh, he was talking with the young woman who brought you and your brother in, and suddenly, I saw his face change—you know how he gets when he's angry. A little like your brother, I might add. Stubborn."

"Mom—"

"The local press has gotten ahold of this, and

382

he went down to talk to them. I have a bad feeling he might add in an opinion on the reputation of your rescuer."

"What? Why would the press care about us?"

"I don't think it's you as much as the fact that it's a small town, and you are big news."

"But why does Dad have to get involved?"

Marjorie raised an eyebrow. "Well, when your father heard that you went up on that mountain, he nearly came unglued. And now we know why."

Oh. Yes. Gage. The guy who led people into danger. Got them killed.

"Mom, Gage isn't the reckless man Dad thinks he is. He was trying to help Dylan stay alive."

"He should have never let Dylan on that mountain."

"Dylan was going up on that mountain whether Gage took him or not. Gage was just trying to keep him safe. But there's more. You need to know something." She sat up, patted the side of the bed. "C'mere."

Her mother obeyed. Ella took her hand. "It was part of the sealed case, but Gage isn't to blame for Dylan's death. Dylan had THC—marijuana—in his system when he died."

She got the response she expected—her mother's mouth opened, her eyes widened. "Oh my."

"Yeah. And we can't know if Dylan was high when he went over the edge, but it would have tainted the lawsuit, for sure. But Gage felt so guilty about what happened, he never pushed his lawyer to find out more, just agreed to the lawsuit terms. And now Dad is going to make him relive it all over again."

"Oh no he isn't." Her mother stood up.

"What are you doing?"

"You're not only your mother's daughter, but you're *my* daughter too. And we both taught you to do what's right, regardless of the cost, right?"

Ella stared at her.

"Like, snowboarding down a mountain that just might get you killed?"

Ella nodded. "Yeah, I guess so."

"You *guess* so? Do you believe that God honors the truth, Ella? Do you trust him?"

She stared at her mother, saw the woman who'd fought cancer, and in her remission wanted to climb back in the ring, do something that mattered with her life.

Oh, how she wanted to be like Marjorie Blair too.

"Yes, I do."

"You got any fight left in you?"

Ella felt a smile nudge through. "Mmmhmm."

"Good." She turned and headed toward the door.

"Where are you going?"

"To get a wheelchair. And then you're getting out of that bed. Senator, it's time to filibuster."

18

Selene Jessica Taggert owed the world an explanation, and Brette was going to get it.

At least that's what Brette had been saying to herself for hours as she surfed the internet, trying to track down information on Jess Tagg. Apparently, when she went into hiding, she'd deleted anything that could track her down to western Montana.

Except for a couple mentions in the local paper detailing recent rescue missions—a grizzly attack last summer, and the same youth group rescue Pete Brooks had been on—Jess stayed under the radar.

No exciting parties, no gala events.

Apparently, Jess had shed her old persona for this down-home girl dressed in flannel.

It made Brette wonder, for a long moment, if she truly had the right person. But Ty had confirmed it. Not only in his guilty expression but in his matter-of-fact explanation to Pete.

Pete Brooks had looked more upset by the fact that she'd kept the truth from him than by her crimes.

What was wrong with these people? Clearly they'd never lost everything due to the actions of others. Didn't know what it felt like to see their world crumble.

Brette set her phone on the bed table. She'd tried to take notes, but she really needed her computer.

No, what she needed was to get out of this hospital bed. But her doctor hadn't yet released her, had mentioned a couple postoperative tests he wanted to run.

She couldn't imagine the bill, but certainly the charity Ty had lined up wouldn't pay for . . .

Oh, *wait*. How gullible was she that she'd believed him? It didn't take much to do the math. If Ty was friends with Selene, back when she was wealthy, then no doubt *he* also had a few million bucks to his name.

And wasn't that just the icing on the cake? Rich *and* manipulative. What else did she expect?

Which only meant she'd have to figure out a way to pay him back.

She stared outside at the falling snow. *Please, let the PEAK team have found Ella and Gage.* Although, with her ordering Ty from her room, probably he wouldn't be hightailing it back to update her.

She picked up her phone and dialed Ella's cell, but it went to voicemail. She set her phone on the bed table, next to the pretty flowers Pete had brought her. He'd seemed so humble, even chagrined, when he brought them in. *"If you want to ask about the stuff that happened last summer, I'll tell you. It's just not that exciting."*

No. Not compared to the world discovering the location and story of Selene Taggert.

She doesn't just get to start over.

The words refused to leave her, just thrumming in her head.

She turned on the television and came upon a local news feed. What looked like the hospital, with a cute reporter with long brown hair delivering an update on a snowboarder who'd been lost on the mountain.

When Oliver's picture flashed on the screen, Brette pumped up the volume.

"He was found early last night by local ski patrol Gage Watson, who, with the PEAK Rescue team, carried him out of Heaven's Peak this morning, along with his sister, Ella Blair. Ella happens to be a senator with the State of Vermont. I got a chance to catch up with her parents earlier today."

The interview flipped to a hurried shot of Marjorie and Mansfield Blair on their way to the hospital, giving a quick statement about gratitude and relief.

The reporter ended with, "We're expecting an update on Ella's and Oliver's conditions coming up soon."

But Brette sat, weakened. They were here, in the hospital. And no, Ty hadn't bothered to stop by.

Not that she should expect him to, after she'd screamed at him to get out.

Still. *"Brette, I do care about you."*

She couldn't get *that* out of her head, either. And wouldn't you know it, her chest hurt, hearing his pleading words. *"I promise you—that kiss, for me, meant something and, please, just trust me—"*

She closed her eyes, trying to get his voice out of her brain. She meant her parting words—she couldn't trust him again.

But it wouldn't matter, because she wouldn't see him again, either.

She wiped her fingers across her cheek, brushing away the moisture there.

"Brette, are you okay?"

She opened her eyes. Froze.

Blinked.

Ty Remington stood at the foot of her bed.

Holding flowers.

"Hey," he said quietly. He looked like a man fresh in from the cold, unshaven, wearing his ski jacket and a stocking cap. He pulled it off now, and his dark hair emerged flattened.

Apology emanated from him in his grim smile, the expression on his face, those beautiful green eyes.

She folded her hands over her chest. "I'm fine. Just waiting on a few extra tests the doctor ordered before they discharge me. I don't want to spend any more of your money."

His mouth opened, just slightly, and she hated herself a little. What was wrong with her that she'd turned so angry, especially toward the one man who'd been kind to her?

Who made her fall at least a little in love with him, only to break her heart.

That was probably what this was about. She was so tired of falling for the wrong men, the ones who didn't care if they trampled over her.

She tightened her jaw, refused to take back her words.

Ty closed his mouth, gave her a tight nod. "I guess it was too much to hope that you wouldn't find out." Then he set the flowers on the bedside tray, next to Pete's.

Gerbera daisies and miniature pink roses.

She liked it. In fact, she had never received so many flowers in her life. But she couldn't look at him.

He pulled up a chair anyway. "I didn't actually lie about that charity fund. My family has a number of them, and, well, I just pulled some strings, got a donation . . ."

She stared out the window at the late afternoon pallor of the day. "That was nice of you. But I'll pay you back."

"It's a lot of money, Brette. Please don't." He was looking at her, and she couldn't help it. She glanced at him, and his gaze held so much emotion, it caught her breath.

What other way could it ever be? I'll never be able to trust you again.

But oh, she wanted to. In fact, she longed to rewind to the moment, twenty-four hours ago, when he'd leaned over and kissed her.

Such a sweet, gentle, perfect kiss. He'd made her, however briefly, believe again in heroes and happy endings.

She drew in a breath. "Why are you here?" And no, she didn't mean it how it sounded, because she suddenly, desperately didn't want him to leave.

"I wanted to tell you that we found Ella and Oliver."

Oh. "Thank you."

"And I was worried about you."

He was? She clenched her jaw.

"And . . . I wanted to talk to you about Jess."

Jess. Of *course* he did. Brette blinked away the heat in her eyes. "What about Selene?"

He folded his hands between his knees. "I have a story you could tell, instead of Jess's."

She frowned at him. "Pete already offered—"

"Not Pete's story, Brette. Mine. About the chopper crash. It might not make national news, but . . . it's a story about a guy who had it all and lost it because of his own stupidity. It's a story of survival—I hiked fifteen miles through a blizzard on a broken knee while my team searched for five days for us. It even includes a miracle. Something *Nat Geo* might be interested in. And it's all yours, if you're willing to trade it for staying silent about Jess."

Brette studied him, the way he offered her a wan, quick smile, the hard swallow that chased his words.

"Ty . . ."

"You told me that you liked inspiring stories. That you didn't do dirt. This story on Jess . . . it's just going to destroy lives."

"*She* destroyed lives."

"Her father was the criminal here, not Jess. And she's paid for his crimes—"

"Hardly."

He closed his eyes, as if pained, and she felt like a jerk.

Because she knew a little about how it felt to lose everything, to start over with nothing. If it hadn't been for Ella in Brette's life, she would have been sleeping in her old Ford.

Maybe Ty had been Selene's Ella.

And here he was, sacrificing his own privacy, his own pain, to save Jess. Throwing himself like the proverbial sacrificial lamb in front of Brette.

Now Brette *really* felt like a jerk.

And not just a little jealous. What might it be like to have a man care that much, to protect her at the cost of his own privacy, his reputation?

"Okay, Ty," she said softly.

He raised an eyebrow, just a little surprise in his expression. Then he nodded. Exhaled. "Thanks, Brette." He leaned back, ran his hands through his hair. "I'm not sure where to start. It was last spring, and we got a callout for—"

"Ty," she said softly. "I'm not telling your story, either."

He stopped talking, just stared at her.

"I came here looking for a hero. And I found one. That's enough for me. You can keep your story to yourself."

He looked undone, his expression hollow.

She offered a tiny smile.

"Brette, I . . . is there any way we could—"

"We're back with that update from Mansfield Blair," the television announced.

He turned, and she wished she'd turned off the television.

Any way we could . . . what?

But Ella's father, every inch the powerful millionaire, in his dark suit jacket, a white shirt, and pressed dress pants, had Ty's attention. Mansfield looked freshly shaved, his dark brown hair slicked back, completely composed despite what had to be a desperate thirty-six hours.

He stood at the front of what looked like the hospital lunchroom, introduced himself, and gave an update on his son. Some sort of brain bleed that, kudos to the PEAK team, had been helped by their quick evacuation.

Brette had the urge to reach out, take Ty's hand, give it a squeeze.

And that's when things turned sour.

"Unfortunately, included in this accident was my daughter, Vermont senator Ella Blair. She is resting comfortably after surgery to repair her broken leg, an injury that would have never occurred if PEAK team member Gage Watson hadn't taken an unskilled, untrained snowboarder along on his search and rescue mission. This is the same Gage Watson who, by the way, was responsible for the death of a snowboarder three years ago on Outlaw Mountain, in Canada."

Ty looked back at Brette, who had sat up.

Their attention turned back to the screen as a voice lifted off camera.

"Wait! I have a story to tell!"

The camera turned and fixed on Ella, dressed in a bathrobe, her hair pulled up in a messy bun, pushed in a wheelchair by her mother, who, as usual, looked like she had stepped out of the boardroom. Or the capitol.

"Gage Watson is not who you think!"

Oh no. Because Brette had seen that look before, the same determination that had made Ella park herself in a helicopter, refusing to leave, only three days ago.

Brette looked at Ty. "I need to go."

And he didn't hesitate, not a pause to question her. He came around the bed and with one movement picked her up, cotton blanket and all.

And then she was back in his arms, hers around his neck as he carried her down the hall.

Yes, probably she could find a way to forgive him.

"Just sit down, Gage," Jess said. She stood in the back of the snack room, holding the remote control, popping up the volume.

Pete sat on a vinyl chair and was staring at the television screen. He'd driven Gage and Ty to the hospital and seen the altercation between Gage and Ella's father.

Probably, Pete's presence was the reason Gage didn't lose it, put the man down in his fancy suit, and fight his way into Ella's room.

No, Pete's hand on his arm, his low counsel to wait until Ella asked for him, had prevailed.

Yes, she would ask for him, and everything would be fine.

Surely.

So Gage had followed Pete to the snack room to grab some quick grub. But not before Pete made him stop by the ER to have a doc take a look at his strained ankles.

Just swollen, no significant injury. And frankly, he felt fine.

Nearly invincible.

He still couldn't believe they'd lived through another avalanche.

And this time, he hadn't freaked out, hadn't

been pulled out broken. This time, with Ella in his arms, he'd held together.

Because accidents did happen, even when he tried to cut the right line. Or tried to follow others.

More, without the accident, he'd still be caught in the limelight, staring at poster-sized images of himself, believing his own press.

Creating a version of Gage Watson he didn't want to be. And that was what Ella gave to him— then, and now. She saw through the veneer to the man he wanted to be.

The man he'd become when he walked through the rubble of his career to the other side.

A man who no longer chased approval.

Gage much preferred the man he'd become to the man he almost was.

About that time, Jess had walked into the room. "You gotta see this." She reached for the remote control to the flat screen attached to the wall. Turned on the television and clicked to the right channel.

Ella's father, standing at a podium just down the hall. Talking about the rescue.

"This is the same Gage Watson who, by the way, was responsible for the death of a snowboarder three years ago on Outlaw Mountain, in Canada."

Gage got up, despite Jess's words.

"Bro, sit down," Pete added. "You're just going to make it worse."

That was rich coming from the guy most likely to do something rash.

But then, "I have a story to tell!"

The camera panned and there she was. Ella, her foot in a cast, dressed in a bathrobe, and looking so darned beautiful he couldn't move.

Until her next words. "Gage Watson is not who you think!"

No, no. He hit his feet.

"Gage!"

"She's going to do something stupid!"

Pete too had stood up and now grabbed Gage's arm. "Dude."

Gage rounded on him. "She has a secret—one that will exonerate me but gets her in big trouble and—"

"What you don't know about Gage is that he's a hero. I demanded that he take me on that mountain, and he practically begged me not to go." Ella's sweet voice cut in and silenced Gage. He stared at the television, his heart caught in his ribs.

"But I'm a good snowboarder, and not only did I trust him but he trusted me. He let me believe in myself to do something I would normally be terrified to do. And because of that, I discovered I am stronger than I think. Braver than I think. And that I don't have to prove anything to anyone but myself."

Gage couldn't move. Pete's hand dropped from his arm.

"But here's the biggest part. I would have never made it down that mountain if it weren't for Gage. He's the best freerider in the world, and he didn't deserve what happened to him three years ago."

Gage left the room.

She was going to destroy everything she had worked for, and, well . . . he didn't need exoneration. He already knew who he was. More, he'd somehow forgiven himself on that mountain too. And maybe that was the reason God sent him up there—to take a good look at himself, at the raw, brutal facts, and remind him that whatever line he cut behind him, grace always lay before him. A pristine, white, unblemished future.

And he wanted to share it with Ella.

He didn't slow as he banged through the double doors to the hospital press room. "Ella, stop!"

He wouldn't exactly call the room packed—just a handful of local stations on hand, but one of them represented the local Fox channel, which would surely make the national feed if Ella were to incriminate herself.

"Stop talking."

She looked over at Gage, her eyes wide, and every camera turned his direction.

"Please, it's done, and I don't care about the past—just . . . please, leave it."

"As I was saying," she said, smiling sweetly

at him, "my brother has trained for six months to ski Gage Watson's epic run, and with Gage's thorough explanation of each section, my brother navigated down much of the course without incident. He fell taking care of his friend, Bradley, who is recovering just down the hall, having been evacuated off the mountain by PEAK Rescue. So, as you can see, without Gage Watson, we'd all be stuck on Heaven's Peak. He's the best snowboarder I know, past, present, and future."

Gage stilled, caught for a second in Ella's smile. She hadn't destroyed herself but had put him right back in the center of the limelight.

The cameras turned and began to flash.

But he ignored them and walked right past the media to crouch in front of Ella's chair.

She put her hands on his shoulders. "The best man I know."

Then, in front of the world, she leaned down and kissed him.

And to the flash of cameras, he kissed her back.

Ty wasn't sure how he'd gotten here, standing just outside the rim of press, holding a woman in his arms while watching his buddy Gage kiss the woman he'd spent three years pining for.

But he certainly wouldn't lodge any complaints.

Especially with Brette's arms looped around his neck. He'd wrapped her like a burrito in her blanket, aware that she was not only wearing her hospital gown but had recently had surgery.

Those extra tests the doctor had ordered niggled at him.

But he'd talk to her later, after she'd had a chance to talk to Ella. He didn't know why, exactly, she looked so desperate to get to her friend, but . . .

Well, he was still reeling from her words. *"I came here looking for a hero. And I found one. That's enough for me. You can keep your story to yourself."*

He didn't quite know what to do with the crazy hope those words had stirred inside him.

Yeah, he could fall in love with this woman if she gave him the chance.

In the room, Gage had gotten up, taken Ella's hand, and was facing the cameras. He grinned, and it seemed genuine, something not canned, but of course, perfect.

Because Gage was a born superstar, so natural in the limelight, he belonged there.

Even when the press peppered him with questions about the rescue, and even the past.

"I regret with everything inside me the decisions I made that cost Dylan his life. And I'm saddened by the injuries Bradley and Oliver incurred by following my route down Heaven's Peak. But anything daring comes with risks, and accidents happen in the backcountry.

The best we can do is try and prepare for them, and trust that if an accident happens, we'll be rescued. I'm just thankful that Ella was bold enough to convince me to go after her brother and Bradley, or they would have died on the mountain. I've never met anyone who fights for the ones she cares about like Ella Blair."

He looked down at her, winked.

"He'd make a great campaigner," Brette said next to Ty's ear.

Ty looked at her. "What?"

Brette shook her head. Then she met his eyes. "I guess I panicked over nothing."

Panicked? Although, well . . . He went out on a limb. "It's not a bad way to get you back into my arms."

He chased it with a smile.

Her eyes widened, and she caught her lip. "Maybe we could . . . I don't know. Start over? Be friends?"

Oh, he wanted much more than friends, but he nodded. "Sure." He'd spied a wheelchair near the entrance and now walked over, set her into it. He arranged her blanket around her, then knelt before her. "My name is Ty Remington. My parents own the Double R, a good chunk of land in northwest Montana. But I work for PEAK Rescue, just trying to help people who are lost, or hurt, or in over their heads." Just like he was. But maybe not so much anymore. His story to

Pete had loosened the fingers of shame around his heart.

Maybe someday soon he would be able to tell his story, the whole story, to the team.

The one that included him falling on his face in the snow and begging for salvation. And not just the physical kind.

Maybe, in fact, that was the first step to climbing back into the cockpit. But, for now, "If you give me the chance, Brette, I promise to never lie to you again."

He held out his hand.

She took it, her smile warm. "I like a man who keeps his promise."

Oh, he wanted to kiss her. His eyes roamed her face and stopped at her lips. But before he could stir up the courage, a voice came up behind him.

"Brette, what happened to you?" Ella. Gage was wheeling her over. He parked her next to Brette, and they hugged.

"Appendicitis. I'm so glad you're okay." Brette glanced up at Gage, back to Ella. "And apparently, you got your chance to talk to Gage." She added a wink. "How's Oliver?"

"He's out of surgery," said another voice, and Ty turned to see Dr. Brenda Watson walking over. She wore her lab jacket, a pair of scrubs. "We were able to stop the bleeding. He's in recovery."

She looked over at Gage. "Well done, son," she said softly and squeezed Gage's arm. He put his hand over hers. Then she bent down to Ella. "I hear you've already met my husband."

Ella nodded. "Glad to meet you, Dr. Watson."

"Brenda," she said. "Likewise, Senator."

"Actually," Ella said, glancing at Gage, then to Brette, "I think my senator season is over. My mother wants to run for her seat again." She looked at Brette. "Have you ever thought of writing the biography of Marjorie Blair, a woman whose family used to run a fishing operation? *The Perfect Storm* meets the Maple Syrup king?"

"I like it," Brette said. She grinned, but Ty couldn't help but notice sweat breaking out on her forehead. Without asking, he touched it with the back of his hand. She felt warm.

Maybe the tests had to do with an infection of some sort. "I need to get her back to her room," Ty said. He looked at Gage. "See you back at the house?"

Gage nodded.

He wheeled Brette back to her room. And she didn't protest when he lifted her into her bed.

"You're not feeling well, are you?" he asked, sinking down into his chair.

"Just a headache. And oddly, my stomach still hurts."

"You just had surgery."

She made a face. "Yeah, you're right." But she held out her hand. "Would you be willing to stick around until I fall asleep?"

He took her hand. "I'm not going anywhere. I promise."

Ella knew this man. The one who smiled for the cameras as he wheeled her back to her room. The one who ordered her pizza and brought it to her bed, shared it with her and her mom.

The one who patiently explained every detail of the rescue to her father.

This man who then went in search of a boy named Hunter, who apparently needed a hero after shattering his femur on the slope.

Pete Brooks had stopped in about then to check on her, and her father cornered him. "Thanks for all you did to help Oliver and Ella."

Pete seemed like a nice guy, and offered her father an "aw, shucks, I was glad to help" kind of response.

"I did some checking, and apparently you have your FEMA incident commander certification," her mother added.

Ella glanced at her, frowned.

"I'm on the board for the National Red Cross. Any interest in helping out nationally?"

Pete was a handsome man, with shoulder-length blond hair that he held back with a bandanna. Probably a lady-killer with that soft smile, the twinkle in his eyes. Her mother's suggestion seemed to make him pause. "Maybe, yes, ma'am."

Oh, her mother was a goner for men who called her ma'am. "I'll be in touch."

Pete turned to Ella. "I saw Gage down the hall, talking to that kid we brought in from the Blackbear. I thought I'd peek in, say hi."

She glanced at the wheelchair, which was still in her room, and Pete seemed to read her mind. He brought it over and helped move her into it. "I'll take good care of her," he said to her parents. "No four-wheeling."

Her mother laughed, and Ella knew he was a shoo-in for the job.

She stayed at the door to watch as Pete knocked, then entered Hunter's room. Gage sat on the kid's bed, talking with him about his descent down Heaven's Peak, giving him some pointers and encouraging him to keep listening to his dreams.

Pete met the boy's parents, and gave the kid a high-five.

A couple of heroes, comfortable in their own skin. For Gage, at least, it was a long time coming.

A fist bump, a handshake with the family, and Ella saw Gage's future.

Maybe a champion freerider again, but more likely a man who continued to save lives.

She was trying to push herself away when he came out of the room.

"You're not that fast, Senator." He caught up to

her, said good-bye to Pete, and wheeled her back to her room. Her parents were gone, probably to check on Oliver, who was now out of recovery.

He scooped her up to transfer her to the bed. She held on just a little longer than necessary, ran her hand along his whiskered chin as he set her down.

"Getting a little handsy there, aren't you, Miss Blair?" But he grinned, cupped her chin in his hand, bent down, and kissed her.

Soft lips, tender, urging her mouth open. A sensuous kiss, one that ignited a simmer of desire through her. When he backed away, meeting her eyes, she saw the promise of more.

She scooted over, patted the bed next to her. "Let's see if the news has a replay of your epic entrance."

She picked up the television remote.

He slid onto the bed beside her and put his arm around her. She settled her head against his chest. "This is so much better than sleeping in the snow."

He laughed, a low rumble that she felt through her entire body.

"You were a hit with the press. I heard that brunette asking you for an exclusive."

"That's Tallie Kennedy. She's a local reporter who's done a few features on the PEAK team."

The television played a lineup of the evening's shows, including a special news spot on local missing persons.

"I was really worried you were going to tell them about . . . well, the case, and Dylan and—"

"I was." She looked over at him. "I wanted to scream the truth, and if my father had kept accusing you, I would have. But then you showed up, and . . ."

"I don't need the world to know, Ella. It's enough that I know. Thank you." He pressed a kiss to her forehead, then leaned back into her pillows. "Actually, I was thinking about what you said. I don't think I want to go back to competing. But"—he gave her a sidelong glance—"I was pretty frustrated out there, not knowing how to help your brother. I was thinking maybe I could go back to school, get a higher degree in emergency medicine."

"I thought you didn't like school."

"I could use a study partner."

"I'm fantastic at flash cards," she said.

His smile dimmed. "Did you really mean it when you said you didn't want to be a senator anymore?"

She nodded. "I'm ready to step out of the limelight. Maybe go back to being a lawyer . . ."

A picture on the screen arrested her attention. She turned up the volume and listened to the description of a missing woman, approximately age thirty, dark hair, high cheekbones. They listed her death as blunt force trauma.

"That's the woman we found last summer,

in the park. Ian Shaw had her face forensically reconstructed," Gage said. "She was featured on *America's Missing* a few days ago. The news must have finally picked it up."

Ella simply stared, everything inside her chilling. No, it couldn't be. "Gage, I know her." She couldn't tear her gaze from the television as the reporter walked the area where her body had been located. She waited until the program flashed her picture again, just to confirm. "That's my friend Sofia. She was one of my housemates at Middlebury. I took her skiing out here with me a few years ago— the year before I met you at Outlaw. She met a guy, I remember that. I think they kept in touch."

"You know her? Are you sure?"

"I thought she'd moved back to Spain, but I haven't heard from her in years. I can't be sure, but, it *looks* like her."

"We'll get another look at the picture to confirm."

"And I'll try and get ahold of her parents. But if that is my friend, Gage . . . I know what I'm going to do."

He raised an eyebrow.

"I'm sticking around Mercy Falls, and I'm going to bring whoever killed my friend to justice."

He nodded. "Of course you are. I wouldn't expect anything less."

EPILOGUE

It wasn't supposed to end this way.

Ty sat in his truck, drumming his fingers on his steering wheel.

The Gray Pony Saloon was rocking tonight, the hint of a spring thaw in the air, and fans of Ben King's first-ever new artist showcase jammed the parking lot. The thump of a bass drum, a steel guitar, the twang of a fiddle wound out into the crisp night. Ben was putting Mercy Falls on the map, with country star wannabes emerging from the woodwork for a shot at a contract with his newly formed Mountain Song Records studio.

Benjamin King had certainly found his way back home after his mistakes.

Ty could make out the silhouettes of Jess and Sierra in their usual booth near the door, with Pete and Gage nearby throwing darts.

From Ty's vantage point, it seemed that Pete and Jess still had to have one very important conversation. But maybe that had something to do with Pete's recent job offer to join the national Red Cross emergency rescue team.

The door to the saloon opened, and Ty watched as deputy Sam Brooks came out, his arm around his girlfriend, Willow Rose.

The sight of it only tightened the fist in Ty's gut.

He wanted to get out of the truck, join his friends . . . but Ella would be in there, probably with Gage, and frankly, the sight of her only dragged up the memory.

He closed his eyes and returned, unbidden, back to the hospital the morning after Ella and Oliver's rescue.

He'd walked into the hospital beside Gage, having followed him in his Silverado, ready to pick up Brette and bring her back to her condo, armed with the suggestion he stick around and make her some homemade chicken noodle soup. Because he meant it when he said he wasn't going anywhere.

Brette hadn't made the same promise, a realization he came to slowly as he entered her room.

He stood there, trying to wrap his brain around the sight of an orderly making up her bed. When he asked a nurse about her, the answer was, "I'm sorry, but she discharged herself, against medical advice."

Against medical advice?

He'd even driven to her condo, armed with the key code from Ella, and found it empty. Brette's bags gone.

He'd arrived at the airport moments after the last flight out of Kalispell departed.

Not even Ella had an answer, and calls to Brette's cell phone went to voicemail.

For the past three weeks.

He wanted to give up. *Should* give up. Clearly, whatever he'd said hadn't been enough.

But he couldn't purge the words from his head. *Against medical advice.*

What advice? But no amount of cajoling with her doctor revealed the reason.

Brette was out there, possibly sick, and there wasn't a thing Ty could do about it.

No, he didn't feel like celebrating.

A knock came at his window and he jerked, painfully aware that he'd just been sitting there, lost in misery.

Ian Shaw stood in the crisp night, the collar on his leather jacket turned up. Ty rolled the window down. "Hey, Ian."

"Are you going in?" Ian gestured to the club.

"I don't . . . maybe not."

Ian glanced at the Pony. "Awful lot of country love songs going on in there."

As if to confirm his words, the door opened and out drifted the heartbreaking tune of a local crooner.

Can't get you off my mind
remembering too well the time
when I held you in my arms
When you said you'd be mine . . .

Ty nodded. "Maybe too much for me." He hung his arm out the window. "How's the search going for Sofia d'Cruze?" Apparently, Ella had recognized the face of Ian's missing person, a woman she roomed with in college.

The thought stopped him. *A woman Brette had also roomed with.*

Brette's sudden, silent disappearance didn't have anything to do with the missing Sofia, did it?

"We got ahold of her family," Ian said. "She hadn't returned to Spain, and they filed a missing persons' report on her over a year ago, but it never made it out this far."

"Any leads?"

"I have hundreds of leads—people who called in from the show. It just takes time to track them all down."

Ty glanced at the Pony. Through the big glass window, he saw that Sierra had gotten up, was trying her hand at darts.

He looked back at Ian. "Need some help?"

But Ian was watching Sierra. She laughed as she clearly missed her target.

Ian sighed, then looked back at Ty, offered a grim smile. "Let's get started."

ACKNOWLEDGMENTS

I love to ski. I learned when I was five years old, skiing a tiny hill near our home. As a family, we eventually graduated to the Colorado, Utah, and Montana mountain resorts. I loved standing at the top of the mountain, seeing the glorious granite peaks touch the clouds, then losing myself in the rush of wind in my ears. I was pretty good—I loved to take jumps, ski moguls, and float down powder. Even had a wicked wipeout on the back bowls of Vail.

I've always wanted to write a story about skiing (or in this case, snowboarding), capture the feeling—and often, the fear—of winging down a mountain. I'm enthralled by freeriders who ski off mountain cliffs and through couloirs and plow through deep powdery fields. It's so dangerous . . .

Some might say reckless.

Not long ago, my son left school to do something rather dangerous. No, not freeriding, but a job that was significantly high risk. My friends asked . . . why did you let him do this?

Um, because he's an adult? And I have to let him make his own choices.

And because God is with him, even in choices I don't agree with.

In fact, my riskiest choices, even if they led to mistakes, were the ones where I clung to God the most.

But what happens when those choices go south? So often we blame ourselves or others — and maybe rightly so. But we also seem to forget that God doesn't stop loving us because we make a mistake or even a bad choice.

Some people, like Ella, live their lives trying to do everything right, fearing that if they mess up, God won't like them, won't rescue them. And others, like Gage, refuse to believe that God could be on their side because of their biggest failures.

Lies.

We can't live a life free of mistakes—they're one of our biggest tools for learning. And God lets us walk into mistakes! He warns us, yes, and suggests we "stay in his line" (to use a snowboarding term), but he not only lets us choose our line but stays with us if take our own course. And helps us pick up the debris when we wipe out.

Not because we're so awesome. But because he is awesome. And he loves us, period. Full stop.

That wild thought makes me feel as if I'm

standing on top of the mountain, the glory of the mountainscape around me, reaching to the heavens, and pushing off into the white grace of unblemished powder.

Freeing. Flying.

May you break free of your fear of mistakes and fly in the grace of God's love.

Thank you for reading Gage and Ella's story! Stay with me for book #4 in the Montana Rescue series as Ian and Sierra finally get their adventure . . . but will they find a happy ending?

My deepest gratitude goes to the following people who show up to help me, story after story. I'm blessed by their faithfulness in this journey with me!

MaryAnn Lund, my beloved mother, who loved me just because I was her daughter. I miss you.

Curt Lund, for your continued ideas, guidance, and support in helping me research the PEAK team. I'm so grateful for your creativity and wisdom!

David Warren, who knows how to manage the erratic emotions of his crazy author mother with fantastic ideas, brilliant storycrafting, and wonderful encouragement. Thank you for seeing my vision and helping me flesh out characters and scenes. I know I've said this, but really, you're brilliant.

Rachel Hauck, my brilliant writing partner.

What would I do without you? Thank you for walking this journey with me. I am so blessed to be your bestie!

Andrew Warren, who is kind enough to feed me when I forget to eat, lost in a story, and wise enough to know when to pull me away because my brain is about to explode. There is no one I'd rather take this wild ride of life with.

Noah Warren, Peter Warren, Sarah and Neil Erredge, for being my people. I know I can always count on you, and that is a rare and beautiful thing. I love you.

Steve Laube, for being the one dispensing wisdom. I'm blessed to have you on my team!

Andrea Doering, for seeing my vision, for your wisdom about story lines and characters. Because of you, I write better books. I am so grateful for you!

The *amazing* Revell team, who believe in this series and put their best into making it come to life—from editing to cover design to marketing. I'm so delighted to partner with you!

To my Lord Jesus Christ, who shows up to protect, provide for, and love me. You make me fly.

Susan May Warren is the *USA Today*, ECPA, and CBA best-selling author of over fifty novels with more than one million books sold, including *Wild Montana Skies* and *Rescue Me*. Winner of a RITA Award and multiple Christy and Carol Awards, as well as the HOLT and numerous Readers' Choice Awards, Susan has written contemporary and historical romances, romantic suspense, thrillers, romantic comedy, and novellas. She can be found online at www.susanmaywarren.com, on Facebook at Susan May Warren Fiction, and on Twitter @ susanmaywarren.

Center Point Large Print
600 Brooks Road / PO Box 1
Thorndike, ME 04986-0001 USA

(207) 568-3717

US & Canada:
1 800 929-9108
www.centerpointlargeprint.com

DATE DUE